WINSTON GRAHAM'S
Brilliant Novel of Love and Intrigue

THE WALKING STICK

Sometimes I woke in the middle of the night and said, you fool, you twisted little beast; and the man beside me was asleep, a heavy young man, solid limbed, white limbed, gentle handed, kind mouthed; so I said, well, there it is, you traded love for integrity . . .

And what is integrity? Can you feel it, can you taste it, as you can feel and taste love?

To whom anyway did I fundamentally owe any loyalty except to Leigh? And I would turn over and try to hold his hand, as if that were the only certain thing in a world that didn't seem to have a lot of certainty any more.

"**THE WALKING STICK** is a thriller which surpasses its genre, a novel in the Daphne Du Maurier tradition . . . An enthralling tale . . . A total success!"

—Peter S. Prescott
Women's Wear Daily

D1133866

the walking stick

by Winston Graham

BANTAM BOOKS
TORONTO · NEW YORK · LONDON

*All of the characters in this book
are fictitious, and any resemblance
to actual persons, living or dead,
is purely coincidental.*

*This low-priced Bantam Book
has been completely reset in a type face
designed for easy reading, and was printed
from new plates. It contains the complete
text of the original hard-cover edition.*
NOT ONE WORD HAS BEEN OMITTED.

THE WALKING STICK
*A Bantam Book / published by arrangement with
Doubleday & Company, Inc.*

PRINTING HISTORY
*Doubleday edition published June 1967
2nd printing .... July 1967*
Reader's Digest Condensed Book Club edition published July 1967
*Literary Guild edition published July 1967
Bantam edition published August 1968*

All rights reserved.
Copyright © 1967 by Winston Graham.
*This book may not be reproduced in whole or in part, by
mimeograph or any other means, without permission.
For information address:
Doubleday and Company, Inc., 277 Park Avenue,
New York, N.Y. 10017.*

*Bantam Books are published by Bantam Books, Inc., a subsidiary
of Grosset & Dunlap, Inc. Its trade-mark, consisting of the words
"Bantam Books" and the portrayal of a bantam, is registered in the
United States Patent Office and in other countries. Marca Registrada.
Bantam Books, Inc., 271 Madison Avenue, New York, N.Y. 10016.*

PRINTED IN THE UNITED STATES OF AMERICA

the walking stick

Chapter 1

The man had been eying me most of the way home, and even happened to leave the bus at the same stop; but as soon as I got off he lost interest and walked away hunching his shoulders against the disappointment and the rain. I walked home, up Holly Hill, the wind beating against my back and legs. The road glimmered like wet polythene. I was late. It would soon be dark.

We lived in one of those big early Edwardian houses, built without taste, but roomy and square and made to last. It had too many steps up to the front door, a semi-basement, two floors above, sash windows, an iron gate that wouldn't shut, and an old street lamp immediately outside. This showed up the brass plate which read J. DOUGLAS DAINTON, M.R.C.S., L.R.C.P.

I opened the front door with my key and went in. They were both at home, and supper was nearly over. We always ate in the kitchen, winter and summer, and even when we had company. It was a long trainlike room, with plenty of space for cooking at one end and eating at the other. It had most of the latest gadgets, for Erica loved gadgets: washing-up machines, mixers, toasters, infrared grills, slicers, potato peelers, bottle openers, electric coffee mills, so that its business end looked like a stand at an Ideal Home exhibition. Cellophaned down one long wall were a selection of paintings and crayon sketches done by all the children, but chiefly by my elder sister, Sarah, whose vision at an early age had been the most primitive and therefore the most prized. The other wall had modern glass cupboards which were full of cooking spices and exotic Chinese teas and highly polished non-used copper moulds and steaming pans.

Apart from my bedroom it was the only comfortable room in the house.

When I got in, Dr. J. Douglas Dainton, M.R.C.S., L.R.C.P., was just scraping the last of a Boursin cheese out of its silver paper and spreading it on a Ryvita biscuit. Propped against a toast rack was *The Informed Heart* by Bruno Bettelheim, which he was trying to read at the same time. Dr. Erica Dainton, M.B., Ch.B., was stirring her coffee and reading an egghead paperback I couldn't see the name of. When she saw me she pushed her glasses up her nose and said: "You're *so* late. Have you been to a party or something?"

It was always her expectation somehow that I was going to break out into a gay life of my own.

"No, there was some work I wanted to finish. Is there anything left?"

"Of *course*. But it'll be cold. The whole thing was served up before Minta left."

My father looked across from his silver paper and smiled at me clinically. "You're wet, Deborah. Thank God I haven't to go out tonight." He picked up the clean knife he was keeping for the purpose and turned over a page of his book.

I went to the stove and helped myself to the remains of a congealed stew. In silence I began to eat. My mother said: "Did you come by tube?"

"No. Bus. It's almost as easy."

"But so much longer, my dear, when you're late."

"I like it better." She knew this already. She knew that I didn't like confined places, tunnels, compartments, boxes, cupboards, caves.

"Sarah rang up about half an hour ago. Asked to speak to you."

"Oh . . . What did she want?"

"To invite you somewhere, I think. She's never very forthcoming about these things."

"I expect she'll ring again."

"Yes, she said she'd ring again."

That rather exhausted the immediate conversation. As a family, although we talked a lot, we were never good on the trivia. When she saw I had nothing to say my mother gratefully pulled her glasses down her nose again.

I flipped through the pages of the evening paper. Sotheby's were in the news again with £7000 paid for a Meissen tea and coffee service of forty-four pieces. Prices went ever up. There had been a murder in Kensington. The Minister of Health was advising doctors to exercise economy in their prescriptions. Wind and rain were forecast for the last week in April.

The telephone went in the hall. They both looked at me. "I expect that's Sarah now," my mother said; and my father said: "If it's anyone for me, say I'm out and'll call them back in fifteen minutes."

"Deborah," said the voice of my elder sister, when I lifted the receiver, "whatever time d'you get back these days?"

"Thursday is sometimes a bit hectic. Why?"

"I'm giving a party tomorrow to celebrate—just a couple of dozen people—eight o'clock. Any hopes?"

"Well . . . thanks." I stared at myself in the dim hall mirror. I hadn't combed my hair since coming in, and the rain had made rats' tails of it. I looked an absolute fright. "Did Erica suggest me?"

"Of course not, you ape. D'you think I take notice of her suggestions anyhow?"

That was true. "What is it, a dance?"

"In a three-roomed flat? But of course. With the band of the Grenadier Guards."

"Seriously. Shall I know anybody?"

"Well, there's me and Arabella. Fruits of the same womb. You'll recognize me by the red rose."

I plucked at a bit of skin round my thumb nail and then bit it.

"Well?" she said impatiently.

"Thanks. Thank you, darling. I'd adore to come. What sort of clothes?"

"Moderately smart. I'm sick of these sordid affairs where everyone comes looking as if they've been washed up with the local sewage."

"Lovely," I said. "What time did you say?"

"Eight or thereabouts. Don't eat because we'll eat."

After hanging up I was a minute or two doing something about the rats' tails before going back into the kitchen. Late invitation for a party? Someone fallen sick? Bitchy. Give Sarah credit for honesty: if she'd wanted me as a stop-gap she would simply have said so.

Pity there always had to be this thing between me and my family. They trying to compensate and be nicer than they wanted to be. Me on guard and not wanting them to be nicer than they wanted to be.

I went back into the kitchen to my father and mother and told them what was on. Douglas was relieved that it wasn't a call for him; Erica made a gallant attempt to be interested in what I should wear, but after a minute or two, when I'd picked up the paper again, she went back to her egghead.

So silence fell, and Erica finished her coffee and Douglas made himself a pot of Soochong tea, and I scraped out the coagulated dish—not all to eat, but chiefly into the waste disposal unit—and sat down with a cup of Maxwell House and we all read.

We had all had a tiring day.

My father at this time was fifty-eight, but I don't think he looked it. He was a very hairless man, of head, eyebrow, chin, legs, chest; and even a photograph of twenty years before showed him to have been just the same then. Otherwise he would have been very handsome, with a clear complexion, a fine profile, and smiling frank blue eyes. I don't really know that he was more honest, more direct, more true, more trustworthy, more sincere than anyone else, but he gave this impression of *shining* candor. If there had been warmth in his eyes as well he

4

would have looked a saint. But there wasn't warmth, or not much, or not much more than the professional man could afford to give off to each patient. To those who knew him well I think even this much was a little too smoothly and evenly spread. You felt if you went to him medically you'd get much the same sympathy whether you had indigestion or angina.

In his youth he'd been a pretty good athlete, and he had kept his figure even today. He always looked astonishingly *clean*—even when he wore a dirty suit you got the impression that his body was clean inside it; perhaps it was partly this lack of hair. His hands were always cool, like his voice. He never perspired. You could hardly imagine him ill or not in command of a situation—though of course his command was that of someone on the General Staff, not in the field of battle.

Some people thought him lazy.

When the Welfare Service came in they were both quite young, with a growing family and practicing together, since it was against Erica's principles to give up her profession to raise children. Douglas had taken one look at the new régime and had opted out of it right away. For eighteen years he had gone on with a tiny but rich private practice, claiming that he made as much outside the Service for a quarter the work. Erica, reacting the opposite way, had at once gone into partnership with three women doctors with a shared surgery in the newer and less prosperous part of Hampstead; no private patients were accepted, and the practice was conducted on strictly business lines, with each doctor having specified hours of work and leisure and no nonsense about personal relationships between doctor and patient.

My mother was a tall woman and a clever one. She had qualified the year of her marriage. I'd heard her say: "Of course I adore children, but they have to be kept in proportion to one's own life. Otherwise at forty-five or fifty you're a dead letter. It's not civilized."

My mother's most stringent criticism was if a thing was not civilized.

She'd been good-looking too, but in a different way

from Douglas, and, unfairly, it hadn't been as durable. The fresh complexion was cottage-womany in a good light. Her curly hair was gray and looked marvelous just after it was done each Friday afternoon. But by Saturday the texture was going and for the rest of the week it was as light and spiky as straw. Her big brown eyes were narrowed with having to make constant decisions, and these constant decisions, because they had to be authoritative, had given her a bossy look.

I suppose you could say they both belonged to the Hampstead intelligentsia. They believed in asepsis, Freud, Aldermaston, the four-letter word, the Berliner Ensemble, the anti-novel, Joan Littlewood, the *Observer,* co-educational day schools, and the use of Christian names between parents and children.

For Heaven's sake, I'm not trying to be cynical or to suggest these things are necessarily either right or wrong; I'm only trying to describe my home as it was, so that what happened can be seen against its proper background.

Perhaps some clever people will be able to see a connection. Or perhaps it was inevitable anyhow.

You could say in a sense that my father and mother were even old-fashioned in some things. After all they were married and had stayed married for twenty-nine years. At least from when I was old enough to take notice, I don't think they ever slept with anybody else. They never drank to excess, or took drugs more awful than the occasional secconal or rogitin—even when packaged and supplied free by the manufacturers. If they were out of temper, their temper hadn't a lot of bite (which is more than I can say of myself). They were never in debt, except to the bank. They paid their taxes, schedule D and E respectively. They'd somehow reared three daughters, who were now all, or soon would be, respectably self-supporting. They performed a valuable service for the community. And they took a month's holiday abroad each year, always apart.

They were in fact two highly successful figures in

urban society; and if they had any failure to irk their justifiable satisfaction, it was me.

I often wondered why it bothered them so much. I suppose they looked on it as a reflection on their own professional competence.

My sister Sarah was a brilliant young woman and had just added another degree to those she had already got, which was what the party was about. After four or five more years in the hospitals she intended to specialize in gynecology. She was tall and a bit big generally but *very* good to look at, with those blue eyes in which even the whites seem to take the color. She had been engaged twice and had always got some young man about her, but the link-up never seemed to last long, maybe because she was too high spirited to stay in the shafts. There was so much in life apart from love. She was probably very much like my father when he was young.

My other sister, Arabella, was only just twenty and was reading medicine at London University. She was tall as Sarah but much slighter, and rather delicate looking, with very sexy blond hair hiding one side of her face and one eye, and a lovely figure. If she got through her studies without being ravished—which seemed unlikely —she would probably go into research, as she was clever enough but hardly had the face or figure for medical practice.

Although I am myself above average height, I always feel a dwarf in my family, with my mother the next shortest at five feet nine.

When I got to Sarah's flat in Ennismore Gardens about half a dozen people were already there. Two of them I knew slightly, the others were already busy talking and drinking happily.

"Hi," said Sarah, peeking down at me. "Lovely to see you. You know Philip, don't you? And Greta? Oh, that's the door again. Could you go and help Arabella pour the drinks?"

There were shouts of welcome behind me as I went

across to the table where the bottles were. Arabella had a new young man called Bruce Spring, who was a Registrar from the Middlesex and had odd Edwardian side whiskers, a hairy mole on one cheek, and pronounced some of his words as if they were corks being drawn out of wine bottles.

The room began to fill up, but as Sarah had said, this was no shabby bottle party with corduroys and woollen shirts and patched jeans. Sarah shared the flat with a girl called Virginia, and they had converted their big bedroom into a dining room for the night. For the first hour we drank and talked in the sitting room, and Arabella and I were pretty busy pouring the drinks. Just as we were about to go in to eat and Sarah had given me the nod not to refill any more glasses, two late arrivals came. One was David Hambro, a young surgeon I'd seen before. The other was a man called Leigh Hartley.

When you get to know someone very well it's often hard to remember first impressions, they come like Morse signals and you don't take the trouble to unscramble them. I remember most his curly hair, his common voice, his look of tormented vigor. He was not tall, but somehow wasn't overlooked by taller men; he had heavy eyelids which could droop over his eyes to give the italics to some word or look; his nose was too narrow for the broad face; his mouth was big and sensitive, the teeth as white as high-gloss paint.

Not handsome. But it was a face that meant quite a lot in a world where so many are anonymous.

The first words he said to me, I remember, were: "Burnt umber."

I looked at him—he was smiling—but I didn't reply, not seeing the joke.

"Break it with Naples yellow," he said, "because of that light coming from overhead. You Sarah's sister?"

"Yes."

"Crikey, three sisters all so attractive! I only met Sarah three weeks ago. Last week it was Arabella. Now you."

"Can I get you a drink?" I said.

8

"Sure. Lovely. Just what I need."

I waited. "Well, what?"

"What?" He blinked with his heavy lids. "Oh, you mean to drink. Well anything that's going. How's the tap water? Is it a vintage year?"

"Yes," I said, "but this side of the valley only."

"Pour me half a glass then and dilute it with a dash of Scotch."

While I did this he looked me over. I suddenly found myself angry with Sarah for putting me behind a table where I couldn't properly be seen and with myself for falling for the trick; or angry with coincidence if that was all it was.

"Seriously," he said, "I do think your hair's great."

"Was that what it was about? Well, thank you."

"Does it ever get out of place?"

"What?"

"Your hair."

"Oh, frequently."

"It *shines*, you know."

He sipped his drink and I sipped mine. Arabella was laughing with her new boy friend.

The young man said: "Maybe I talk too much."

I half-smiled but did not look at him.

"What's your name?"

"Deborah."

"Mine's Leigh. Spelled with a gh. Leigh Hartley. You a doctor?"

"No. I work in the West End."

"The only unmedical Dainton, eh? Thank God. I'm always scared of doctors, even those I know well. And women doctors frighten me even more."

"Why?"

"Why? Oh, I don't know. Because they're somehow the wrong sex for the job, I reckon. And people who are the wrong sex for a job are always slightly more sinister than people who are the right sex . . . like male nurses, f'rinstance."

Sarah was leading the way into the bedroom for supper.

9

I said: "Your ideas are a bit Victorian, aren't they?"

"Old-fashioned, maybe. But why blame the poor old Queen? There weren't any women doctors in Edward's day, were there? Or the earlier Georges or the Stuarts or—"

"Well, they burned them then," I said. "Perhaps you think that's a good idea." I picked up my stick. "Supper's ready."

"Can I sit with you, d'you think?"

I smiled. "No. I have to help. You follow Arabella and then you won't lose your way."

He smiled back at me and turned away glass in hand. Before he could move far I deliberately came out and limped beside him to the bedroom door. "In there. I *think* there are enough seats, but I'm afraid it's going to be crowded."

He pretended not to notice and nodded and slipped in.

Actually I didn't help much because it's always hard for me to get up and down in a hurry, and anyway the kitchen would hardly take more than three. So after passing a few things I grabbed a plate and a glass of wine, and a couple of people made room for me sitting between them on a bed.

There was a biggish round table which was normally in the living room, and that took seven. Three or four more sat around the low dressing table, and the others sat on or between the two beds or stood or squatted on the floor. Leigh Hartley was at the dressing table and spent most of the meal talking to a stout dark girl whose name I never knew; but every now and then I could tell his head was turned and once I glanced up briefly and met his look.

We ate for about an hour. It was Spanish Chablis, with vichyssoise, followed by *jambon à la crème*. Virginia fancied herself with her foreign menus. But actually it was very good. The man next to me was a doctor and the man on the opposite bed was a doctor and they were discussing the opening of a new psychiatric ward. The man next me said: "What I'd really like is a selection: about

10

fifteen schizos, five paranoids and a dozen manic depressives to begin. That's about the right proportion. It doesn't do to get out of balance right at the start." He sounded as if he was ordering plants for his herbaceous border.

"Well maybe we can fix that," said the second man. "I'll talk to Villars-Smith in the morning."

The man on the other side of me had just come back from a skiing holiday in Norway, and if supper had gone on another hour he might just have been able to get the whole thing out of his system. I sat there listening and saying yes and no and watching his red young self-important face swelling up like a frog as the room got hotter: a perfect subject for a coronary at forty-eight; but he'd still got twenty years ahead of him of swelling and shouting and accidentally spitting out bits of food. One couldn't help but speculate what he would be like as a husband. Some poor girl . . .

Supper finished about eleven, and everyone was very jolly and talkative. I went into the kitchen, but after a bit Sarah pulled me out. "I've told you before, Deborah, you *are* an ape. We *pay* to have this cleared up. Come and talk."

So I went in and somebody found me a chair, and in about five minutes Leigh Hartley had edged over to sit on the arm of the settee nearby.

"Hello," he said. "Remember me?"

"Not very well."

"I'm that fresh guy who insulted you by admiring your hair."

I didn't reply, and after waiting he said: "I suppose the old cold shoulder is the easiest way of keeping wolves like me at bay."

I met his eyes. They were gray, absolutely clear gray, with whites nearly as bright as his teeth. "I haven't any trouble usually. After the first howl or so, they don't come after me."

He continued to look. "Because you're lame, you mean?"

Most people weren't quite tactless enough to spell it

11

out. But all I said was, "It could be," and turned to speak to David Hambro, who was squatting on a cushion nearby. I carefully didn't turn back for quite a time, and knew he was sitting there more or less isolated, because the girl on the settee was chatting to Arabella. I tried to think of a way I could get up and leave without speaking to him again, but presently he got up himself and crossed the room. It was funny how angry one could still become, because it probably hadn't been intended as offensive. You shouldn't victimize a man for speaking the truth . . .

He came back carrying two glasses. "You were nearly empty so I've brought you a refill," he said.

"Thanks, but I'm fine with what I've got."

"Well, let me exchange a new one for the old. It tastes better out of a clean glass."

I smiled at him. "No, really, I don't slobber. This is perfect, thanks."

He sat down on the arm of the settee. "O.K., I'll drink them both."

That ended diplomatic relations for quite a while. About midnight one or two couples began to dance, and David Hambro asked Arabella. Hartley slipped down onto the cushion and hugging his knees looked up at me.

He said: "You're quite right, you don't slobber. I've been watching." He went on: "I'm not really a wolf, you know. Haven't the time."

I smiled again, but thoughtfully.

He said: "Well, stone the crows, but you're really beautiful. Maybe it is a bore to you, but think of the kick it gives other people."

The disc ran out at last, and couples stopped dancing, and Sarah went to turn the thing over. It was long-playing and I could see I was stuck for another twenty minutes.

"Why haven't you the time?" I asked. "You should make it."

"I'm sorry," he said, "but sarcasm is almost always lost on me."

"You still haven't answered."

12

"I paint." He bit it off with his teeth, like someone biting the end of a cigar.

"Oh, I see, that explains the yellow."

"What yellow?"

"You said something about Naples yellow before supper."

"Well, yes. Well, it explains me, see. I'm the uncouth type. Haven't had time to pick up the graces of society."

I looked at his hands: they were broad and stubby; he might more probably have been an engineer or a carpenter. His clothes were odd too, quite good but overstyled. A few people were going now; two of them came across to say good night to me. My stick got in the way, and one of them stumbled over it. The music was late-night music, dreamy, beat stuff suitable for amorous couples and a crowded floor. I wished I hadn't come. I wished so much that Sarah wouldn't ask me. She did it always out of a loving goodness of heart and trying to draw me into the circle of her friends, and always it was a failure.

"What do you paint?"

"Pictures. You know. With a brush. Oil on canvas. Or hardboard when I'm short of cash. Or canvas paper when I'm broke. It's a simple question of economics."

"What isn't?"

"Well, you aren't . . . I shouldn't think so anyway."

"Are you a good painter?"

"No." He stopped looking at me and looked through me. "I'm a good draftsman. But that isn't enough."

That was original anyway. Or maybe it was just a new line. "You're modest."

"No—clearsighted."

"In that case, why do you still go on with it?"

I thought he was staring at my bad leg, and moved it for him to see better.

He said: "Why do you go on breathing?"

"Do you sell your paintings?"

"One or two."

"Do you work at something else, then?"

"No. I've a bit of lolley from an aunt. She married an

13

ironmonger in Dulwich and I was her only blighted nephew. It just about keeps me above the Chinese famine
level." He gulped his other glass of wine. "Can I take you
home?"

"Thanks, but I'm spending the night here."

"You don't live with Sarah—not normally, I mean?"

"No, with my parents in Hampstead."

His face set into fixed angular planes. "Will you come
out some evening with me?"

". . . I actually don't go out much. I get home latish
most evenings."

"A Sunday then."

"Well . . ."

"Good, that's settled. I'll ring you. Or what about next
Sunday?"

"No, I'm booked."

"O.K. I'll ring you." He looked round. "I don't know
anything about *you* yet. Odd, isn't it? But you're beautiful
—or nearly beautiful. Been watching you. With some
expressions and in some lights it's like catching light on
water. Quicker here and gone than a rainbow." He
brooded. "It's so unfair."

"What's unfair?"

"Beauty. It does things to you. Doesn't it?"

So did ugliness. But when he rang I could be out.

He said: "There's no Goddamn fairness in art. What
you feel is absolutely no guide to what you can express.
We can all be Rembrandts, Rouaults, Picassos in what we
feel and what we get fun out of and that sort of thing; but
not one in a bloody million can *express* it."

Most people were going. Release was not far off.

He said: "What do you do? You've got a different face
from your sisters. You musical?"

"No."

"They've got long faces really. Modern faces. Yours
isn't. It's oval—a good bet for old man Rossetti. It's nine-
teenth century. Very out of date."

"Thank you."

"No. It's got something. It's sensitive, and *gentle*. Of
course, I can see you aren't a bit gentle really, but that's

14

not what I mean. You *look* romantic, even though underneath you may be—"

I didn't learn then just what else Leigh Hartley thought I might be underneath, because Sarah came across and interrupted us, bringing with her a girl neither of us had yet met. I waited until the conversation got going and then slid away into the kitchen and saw no more of him that night.

Chapter 2

I work for Whittington's, the auctioneers. This might seem a bit of a comedown in a professional family like ours, if it hadn't been Whittington's.

When I left school the one thing I was certain I wasn't going into was medicine, so my mother sent me off to France where she had a married cousin. I stayed there, outside Avignon, and read for university entrance but never got far as I'm not really the academic type. Being laid up so long has fostered the reading habit without giving it discipline, so that I can always read and study and pick up quickly what I am interested in, but what I'm *not* interested in simply slides away and my memory of it is as blank as a cinematograph reel that hasn't been exposed to the light.

My half uncle is an archaeologist and writes popular books on Pompeii and Arles and Perpignan for the French public. I read these and they touched off a fuse, so that I went back to the scholarly works from which he'd got most of his facts, and then I couldn't read enough about it.

So later I had gone to Whittington's. It was a time when employment by any of the big three was just becoming fashionable. Even Debs applied for jobs in Whittington's or Sotheby's or Christie's, and when I put my name down I was at the foot of a long list. But it wasn't long before I got a second interview, and with it, at nineteen, a job as a receptionist clerk. There were, you see, certain things in my favor. Already I knew quite a lot about early art. And Mr. Hallows, who first engaged me, must have reasoned that it was unlikely I should get married. In a world where woman-wastage must reach about 90 percent, this virtue isn't to be sneezed at.

So after two years I was put in the antiquities department, and then later transferred to the porcelain which was much larger and really covered most of the things I was interested in. A year later I became a cataloguer, and now I was Mr. Mills's right hand and usually went with him if there was a china or porcelain collection to be itemized out of town. On smaller jobs I often went alone.

Whittington's is the smallest of the big three, but in some ways the most select. It is just the oldest, by a matter of five years, and its links with English aristocracy are secured by long custom. All the same it was slower than the other two to discover that even tradition must give way to progress, and in the postwar period—when I was still a child at school—it nearly ran on the rocks. Then a new generation of directors grew up and shook it out of its dying sleep and put it on its feet again.

He rang me on the following Wednesday about nine in the evening.

"Look," he said, "you free this coming Sunday? I'm a member of the Seven Arts Club and we have a film show every Sunday evening. It'd be interesting this week—"

"Sorry," I said. "I'm already booked up."

"Oh." He sounded really disappointed. "Pity."

"Yes. Thanks all the same."

He sensed I was going to ring off and said quickly: "That's a pity because it's the Picasso film—it's an old one, made ten years or more ago, but I've never seen it. The old boy in action. People who've seen it rave about it."

"Oh . . . Yes, I have heard of it."

"Not that the Seven Arts Club is often much to write

17

home about. I sometimes reckon it's more an excuse to watch blue films than anything else. But every now and then they turn up something real good."

"Like this."

"Yes, like this. We wouldn't need to get there till nine. What hopes?"

"No hopes . . . Sorry again. I must ring off now, as I left a kettle on."

"O.K. . . . Deborah?"

"Yes?"

"When is your next free Sunday?"

Damn the man. "Well . . . I'm not *absolutely* sure. Perhaps next month."

"As long as that? Anyway, I'll ring again."

"Yes, all right. Goodbye."

"Bye."

In the drawing room my mother had just finished playing the piano. It was an ascetic, sterile room, with two small Hamadan rugs on the polished oak block floor. The charcoal leather settee was without cushions. The Bluthner six-foot grand in black veneer had an Anglepoise lamp on it. That was all there was in the room except for three framed reproductions of paintings by abstract artists, two small pieces of modern sculpture, and three chairs. Douglas, my father, always said that if one's intellect was worth while, that furnished any room adequately. People cluttered their rooms, he said, as they cluttered their minds. (Yet, of his three daughters, I collected porcelain and Sarah collected old silver. Arabella so far only collected young men.)

Erica wore an expensive but seventh-winter gray barathea suit.

"Was it for you?"

"Yes."

"Not one of the girls? Because I wanted to ask Sarah—"

"No, it was somebody I met at Sarah's party."

"They were inviting you out?"

"No. They wanted an address."

Up in my bedroom I had a moment's regret. The Picasso film was one I hadn't seen, and God help me, it

18

couldn't have hurt to go out one night with a man. And I could surely handle Leigh Hartley, in the very unlikely event of his needing to be handled. (A *few* men had been interested in me in my life, but very few. In most cases the sight of a withered leg put them right off, and in others I think they felt I was delicate and they'd be taking advantage of an invalid.)

I stared at the slightly damaged Italian majolica dish I'd picked up in a shop in Brighton. A gorgeously rich ruby luster, and the central picture was of God turning Adam and Eve out of the Garden of Eden; it had probably been painted by one of the Grues of Castelli. The plain answer to my question was that men really weren't for me. Any more, perhaps, than they should have been for Eve.

Leigh Hartley in his obtuseness clearly hadn't come to appreciate all this, for he rang me the following Monday evening and told me that because of its great success the members had managed to get the Picasso film for a further evening. Could I come next Sunday at nine?

I said: "You've seen it once. You don't want to see it again," and then cursed gently under my breath while he reassured me he was going a second time in any case. When you've not said no at the very beginning it's harder halfway through. Of course I should have said: "For God's sake go away and stop bothering me!" But last week's thoughts were still in the back of my mind; and, after all, the poor fellow didn't mean any harm. His rather humorous blunderings were better than the glassy-eyed self-adulation so many young men have.

So I found myself weakly agreeing to meet him at the Hampstead tube at 8:30. He would have come to the house, but I couldn't bear the thought of leaving under the speculative eyes of my parents. I never really knew how they felt about this sort of thing.

This Sunday evening was the first Sunday in May, and when I got to the tube he was waiting standing beside a very small red sports car. I got across the road without him noticing, and came up behind him. His face lit up when he saw me. He was younger than I remembered,

19

probably *years* younger than I was; crikey, he must *still* find me attractive, I thought; odd, is he a "case"? but generous and warm; give him his due; pity about his bad voice—just flat rather than accented, and thin in timbre; a sort of cockney voice without the accent; it didn't go with his physique, which was husky and strong. Artist barrow boy? And those clothes.

"Can you fit in here? Let me take your stick. That bogie across the way has been looking pretty nasty, I reckon one shouldn't park here. Mind your coat—this door has to be *slammed*. Good. Hold your breath and we'll see if it starts."

The show was in a little cinema in Wardour Street, and had just begun when we got there with a short film about sculpture in Japan. When it was done we ran straight into the Picasso. I'd never studied painting as such; but inevitably as pictures and furniture were the two biggest sections of Whittington's, one came to know a certain amount about them.

When the lights went up we had drinks at the bar there, but it was crowded and noisy. So he said, let's go round the corner and have coffee in peace. This we did, and sat in a cafe and talked in quite a friendly way for a while.

Then he said: "You didn't want to come out with me tonight, did you?"

I picked at a flake of skin on the edge of my finger. "Not particularly."

"You reckon I'm a smart Alec, who won't take 'not particularly' for an answer." He was smiling, but one really got the impression he cared what I said next.

"It isn't *quite* that. Maybe I'm a bit abrupt—a bit rude. Or seem so. It isn't that I intend to be."

"Good. I'm glad to know it."

I said carefully: "Of course I enjoyed the film, and of course I wanted to see it. It was fun . . . I get a great deal of fun out of life, but it isn't always quite the *same* fun. I mean the same as other people's."

I paused. He said: "Well, go on."

"There's not much more to say, is there?"

20

"D'you mean because you're lame?"

It was the second time he'd mentioned it, and emotionally I still resented this.

"As you say. But I'm quite happy, I assure you. Really *perfectly* happy, thanks."

He thrust out his bottom lip and sucked at his coffee. "O.K., O.K. You're happy. That's fine. Couldn't be more pleased. But I'm trying to separate this up, see. I am trying to sort it out. If you wanted to see the film, why did you 'not particularly' want to come out and see it with me? Have I got smallpox?"

I stared past him at a dark young man in the corner who was eying me.

"What's the matter with you?" Leigh said. "I mean, why are you lame?"

"It's a fine evening, isn't it?"

"Oh, I get the danger signals. So tell me just one thing. Why does it make you different from other people? I know, maybe you're not good at ballet or skiing. So are seven million other girls not good. In what other way has your fun got to differ? Eh? I'm interested, Deborah. I want to know."

I lifted my coffee cup. There was a thin circle of brown in the saucer. Someone had just put sixpence in the juke box, and it was thumping out one of last year's pop songs.

"If you're white," I said, "why want to be brown; if you're brown why want to be white? If you've straight hair, why pine for curly? If—"

"That doesn't answer a damned thing. You're only evading the issue."

"All right, I'm evading the issue!"

We were silent for a while. Then he said:

"What's your work? Some sort of secretary?"

I told him.

"Hm. Interesting. I thought perhaps you were shy, but you must have to deal with people all day long."

"Oh, yes, but that's in the course of business."

"Well, how about treating me as if I was in the course of business?"

I laughed. "What have you got to sell?"

"Myself."

We looked at each other. *"Make no mistake,"* said the disc, *"you gotta be certain in love. No mistake, no mistake, no mista-a-ake."*

I said: "Phew, it's nearly eleven-thirty. I think I must go."

"Come round to my place for a drink."

"Not now, thanks."

"You'll come out again?"

"Find me another Picasso and I will."

"Next week it's some nudist film from Sweden. But I'll shop around. We'll find something."

The dark young man in the corner was just leaving. I was glad he'd be gone before I had to get up.

Leigh said: "D'you have a lot of friends?"

"Oh, yes, a lot."

"How about including me in?"

"But of course."

He blew out a breath. "O.K. Let's go."

"Why d'you sigh?"

"Because you said 'But of course' in a Goddamn party voice that meant nothing at all. I reckon I ought to know when I'm beat."

Something moved me to say, "Sorry."

"No, no, if that's the way you feel, that's the way you feel. It's a free world. Look, you wait at the door and I'll get the car."

He got the car, and we drove back to Hampstead in a sort of cold-war silence.

"Don't bother to drive up," I said. "It's a nasty hill and One Way."

"No. Party manners'll triumph even over the brush-off."

We roared noisily up Holly Hill. "Which way now?"

"Fork right. That's it. And it's the third house on the right."

We stopped just short of it. I said: "Thank you. It's been *very* nice."

"But you don't want to come out with me again?"

"Well, it's just a question of looking the facts of life in the face."

"Such as?"

"You've already spelled them out. Good night." I began to get out of the car.

Another car came up behind and turned to go into our garage, which I hadn't noticed was open. The headlights lit up Leigh's tiny sports car. "Hold it," he said, "I'll just draw ahead to let this character get in. One of your household?"

He drove on a few yards, and I knew by the rapid expert swing of the other car into the garage that it was my mother driving.

"I'll go now," I said. "Thank you very much. Good night."

Of course he had to get out and help me out, though Heaven knows I've learned to be quick enough at that; but my stick had got lost somewhere behind the seats, and by the time he'd found it Erica was on us and I had to introduce him. We talked for three or four minutes and then he drove off and we went in.

"Are you on duty tonight?" I said, hoping to head her off the subject.

"Well, of course, otherwise I should not have been called out. Who's the young man? Was he bringing you back from Sarah's?"

"No, he took me to see a film."

"Odd voice. Where did you meet him?"

"At Sarah's. He's an artist."

"Oh?" It was a mistake to have told her that. An interest stirred in her voice. "Ask him in for drinks sometime."

"Yes . . . sometime."

We went up the stairs. "You really should have more men friends, Deborah. There's absolutely no reason why not."

"No. No reason at all."

That night I had my old dream back. I dreamed that I was in a coffin but somehow it wasn't long enough and

23

my head stuck out through a hole in the end. My hands and arms and legs were tied and I couldn't move a muscle. People were looking at me—three or four of the undertakers—and I knew that in a matter of minutes I should be buried and the earth would be shoveled into my mouth. I tried to protest, to scream, to explain that I wasn't really dead, that only my body was dead and my head and brain were very much alive. Each time I tried to speak to the undertakers they turned away.

Then I knew really that it wasn't just burial they intended but a kind of torture. All the time there was this terrible sound of a great animal breathing: I couldn't see it but it was somewhere near; and all the time the men were watching the dials on a kind of clock to see how much pain I could stand. And the pain wasn't yet there, but I *knew*, I knew it was going to *start*.

And then one of the undertakers came forward with a long rubber tube and began to push it up my nose, and every now and then he said "swallow" and pushed in a bit more; and then I had no breath but only pain, no breath to speak, no breath to call out, no breath to exclaim. The weight of burial was on my chest. I was dying, dying; and the pain, the terrible pain, and the suffocation . . .

I rocked backward and forward as Erica gripped my shoulder and shook me awake.

"Deborah! You'll disturb your father!"

No one, *no one* who has not suffered such nightmares can understand the inexpressible bliss of waking to find a familiar bed, a familiar room, movement in one's limbs, easy breathing, no burial or intended burial, a stern but familiar motherly hand. And no pain anywhere.

"Sorry," I said, struggling still. "Did I wake you?"

"Yes. You were crying. That awful whimpering sound. It's only about two o'clock. I must only have just gone off."

"Sorry, Erica. So sorry. I'll be all right now."

"Did you get overexcited tonight?"

"No, not a bit."

24

"I wondered if going out with that young man. It's years since you had one of these turns."

I struggled up in bed. "Don't call them *turns*. I'm not having fits or anything. They're just horrible nightmares. I'm all right now. *Sorry* to have got you out of bed. Really, I'll be all right. Like me to make you a cup of tea?"

"No, no," said my mother horrified. "That really would end the night. Tannin is as stimulating as caffeine."

I lay back and stretched luxuriously in the bed. Even my bad leg felt cool and comfortable.

"Thank you for coming. I was just being buried alive."

"*Really,* Deborah. Sometimes I think you glory in it."

"No glory, darling," I said. "But it's glory to wake."

Chapter 3

I sometimes think that the most threadbare things in the world are yesterday's smart ideas; and surely one of the most dated of them all is calling one's parents by their Christian names. The notion, of course, is that if everyone gets on a matey first-name basis from the start, it helps to abolish the gap between the generations; with resultant reduction in tensions; but this really is most awful nonsense, because nothing can ever abolish a gap of twenty to thirty years. Far more important is a good imagination on the child's part and a good memory on the parent's; and the second is the most obligatory; because a child can only *try* to imagine what it must be like to be a parent; a parent ought to be able to remember what it's like to be a child.

Erica, in spite of all her forward-thinking ideas, didn't seem to be awfully good at this. Maybe too much clinical experience had rubbed away the sensitive feelers that enable one human being to apprehend how another is feeling. She was terribly proud of her other two daughters but was always making gaffes about their love life; and her attitude toward me seemed to vary between trying to thrust me into personal relationships with outsiders and trying to guard me against them.

All I really wanted to do was live the life I'd worked

out for myself. I hoped I hadn't got a chip on my shoulder about a comparatively minor disablement; I tried to be realistic about it; for the rest I was busy and content and just wanted to be left in peace.

But no one seemed particularly willing to co-operate in this, except perhaps Douglas, my father, who constitutionally favored any line which required no effort on his part.

On the next Saturday we all met for supper, Sarah and Arabella, too, and we had hardly got through the grapefruit before Erica was saying she had heard this young man Hartley twice ringing up, and me telling Minta to tell him I was out.

So then we all had to discuss him and to discuss whether it was a good thing or not that I should choke him off. Everybody studiously avoided mentioning that this must be the first young man I'd had for about four years; instead they talked about *him*. Sarah didn't know much, except that she had met him at David Hambro's, and David Hambro had met him through an antique dealer and had gone to see an exhibition of his at some East End gallery. She said she'd ask David about him next time they met, and I said for Heaven's sake, and she said but tactfully, of course, ducky, without mentioning your name. And I said, This family is disgusting; it will leave absolutely nothing alone.

The following week we were pretty busy in Whittington's, and on the Tuesday I had coffee and a sandwich for lunch and did not slip out until four for a cup of tea. (Whittington's office tea is awful.) As I came out into the thundery gloom of Grafton Street a voice said:

"Do you know that the Kingdom of Heaven is on hand?"

I should have recognized his voice, but just for a moment I hadn't, and he must have caught the expression on my face.

He said: "Who shall abide in thy tabernacle? Who shall dwell in thy holy hill? Only Deborah Dainton, who now turneth a cold fish eye on him who waiteth."

I said: "What *are* you doing here? How did you know I should be coming out now?"

"I didn't. My flat feet were not flat earlier in the day."

"You don't mean you've been here for—since lunch-time?"

"I came at twelve. But don't be unduly impressed. It's no more than I'd do to see Charlton Athletic."

I felt very peculiar for a second or two, flattered, angry with myself for feeling flattered, angry with him for making me feel angry with myself, very slightly happier than I'd been two minutes ago, but still wanting no part in any of it. I turned and walked on, and he walked with me, taking the side that my stick wasn't.

I said: "You must be—crazy. Don't you ever work?"

"Constantly. But look at the day. This light is impossible."

"So you . . . But there are other things you could have . . ."

"Oh, yes. Where are you going? For tea?"

"Yes." Somehow from the beginning the conversation had got off on a different level. "Why can't you—"

"What?"

I was going to say "leave me alone," but the words did not come.

"Join you?" he finished.

"If you want."

"I must have made my wants clear by now."

We turned into Bond Street, and crossed. There was a cafe nearly opposite that tried to look Continental, with a sunshade in the open entrance and an artificial palm. We went in there. He ordered tea and toast. He was always heavier than I remembered him. He sat on the edge of the tubular chair with an air of nonconformity, like a carpenter invited into the parlor during working hours.

He said: "You're always out when I ring."

"Well . . . I often am out. I—"

"Last time we met, you asked me to look the facts of life in the face, didn't you? Well, most of the facts of life I know begin with boy meets girl. Clue me up with the special ones in this case."

28

I fumbled in my bag. "Well, as you pointed out when we first met, I'm lame."

"What's wrong with you?"

"I had polio."

"So?"

"So I've got a rotten leg. Understand? It's about an inch shorter than the other. Also the muscles have wasted. It's as thin as a stick and as much use. Can't you see for yourself?"

"Is that a good reason for hating me?"

I said angrily: "Can't I have likes and dislikes of my own?"

Just then the waitress came with our order and he glowered across the room as if thinking he'd get up and leave. But he stayed on, and with fingers shaking with annoyance I poured the tea.

He said: "How old are you?"

"Twenty-six."

"I'm twenty-five. I want to paint you."

"Oh, so that's it . . . And all the time I thought you were attracted by my exquisite charm."

"I am, God damn you."

"Sugar?"

"No . . . I reckon you don't take me seriously at all."

"Should I?"

"Yes."

We looked at each other like personal enemies. Bond Street roared by without anybody taking the least notice of it.

"What time d'you get off tonight?"

"Why?"

"Never mind. Tell me."

"Oh, it'll be late. Six-thirty or seven."

"I'll wait for you."

"You're wasting your time."

"Well, it's my time, isn't it?"

I sipped the tea and burned my lip.

"I live in Rotherhithe," he said. "D'you know where that is?"

"Near Tower Bridge?"

"Fairly. I've got a studio near what's called Cherry Garden Pier. It looks over the river. I'd like to show it to you."

"All right," I said.

"You'll come?" He looked really astonished, staggered.

"Yes—to see it—I don't mind."

"When—tonight?"

"Yes—just to see it. But not—forget this idea of painting me—tonight or any time. That's out."

"O.K., O.K. I only asked."

"Yes, but is that why you wanted me to come to your studio?"

He took a bite of his toast. His teeth I remembered as soon as I saw them again. "I wanted it for every reason, Deborah. You can't hardly have failed to notice that, can you. But so far I've had no encouragement. Damn all. Well . . . this is encouragement—"

"Yes, but—"

"Wait. This is encouragement but no more. Message received. I deal but you play the hand. Right? I'll meet you at six-thirty. The bloody parking meters will be off duty by then. I'll be outside the front door or as near as I can get. Agreed?"

"Agreed."

He looked at me. "You're not going to nip out of a back entrance while I'm not looking?"

"Why should I?"

He shrugged. "Why should you? No reason, except that maybe you've suddenly gone dead easy, and I'm scared of the double cross."

"No," I said, "I haven't gone dead easy."

In fact, the thought had crossed my mind to do what he suspected; but you can't sink quite as low. He was waiting for me in that little uncomfortable red car and we drove south across Westminster Bridge and then took the New Kent Road. "Traffic's always grotty at this time of day," he said, his face in uncomfortable, wry planes as he stared at the car in front, "but this way round is better than going straight."

30

Up Tower Bridge Road there was a break and he accelerated away. The car was open and the back draft blew my hair over my eyes. I put up my hands to hold it back, but he said: "Let it blow; it looks fabulous."

We turned right some way before the bridge and came into a lot of new property, council houses, flats and children's playgrounds, and then dived up an alley with derricks at the end of it. Another couple of turns, and he stopped in a narrow chasm of a street between two warehouses. "If you'll hop out here I'll drive the car on the pavement."

After we'd done this he opened a gate with an open padlock on it and led the way beside the warehouse to a shabby brick wall with an old Victorian-style door up three steps.

"Up here. I'll go first. This is it. Mind your head."

We went into a big long room with a low ceiling at the sides but rising to a high peak, with open rafters. There were two big windows and also a skylight. The room was littered with easels, cloths, cushions, painting knives, brushes, tubes of paint; it was in an awful mess; the furniture, what you could see of it, was of worn dusty green velvet. The windows looked right over the river.

"It was stables at one time," he said, taking out a comb and combing his hair. "It should have been pulled down with the two cottages that used to be here; but Mr. Taylor and Mr. Woodrow, who built the warehouse, didn't need this bit of space in their setup, so I clung on. Of course it's only a stay of execution."

He was nervous. An odd change.

"Lovely view," I said.

"Come to this window, you can see Tower Bridge from here."

The river was lapping at our feet. It was iron gray in the sultry evening, with little grins of sharper light where it was broken by movement or reflection. Twenty steel derricks bent over the water like birds drinking; tugs and barges passed and glided, smoke rose and eddied; seagulls swooped; it was a different London, one I didn't know.

"Swans!" I said.

"Yes, they've seen us. I often feed 'em about this time. Wait a minute."

He went through a door and came back with half a loaf of bread. "We can get out this way."

There was a door beside the window and this led out onto a concrete platform only just above the river.

"At high tide my balcony's under water, so I don't keep chairs out here. Don't fall in!"

Six swans came round, and he handed me a piece of the loaf and we fed them in turns. They paddled and gobbled and maneuvered and came for more. The air was fresh and tangy and smelled of the sea. A flag fluttered from Tower Bridge. I felt good.

It's not easy for me to crouch down for long because all the weight has to be taken by one leg. I moved to get up and he helped me.

"I envy you this!" I said.

He smiled. "Robinson Crusoe on a desert island surrounded by commerce. It's hell when they're unloading. But this view's here day and night, winter and summer the same. *Son et lumière* without an entrance fee . . . Like a drink?"

We went in, and he mixed two gin and tonics. The room really was in a mess. It smelled of resin and varnish and glue, and there were bits of paint-stained cloth on the floor, and stretching wedges and canvas pliers. I deliberately didn't look at any of his pictures, which were stacked in heaps.

"The air's lovely here," I said. "Where I work in Whittington's, when I'm cataloguing, that is, I'm in a sort of basement cellar, which gets oppressive after a while."

"Tell me about your work."

I told him, and he listened intently, as if he were really interested, not, as some people do, with too many nods and grunts so that you know they're waiting for you to finish.

"D'you get well paid?"

"A thousand a year."

"How d'you mean, you work in a cellar?"

"Well, Whittington's is like a rabbit warren. The office

where I catalogue actually is under the pavement of Grafton Street. If you look as you pass you'll see the heavy opaque glass squares that let in the light."

"I'll remember to stamp next time. Three bangs means, I'm waiting to take you to lunch."

I laughed and he said: "Can you find somewhere to sit? In my life chairs aren't for sitting on."

We sat by the bigger window watching the scene changing in the early evening light.

"Do they teach you anything about painting in your job?"

"They don't *teach* me anything. One picks up a bit about values."

"Well, I wouldn't say I wasn't interested in that!"

"I talked about pictures to Smith-Williams the other day, and he did rather confirm what I thought."

"What did you think?"

"Oh, I mean that our business—Whittington's business —is not to sell new things but to sell things that have become old and acquired a value. You see, if a new painting *had* a value, it would be much more likely to fetch it in a gallery, in an exhibition, than in the sale room."

"Yeh." He swallowed a gulp of his drink. "But who says your painting has a value, and where do you get your exhibition? That's the crunch."

"I though you'd recently had an exhibition. I thought David Hambro said you'd had one."

"Oh, that. In a flea-bitten hall in Southwark." He breathed through his thin nose and rubbed a smear of paint off a finger. "D'you know, Deborah, how artists live —outside of a little circle in Bond Street and St. James's? Eh, do you? Well, the answer is they don't! They paint —and then what? If they're lucky they get a few hung in the local pub, in the hope someone may come along and take a fancy to one of them—then it's not likely they'll want to pay more than a fiver. Or, if they know the right guys on the local council they may get put up to do a mural or a water color for the civic center or the new secondary modern. And that's your lot. After that they can hawk 'em round the art stationers and the fancy shops or they can stack 'em away like I do, one against the other till there's too many of 'em, and then I have a bonfire, or if it's good canvas I start painting over the top!"

Out of the corner of my eye I could see a painting of a river scene.

"I suppose that's so. People, quite a lot of people, buy paintings nowadays, but I suppose—"

"The paintings buyer is a special breed," he said vigorously, and finished his drink. "Another?"

"Not yet."

"Or two breeds. The paintings buyer is two special separate breeds really, you know. Quite separate, see. There's the one kind—the With-it, Art-conscious, glossy-magazine-buying, Demi-semi-avant-garde junior executive. You know. Him and his wife go off to Spain and buy an antique tile and stick it up on the wall and consider it 'terrible fun.' And every now and then maybe they've a bit of money to spare for a painting for their flat; but it has to be so with-it that they can never afford a genuine one, so they get a reproduction of a Braque, or a Dubuffet."

"Yes, I know the type," I said uncomfortably.

"The other breed . . . the other breed is all money and no taste. They buy paintings like they buy stocks and shares, spotting a winner or selling a loser. They fill up their houses with paintings they only really enjoy for their money value. They couldn't bear having a painting on their walls that wasn't *worth* anything, however beautiful it was. Well, what good are people like them? For the *average* artist—not the lucky one or two—for the *average* artist, what bloody good is either breed to him!"

"None," I said. "I know."

There was silence while a barge stage-managed a pile of timber slowly past the window. Then suddenly Leigh laughed. "Well, God bless Aunt Nellie. Her little nest egg will keep me for a while yet. Let's go out and eat somewhere."

"May I see one or two paintings first?"

I felt he must have expected me to ask, but in fact he seemed genuinely to hesitate. Then he said: "O.K. But the light's bad now. There's half a dozen here that'll do."

They were all river scenes. They had a factualness and a fidelity that appealed—you could put one on a wall and think that's how it would be if I had a window on the Thames. But their very fidelity would, I could see, be a disadvantage today. I remembered his remark at Sarah's party when we first met. "I'm a good draftsman but that isn't enough."

This time he said: "O.K., O.K., that'll do for a first dose. I don't want to make you gag. Sure you won't have another drink?"

"Sure, thanks."

"Oh, Lord," he said, "you got a spot of paint on your frock. Stay still."

He'd pointed to a spot on my shoulder I could only just see by twisting my neck. It didn't look much.

"Stay still," he said again and took out his handkerchief. "Next thing we know you'll be getting it in your hair."

He spat on the handkerchief a couple of times and rubbed and then stopped. "I think it's come out. You look when you get your frock off, but I don't think it'll show. This bloody place needs a spring cleaning. Sorry."

"It's all right. It's nothing."

He was very close. "Sorry," he said again. Eyes weighted with some purpose. Should have known the purpose. At twenty-six should have known the purpose very well; but that's the trouble: learner driver, everybody's got to learn, even late in life.

He kissed me. Anyway, he tried but I turned my mouth away. Kissed my cheek. Fumbling a bit with his hands about my body. Then he gripped my arms. I put my hands on his chest. He hugged me, suddenly, convulsively, like a bear. Didn't have a chance then. His cheek was against mine. Then we were separate. "Sorry," he said for the third time. "I reckon this isn't in the auctioneer's handbook. Never try to claim goods before the hammer's down."

I was choked with anger and contempt and embarrassment, so because of the last of these I said nothing at all.

He picked up the pictures and began to stack them. I went across and picked up my summer coat, put it on, looked for my stick but couldn't find it.

There was a knock on the door. Leigh swore under his breath and stopped to comb his hair. Then he went and opened the door. There was some muttering and a man came in.

". . . Well, he said to bring it now. I just dropped in, like. It didn't make no difference to me. Oh, sorry."

Leigh said: "This is Ted Sandymount, friend of mine. Miss Dainton."

"Pleased to meet you, Miss Dainton. How are you? Muggy weather, isn't it? I just dropped in, Leigh, with this packet. It didn't make no difference to me. Jack said to come, and I was passing near."

About forty, well-dressed by Carnaby Street standards; brown wavy hair, very thin and brushed back like the grain in wood, a smooth tanned face, a nervous twitch to the nose and eye that was half a wink and half a sniff. He padded across on flat feet and shook my hand and eyed me knowledgeably, as if he'd seen me before, or heard about me. But perhaps it was just that he was used to finding girls here.

Leigh said: "We were just going out to eat, Ted. Otherwise I'd say stop and have a drink."

"No, no, I'm on my way. I just dropped in." Ted Sandymount winked at me. "This is a bit of old London Londoners don't often see. Where the work's done, mind, where the work's done. West End couldn't live without the East End, that's what I always say. There's the back door and the front door to every city. Can't get away from it."

"Who wants to?" Leigh said.

Ted laughed at nothing. "Who wants to? Some of those duchesses you see in Fortnums. They don't know how the work's done and don't care: what d'you say, Miss Dainton?" He looked at me with bloodshot, selfish little eyes, and you could tell that what he was saying had nothing whatever to do with what he was thinking. What he was wondering was what I would be like in bed. I seemed to be striking it rich all of a sudden.

"Yes, well, maybe," said Leigh impatiently. "I'm hungry; so thank Jack, will you, if you see him before I do. I wasn't in all that hurry for the paints. So long now."

"Bye bye," said Ted Sandymount, twitching. "Bye bye for now, Miss Dainton. See you again sometime. Bye, Leigh. You'll be in tomorrow?"

"Sure, sure: I'm always in."

I found my stick. "We can all go at the same time," I said.

Chapter 4

"Miss Dainton," said the girl at the desk, "there's a lady here with a couple of little bottles that look as if they would interest you. A Mrs. Stevenson. She hasn't been in before."

"All right. I'll come up."

I left the office and made my way through the dusty cellar where the pictures were stacked before cataloguing, skirted the accounts department, climbed the steps, along the corridor by the auction rooms and reached the counter where Janet Browne was talking to an old woman in a torn raincoat.

He'd torn the lining of his coat last night on the brake lever as he got out of the car at the little cafe where we ate. It had been a silent sort of meal that I would have been glad to escape from, but I didn't want him to think I was a Victorian heroine shrinking from a first kiss. A little pub-cum-cafe off Jamaica Road, where there was an odd assortment of seamen, tarts, shopgirls, lorry drivers; interesting if in the mood. I thought once of borrowing a needle and cotton from the waitress to stitch the tear, but thought it might give him the idea I was feeling domestic. "Ted Sandymount's an electrician," he said after a long silence. "Does work for ships and river men. Small way of business but I reckon he does quite nicely. Any form

38

of trade is in his line really. Good chap, you know, under his smoothie looks. Would do anything for me. Generous to a fault."

Mrs. Stevenson said: "I brought these little things in. I really couldn't say if they're of any value, but I think they must be, as my dear mother kept them in her cabinet. Trinkets really. Pretty trinkets." She had a voice like an old 78 gramophone record of Caruso played too often and nearly worn out. I unwrapped the rough brown paper expecting the usual junk: Toby jug or sham Rockingham. I found a shepherdess guarding a lamb, not bigger than four inches; an even smaller group of three birds.

"My husband," said Mrs. Stevenson, "my husband often urged me to give them away to his favorite niece, Emma, but somehow . . ." The needle stuck, and for a moment there was nothing but hissing and grating. Then she coughed it into its groove again. "Sentimental value. My dear mother prized them, and now—"

The head of the shepherdess came off, beautifully fashioned, with a little cork inside. *All three* birds had detachable heads. "Why," he had said last night, "did you not let me kiss your mouth? It looks nice. Isn't it for use? Or have you taken a vow?" This suddenly in the car on the way home. "You don't realize," I said. "Realize what?" he asked.

"These are scent bottles," I said to Mrs. Stevenson. "About 1750. Oh, yes, they're valuable. You want us to dispose of them for you? We haven't a porcelain sale until June the twentieth. But we could include them in that if you wanted. The catalogue is just going to press."

"Yes . . . Well, yes." Old eyes wrinkled like leaves, suddenly speculative, cautious. "Valuable? How valuable?"

"I could only give an estimate. But they're Chelsea and the best period. They'll probably realize between £300 and £400 each."

"Realize what?" Leigh had asked again.

"Realize," I said in livid anger, "that I don't *want* to get involved with *anyone!* Apart—absolutely *apart*—from whether I want to get involved with *you!* Are you a com-

39

plete fool? Do I have to spell it out all over again? Now leave me alone! For God's sake leave me alone!"

Mrs. Stevenson picked up the shepherdess, and her hand shook as if she were using it as a pepper pot. "My —er—my dear young lady . . ." I took the scent bottle gently from her and put it in safety on the counter. "My, oh my, oh my! . . . Are you sure? You look very young . . ."

"Yes, I'm sure. But I can get it confirmed if you care to wait."

"I can hardly believe it. My dear mother would, I'm certain, be quite surprised. You know"—her Adam's apple moved up and down—"you know, I'd thought about —about £20. I'm a little short of—of money, you know. I thought about £20. I thought to myself . . ." She went on talking, like the long-faded Caruso in a recitative. There was a smell of Wincarnis on her breath. The gramophone would soon need rewinding.

"Let me give you a receipt," I said. "It'll be the twentieth in the morning, Mrs. Stevenson. Your address is? . . . Yes, of course you can come to the auction if you want to. No, just come to the front door in Grafton Street at about 9:40 and explain to the Commissionaire."

When I got back to the department Maurice Mills and three or four others gathered round in admiration of the prizes. So often, all too often, it was the other way round —people came in with precious possessions handed down from grandparents, highly prized, convinced of their certain value; and then you had the job of disillusioning them—the heirloom was paste or imitation or otherwise worthless. Worthless. Worthless. Like my friendship with Leigh Hartley. Utterly worthless and foredoomed. But these two little figures were exquisite, much sought after, the work of rare, delicate craftsmen. One smoothed them, cosseted them, would hardly be able to bear to see them sold.

A fatal mistake. One mustn't get attached, not even to Chelsea figures.

"Have you been out with Leigh Hartley again?" Erica asked. "Why don't you invite him in? I suggested it before, you know. If he's an artist Douglas and I would find him interesting."

"Maybe, sometime."

"When am I going to see you again?" he'd asked. I said: "Don't you ever take no for an answer?"

"Why don't you ask him for drinks next Sunday?" Erica said, fingering the rather handsome pearls she always wore. One would have hardly thought her dressed without them. "Arabella will be here and there are sure to be a few other young people around."

The Chelsea figures were beautiful, but you couldn't spend all day admiring them. Back to the old grind of cataloguing. (But it wasn't really a grind because every piece was different and many beautiful.)

Weak—how weak could one get? That was the precise moment to finish it, inside his car just parked near the brass plate which read J. DOUGLAS DAINTON, M.R.C.S., L.R.C.P., just as I reached for my stick to get out. But I hadn't finished it. Perhaps I hadn't *wanted* to at that precise moment. Of course later I'd certainly wanted to, sitting in my bedroom thinking it all over, telling myself I was a feeble fool, but by then it was too late. I'd said: "Oh, perhaps next week." "What day?" "I'm not sure." "Make it Monday." "I'm going out Monday." "Tuesday then." "All right, Tuesday."

"I don't think he's quite your type," I said to Erica.

"My dear Deborah, when I think of some of the very advanced young men Arabella has brought home . . . Douglas and I, as you know, pride ourselves on being able to talk to the young in their own language. It's an attitude of mind."

Everything, it seemed to me, was an attitude of mind. Sex included. My two sisters differed about this. Sarah had had at least six young men passionately attached to her in the last few years, but at twenty-seven had given herself to no one. "When I marry," she had said to me once, "I shall marry for love and I don't believe in being secondhand goods." Arabella at twenty I knew was already sleeping with someone.

And what about their middle sister? Chance is a fine

thing. Who wants to sleep with a girl with a shriveled leg? It turns you up really to think of it. Just imagine in bed, one nice leg and one thin, cold one. Then what the hell did Leigh Hartley want?

Lot 242. Brown glazed stoneware jar. Kwang Yao. Lot 243. Meissen May flower vase, blue, mounted in ormolu. *Pâte dure.*

Arabella had said: "I don't in the least feel I shall be secondhand goods. That doesn't enter into it. Sex is only like anything else. If you kiss someone you don't have a secondhand mouth. Aren't we born to live?"

For what purpose had Leigh Hartley been born? There were plenty of pretty girls around, glad of a robust young man and not particular about an accent, without him picking on me. Leave me alone in the quiet, evenly balanced, interesting life I'd found for myself.

"I wish these patent medicine firms would leave one alone," said Erica, screwing up a handful of pamphlets. "I feel like writing to our M.P. about it. Do they *really* think we're so ignorant as to suppose that the more complicated the synthesis the more likely the cure?"

Lot 251. Persian Ewer, white ground; with pattern in Iranian copper luster, eighteenth century.

Lot 252. Wedgwood . . .

What was the synthesis in my case, and what the cure?

John Hallows, who was the youngest director and dealt with jewelry, came in just then with a ruby ring he wanted Maurice Mills's opinion of, and I slid off my stool to look at it too. It had come in by registered post today from Norwich. The registered cover had been for £20 and the likely value of the ring about £600. People often did that sort of thing.

I stood talking to them, conscious that my leg was aching a bit. Odd, for it seldom did. "Stick your leg out," the physiotherapist had said. "Straighten it! *Push.* Just a couple of inches toward the sling." One fairly sweated in those early days, trying, trying. Odd that one had absolutely no control over that piece of bone and muscle that used to be a part of one's personal body. It just hung there like the discarded tail of a lizard. But the trouble was it wasn't discarded. You couldn't leave it behind and you couldn't do without it. Of course I was very lucky compared to many I saw.

"Sitting in at the sale tomorrow, Deborah?" John Hallows said. "We've got some pretty luscious pieces coming up, apart from the Leipzig emeralds."

John Hallows was the type of man I would have liked for a brother: good looking, kind, sharp as a needle in his job, but very alert to other people's feelings. We liked and respected each other.

"I don't care for morals," Arabella had said on her eighteenth birthday. "Morals are what other people think you ought to do. I only care what I think myself. I'm not going to be anybody's easy lay, but if I want to go to bed with a man I shall do so."

"Darling, you may think you're your own best judge," Sarah said, "but there's only so much to life, only so much experience, whether it's sex or any other sort. And if you fritter you fritter. And as you fritter you cheapen. What do you say, Deb?"

What I had said I couldn't remember because anyway what did it matter to me? But I was very lucky. "She's been very lucky," Mr. Adrian had said, "complete recovery of her breathing and of the right leg, and muscles of the left hip are perfectly sound. Wastage will probably not develop much above the knee. She'll be able to lead a full life." Odd to hear doctors being advised by doctors. Mr. Adrian was the great man on polio. He kept people with paralyzed throats alive by performing tracheotomies on them and pushing a tube into their windpipes. Then they lay there like stranded fish for the rest of their lives gulping air through artificial lungs.

That day I was almost afraid to go out to lunch in case Leigh was waiting on the corner, so I slipped out by the back entrance and ate in a dive in Lancashire Court. On the way back I went in the front way and there was no one there. Odd then if he never turned up again. Why should he? Perhaps he'd decided to leave me to my nice little quiet life after all.

"If you can promise to get hold of your friend," my

mother said, "I'll work off one or two other invitations at the same time. There was that fresco artist in Holly Hill, and the two people from Chelsea—what's their name?— Evans or Jones. They paint jointly by a new process— something like *gouache* but their own invention."

"Not this weekend. I shan't be seeing him till Tuesday."

"Well, that's awkward because the following Sunday I'm on call. Why don't you ring him?"

"I don't think he's on the phone. Anyway I don't know his number."

"What does he *do* all day in the East End, one wonders?"

"Work."

"Work," Leigh had said. "I'm like a man whittling away at a stick. I do it because I want to but the slivers are of no flaming interest to anyone else. It drives you up the wall. Of course I'm learning all the time, but it drives you up the wall."

"Is he at a school, d'you know?" asked Erica. "Has he a teacher?"

"No. He says he wants to paint the way he wants to paint."

Erica nodded approvingly. "How right. One thinks of the St. Ives primitives. How they would have been ruined . . ."

I said to Mr. Smith-Williams: "If one wanted to help a young artist, how would one go about it?"

"What sort of a young artist?"

"Well . . . twenty-four or twenty-five, lives in the East End, has been painting quite a while. But he doesn't seem to have had much recognition so far."

"That's not unusual. Do you know his stuff?"

"I wouldn't like to judge it."

"Has he tried the West End galleries?"

"I expect so. Some of them."

"Well, that would be the first step. Get an opinion from two or three of the more honest of them. See if they'll take a few of his paintings, and if they won't, ask them why."

"Who particularly?"

"Well, the Maud Brothers I'd go to first. They're absolutely straight and would give you a completely unbiased opinion. After that Arthur Hays of the Cheltenham Galleries."

"You wouldn't give one yourself?"

"Not wouldn't but couldn't—with anything like their authority anyway. You know Lewis Maud, don't you?"

It was raining on the Thursday, and Leigh was waiting for me outside.

"I can't—" I began.

"I've come to take you home."

There was a glint in his eye to show he knew I was going to say I couldn't go with him, so he'd chosen the answer that silenced me. As he tucked me in and shut the door he said through the swivel window: "Well, it's better'n waiting for a bus, isn't it?"

We had to make a detour to get out of the one-way streets, and while we were waiting at a traffic light, I had a good new look at him, trying to see him afresh. He was wearing a pink linen jacket without lapels and fine corduroy trousers of the wrong brown, and just too tight.

He said: "One day next week I want you to come skating with me at Queensway."

"What *are* you talking about? You must be crazy."

"Because you've only got one good leg? Well, Christ, that's three between us. It's *plenty*. Wouldn't you like to try?"

"No."

"I reckon you could do far more than you do."

"Thanks."

"Do you ever swim?"

"No."

"People in England are crackers. They're scared of going on a beach if they've a varicose vein. In Italy or Spain nobody cares: cripples, old people, fat people, they all enjoy the sun."

45

We broke free of the grip of the traffic and raced four abreast up Gloucester Place.

"As a cripple, an old person or a fat person," I said, "I enjoy the sun very much in my own way."

"But you're afraid to enjoy it in ways that might make you be looked at. It's a great mistake."

"It's a great mistake," I said, "to suppose that this line is going to get you anywhere."

"Where I want it to get me—where I want it to get us both—is to the ice rink next Tuesday."

I sat quiet and watched the traffic creep and clot and spurt, creep and clot and spurt.

He said at length: "Deborah, come off it. I'm not trying to needle you or improve you or shove you around, see. I just *like* you and I want to be your friend."

We went up the Finchley Road and came to Swiss Cottage, juggled with the involved traffic lights and hummed up Fitzjohn's Avenue. His car was a Triumph Spitfire. It was old and the hood rattled. The engine seemed all right. His big square hands were stained in two places with ultramarine.

I said: "I know, Leigh. Or should know, I suppose. I suppose I've snapped at you a lot."

"Not as if you meant to bite."

It had nearly stopped raining. The road here had just been relaid, and it shone like a slab of newly split coal.

"You understand . . ."

"Oh, yes," he said, "I reckon I understand all right."

We roared up the hill.

"See you next week then," he said.

"If you want to, but not—"

"On ice?"

"Not on ice."

"O.K. You're the boss."

His phases were still all wrong, but I didn't know how to put them right. I couldn't go on contradicting him forever.

We came to a stop. "Tuesday, then?"

"Tuesday then."

"Fine."

This time he let me get out of the car without getting out himself. I wasn't quite sure what that implied, whether it was a little victory for me or a little victory for him.

Chapter 5

And then he turned up at the cocktail party after all. I don't know who had been gulling me most—my mother had apparently got an invitation to him through David Hambro, but she never breathed a word to me; and I couldn't help but suspect when I saw the look in his eye—like a horse that means mischief—that in fact he'd had the invitation when we last met.

Erica normally has the average woman's approach to cocktail-party-giving—that is, she drags together a group of ill-assorted people, crowds them in a room with plenty of gin and smoke and allows them to shout at each other at the top of their voices for two hours. But either some didn't run up this Sunday, or she'd decided that this was to be one of her refined, arty evenings, for the total number was ten, and seven were painters, all of them abstract except Leigh. Two were French, one an Italian who spoke no English. One, a man called Collins, was interested in expressing pure psychiatry on canvas, which interested Douglas. Another had given up oils and was trying to advance the technique of collage by cutting holes in his hardboard panel.

I found it all rather tense because I could see in the middle of the talk that my family was trying to size Leigh up. Erica several times edged him into a group arguing about the geometric disciplines of form, but he wasn't having any. He might have been an engineer among musicians. Probably most of the other artists there were too self-centered anyway to realize that he was a painter at all.

For the most past he talked to me or flirted with Arabella, who wasn't above that sort of thing; and once or twice when I wasn't within hearing I saw him talking to Erica and Douglas. I noticed him eying our pictures, the prints of Paul Klee and Vasili Kandinski. It occurred to me to be surprised that I cared what *he* thought.

When they all left about nine, I ate a sandwich and made some coffee and took it in to Erica who was still in the drawing room emptying ashtrays and looking tall and flushed and wispy-haired and exhausted. Douglas had gone out about half an hour ago to see an old patient, so there were just the two of us.

Erica said: "Well I did think of asking Claude Collins and your man to stay on for an omelet and wine, but somehow they didn't seem to get on. Your man's not articulate, is he?"

"Sit down and put your feet up," I said good-humoredly, "and don't call him my man. He's got a name and he's articulate enough when he feels like it. But I told you, he doesn't fit into the usual *pattern*. You got what you deserved asking him here behind my back."

"My dear, you were so preoccupied—and so obstinate. We're much concerned for your future—Douglas and I —so naturally we want to *meet* your—your young men. And seeing them here in your own home, will help you to bring them into perspective."

She sat down suddenly with her coffee and began to sip it. The steam misted her glasses and she took them off.

"He left me something, by the way. A brown paper parcel. He left it by the front door. If you're not too tired . . ."

I hastily swallowed a mouthful of brown bread and butter and chicken and lettuce, and went down to get the parcel. As soon as I saw it I knew what it was.

"He said it was one of his paintings." Erica looked

older and more tired than ever without the frontage of her heavy glasses. Like a book without its glossy jacket. "Very civilized of him. Though I must say in conversation it was quite hard to pin him down to opinions."

She unwrapped the painting. It was quite small, I suppose about 16 × 10. Half done she paused to drink more coffee. The last bits of brown paper came off and we looked at a scene of London Docks, with the heavy cranes in the foreground, and a tug bringing up a string of barges.

"Very—civilized of him," said Erica staring at it fixedly and fingering her pearls.

I reached over and offered her a sandwich but she shook her head. I realized I wasn't very hungry after all and dropped half of mine back on the plate. Erica put on her glasses and tucked away a few spidery ends of gray hair. They sprang out again. I wondered if in thirty years my own hair would be like that.

"Really," she said, taking her eyes off the picture at last, and looking round, "even a dozen people turn a room into a shambles. This will have to be put right before Minta comes in the morning."

There was the sound of a car outside. I stared at the picture.

"She's getting more and more temperamental," Erica said. "It always happens with these women who begin as treasures and stay with one family half their lives."

It was Douglas back. I got up and began to empty the rest of the ashtrays.

"They realize they have power over the family they serve, that's the trouble, and the power corrupts them."

He'd been drinking whisky, not gin. There was some left in his glass but it was mainly melted ice. One of the Frenchmen had drunk *crème de menthe* and soda all evening. Very odd.

I said suddenly, with a breathless anger that didn't quite get out: "I think it would be better if you considered my room possibly empty too."

Erica finished her coffee and put some of the brown

paper back round the picture. Then she propped it distastefully against the leg of a chair.

"Whatever makes you say that?"

"It would be so much better if I didn't live at home. You'd have me less under your feet, feel less responsible."

"I wouldn't want you to leave, Deborah, you know that. We've had all this out before. It would be a great mistake."

"Mistake on whose side?"

She didn't answer. The glasses tittered together as I put them on the tray.

She said: "You know, we weren't trying to *interfere* with your friendship with Leigh Hartley, asking him here. It seemed simply the polite thing to do. I quite thought you'd appreciate our little gesture."

"Well, I didn't and I don't! Anyway, this house is too far out. It's too far every morning and evening!" I dropped a glass and it shattered. I knelt awkwardly and began to pick up the bits and put them on the tray.

Erica said with false patience: "Don't get into one of your tempers, Deborah. You're getting excited over absolutely nothing . . . As for responsibility, of course we feel responsible, and should wherever you lived, because love *creates* responsibility. We feel just the same for Sarah and Arabella—"

"Not in the same way."

"Yes, in just the same way. But I agree, the essence of good family life is that every member of the family should feel free within it. It's what Douglas has always said. It's the only psychological basis."

I went to the window fuming, not perhaps absolutely clear in my own mind yet why I was so suddenly angry, only aware that Erica had mistaken the cause. It was not the interference that I found intolerable but this sudden judgment of his work which had taken place, casual, Olympian, absolute. I banged the window open to clear the stale smoke. Douglas was just coming up the steps. His head shone smooth and pale and civilized in the lamplight. I realized I had very little in common with Leigh Hartley, except that, temporarily, I was on his side.

In fact I had nothing at all in common with him; but I had never deceived myself as to that. If I was getting emotionally involved, even in the smallest and most immature way, at least it was not without awareness of the mistake; it was against my conscious, educated judgment. One couldn't do better than one's best.

On the Tuesday we met again and drove to a sort of club in Wapping, where he said artists sometimes met. It was a fairly sleazy place, with a hard-eyed manageress and brassy barmaids, and a clientele to match. For a minute or two we saw Ted Sandymount again, and he looked thoroughly at his ease here, like a fish in water. Then after he'd gone a big man called Jack Foil came and sat down at our table. He was about fifty with a fleshy, heavy face and thick gold-rimmed glasses in which the pebbles really looked like pebbles. He wore a signet ring on either hand and smelled of carnation. He was a promoter and antique dealer.

He and Leigh talked about the exhibition Leigh had had in Southwark. Jack Foil had helped him to put it on, and he thought they might arrange another in a few months. I thought Leigh was more tentative than I'd known him before, anxious to agree with whatever Jack Foil said. Foil's voice was not uneducated but it was deep and thick and pompous. From the size of the cigar he smoked he must have promoted other more profitable ventures than art exhibitions.

I was not at all made to feel unwelcome—in fact Mr. Foil went out of his way with a sort of elephantine politeness to keep me in the conversation. He seemed to look with a paternal pebble on Leigh, and I was more or less included. When he got up, grunting and hum-humming, he did in fact say, "Bless you, my children," as his parting words; but I thought his square back looked formidable. He would be a good man to be on the right side of.

It was an alien world. I asked Leigh if he had been born round here.

"Good grief, no, I come from Swindon. My old dad is an inspector on British Railways. My mother was a schoolteacher, an arts mistress at Swindon High School; she didn't do much painting after she was married because she had three kids and then died. I went to Swindon Secondary Modern and first got a job as a clerk; but when old Aunt Nellie coughed up this money it seemed time to cut loose."

"Since when," I said, "I suppose you've had a lot of paint and a lot of women in your life."

He showed his teeth in a sudden grimace. "Yes to number one, no to number two. There's been one woman —one other woman. You don't latch on, dear, you're too conventional, you think all artists are like those lily-necked twits your mother dragged out from under some Chelsea stone last Sunday. You think all an artist does in life is hop in and out of bed with unwashed women. It's a big laugh. The true artist hasn't got all that much *time*."

"You think of yourself as a true artist, then."

"Christ knows. Maybe I'm old-fashioned. But all this swank, all this cult wind they blow out. To me art is hard work and more hard work. It's not a high-class gab shop!"

"And where do people like Ted Sandymount and Jack Foil fit into your artistic world?"

"They don't. But they're part of the *real* world, and that counts, doesn't it? Just as much part of the real world and the East End as the tugs and the derricks. They're people I knock along with. I understand them, see. They get on with the business of living and don't wrap their notions up in fancy paper and colored string."

"Unless," I said, "it happened to be black market string."

He looked at me. "You're a sharp little devil, aren't you? And I love you for it. Tell me about your illness."

"What illness?"

"Your—this polio thing. When was it?"

"Years ago. I've forgotten all about it."

"Well, what's wrong with your leg? Tell me exactly."

53

"You can see. It won't work much from the knee down and it's not absolutely right from the knee up."

"I thought that most of that was done with now—thanks to a gent called Salk."

"I was pre-Salk. I tell you, it's prehistoric. I was ten at the time."

"Are you ever ill now?"

"I had flu the winter before last."

"Don't be silly. I mean this look on your face. It sends me. Like a—like a madonna who's had a car accident."

I laughed. "Can I quote you?"

"Not to your other boy friends, you can't. But it's there, Deborah. Blessed Damozel stuff. Does it hurt to walk?"

"No, not really. One doesn't do it as instinctively, as forgetfully, as a normal person, that's all."

"Why can't I paint you?"

His hands were both on the table, palms downward, showing the freckle of dark hair from fingers to wrist. One as usual had a smear of paint.

"Have you ever done portraits?"

"Oh, yes. Not much good, but then . . . If I could paint you, it would be a real big help to me."

". . . I'll think about it."

"Think hard."

A half-dozen colored men came into the club. Their shirts were puce and vermilion and acid yellow and pea green.

He said: "Tell me about your job."

"I've told you."

"No, everything."

"Why?"

"Because I'm interested in everything you do."

"You'd be bored."

"Try me."

I tried him. Later we drove home, and I agreed to meet him on the following Tuesday. He said why didn't we meet every Tuesday and Thursday. It seemed a good idea, he said, to have a regular date. I said no, I sometimes worked late and could never be sure more than a

54

day or two ahead. This was true, but not the whole truth. Really, I was still struggling not to get too committed. The fish, you'll notice, always does struggle, even when it's firmly on the hook.

John Hallows was flying to Geneva next week to pick up an important piece of jewelry which a Viscount Vosper was going to put in our next sale. There was a rumor that Lord Vosper also had a collection of valuable resist lusterware that he was considering selling, and some discussion took place as to whether I should go with John Hallows to see it. But in the end it was felt that it might be better not to push the viscount into some sale he was not quite decided on.

This discussion took place on the Tuesday at 6 P.M., and as a result I was pretty late meeting Leigh. But he took my explanations patiently enough and drove me off along the Bayswater Road.

"You hungry?" he asked.

"Not particularly."

"Well, we can eat when you like."

We turned off and stopped outside what looked like a cinema. Somebody was just driving away, so Leigh put his car in the convenient place.

My mind still on the recent meeting at Whittington's, I said absently: "The movies again?"

"Sort of. It's a place I go sometimes."

As we went up the steps a commissionaire opened the glass doors for us. Leigh went to the pay desk and bought tickets. Somewhere was the sound of music. Glittery, even for a cinema, with a lot of massed lights over the stairs. Then suddenly I knew.

"Leigh! You fool! I told you."

He caught my arm as I turned to go out. "We can watch, Deb. No call to do any more. Be a sport."

"It isn't a question of that." I hesitated, wanting to leave but not wanting to let him or anyone else see that it meant anything to me.

"Well, let's just go and look-see. We can always come away if it's a drag."

As we went down the stairs the cold greeted us. Piped organ music was encouraging some sixty or seventy-odd people of varying degrees of skill, and lack of it, round a big oblong rink. The ceiling was dark blue dotted with stars, and there was a sort of sham Gothic castle at one end. We took seats outside the wooden barrier and watched in silence.

As so often, his action had roused conflicting feelings: anger at being tricked, a back-of-the-mind awareness that the whole thing was too trivial to be worth anger; disgust at his obtuseness, annoyance with myself that I was still far too sensitive; a wish to throw him over and a knowledge that if I did I'd regret it.

Presently he said: "O.K. now?"

I didn't speak. Three quarters of the girl skaters were in flesh-colored tights with tiny frilly skirts. They all had the most beautiful legs.

He patted my hand.

"Leigh," I said, "we shall get on so much better if you treat me as a grown-up human being and not as a retarded adolescent who has to be coaxed and cheated into doing things."

He still had his hand over mine. "Crikey, I *like* coaxing you, Deborah. It's nice for me and it's good for you. Honest. What harm have I done? Tell me. Just tell me how you've come to any harm through coming here!"

I sighed. "Sometimes we don't talk the same language, do we? We—we need an interpreter." Two beginners came sliding past us, clutching nervously to the rail.

He thrust his bottom lip out and wrinkled his forehead. "Maybe, maybe. I'm not subtle. Even my best friend wouldn't accuse me of being subtle. I just go on simple primitive instincts, and one of my instincts is to try to give you pleasure. But pleasures aren't always pleasures right off. Sometimes they hurt at first. Have patience, lovey. Don't shoot the pianist just yet."

We sat for a time. Then he said would I like something to eat and I said yes, so we went to the restaurant upstairs which looked out on to the skating. The warmth was very welcome after the chill of the rink. We had ham omelets and salad and beer and Cheddar cheese and biscuits. While we were there the floor was cleared of beginners and the experts had a session for dancing. This was much pleasanter for me to watch. In the same way I could enjoy Wimbledon but not the local tennis club.

About eleven he drove me home. Outside our house he leaned over and kissed me. I didn't turn away. He said: "Debby, Debby, Debby, what a gorgeous kiss. I love you. You weren't meant to be a nun. Remember that, can you, till Thursday?"

I remembered it till Thursday.

We went to Rotherhithe again but not to his house. We went to Ted Sandymount's flat. Ted, having just been turned out of a condemned building, had been rehoused on the sixteenth and top floor of a new block of flats. From his picture window you got a dream view of London's dockland, stretching from Tower Bridge to Greenwich. The river curled like a dangerous snake slipping half-hidden through the undergrowth of the city.

I couldn't bring myself to take to Ted. He might be big-hearted, as Leigh said, but he represented most of the superficial things I sheered away from in a man: a sort of vulgarity of outlook which cheapened what it touched. He had to perfection what Sarah had once called "lavatory-seat humor." I couldn't see how he appealed to Leigh who, for all his faults, wasn't really at all like that.

But that evening Ted seemed to be laying it on for me. He pushed forward the easiest chair so that I could sit and look out of the window, and rushed down in the lift to get a tomato juice when I said I didn't want to drink any more. He asked my opinion about things and instantly gave way if we both happened to speak at the same time. I thought Leigh must have given out that he was more than ordinarily keen on me, and Ted was doing his best as a friend to help the thing along.

As the evening waned lights began to wink in the streets below, and quickly the contagion spread until the whole city was like a hoard of jewels that had been raided and scattered. Ted said "You'd pay £20 a day for a view like this at the Hilton," and sniffed and twitched his way into the chair beside me.

"Some day," Leigh said, "I'll come up here and paint it. Sort of aerial view."

"I don't know why you don't paint Deb," Ted Sandymount said. "She's looking as pretty as a picture right now. All radiant, like. What's she done—won a prize in something?"

"I'd paint her like a shot if she'd let me," said Leigh. "I've asked her over and over. It's just what I need."

"Why?" I said.

"Because," he said.

"No, why?"

"I've told you often. You don't want me to say it all over again in front of Ted, do you?"

"Here, what's all this?" said Ted, his face as full of eagerness as a TV commercial. It should have jarred but for the moment didn't. "Why can't he paint you, Deb?"

"Maybe some time."

"Saturday?" said Leigh.

"Not Saturday."

"Why not Saturday?"

"I don't know. It's—too soon. I've got to think about it."

"Saturday," said Leigh.

"I have things to do at home."

"I'll call for you Saturday," he said, "if the light's good. It's the thing I need. For my painting. It's easy to be snide about inspiration, I know; but what else can you call it? It's the spark that sets the engine going. The split atom in the reactor, the—the . . ."

"The thing that makes the world go round, eh?" said Ted, patting my good knee. He always had to be patting. "You see Leigh needs you. He can't ask better than that. What d'you say? Give him a break, eh? Be a pal."

Chapter 6

He said: "Here. This way. I want you three quarter face, see. That's about it. Head up a fraction. Now . . ."

He stepped back and stared at me. I was sitting on a high chair looking more or less out of the larger of the two windows. It was a bright morning with sun and shadow falling in turns over the river. Leigh said it was perfect for work but he was fussing a lot about getting the sitter right.

Now after a minute or two's silence he said: "Mind if I use my comb?"

"What on?"

"Your hair . . . See . . . D'you mind?" He put his hand on my head and began to fiddle with the comb.

I hadn't realized how intimate the painting of a portrait can become. He used any excuse, putting his fingers on my neck to turn my head, grasping my shoulders with warm hands, smoothing the dress round my hips. It was a sort of mock love-making in a Laurence Sterne way, and I cursed myself for being such a fool. But I didn't all that much want it to stop. That was really the awful thing.

When he'd fiddled about with my hair he drew back and at last gave a grunt of approval. "That's better. That's about right. Hang on, I'll take a snap . . . I'll just get a bulb. Now hold it."

I waited until the flash had gone before I said: "Isn't this supposed to be a *painting?*"

"Yes, but I reckon to have a snap too. It helps me to get perspective."

I thought how shocked Erica's friends would be.

"Do you take photographs of all your subjects?"

"Not river scenes. The few portraits I've done, sure."

"Who else's have you done?"

He was at last making a few preliminary lines on the canvas. "Oh, nobody particular—a few friends."

"Girl friends?"

"Not specially."

"What about the one you mentioned?"

He looked at me for a long time. "Which one?"

"The other one. You said there was one other one since you came here."

"Oh, her . . ." There was a long pause. "That's ancient history."

"Tell me about her."

"Look, I can't concentrate if you talk all the time."

"I thoughts artists talked to put their sitters at ease."

"Well, this one doesn't."

Silence fell for about half an hour. Then I said: "I'm getting cramp."

"All right, relax. I'll shove some coffee on."

"Can I see what you've done?"

"No. Stay where you are." He went into the kitchen.

"How many sittings will this take?" I called after him.

"What? Oh, about three. Three or four."

I walked to the window, massaging my neck. It was low water. Two tugs were passing, their bright funnels puffing like Roman candles just alight before the first stars were sent up.

"What a marvelous place for fifth of November fireworks," I said.

"What, here?" He came back. "Where?"

"On this beach. You could even have a bonfire."

He laughed. "Go on with you. You'd have the Dock Board down on you." He put his arm round me and kissed my neck.

"Tell me about her," I said.

"What—this other girl? Why? It's a drag. It's done with."

"Was she just a casual caller like me?"

"You're a lot more than that."

"And the answer?"

"The answer's no."

"Was she your mistress?"

He put his face against my hair and sniffed. "The answer's no."

"Tell me about her."

"I don't want to. She was just someone I was keen on, but it didn't figure." He turned away from me and back into the kitchen.

The tugs had disappeared round the bend toward Surrey Docks. Rowers from the various clubs were out in force this morning. Those going with the tide moved with effortless speed; those against had to strain for every yard.

He came back with the coffee, and we sipped it together in companionable silence.

"Was she from round here? Was she an artist?"

He gave an irritable hunch of his shoulders. "She came from Ireland, if you must know. Her name was Lorne. She was twenty. She's now living in Stratford-on-Avon working as a receptionist at a hotel. She was five feet four and dark, with blue eyes, and I painted her six times." He added roughly: "Now tell me about *your* love life."

"Sorry."

"No, no." He swallowed, and took out the comb and ran it through his hair. "I should be flattered that you're curious. Crikey, I should be pleased."

In silence I got back on my chair and he lifted my chin an inch and then went back to his easel.

"D'you believe me?" he said.

"About what?"

"About other women being unimportant."

"I don't know."

"What don't you know?"

"I don't know enough about you, Leigh."

61

"D'you think I don't mean what I say?"

"Oh, no . . . I think you do. But it's hard to judge— we've known each other so short a time—it's hard to judge."

"What?"

"Well, how far you forget what you felt for other people, how soon you'll forget what you think you feel for me."

He was painting now. "I've told you—you've got it all wrong about me. I'm not the type. You've got this kinky view of artists—"

"Perhaps it's just a general view of men."

"Well, stop being in a groove. It's not like you."

Silence fell for a bit.

"There's another thing I want you to try," he said.

"What's that?"

"Skating with me on Tuesday."

I went skating with him on Tuesday. I wore a pair of stretch pants I had bought in France, and these hid quite a lot.

We hired skating boots and went down to the rink. He insisted on putting mine on for me. Something about the intimacy of the Saturday portraiture continued on. He took off my built-up shoe and fitted the boot on to my thin foot, with an extra sock inside to prevent it rubbing, and presently, when he had put on his own, helped me to get up and limp to the edge of the rink.

My face was hot before I even started. I felt everybody in the place was staring and sniggering as I put a scared wobbly skate on the ice. In spite of the disguise of the slacks I had a pretty fair idea what I looked like, and I hated him for that awful humiliation of it.

He said: "Don't think about slipping, see. Just try to stand up and hold on to me."

He got on the left side of me so that my weak leg was in the middle of us and pushed off with his left leg. My good leg at once wanted to shoot from under me. I put the bad one down and somehow we glissaded into the side and all but fell.

I swore deeply in my heart but said nothing. After all it was no good being angry again with him—only with myself for being such an utterable fool.

So we tried again and again nearly fell. "Good," he said—the idiot—"another try; we damn near made it that time."

At the seventh attempt I said breathlessly: "Let me *go*—it's no *good!* For Heaven's sake, let me *go*, Leigh! You go on your own."

"Another one—just for luck. Just once. I thought we were getting it. Nobody's looking."

I bit my lip and we started again. This time we began to go. His strong sturdy body was like a rock against mine. We began to go round the ring. We almost made a complete circle, before somebody sweeping across made him swerve and we had to fetch up hurriedly at the side.

"You see!" he said laughing. "You really *did* it! If that nit hadn't got in our way we'd have gone on forever!"

Breath back and begin again. And this time it really did work. Round twice, shakily but no fall. My left leg had just enough power to push at the ice and he showed me how to turn it to gain a grip. This I could do not from the calf and ankle where it should have been, but by turning the thigh.

Hot all over; hands in his clammy with sweat. But his triumph was so real that he might have been celebrating some feat he'd pulled off himself; I found myself laughing with him. We sat and rested and then tried again. Again no mishap. We went round six times before giving up and taking coffee and sandwiches in the cafeteria.

"There," he said, "you see! It's quite possible. And next time it'll be easier still."

"There'll never be a next time!" I said, knowing that there would and that he knew that there would.

He held my hand, fingering it as if he would feel each individual bone. "There's other things yet, in time. Swimming—that ought to be easy; golf—I've never played golf, we might start it together; dancing . . ."

"I *can* swim."

"But do you?"

"In the physiotherapy baths."

"That's no good. South of France is the place. We could go on a trip . . ."

I didn't try any more to discourage him. I knew it was no good. Anyway just then I didn't feel in a discouraging mood. Tomorrow both legs would be stiff, but I was feeling as ridiculously pleased as he looked. And so well, so very, very well. I felt like someone who has been out riding on a cold, wintry morning. Tired but relaxed, skin tingling, appetite keen, lungs full of air, and alive, alive, alive.

He looked at me and smiled his all-embracing, rather contorted, rather beautiful smile.

"You've had enough for one night, Deborah. I'll take you home."

Friday at Whittington's. A day like any other day. Cataloguing completed until some new stuff came in on Monday, I was doing a few letters in reply to inquiries. Letters were always coming in: "Dear Sirs, I have for long had on my mantelpiece two beautiful vases of what I believe is called Cloisonné ware . . ."

Upstairs Smith-Williams was conducting a sale of English water colors and early drawings. Only small sales were held on a Friday, such as would be completed by noon. A furniture van was outside our back door in Bruton Lane unloading some furniture which had been sent down from Scotland.

A telephone rang in the office of Peter Greeley, the head of the firm. It was from Switzerland, from a hospital in Geneva to say that John Hallows had met with a car accident ten miles outside the city and was in hospital with concussion.

Greeley called Maurice Mills into his office, together with three other directors who were in the building, for consultation, because Hallows was expected back on the 14:30 plane with the Vosper tiara he had been sent to collect. One of the emigrant English, Viscount Vosper had tax-dodged himself abroad ten years ago, but had been living beyond himself and had decided to realize on the diamond tiara which had belonged to his mother and which was valued at £40,000. John Hallows presumably now had this with him, but it had been a member of the hospital staff who had telephoned, and Greeley had not liked to make public the sort of cargo that John Hallows was carrying. After a few minutes it was decided to ring up Viscount Vosper to see what he could do on the spot, but before Peter Greeley could put through the call, another ring came through from Geneva, and it was John Hallows himself to say that his injuries were slight but that the accident had been a put-up job and that he and the chauffeur had been set on by three masked men and the tiara was gone.

This news ran through the building like a short circuit, and only Smith-Williams, on his rostrum in his expensive charcoal gray suit, went on in ignorance. Peter Greeley decided to fly out with Maurice Mills to Switzerland at once, and they left to catch the 13:15 plane.

All this meant extra work for me, and I didn't get home until eight. We had been skating again on the Thursday, and it was tiring me even more than I'd expected. The following morning I slept on and was still in my bath when Leigh called at ten. Fortunately it was Erica's morning on duty so they didn't have to meet.

On the way to his place I told him what had happened to John Hallows. He whistled.

"Somebody's been pretty sharp. Also somebody's been pretty dim-wit."

"In what way?"

"Well this man Hallows; you really sent him off to collect a valuable tiara like that without any guard at all?"

"Often it's the safest way. The less publicity the better."

"Yes, if someone isn't in the know. But what about this Viscount fellow in Switzerland? How is anybody to know how many in his household knew about it? Your man ought to have had a guard."

"Maybe."

"Of course, it'll be insured."

"Oh, yes."

65

When we got to his studio I found the chair and easel ready, and he fussed less than the first time. But the painting was covered until I was settled, and there was no chance of seeing it.

"Has the photo come out?" I asked innocently.

"Oh, yes," not noticing any irony. "It's just good enough to keep me on target when you're not here. I've done quite a bit of the background since last week."

I sat for about twenty minutes in silence while he painted away. Then he said:

"You know these characters who do these robberies—you can't help but admire 'em."

"Admire them?"

"Well, not exactly admire them, but . . . See I reckon, Deborah, that there's two sorts of crimes, isn't there? There's the anti-human and the anti-property. I've no room at all for the first—the lout who clobbers an old woman and steals her bag; the man who shoots a bank messenger; the sneaking sex criminal who lurks in bushes to attack little girls. God, I'd belt 'em all!" He dabbed at his palette. "But the type that only goes for property—and not personal property but company property, insured, gold in a vault, £5 notes belonging to a bank, that sort of caper—the man who pits his wits against the law, playing the game to the rules—no violence or the minimum—nothing that'll harm people as people . . . You know, you can admire their cleverness, their guts, their nerve."

"I don't suppose John Hallows will."

"I don't reckon he will. All the same, I still think your firm ought to start using its loaf."

"There are still an awful lot of honest people in the world," I said. "Most business goes on in that belief—just as you live assuming that most people are sane. If you didn't you could hardly live at all."

I watched his face as he worked. The concentrated H lines of a frown between his eyes, the thick short curly hair, never tidy but too often combed, the big mouth with its thin sensitive lips parted. The poised right hand moved swiftly between palette and canvas. Was it creating an immortal work or an amateurish botch? From here I couldn't tell. The concentration was the same, the muscular movements, the degree of mental and spiritual effort, the quality of canvas and paint. Who knew? Who was to decide?

He said: "Tell me something. How do you think on morals, Deborah? How does your mind work? Not just sex morals but ethics generally." He called it ee-thics. "D'you reckon to still believe in all those old Commandments? Steal, adultery, murder, the lot."

"Why?"

"I just wondered."

"I don't know. Why?"

"I just wondered."

"And you?"

"Oh," he shrugged. "Maybe I'm poor enough to wish I'd the knack of making money in some big quick way. Too many Cheap Jacks, too many Smart Alecs, too many Smooth Operators are striking it rich these days for me to feel much of a twinge of conscience if I could come by money quick and easy . . . So it's lucky the chance isn't likely to arise."

"You've money enough to go on with?"

"Oh, scraping along . . . Maybe it's the best bet. Honest Jim in his garret. Of course if I could make money out of painting that would be different. Then I'd feel I was really on the way."

I tried to stretch without moving. My limbs felt tired and stiff.

"Of course," he said, "your background's so different from mine. You've never wanted for anything since the day you were born. Delicately nurtured they call it. Money can't ever have the same importance—"

"It can have plenty!"

"Yes, but look at my old man on the railways. He's got a safe job, I'll grant you, but one of the worst paid. A declining industry: nobody cares a damn for railways any more; and no hope himself of getting any higher; his union fights a battle and he gets an extra 12/6 a week, and tax at once takes off 4/—. Just standing still, with the rise in the cost of living, just standing still costs him more than 8/6 a week more, but unless he goes out cleaning cars of an evening he hasn't a hope in hell of laying his hands on another penny piece. Could you blame him if he cooked some figures to wangle a few quid out of the post office."

"Did he?"

"Did he? Not likely! It would be against the principles of a lifetime! But you see what I mean. Living with someone like that makes you think. I'm not sure his son might not be tempted if the chance came his way . . . Ah, you've moved!"

"I must have been shrinking away from you in horror."

"That's it. Well, it's time for the coffee break anyway. I'll help you down."

Instead of helping me he lifted me, and then lowered me gently, but kept his arms round me. I smiled. But he wasn't smiling.

"Deborah Doolittle."

"Leigh Do-Nothing."

"I got a much tougher job than old Higgins or whatever his name was. I have to breathe on you and rub you gently like a—a sort of angel with frostbite. It's a thawing process, see, and a waiting process. Real good for me."

"For you?"

"Yes, for me. I got no patience in the ordinary way—can't wait—must grab at life. But this—this being with you—it teaches me patience—Chinese patience nearly. Chinese torture sometimes."

"As bad as that?"

"As bad as that and as good as that. Only one thing could do it, you know. Only one thing could ever make me so patient."

"What's that?"

"Don't you know? You shouldn't even have to guess."

He put his mouth against my cheek and kissed and sniffed. It was as if he was suddenly tired and wanted rest. I put my hand up and smoothed his hair.

There was a couch that a step or two back took us toward and he bent and swept newspapers and other litter flying. I lay on it and he knelt beside it, stroking my face and then my breasts and legs. He began to kiss me on the mouth, neck and arms, then unbuttoning the front of my frock, pulled shoulder straps down and put his lips about the top of my body. A wave of sudden sexual emotion sluiced over me and I'd no more control of thought or direction than a branch caught up on the crest. His mouth came up to mine and his hands were like warm snakes making magic life and a fiery compulsion that had no end but acceptance. Sanity was falling out of the skies and darkness shone through the sunlight, and I was sitting up and he had moved back to squat on his haunches, drawing deep breaths and his gray eyes pale as paint.

A tug hooted in the river. I dragged together the neck of my dress.

"Patience," he whispered, and swallowed, not sure of me. "Christ!"

The tug was bringing up a vessel of some size which looked to have a Norwegian name on its bows. They would have to open the bridge. All my life I had never seen them open Tower Bridge.

He said: "I'll get the coffee."

When he was gone I tried to stand up, but even my good leg was groggy. I flopped back on the couch and began to pick up the newspapers and fold them and stack them beside me. Just for something ordinary to do. Just to keep in touch with ordinary life. My mouth was as unstable as a drug addict's. As he returned I managed to get up and peer out of the window at the cargo boat so that he couldn't see my face. If he had come back for me to take me then I'd have gone like a straw.

"Coffee in a minute . . . Deborah." Instead his voice was supplicatory.

"Yes?"

"You got to admit until now I've been patient. This was—a sudden crack, see. I'm still ready to go at your rate, if you know what I mean. From now on."

"Yes."

He went across and dragged forward a chair. "God, my hand's like I've been shell-shocked. Doubt if I shall be able to paint."

The tug was belching black smoke. Any moment now the bridge would begin to open. The central platforms would lift and separate, opening like two giant hands raised in praise and prayer. Traffic was stopped. The Norwegian vessel was drifting slightly with the tide. A barge altered course to move past it.

I hadn't done up the top button of my dress.

I turned and limped blindly toward the kitchen.

"Where are you going?"

"To make the coffee."

Chapter 7

It was heavy and still that night when he drove me home, but glimmerings of late daylight latticed the clouds over Harrow. In the open car whiffs of lilac and wallflower surfaced through the tire-tarmac-petrol smells. Houses glimmered like lighted barges, Euclidean problems jostling against each other full of unsolved areas and unmeasured angles.

After another hour in the studio while he had tried to continue the portrait, we had gone out to lunch at the Spanish Galleon, and then had gone aboard the *Cutty Sark,* whose magisterial masts dominated Greenwich. Afterward we had walked beside the river and sat for a time in the temporary sun on the soft sand where there was the notice which said DANGEROUS FOR BATHING. We had had dinner in Erith and had taken a roundabout way home.

No more said about that five minutes in the studio but it lay in the back of our minds. It couldn't be ignored. It didn't have to be.

Because I wasn't in the least unhappy that it had occurred. And that made it perfectly clear that, unless I took some pretty drastic decision here and now, it would happen again even more unmanageably in the near future.

71

Not a problem then? Arabella wouldn't think so. I still did.

Who to ask? Advice from Sarah? She was the sanest, most down-to-earth of my family. But what use advice? One would ignore it. Help, then? What sort of help?

At the door of our house he kissed me just once. Affectionate, without obvious passion. Being patient, no doubt, as promised. Or had something this morning not been quite to his liking? Perhaps he'd come to the concluison that I was delicate, too delicate for all that sort of thing.

"Monday?"

I had the grace to say: "Not Monday."

"Tuesday, as usual, then?"

"Yes . . ."

"Skating?"

"Perhaps."

"Mustn't overdo it. It was a long session on Thursday. See how you feel."

Invalid. "All right."

"Night, love."

"Good night, Leigh."

I stood and watched him drive away. His car had a curious exhaust note, like a very cross fly caught on a very big windowpane. I took a deep breath. I was happy. Life was good enough, big enough, and I was strong enough. That was what mattered.

All weekend—two days—to think, to decide, to remember, to weigh up, to reason it out. To remember. Two days. Didn't need even to begin to think until tomorrow.

Tired, pleasantly tired, and sleepy. I looked forward to pulling the cool sheets up and lying with my eyes just clear, not to read but just to look at my treasures—and think. To remember. To think.

It being Saturday, Arabella was home; the strains of her record player coming from the drawing room. In our family even Arabella preferred classical music, but the fact that she was playing a Beethoven trio told me that my father was out. Douglas couldn't bear Beethoven's music. "All triviality of theme and ponderous Germanic decoration," he called it.

I found her stretched on the one uncomfortable settee but draped over it in such a way, blond hair voluptuously falling, that she contrived to make even our stark room exciting. She was reading the Kama Sutra, but she dropped it when I came in. Erica had gone to bed with a headache, she said, but had taken a pile of B.M.J.'s with her for light reading. I remembered Arabella as a thin straggly little girl inclined to malicious teasing of her lame elder sister, and this had gone on until she was sixteen. Then, almost overnight, her sallow, spotty skin changed, her hips and calves and breasts developed fashionably gentle curves, her eyes grew bigger—her hair more glossy, and every second man eyed her with interest and appreciation. At roughly the same time her nature had seemed to alter, had become less aggressive, less prickly, and we had scarcely exchanged a hard word since.

Not that we were very close—it was a light, easy relationship—and I found I couldn't ask her about Bruce Spring. Even though we normally discussed everything under the sun on a skim-surface level, like swallows over an evening lake, we never plunged in. She had no hesitation in openly asserting her right in principle to sleep with whomever she pleased, but I couldn't say to her as a personal question: "Are you happy? How do you feel? What's it like? How does it work out in practice?"

So in a while I put the needle back on the Beethoven and left her to her music and her Kama Sutra, and went up to bed. The light was underlining Erica's door so I tapped and went in.

She was sitting up reading in a blue silk bed jacket, her glasses half-down her nose, the white satin counterpane carefully folded back, a smell of Eau de Cologne, the lights too bright for a bedroom.

"Hullo, darling," I said. "Headache?"

"Oh, Deborah . . ." She ran her middle finger along the bone of her nose to push her glasses up. "Mavis left an overspill of work when she went on holiday, and difficult cases always come in blocks."

73

"Can I get you anything?"

"No, no. Just a little tired."

"Couldn't you do with some more frivolous reading?"

"One has to keep abreast of things. And you?"

"Yes, fine, thanks."

"With Leigh again?"

"With Leigh . . . What did you do with the picture he gave you?"

"It's in Sarah's room. Have you been to his studio?"

"This morning."

Douglas's blue Viyella pajamas were laid out on the other bed. Erica was a stickler for some of the niceties, even though she despised others. A few years ago she had tried to convert us all to nylon sheets, but led by Douglas we had all rebelled. And he still refused to be dragooned out of his warmer nightwear.

"I asked Sarah," Erica said, "to ask David Hambro about Leigh Hartley. You remember I asked her when you were there."

"Oh, yes?"

"It seemed odd, this young man, living alone in the East End. Of course David confirms what Leigh told you. He came to London a few years ago on a legacy and has been painting on and off since."

"Well, I didn't suppose he was a liar."

"No. Oh, no. Of course not. It wasn't for that reason that one asked."

For what reason then? "I think I'm off to bed," I said.

"Did you know," Erica said, "that he was married?"

"Who? David Hambro?"

"No, Leigh Hartley."

On the table beside Douglas's bed was this thin pile of brightly colored folders. Greece. Corfu. Yugoslavia. Erica's holiday in Ireland had been fixed months ago. Douglas never made up his mind until the last minute.

"Oh, Leigh," I said. "Yes."

"You knew?"

"Yes."

Erica picked up her article, which seemed to be on contraindications of the barbiturates.

"Have you met her?"

"Who?"

"His wife, of course."

"Oh, no."

One advantage of my father and mother working in different practices was that they could both be on holiday at the same time, even though they went in opposite directions. Opposite directions.

Something fought its way up into my mind. "She lives in Stratford-on-Avon now—works as a receptionist at a —at a hotel."

"Are they divorced?"

"I've no idea."

I was trying to swallow something sour that had come into my throat. It was as if I had vomited and couldn't get rid of the taste. "You're so civilized, Erica, it's strange you don't believe in Platonic friendship."

"Not with him, I wouldn't."

"Why? Does he look so sexual?"

"Not in so many words, no. He may be a very agreeable fellow. But there's an earthiness about him. It surprises me . . ."

I didn't ask what surprised her. If only I could escape now—escape on the right note, without giving any appearance of running away.

"Where's Douglas?"

"He went to a meeting at the Joe Rogerson's."

"Oh, yes," I said.

She pulled her glasses down an inch again and looked over them at me. "Will you be in to lunch tomorrow? We've got the Mayfields coming, and you know how fond they are of you."

"I'll be in to lunch."

The piece of the Attic black figure vase had been let into a thin wooden frame for safety. It depicted, so far as one could tell from the fragment, a drunken dance. It was made of a high quality clay of about the sixth century B.C., polished and orange-red in color with the scene painted in what then must have been brilliant black. One pictured it complete, as it had been first moulded: a graceful urn-shape with slim handles like ears and a flat black lid. I liked to believe it had been painted by Exekias.

It represented perhaps the limit of perfection in a style which soon after had changed to red-figure and thus set off a new chain of invention and inspiration. A few months ago a good example of the red-figure style had come into Whittington's but it had gone for too high a figure for me to buy. I would have loved to have stolen it.

Perhaps I had no higher a moral standard than Leigh. He would steal if he could; he lied (by omission) when it suited him. Who cared for ee-thics these days? He had hinted at that to me but had not liked to say it any plainer. Life was a free-for-all, and devil take the fools who were gullible enough to think otherwise. Lovely fragment of a purer age.

I shut my eyes but didn't put off the light. Light was my only company. For the time I couldn't do without it. Dark would bring a shutting in of thought.

She came from Ireland. Her name was Lorne. She was twenty at the time.

She was five feet four and dark with blue eyes, and he painted her six times. Also, quite by the way, he happened to marry her. A simple little accidental occurrence not worth mentioning. This morning his hands had been on my naked body, on my breasts, the first man's ever. Swallow the poison, it meant nothing these days. What did jealousy and hate have to do with a simple light-hearted piece of petting? A civilized girl didn't get angry, blood didn't beat, heart freeze, passion and pain breaking. Fun, fun was the thing; have fun. Come then, kiss me, sweet and twenty, youth's a stuff will not endure. But when you're sour and twenty-six and twisted of mind and body?

Two lovely plates, think of them, rest, cool one's soul on them. One on either side of the long mirror. The first, a Rockingham in apple green, had been a birthday present last November from Sarah and Arabella. Ornately scrolled, with a harbor scene, a sailing ship at anchor, land and castle behind painted a delicate apricot. On the other side was a Coalport I had bought myself, simpler as to design but rich in color, painted with flowers by William Cook and rimmed with gold.

To get away, that was the thing, to get away. Time to reason, to think, to forget. I ought to put the light out. Sleep might come. Needed a couple of sleeping pills. Some downstairs, no doubt in the room at the back where Douglas kept his stuff; but how to know one pill from another?

Sleepless then. John Hallows in hospital; Maurice Mills flying home; Viscount Vosper protesting. Who shall abide in thy tabernacle, Who shall dwell in the holy hill? I'm crazy about you, Deborah. Get that? Let your hair blow, it looks fabulous. Among the productions of the Dutch potters must be noted the figures: miniature pieces such as vases and dishes, dogs, violins, slippers and ewers. You really should have more men friends, Deborah. There's absolutely no reason why not. At high tide my balcony is under water. Why did you not let me kiss your mouth? It looks nice. Isn't it for use? She's having one of her turns, says Erica, we really must wake her.

I start up with a jerk, look anxiously round the room. Empty and quiet—no one here—the light still burns. Twenty past three. A pain in my solar plexus.

A small Rakka jar from Mesopotamia; not such a good color but cheap at one of the sales. In a year or two would sell it, buy something Greek in its place. There was a Turkish Isnik dish I coveted in the coming sale. The *arcanum* or secret of making porcelain was closely guarded . . . from 1744 . . . Sleeping pills. Put the light out. Mustn't be red-eyed in the morning or Erica will suspect. *Out* with the light. . . .

Heart goes thump, thump, thump. Not ready yet for the coffin or the grave. But how am I alive at this moment in inky darkness? Only because I can feel pain and hear the ticking of a clock.

Only perhaps because I can feel pain.

I got up about seven and took an early bath. Sunday

was a late day for everyone unless there was some unexpected call out. Douglas had once said that a moratorium should be declared on all illness between six and eleven of a Sunday morning.

I crept down and got one of the papers and spread it and stared at its black and white surface over a cup of tea. No communication passed, so I went back to bed and lay there very quiet till nine. I dressed then and rang Sarah. We had a long conversation.

Over breakfast I said to Erica: "I'm thinking of going to stay with Sarah for a bit. Virginia Fisher is starting her holiday on Thursday, and Sarah will be alone."

Erica spread butter thinly over a piece of Ryvita. "She often has been before."

"Well I've often stayed with her when this house has been closed. And she's working all hours."

"I'm sure you're better here on the whole, Deborah," Erica said. "Generally speaking you get regular meals and lead a settled life."

"I thought of going on Tuesday," I said. "Just for a few weeks."

"But that would take us up to the holidays! You'd be there seven weeks at least."

"Not if I come to join you."

"If you did."

"Well, I might well. I've no plans for the holidays."

"If you go and stay with Sarah," Arabella said, "you might be able to sort out how serious she is over Philip Bartholomew. I'm not sure if she hasn't caught the bug rather badly this time."

"Who's Philip Bartholomew?"

"You must remember him, Deb. He was at that party and doing a fly-round-honeypot act. Serious type. Too serious I'd have thought for Sarah."

"No, I don't remember." Perhaps because someone had been doing a fly-round-honeypot act with me. Someone who was a liar (by omission) and not at all the serious type.

"What does he do?" asked Erica.

"He's in law. His father's a judge. They met at some 'do' in the Temple."

Highly respectable, highly suitable. Not East End and fly-by-night and slipshod and needing a bit of sex to keep things going. The son of a judge, not a railway worker. The friend of law and order, not the friend of Ted Sandymount and Jack Foil.

Douglas came in looking shiny and hairless and clean from his long immersion in the bath. He greeted his family with engagingly frank, cool eyes, and his family got up and made fresh coffee and put on his eggs and bacon. I wondered how far he was in Erica's confidence, how much he knew of my friendship with Leigh Hartley, more important how much he cared. I would have *loved* to have gone to his room after breakfast and told him everything. Whether he offered advice or not, the mere act of telling someone sympathetic and understanding and wise. . . . But I knew it wouldn't work. If I went and asked him about any general, impersonal subject—from Taoism to Lesbianism—he would talk intelligently, clearly and with great understanding and sincerity; and moreover he'd listen keenly to anything I said. But if I went to him with a *personal* problem—not what should one do in principle but what should *I* do in *fact*—he would shift mentally a foot or two away as if close contact were to be avoided. Douglas, I'd say, I'm involved, half caught by a man and spinning on the edge. Now I learn . . . He never told me . . . We've about a quarter made love . . . He was persistent, pestered . . . How should I break altogether? Somehow it's much harder for me. It was harder to go with him in the first place; now it's harder to stop. There's no doubt he's attracted to me, physically attracted. But what does it mean in his language? I don't *want* to get involved any further now, now this has happened. But how can I make a break?

They'd surely done their best, both Douglas and Erica. The taboos inherent in any parent-child relationship had been knocked over one by one. We were on a level; friendly, companionable, appreciating the same jokes, dis-

79

cussing the same articles, arguing with the same balanced appreciation of the other person's point of view. The only things lacking were involvement, loving kindness. Did I ask too much?

"The egg's double-yolked," said Erica. "They're three-pence dearer than the others, but very fresh."

The plate was put in front of Douglas as he opened his newspaper.

"Ah," he said with satisfaction. "I see there have been more protest marches in Madrid."

Chapter 8

John Hallows was back as usual on Monday morning, a plaster on his cheekbone. It was the day of the porcelain sale and I sat almost all day in the sale room, noting purchasers and prices. I didn't see old Mrs. Stevenson there but her two little Chelsea scent bottles fetched £325 and £375, so my estimate hadn't been a bad one. The Turkish Isnik dish didn't fetch as much as we had expected but I felt too miserable and unsettled to bid for it.

On the Tuesday I telephoned Whittington's and told them I had a sore throat. Then I packed a bag. I just took three frocks and some underwear and a nylon dressing gown and a few personal things, as if I were going only for a week or so. In the top of the wardrobe as I reached for a new scarf, my fingers closed over the irons I'd worn until I was twenty. I took them out and tried them round my leg, and it seemed as if the leg had filled out a bit since then.

Erica was just leaving for her surgery. She said: "And what if people ring? Do I tell them where you are?" "Of course," I said, "I'm not in hiding, darling." "Well, one just wishes to know," she said. "I never ask, but do you still do the massages regularly?" "Not regularly but often enough." "I'll say no more, as I know how you hate being

fussed over." "It's bad for me, darling, you know that.
Bad psychologically. Isn't it, Douglas?"

Douglas said: "It rather depends who does the fussing.
One mustn't interfere with the age-old struggle to be free.
Be careful how you get your car out, Erica. I drove mine
in rather carelessly last night."

It was on this note that I left home.

That evening, Sarah being on hospital duty, I persuaded Virginia to go with me to the cinema. We went to
the last house, and were not home until eleven-thirty. The
telephone didn't ring that night.

Wednesday I went back to work. The difficulty of
course with a place like Whittington's is that it's not like
a big office or a bank or an insurance company, which no
one may enter unless he has legitimate business. People
wander in and out of the showrooms all day inspecting
the stuff on show and, although technically they have no
business downstairs where the assembling and cataloguing
of the goods takes place, no one really questions the occasional intruder, and I thought all day that Leigh would
suddenly appear, squeezing his way among the furniture
and the stacked pictures.

I didn't go out for lunch, and in the evening I slipped
out of the back entrance into Bruton Lane.

Philip Bartholomew came to dinner at the flat, a thin
young man about Sarah's height, with a desperately pale
complexion as if his skin never saw the sun. Virginia was
very excited about her holidays which began next day, and
we had a jolly evening. Or they had anyway.

Halfway through dinner the telephone rang, and Sarah
came back from the bedroom to say: "It's for you, Deb."

I picked up the telephone without an idea in my head
what I was going to say.

"Hullo."

"Hullo, Deborah. I've caught up with you at last."

"Who's that?"

"That man Hartley. Who you had an appointment with
last night."

"Oh, Leigh. Oh, yes, sorry; I had a bit of a throat."

"Are you better?"

82

"Yes, thanks."

"Really?"

"Yes. Yes."

"We'll meet tomorrow as usual, then?"

"No, I can't tomorrow. Virginia Fisher, Sarah's flat mate, is going abroad for her holiday and I've promised Sarah to help her rearrange things."

"Oh . . . I'll call for you Saturday morning, then, as usual."

"No, I can't this Saturday."

"Hey, hey, what's the matter?"

"Nothing. I just can't make it."

"Oh, but we were in full flight on the painting. Too long a delay might spoil things."

"Sorry."

A pause. I could picture his knitted frown, heavy lids down, lips drawn.

"Is it because of what happened last Saturday?"

"D'you mean? . . . Oh, no."

"Of course you know what I mean."

"Yes, I know. And it isn't."

"I reckon maybe it is. Look, Deborah, it was the sort of thing could have happened to anyone. I love you. D'you latch on to just what that means? What happened was because of that. Anyway there was nothing wrong. Don't be afraid of it."

I bit the skin on one finger. "I'm not afraid."

"Then when will you meet me?"

"Not for a while."

"Crikey, I just don't get this! I can't believe you don't feel something for me, being the way you were on Saturday. It doesn't make sense. So why try to strangle something, now that it's just come alive? Why run away?"

"I'm not running away! I just think I'd like a break."

"Give me a chance to finish this portrait. Another couple of sittings will do it. I swear to God I'll not touch you again."

"That isn't the *reason*, I keep telling you! But I just want a break!"

"Darling, what's the matter? If you—"

83

"Goodbye, Leigh." I slammed down the receiver and sat there with trembling fingers, angry and more miserable than I'd ever been in my life.

I couldn't face them for a bit. I couldn't go back and go on with my dinner. So I went into the bathroom and sat on the pink-toweling-covered lavatory seat and said, stop, stop, *stop*. It's not important; it'll all be the same in a hundred years, in five years, in one year. I shall look back and think, what a *fool* I was to get upset about such a trivial thing and such a trivial man.

So presently I stopped and blew my nose about a dozen times and took a few deep breaths and tried to put it all away from me. Proportion, that's the most important word in life. If you can see things in proportion half your troubles are not troubles at all.

The "spare" bedroom in the flat in Ennismore Gardens was so tiny as only just to admit a single bed and a cupboard which did for a wardrobe. At night the walls were so close that I had to fight the old battles with claustrophobia. So when Virginia left, I moved in with Sarah.

I told Sarah that Leigh had become too persistent and I wanted to choke him off, so she must help. Sarah said: "Anything you say, duckie."

I saw nothing at all of him that week.

On the Monday John Hallows had to go back to Geneva, and Maurice Mills left with him, so I was in charge of the department. This meant my working late both on the Monday and on the Tuesday. By Tuesday evening I didn't feel much like queueing for a bus and then walking, so I took a cab back to Ennismore Gardens.

It was a light, warm and dusty evening, when there didn't seem much sap left in anything and the leaves of the trees made thin scratching noises in the breeze. The declining sun was flooding the eastern side of the square. Two dogs dodged aimlessly among the rows of parked cars, playing hide and seek with each other.

As I got to the door and put in my key I heard Leigh's step behind me.

He said: "I thought you must come in sooner or later."

I stood there, feeling the ridges on the cane of my stick. "Have you been waiting? Sorry."

"Sarah went out half an hour ago. Can I come in?"

"I'm tired. I'd rather be alone."

Reflection of the sun in his eyes as he looked up at me.

"What's wrong, Deborah? Why've you thrown me over?"

"I don't think there was all that much between us, was there?"

"I reckon so!"

"Well, perhaps we can talk about it sometime." I moved to turn the key.

"No!" He put his arm across the door. "I must know. It's only *fair* to tell me what's wrong, to say something, to explain."

I stood there feeling pretty sick.

"Let me alone."

"No. Come out to supper with me."

"Just give it up, Leigh."

"No."

I leaned against the side of the door farthest from him. "Go back to your wife."

He stared at me and took a breath. "So *that's* it."

"Not altogether."

"So that's it! My God, I might have guessed it was that."

"Not quite in the way you probably think I mean it."

"Who told you?"

"As if that mattered. It's true, I suppose?"

"Oh, it's true. But I haven't so much as *seen* her for over a year."

"Isn't it time you did?"

"No. It's washed up. Done with."

I said exhaustedly: "Leigh. In a minute I'm going in —and if you don't let me I shall call a taxi and drive to Hampstead. But before I go I want—want to make it clear about this—about us." I swallowed and tried to get my thoughts in line. "I—I don't know what the rules are of this game. Perhaps there aren't any. That would be nothing new. But I have to have *some* rules to go by—it so happens—rightly or wrongly I can't do without them —and if they aren't there I slide gracefully out. That's what I'm trying to do now if you'd only let me!"

"But surely—"

"Wait. If I could finish, and then . . . Leigh, if I fell in love with somebody—*if* I did—and he was a married man, it would matter, but it wouldn't matter all that much. There's divorce—or in certain circumstances no divorce—whatever the situation was, it couldn't be the *deciding* thing. One could only judge—could only go on how it looked. But . . . but if I fell in love with a married man and he didn't *tell* me he was married, *that* would be the deciding thing because that would mean he was cheating from the first step. If—if there's anything in life at all, one of the fundamentals, surely, is that you don't cheat people you care about. Or, if you *do* cheat them, then you can't care about them in the way I mean."

His face was set in a sullen narrow frown, almost pouting. After a minute he took his arm from the door.

"Sometimes," he said, "it isn't just quite so dead easy as all that. It isn't step one, step two like some goddamned ballet dance. Sometimes you're so blind scared of scaring off the person you're in love with—especially when she's *difficult* and *touchy* and *independent,* and can't bear to be *pitied,* and liable to fly off at the slightest thing and doesn't care for you much at the start *anyway*—sometimes then you're so blind frozen scared of frightening her off that you don't dare tell her a single thing she won't like or you may lose her in a flash—snap and she's scarpered. Just that! Just that, Deborah."

As he was speaking we both saw Sarah coming round the square with Philip Bartholomew, and when he'd finished there were about a dozen seconds before they came up with us. Those seconds passed in silence.

Then all was talk. They hadn't yet had supper and it was waiting inside—cold meats and things—so we could go right up. Sarah obviously thought of inviting Leigh to join us, but she glanced doubtfully at me.

"Then I'd best be pushing off," said Leigh. "Nice to have seen you, Philip. And you, Sarah. See you again sometime. Bye, Deborah."

And hunching his shoulders as if it were raining he turned and went off toward his little red car on the other side of the square.

Chapter 9

Wimbledon and Henley came and went. It rained in Ascot week. My father and mother left on their separate holidays on the fourth Sunday after Trinity. London was full of foreign visitors. The season began to look tired and dusty. Whittington's always closed for the month of August, except for a skeleton staff for receiving goods for future auctions—and auctions did not begin again until the middle of September.

I was left in harmony and peace, just as before and just as I wanted to be again: a quiet ordered life; no firm hands touching and grasping my body in strange ways, no questing lips, no heavy-lidded, anxiously admiring eyes.

Peace.

Time on my hands.

Sarah's friendship with Philip Bartholomew grew. Since she was so tactful about Leigh, no questions for her; but it looked like the real thing. I came to like his seriousness: it wasn't a dull moral attitude but seemed to spring from a fundamental belief in the value of human beings. Unusual these days. And it didn't at all stop him from being lighthearted or jolly.

Arabella's affair with Bruce Spring was going through as many vicissitudes as a barometer in the monsoon season. It was fascinating to see. Maybe I'd have been better that way instead of sitting on my feelings like a repressed Victorian.

One day in the showrooms of Whittington's, a voice said: "Miss Dainton."

Jack Foil. The stout, elderly man whom I'd met with Leigh at that club in Wapping.

"It is Miss Dainton, isn't it? Do you work here, then?"

We talked for a minute or two. Very friendly and polite. Behind their thick lenses, his eyes wobbled like lightly poached eggs. He was here, he said, looking at some Oriental rugs. He wanted two for his dining room. His wife had a fancy for them. And there was a Sung baluster vase catalogued that he was interested in professionally. Did I know where that was?

Yes, I knew where it was, and led him to it, while he told me that his antique shop was in Brompton Road and invited me to call in any time I was passing. Was I interested in indoor plants? It was his hobby.

We stood and looked at the baluster vase and he puffed out his thick lips and he asked me why it was so called, and I said its real name was Mei-ping, which referred to the shape of the mouth. But of course, I said, he must know all this, being a dealer.

"No," he said. "This isn't really my line. Furniture and silver mostly. Is this genuine, this vase? I mean is it a genuine Sung?"

"No."

"No? Oh, I see the catalogue only claims . . . But how does one know?"

"If you lift it up you'll see something has been ground out of the base. It was a reign mark, probably. The reign in which it was really made. It wasn't *intended* as a forgery, only as a copy."

"It's really Chinese, then?"

"Oh, yes. Probably Yung Cheng. And quite valuable."

"How clever you are. Have you worked here long?"

"About seven years. But porcelain and antique pottery are my subjects. I don't know much about rugs, I'm afraid."

He took out a heavy cream silk handkerchief and

wiped the outside corners of his eyes with it. It smelled of carnation.

He said: "To be frank, Miss Dainton, I don't think I should have been so sure of recognizing you this morning if I hadn't been looking at your portrait the other day. I haven't a good memory for faces in the ordinary way."

"Oh," I said, color coming somewhere. "You mean Leigh Hartley's painting."

"Yes, it's splendid, isn't it?"

"I haven't actually seen it."

"You haven't . . ." He put the handkerchief away, and his signet rings flashed in the light. "Oh, hasn't he let you see it yet? Well at your next sitting, maybe."

I folded my notebook over. "I think I must be getting on. I was looking—"

"Of course. Don't let me detain you, Miss Dainton. Working hours etc. But I must tell you, I'm very struck with that portrait. It's much the best thing Leigh has ever done. If you don't want it yourself when it's finished, I've offered him a hundred guineas for it. Not to resell, but for myself."

"For that?" I half-laughed in surprise and embarrassment. "*Really.* He'll be pleased, I expect."

"Yes, he is. He's still groping his way in art, you know. It's hard for a young man who's not an absolute genius to develop a distinct and personal style. Young artists often spend years doing what other people have done better before. This, this portrait he's done of you, is the first sign I've seen in him of an important development."

It was one of those things in life when because everything moves as usual, nothing seems to move at all.

On July 21, which was a Friday, I felt I just couldn't go back to the flat and spend the whole weekend there, so I went on my own to the Academy Cinema to see a reissue of the Bergman film *Wild Strawberries*. I got a seat at the side away from everyone else and watched the remaining few minutes of the secondary film. As the big *Fin* showed up larger and larger through the last sunset someone walked along the row and sat next to me.

The lights came up slowly. People stirred and yawned and looked about. A girl came up the aisle selling ice creams and soft drinks, and a little cluster formed around her. The dull discomfort in the middle of my body, which had been with me so long, turned and twisted into life.

He said: "I couldn't believe my eyes. Honest I couldn't."

I moved my stick to the other side of the seat, out of his way. I was wearing my old office dress, the gray linen one with the wide green belt.

"Have you seen the main film?"

"No."

"Nor have I. Mind if I stay here?"

"As you please."

"I've only been here about ten minutes. How long've you been here?"

"About the same."

"As soon as my eyes got used to the dark I looked around and there you were!"

It didn't seem likely. Probably he'd followed me from the office. I stared at the advertisements trying to empty mind of thought and heart of feeling. Blood and nerves obey. Be cold, detached, secure, an iron tower in a wind, not a frail surface-rooted tree.

Brown suède boots crossed themselves beside me. Dark brown small check trousers, a cinnamon shirt with white collar and a green knitted tie. No jacket. Probably he was frowning at me; if I looked up he'd be staring at me with those contorted lines over nose and brow.

"It's been hell not seeing you," he said.

More people coming in now for the beginning of the big film. Two sat down behind us, began to rustle chocolate paper. Hell? But why? There are other women. Dozens and dozens all able-bodied, glad of a strong vigorous young man. Then what? He wants me. That's it. And no one else'll do. For some reason. And I?

He said: "Been to the ice rink since?"

"No."

"I went a couple of times, hoping you might be tempted or perhaps go with someone else."

91

The advertisements were over. Music played. More people, filing in, settling.

"You living with your sister all the time now?"

"Yes."

"Don't your father and mother mind?"

"They're both away."

"When do you have your holidays?"

"Week after next."

The lights began to go down.

He leaned over. "Look, Deborah, you think I did you dirt not telling you about Lorne. I *did*. But it was for fear of losing you. I told you that, tried to explain. Didn't I explain that to you? Every time it came up and I was going to say something, I just looked at you and thought, if I tell her she'll walk out."

"Perhaps I would have."

"Well, then."

The curtains were sliding back as the taped music died and was superseded by the soundtrack of the film.

He sensed he had a good arguing point. "What *should* I have done? Tell me. How could I have done it?"

I sighed: "I don't know. It's difficult to answer when you—"

"There you are, you see. Look, Deborah, when this is over—"

"Ssh. Ssh!" said someone behind us.

"Let's go," he whispered, making a move.

"No. I want to see the film."

"I'll talk all through it."

"Don't you dare."

He subsided, but I didn't know if he'd stay quiet for long. He put his hand on my arm. Though I made no response, I didn't take it away.

So we sat through that strange somber classic. At first I couldn't follow it for thinking of the choice I'd to make when it was over; but when I did follow it it seemed as if it was my own life. Infinite pathos of lost youth, joys of childhood fading into the past, sound of dead voices, echo of laughter; these seemed to fill and flood my memory. The tension of my half-broken love affair heightened every light and shadow so that I was caught up in it and became a part of the tale. I felt the loss of an emotionally rich life that hadn't ever really been mine. In the end I shed no tears. but there were tears in my heart.

When it was over we moved together slowly toward the exit, going with the crowd. I didn't know what effect if any the film had had on him. Fragments of the conversation of others drifted around.

Outside he said: "Coffee?"

"No, thanks."

"Drive you home?"

"Thank you."

"Ennismore Gardens?"

"Yes."

Little red car. Same smell of petrol and leather and paint. Same rattles. The wind blew back on to my hair. London was warm and traffic fairly light. We could have raced down Park Lane, but he kept to a moderate speed.

Seeing a film like that gives a new look to your own life. When you've been concentrating on the eternal verities, temporary misunderstandings look pretty trivial. It seemed to me just then that childhood, maturity, marriage, old age and death were each no more than the turning of a page; and soon it's all gone, and nothing's left but the sad wind sighing in an empty garden. Just how big did my own doubts loom in this context? They made no louder sound than a pin drop in a great hall.

After the car stopped we sat in silence for a while.

I would have loved to talk to him about the film, to tell him what I felt, to say that tragedy of this quality had a liberating effect on tired and twisted emotions. One wanted to *proclaim* that there was some justification to life, that there was *some* purpose to it more dedicated than the blind reactions of an amoeba, that all one could do was reject and throw out the trivial, the petty, the cheap, the vulgar, the shoddy, the sham. And say, I am a human being, and as such am greater than the sum of my parts. I live. I breathe. I am. Let the pages be turned . . .

But he didn't speak and I didn't speak, because I was afraid he wouldn't understand.

The sky had a whiteness that comes only from the moon; it encroached even on the cinnamon glow of London.

"Do me a favor, Deborah?"

"What?"

"However you feel about me, give me a chance to finish the painting. You don't need to get any more fenced in. But I'm stuck, and it's hell to be stuck. One more sitting might do. Two at the most."

"All right."

He took a breath. "Thanks."

I opened the door, anxious to be gone now.

"When? Can I come for you tomorrow morning?"

"If you want."

"I want."

I opened the door, got my stick and went in. After shutting the front door behind me I stood back to it for a minute or two, waiting for his engine to restart. I couldn't forget the strange dream in the film of the coffin and the dreamer seeing his own face as a dead man.

At last I went into the living room. Sarah called from the kitchen.

"Good film?"

"Great, thanks."

"Coffee? I'm just making some."

"Lovely."

After a minute or two more I went to the mirror and pushed my hair back more or less in place. I ought to wash it tonight. Sarah was still in the kitchen. I went to the window and parted the curtain an inch. He was still sitting there in his car smoking a cigarettte.

Chapter 10

While I was sitting on the Saturday morning, he said: "I'd like to tell you about Lorne."

"Oh . . . It doesn't matter."

"It matters to me. I want you to know about it."

"She was five feet four and dark, with blue eyes."

He painted steadily for a minute, refusing to be put off. "And twenty years old. She'd come from Cork and had got a temporary job as a receptionist to a colored dentist in Jamaica Road. I had a toothache and went along to the first brass plate I could find. She let me in."

I stirred.

"Don't move. It's just great as it is . . ." He picked up a tube of paint and squeezed some onto his palette. He dabbed it with a brush and began to mix. "She was horribly lonely, see? She couldn't bear London. She knew nobody out of all the millions. They'd no friendliness, she said . . . I suppose it attracted me, her being like that . . . She was pretty in a way. I was her only real friend in London, she said. One day we decided to get married."

A cloud moved over the sun and he looked up, scowling, as if someone were standing in his light. He said: "Living together's different from loving together, isn't it. We never somehow made it. I've always heard of the Irish—haven't you—as being happy, easygoing, careless,

95

untidy, willing to live in a mess. Just like me in fact. She wasn't like that. She was all for neatness, carefulness, looking after details. And she always worried. If I'm painting I like to stop when I want to stop, not when the potatoes are ready. And when I stop I like to drop things where I can pick 'em up next day. She was forever struggling to make me live as she thought I ought to live, quiet and orderly, see, and it just didn't work."

"You don't like order?"

"I don't like someone who *worries* about it. But Lorne never settled here in this studio, she never settled in this district. She thought it was ugly and everything about London was big and hard and cold and gray. She made no other friends. And the break up was partly my fault. In those days I expected people would like what I painted and want to buy it—some of it at least. I wasn't—geared down to failure, as you might say, and that made me pretty short tempered. She was nearest to me, living here, and got what there was. She didn't like it. I don't blame her for *that*."

"Generous of you."

He smiled. "Well, I wanted you to know it wasn't some grotty Bohemian affair, it was a genuine marriage that genuinely went wrong, the same as it can in your swank Hampstead circles. We haven't divorced, because she's a Catholic, but she left me eighteen months ago and I haven't even seen her for twelve."

"Why don't you try again?"

"I don't want to. No more would she."

When we'd finished that morning he said: "One more sitting'll do it. Like to see it now?"

I slid off the chair and limped to the easel. One isn't ever much of a judge of one's own portrait, and I couldn't decide whether the girl with the coppery brown hair and the dark eyes and the fair complexion was like me or not. I thought I looked as if I were listening to something. Somehow he'd made me look a bit more lush, a bit more sexy than I really was, as if he was maybe reading into me what he wanted to see there.

I said: "Did you mean it, what you said just now? About being geared down to failure?"

"What?" His eyes were suddenly a very clear gray as he blinked toward the river. "Oh, that. Yes. Nasty medicine, but better to swallow."

"D'you think being reconciled to failure at twenty-five is a good thing?"

"It's better than living among the ostriches . . . But of course I'm making a big drama of it. I don't really think my stuff's hopeless, otherwise I wouldn't push on. I mean failure in a money sense."

"Hasn't Jack Foil offered you a hundred guineas for this?"

"Who told you?"

"He did. He came into Whittington's a couple of weeks ago."

The morning was cool, and I'd brought a light linen coat with me. I went to pick this up.

He said: "Can't we lunch somewhere before I take you home?"

"Leigh . . . I know lots of the people who run the galleries in the West End."

He was putting his brushes in their jars of turpentine. "Can we lunch?"

"Yes. I ought to be back by three, as Virginia is coming home."

"I'm afraid of going to these West End sharks. They're interested in nobody but the latest French discovery or some gimmicky bloke who frames his pictures with old lavatory seats."

"Not these. Of course they run with public taste—they have to if they're going to live. But I'm sure they'd be absolutely honest with you."

He put out his bottom lip doubtfully.

"How long is it since you tried any gallery in the West End?" I asked.

"About eighteen months."

"Well, haven't you improved, moved on since then? Just this portrait seems an advance to me. Jack Foil thinks the same."

"I know." He wiped his hands on a much stained cloth. "All right, if you think so. And thanks for the interest. That's the one certain good thing that can come out of it."

Through Smith-Williams I was able to make an appointment with Lewis Maud, the older of the two brothers, for Friday at three, and another with Arthur Hays of the Cheltenham Galleries at 4:30.

The Maud Gallery was at the smarter end of Grosvenor Street, but its windows were old-fashioned, and they'd done nothing to liven up the inside with modern furnishings. All the same its turnover was probably as big as any in London. Lewis Maud was a third-generation English Jew of about fifty and was the sort of man you'd never notice in a group. Quiet spoken, badly dressed and casual, he had no pretensions and no side. Everything about him was strictly workmanlike, and he'd no room for theories and schools. For this reason I thought he would appeal to Leigh; at least they could talk the same language, whatever was said in it.

Leigh had brought four paintings. I felt apprehensive about the whole thing now it was on me, but hopeful and excited as well. I introduced them and they talked amiably enough, and Lewis Maud pointed out one or two new names among the pictures on his walls. We trailed about the gallery, Leigh making a few assenting grunts and I trying to comment intelligently. There was no one else in the place, but after a few minutes Maud led us into his office at the back, in which there was nothing much but a desk and an easel, and said: "Well, I think we have to see these paintings of yours, Mr. Hartley. If you'd be obliging enough to put them on that easel one by one, I'll sit here. The light's good. Sometimes in the winter it's dark in here . . ."

So Leigh untied his parcel and dropped brown paper and string on the floor and took out the first painting and put it on the easel. His face was dead pan.

A painting of two tugs passing in the river, a barge, the derricks against a cloudy sky, swans in the foreground.

"Yes," said Lewis Maud thoughtfully. To me: "Do you smoke?"

"No, thanks."

Silence fell. Leigh put up the second one. It was the interior of his studio, littered with the stuff that usually lay about: old cushions, paint brushes, magazines. Light fell through the window, fell obliquely, cleverly, I thought; dust hung in it.

"Yes," said Maud. "Yes, I see what you mean there."

Leigh took down the first two paintings, propped them against chair legs. All around us in that small room were other people's works, clamant, rival, accusative. A drawing of an old boat by a modern French painter priced at £850. A couple of little impressionist paintings of St. Tropez in the nineties, probably worth £7000 the pair; a Pissarro in a corner.

Leigh put up his third, the second river scene. A much darker work, almost colorless, done in black and white and metallic grays. He looked at Maud and then at me.

Maud struck a match and lit his cigarette. There was room on the easel for the fourth painting, and beside the river scene Leigh put my portrait.

"That's unfinished," he said. "I need a couple more sittings."

There was a squeal of brakes outside and the blaring of a horn. Lewis Maud looked up absently. "This traffic," he said. "You're better without a car these days."

"Yes," said Leigh. "I had to park mine in Brook Street. You feed a meter sixpences like giving sweets to a greedy kid."

Maud tapped the ash off his cigarette and brushed a freckle off his sleeve. "Well, Mr.—er—Hartley, I know you'd want me to be frank, wouldn't you?"

"That's what I came for."

"That's what you came for. Yes . . . Well, I'm afraid I have to tell you that these paintings are not at all in my line."

Leigh stood back and put his hands on his hips, staring at the paintings himself with a painful air of assumed detachment.

Lewis Maud glanced apologetically at me. "They're really not in our line, Miss Dainton, not in the tradition of what one comes to appreciate and look for after thirty-odd years in the business. But of course it's a personal view."

"Yes," I said.

Maud went on talking half to me and half to the pictures, rather avoiding looking at Leigh. "If I said that they were not in the tradition of modern painting, that might make you think I meant modern fashion. I don't. I mean in the development of technique, the—the *understanding* of technique. These are—pictures, if you know what I mean. They're no better and no worse than hundreds of others about. But they're not really—forgive me —paintings, as I understand the word."

"Well," said Leigh, "that's straight enough, isn't it?"

"Look, Mr.—er—Hartley, don't think I mean this the wrong way. In this country alone there are hundreds, thousands of painters, amateurs, who paint for their own pleasure. It's a wonderful recreation for them. But that's rather different from the professional with something to say, some original vision, the spark that sets him above his fellows. That's what we all look for. But he's hard to find, and . . ."

"Surely," I said, trying to pick the right words, "isn't it partly a matter of development, of trial and error, of hard work and extending one's vision . . ."

Lewis Maud worried his cigarette with fingers and lips.

"Mr. Maud doesn't think so," Leigh said.

"No, I don't," Maud said. "If the spark is there, *then* the hard work, the development, the extending of one's vision—these are all necessary, vital. But—"

"Do you not like the portrait?" I asked.

"I think the portrait has more feeling. But it's—romantic, old-fashioned in its approach. Look." Maud got quickly up and went to fumble among the stacked canvases and presently came back with one that he put on the easel beside Leigh's river scene. It was a painting of an old woman lying on a bed. "What I am trying to say is that you may well be able to sell your paintings at a fine arts shop where people go who want a picture of what their own eyes would see, a painted photograph. Fine. But it's a surface thing, an imprint, unrealized. Look at this old woman. The Frenchman who painted her saw her lying just like that, but he didn't put down *just* what he saw. He built her up, first bone, then flesh, then clothes, so that now she's not just a black design against yellow and blue but a great heavy lump, solid, sculptural, pressing down the bed so that you can hear the springs creak. You can smell the old black woollen jacket and the black serge skirt. Mind, I'm not saying it's a great painting, but it's a good one, and I'd back my judgment on it. But look now at this river scene of yours. Do you feel those tugs have got machinery inside them? Can you smell the seaweed and the oil and the smoke? No. It's the work of an illustrator, not of an artist. It may well appeal to people who want just that, a conscientiously drawn and painted illustration. It may sell, and others like it may sell. People will pay twenty or thirty guineas for that sort of thing. But I don't think the London galleries are the place for them."

"Well, thanks," said Leigh grimly. "Thanks a lot."

Maud looked at him briefly, assessingly. "I'm sorry. Too many people paint, you know."

"Or too many people take themselves seriously, you mean?"

"Well, yes. Art is a wonderful recreation. I paint myself. But it's a terrible way of making a living. It's the old story of many being called and few chosen."

Leigh began thoughtfully to wrap up his four paintings.

Maud said to me: "Mr. Hartley is modest in his approach. I only wish I could help him. I get so many people offering me their paintings—a dozen a week—and the worse painters they are, usually, the more insanely conceited they run."

"Well," said Leigh. "Glad to have stepped out of the ruck in one respect anyhow. Goodbye to you, Mr. Maud."

I'd thought he would refuse to see Arthur Hays, but with a sort of grim patience he went along and I went

101

with him. Mr. Hays was an altogether more polished person than Lewis Maud, but although his response to the four paintings was suaver and more oblique, it was equally dismissive. We came out and walked back to the little car. Leigh opened the door for me, thrust the parcel into the space behind, and then got in beside me. We sat in silence.

"Did you get the feeling they didn't like my paintings?" Leigh said.

I stirred uncomfortably and bit at the skin around my forefinger.

"Definitely," he said, "they don't recognize genius, that's what it is. Every artistic Messiah is rejected by his own generation. Wait until I'm dead."

"I'm *sorry*," I said miserably.

"Not to worry. That painting of you, in a hundred years it will be in the Louvre and called the Mona Deborah, and beginners'll sit round it trying to fathom the secret of its smile, see. And I in my pauper's grave won't be able to tell 'em. Cup of tea?"

"Anything you say."

"We'll have to move from here, anyhow. I borrowed somebody else's unexpired time, and a bloody little Blue Boy is watching us."

We had tea in a cafe in Piccadilly. After his brief rally of jokes he sat silent, sipping his cup and staring out at the traffic.

I said: "I'm sorry I took you now. But it's got to be kept in proportion. We're no worse off."

"Well, thanks for the 'we'."

In fact I knew we were both worse off. He, because no one is the better for having his work damned. I, because I'd hoped so much that there was something there.

The following week I was going to join Erica in Ireland, and there were things to do, washing and ironing, clothes to pick up from Hampstead and another suitcase. I had intended to leave him after the two interviews. Now I found I couldn't. We sat for a long time over tea.

He said: "I think I'll get away for a bit if you're going away. To Paris and Rome, look around. I've never been abroad. Never had the time or money. Maybe I need time to think. Get a new direction."

"Can you afford it?"

"If I sell this portrait to Jack Foil."

We got up, and he drove to the Queensway rink, but it was closed. Rain was falling and we sat in the cramped little car not speaking. He bought an evening paper and looked through the cinema advertisements, but there was nothing we wanted to see.

"Do me a favor?" he said at last.

"I'll try."

"Come home and let's cook a meal. Are you a good cook?"

"No. Moderate. But I—"

"I'm moderate too. Two 'moderates' might make a 'good.' We could pick up a cooked chicken some place and start from there."

I knew I should say no, but I felt desperately sorry for him, and this was a new feeling flavoring the old one.

Most shops were shut but we found an uncooked chicken—which they jointed for me—and some stock cubes and a few vegetables, and drove out to Rother-hithe. The studio was tidier than usual—Friday was the day he had a charwoman—and with the lights on and the curtains drawn we shut out the wet evening. As soon as that was done he began to kiss me. I'd known he would and had been waiting for it. He buried his head in my shoulder and we held each other tight, as if with a mutual recognition after separation, as if for comfort after deep disappointment, as if for joint protection against the hostility of the world.

. . . Presently we had drinks and then I went to the kitchen to prepare the chicken. In a few minutes I heard a thudding noise and limped out to find him breaking up his canvases. In the room were three ladder-back chairs with long protruding knobs at the top. He was impaling his canvases by banging them on to these, so that each one was crowned with a broken picture in its wooden stretches.

I shouted: "Leigh! Don't! Stop it! Stop it!"

He didn't look very angry when I caught his arm. He scratched his head and then shook it as if to clear it. The picture he held in his hand he resignedly skimmed across the room till it landed by the door.

"You're right—it's—it's . . . But hell, I have to have one show of temper, don't I?"

"But that's no good. Doing that is no good at all."

"What's any good?"

"Supper. Come and help me. I want to try to do a fricassee of chicken in white wine sauce."

When I got him into the kitchen he said: "Anyway, there's no white wine."

"Red will do."

He sat down on a chair and put his head in his hands. "Christ, I feel a mess."

"Help me. Have you a casserole?"

"That cupboard over there."

"And the wine?"

"There's three or four bottles under the sink. God, I think this is an all-time zero for me."

I poured him another drink and he took it, swallowed it at a draught. "Now you."

"I'll have some with supper."

"No, now."

"All right."

After ten minutes or so, during which I got the chicken ready for the oven, he stood up. "Picture of the artist wallowing in self-pity."

"Don't be silly. It's only the opinion of two men."

"Is it the opinion of one woman?"

"Who?"

"You."

"This interests me," I said.

"Why?"

"Haven't you always been preaching the virtues of courage and perseverance to me?"

He put down his glass. "On target, that was. Bang on target. Every time a coconut."

I put my head on his shoulder. "*Sorry*. I know how you feel—how you must feel."

He put his hand round my legs. It closed on my knee and was warm there. It was the wrong knee.

"Don't."

"Why not?"

But I had moved away.

We ate about nine-thirty. The cooking had come off well—never a certainty with me. We drank a bottle of wine between us. He went into the kitchen and came back with another one.

I laughed. "No more for me."

He filled my glass and then his own. His face had paled with the food and drink.

"Do me a favor?"

"It depends."

"That wasn't what you said earlier. Then you said 'I'll try'."

"Drink makes me cautious."

"Well, just *tell* me something then. Am I a failure in other ways?"

"Oh, that's not a question you need me to answer!"

"What I mean is: Am I a failure in the other big way? With the girl I love."

I sipped at the wine and then put it down. "How can I answer that question?"

"Truthfully. On the chin."

"And if I said yes?"

"I reckon I'd jump in the river."

"So it's blackmail."

"No, I want the truth."

"Well, you can stay out of the river." My heart was thumping, and that was not the effects of wine.

"Really? Really, Deborah?" He didn't smile, but the tight creases in his face changed and lifted. "That makes a lot of things worth while."

"What sort of things?"

"Breathing for one."

I laughed again.

He said: "Can I ask that question again? Do me a favor?"

"What?"

"Stay here tonight."

I looked at my glass. It was still nearly full. The wine was a sort of old rose color. For wine is bright at the goblet's brim . . .

An answer; you're twenty-six; you know your own mind; it's out of the question; say no before he gets the wrong impression; sleeping with him, naked together, a whole night, you, a cripple; you must be insane even to think of it. He's insane to ask. But nothing's insane for him to ask, or to do.

A shiver (try to suppress it) went corkscrewing in womb-dark depths. Over. Now sense. Take it easy.

"Deborah," he said. "Please . . ."

He did not wear his scarlet coat, For wine and blood are red . . .

This isn't love, this violent passion, taking the breath, making the blood drumbeat; it's a sexual hand, clutching. But such a nice girl with a good upbringing and such intellectual parents. This man, over here; this one waiting; not next week; tonight; in half an hour; the unutterable invasion of privacy; intimacies often considered but never known. Put it off. In a month, two months, not now.

"Deborah," he said, still not moving, but eyes weighing, gray eyes darker with need.

Well, all I had to do was say no. Tongue against top of palate—the easiest monosyllable. He wouldn't, couldn't stop me from leaving. I was my own mistress.

Or his.

"If you want me to stay," I said, "I'll stay."

Chapter 11

I suppose I should be all agog to set down in detail the very first experience of a hitherto sexually deprived girl of twenty-six. At this distance, short though it is, I suppose I'm now detached enough to separate the pure physical act from what you might call its emotional overtones, to see the struggle between withholding and giving as a struggle between different sides of the same impulse, to weigh sheer awful pleasure-killing embarrassment against an absolute resolve of the intelligence to find a rationalization for it all.

Maybe we're all egoists and think our experiences are different, whereas really it's only a million million variations on the same theme. That I was lame and withered and painfully innocent only added and subtracted shades of meaning to a cliché that is current everywhere. It's probably not even far from unusual that our first sexual meeting should have been emotionally taut, exciting, rubbing the senses raw, nervously exhausting and inexpert to the point of failure. (Although I knew so little I knew instinctively now that he had had quite little to do with women.) Nor can it be unusual that later in the night, perhaps about one, with the shaded light still burning—shaded by a tea cloth that later we found blackened through by the heat of the bulb—and in the drowsy, bittersweet, half acrid-seeming warmth, when limbs touched again and urges rewoke and inhibitions were taken unawares, that what passed then for completion came to us.

The following morning I slid away from him early and took a bath and cooked breakfast almost before he woke. Then after breakfast he drove me to the nearest telephone box and I rang Sarah. To my relief she had come home late and had thought me asleep in my room. I said I'd been visiting a friend, and would be home tonight. She said, what time was my plane to Dublin tomorrow, and I said not till the afternoon, and she said in a cool casual voice: "You're all right, Deborah? Not ill or anything?" And I said in the same sort of voice, "No, I'm fine, darling. See you tonight."

Then we went shopping and I bought enough for lunch and dinner, and the Sunday newspapers, and some more bottles of wine, and a new tea towel.

It was a lovely day with a warm wind directing the clouds like traffic past the sun, and when we got back we sat on the balcony in a couple of deck chairs basking. There wasn't much talk. He made coffee, and the smell and taste were delicious in the sun-warmed air. Very little moved on the river, and today all the derricks were silent. It was like being in some foreign city a thousand miles from London.

At last he said to me: "D'you *have* to go to Ireland?"

"I've booked a flight."

"Scrub it."

"I shall only be gone ten days."

"Come somewhere with me instead."

"Oh, no."

"Oh, yes."

"Erica is counting on me."

"Let her count, Deb. I'm afraid."

"What of?"

"Of your damned hygienic dehydrated pre-packed medical family. Once you get back among 'em."

"What?"

"You'll discover it's an intellectual error to have an affair with an unlettered burke like me. You'll talk it all out on an academic level until there's no real feeling left."

"Don't you think I've a mind of my own?"

"That's what I'm afraid of. At present I'm only appealing to your body. At least I hope I'm doing that?"

"Don't talk of it. It's you that's analyzing now."

"You shivered. Are you cold?"

"Very warm, thank you."

"I want you again, Deborah."

"Oh, God, be quiet."

"Are you scolding me or God?"

"Don't tease. Enjoy the sun."

"I want to enjoy you."

"Sometime. Sometime. Don't talk. Let it be. Wait."

We had lunch on the terrace; some of the cold chicken, with cheese and grapes and wine. We drank too much wine. We didn't get drunk, but the feeling of being heady and relaxed and high-spirited and giggly and uncaring was new to me. Everything we said to each other was very funny. We laughed, and loved with our eyes, and the sun was warm and the grapes were sweet.

When the last was gone he said: "Let me paint you. Let me start another canvas absolutely different. Let me paint you different. The way all artists want to paint their women."

"No."

"Oh, yes. What's wrong with it?"

"Others might see it when it's done."

"We'll not let 'em see it. I'll promise to give it you if you want it, and you can tear it up."

"No."

"Why not? *Please*. Look, I tell you what. If you want, if you still feel the same way about your leg, in spite of everything I've said and done, then let's do it from the waist up only."

"I couldn't."

"What difference does it make? There's no one else to see."

What difference did it make? I took a gulp of wine.

"Look, the sun's going round and the light won't be so

good in another hour." He got up. "I'll get the easel and the chair ready."

He stumbled as he went in. Perhaps he would paint better this way, slightly drunk and inflamed with desire. Could I claim I was any different? Or wanted to be any different. Embalm this moment. Food and wine and love and sun and no thoughts. If one could stay like this, lifting away the upper cerebral cortex, stuffing it on a shelf somewhere and allowing all the physical instincts their proper place. Some people went through life that way— and made a thorough mess of it. But was theirs more of a mess than when one tried to live entirely by reason and self-awareness? Was there no happy mean, where one need be neither overcivilized nor the complete savage?

It was agony to know the name for everything, to know all the smart tags. To know exactly what all the educated and over-educated would say. If they saw me at this moment, drowsy and sensuous and warm, how easily they'd explain it all in words of five syllables, how cool and appraising they'd be, those that weren't hiding their laughter. Go away brain, leave me alone . . .

So when he came out, tight faced and heavy eyed and said it was ready, I got up and went in, trying not to stumble and trying not to limp, and sat on the stool and took off my clothes, and he wrapped a piece of crimson curtain around my legs and kissed me and gave me a glass of warm wine to hold, and I gulped at it, and he went away and began to draw.

But of course it was no good. Five minutes perhaps it lasted while he scrawled the outlines. But then he had to come over to move my head. I gave him the glass to drink and he sipped at it and held it for me to drink, and his hands were so unsteady that he spilled the warm wine over my breasts, and when I smiled up at him he allowed the glass to tilt again and it all spilled everywhere, running down my arms and hands like fine blood.

After that, as I suppose we really knew from the beginning, no painting was done.

That night I wired Erica to say I'd changed my plans

and was not coming to Ireland. About eight Leigh drove me to see Sarah at the flat. I told him to go and I would follow him by taxi, but he said he'd wait and it didn't matter if it was hours. He'd wait in his car on the other side of the square. He had, he said, plenty to think about.

Virginia went home every weekend, and Sarah didn't usually see Philip Bartholomew on Sunday evenings, so if she wasn't working I was fairly sure of finding her alone. I did.

When she saw me she said: "Lovey, what *have* you been doing? You look as if you've been taking Purple Hearts. And you're sunburned!"

"It's the day," I said. "We sat by the river. His studio is by the river, you know."

"Leigh again?"

"Yes . . . We—sat by the river."

I put down my stick and untied the scarf that I'd put on because of the open car. "Sarah, I've got to talk to you. I've got to tell you something."

"D'you want anything to eat? There's some cold ham in the fridge and a crumb or two of *pâté*."

"No. I'm not hungry."

She put down the stocking she was examining for ladders and crossed her slim strong beautiful legs. "Say on."

"Sarah, I'm not going to Ireland. I'm going away with Leigh."

She pursed her lips as if to whistle and then didn't. "So I shall be the only bastion of purity left in the Dainton family."

"Don't joke."

"Sorry. Of course you're not going into this in the light-hearted way Arabella does. But it's happened suddenly, hasn't it? A couple of weeks ago you were in the middle of a cold war."

"I know. But probably that's not unusual, is it? You quarrel—then come together again—and all the time you've been apart the—the chemistry has been working . . ."

She looked at me. "Does Erica know?"

"I've wired I'm not coming. She doesn't know anything

111

else. And for a time I'd rather she didn't know. At least
. . . I don't want to cause her any worry—or Douglas—
but I don't want her *mind* turned on this. I don't want
what I'm doing analyzed and parsed. I've as much right
as anybody to be irrational for once."

Sarah smiled. "Of course. Where are you going?"

"Spain probably."

"Tomorrow?"

"Yes."

"D'you want me to help you pack?"

I got up. "I—want to tell you more about it; and yet I
don't want to. That's irrational enough, isn't it?"

"You mean you want female counsel without the great
Dainton brain?"

"Yes! . . . Oh, darling, yes, I do . . . Or not counsel.
Because what's done is done, what's decided is decided.
But I'd like to—to just . . ."

She got up too, topping me by five inches. "You look
as if you need an old-fashioned cup of tea. I'll make you
one. Put your feet up, and I'll be back in a jiffy."

While she was gone, I kicked off my shoes, the heavy
one and the light one and put my stockinged feet up on
another chair and wriggled my toes—or wriggled those
that would wriggle—and stared at them complacently. Either I was still full of wine or love or something, because
the fact that my feet didn't match seemed for the first
time ever not to matter.

When she came back I told her the rest—edited here
and there—but no doubt she could read between the
gaps.

She said: "What does he intend, do you think? To get
a divorce somehow? Or isn't that in the book?"

"Just at the moment I'm trying not to think or plan or
contrive or *anything*. All my life things have been
planned ahead, arranged, ordered—not unpleasantly; I
don't at all complain. But this is different. I'm going to
live from day to day."

"And enjoy it . . ."

"I think I can."

She stirred her tea and sipped it thoughtfully. "Send me a postcard."

"Yes."

"You'll write to Erica?"

"I shall write something."

"One thing . . . I think you ought to try and play this all on the same level, Deborah. You've always been one to feel things quite a bit, haven't you? Arabella will have a broken heart six times before she's our age, and it'll mend again quick as a wink. You're the type to sink in deep and nearly drown." With an absent-minded hand Sarah fluffed out her hair. "Well, you say you're going to enjoy yourself and live from day to day and be happy. That's Arabella's way, not really yours. So if you play this Arabella's way then you ought to try to keep to her rules . . ." She stopped. "Have you the least idea what I'm trying to say?"

"You're trying to tell me not to get too involved, just in case."

"*Roughly*, yes. The wording's confused but that's the message. It's a *precaution*, Deb, if you know what I mean. Like fastening your seat belt. It's just a general thought I have. Not knowing him, but knowing you. I *like* him; there's nothing more in this than what there seems. I'm only suggesting you should watch yourself—as a precaution."

I patted her hand and then bent to put on my shoes again.

"Maybe I already am too involved, Sarah. How d'you measure out love? By the spoonful or the square yard? Probably there isn't any way . . . I'm going in with my eyes open. From now on it's just as it comes."

Chapter 12

We flew to Gibraltar and hired a little car there. We got into Spain the following day and drove along the west coast toward Cadiz. But we stopped short at a motel about five miles north of Tarifa. Being August there would be crowds at all the popular places, but here there was nowhere to stay except at two motels on a three-mile stretch of beach. It was very hot, but all the time a strong breeze blew off the Atlantic. The sea was white with surf and the bathing not too safe, for the pale fine sand fell away in a bar that was covered on all but the low tides, and one was suddenly out of one's depth. I'd refused to go into a shop in Gibraltar to buy a costume, but Leigh had bought two for me there by guess, and they fitted well enough. I'd never imagined it would be possible in August to find so quiet a place; but you only had to walk a few hundred yards round a point of rock and there was no one at all. So I bathed about four times every day. This was heaven.

When we were having breakfast one morning on the balcony I asked him how he had known of such a place when he had never been to Spain before.

He said: "Jack Foil told me about it. He came touring this way last year."

"D'you mean he knows we've come here now?"

"How could he? No, but when we were coming I remembered what he'd said. Luckily."

"Luckily indeed."

"Deborah." His smile was half a frown in the bright light.

"Um?"

"I've been thinking about your leg, about your walk, see. D'you have to wear that built-up thing—that extra thick shoe?"

"Afraid so. Sorry."

"But I've been watching when you've walked to the sea, no shoes, no stick. You limp less, you do really."

"I walk on my toes, that's why."

"Why not try that with an ordinary shoe?"

"I was told not to. I was told it would throw my spine off balance."

"Wasn't that when you were growing up, though? I can't see why it'd put you off balance if it makes you limp less."

"I haven't any normal shoes—I mean a *pair* of normal shoes—if I wanted to try."

"Let's drive into Cadiz and buy a pair."

"It's miles. Let's wait for a wet day."

"The sea's rough and the tide's out now. It'd take us a couple of hours each way at the most."

"I'll come for the drive."

"You'll come for a pair of shoes."

On the way there I said: "Leigh, we've been away five days and you haven't let me pay for anything so far. That's ridiculous."

He fiddled with his sunglasses. "It's the principle of the thing."

"I thought you claimed not to have principles."

"I've my own set, made to measure, see. I'd never mind pinching someone's tiara or traveling by air on a forged ticket—but I don't take a girl on a holiday and expect it to be a Dutch treat."

"It's as much my pleasure as it is yours."

He glanced quickly at me. "That's the nicest thing you've ever said to me, Deborah."

115

"I must have said nicer things than that."

"Yes, but when we've been making love. Anyone says nice things then. This is coolly, in the light of day, like."

We traveled over the long empty road, broken only by the occasional clump of pines, the distant white-walled farm, the advertisement hoarding for brandy or sherry.

"You've never told me," I said, "how much money you have to live on; how much your aunt's legacy brings you in."

"Oh, I'm spending capital. I told you that when we first met."

"It's not a very good idea, is it? How long will it last?"

"Not long. When it's gone it's gone."

"And then?"

"Then I'll work at something else. Maybe before it's gone. I've not much encouragement to go on wasting paint."

"What will you do?"

He shrugged. "Haven't thought yet."

We reached the causeway to Cadiz about eleven and got to the town in time to do some shopping before everything closed for the afternoon. We found a square in the center of the town and a place to park the car, presided over by the usual Spanish cripple, this one in a wheel chair. A fellow feeling, a sympathetic twinge.

We wandered down the narrow slits of streets and soon found a shoe shop. The shoes were cheap and of good style and quality, and, gripping my arm, Leigh pushed his way in through the bead curtains. I bought two pairs of shoes. My feet weren't all that much different in size, and I didn't try too hard, as I was convinced I'd not be able to wear them. But just as we were leaving the shop I pointed to a pair of high-heeled crimson kid with a bow in front and said: "Aren't those lovely!" And he said: "Buy them." And I said: "That's impossible." And he said: "Just for the fun. You can wear 'em in bed." And I laughed and said: "I've never owned a high-heeled pair of shoes in all my life." And he said: "Now's the time to begin," and we turned back.

After lunch we drove to the beach and Leigh bathed,

116

but I wouldn't because the beach was crowded and there were a few English and Germans about. Later we went back for tea in the town, and I said: "Leigh, there was a good man's shop on the other side from the shoe shop. Let me buy you something. There was a sweater and one or two other things."

His eyelids drooped. "That's because you don't think much of the clothes I wear, isn't it?"

We went back to the narrow street which now in the slanting afternoon sunlight was thronged with black-coated people; and there we bought two sweaters, a pair of beach trousers, shorts, a smart jacket in fine blue wool.

We drove home, watching the sun sink itself into a raft of cloud floating over the sea. The old ramparts of Cadiz were black against the vanilla sky.

As we came through San Fernando, Leigh said: "I reckon you're taking me in hand, aren't you?"

"What d'you mean?"

"Well, these clothes. Quieter. A bit less juke box."

"Don't you like them?"

"Yes, sure. They're O.K."

"Well, then."

"And this business of stopping me combing my hair. That's another thing. Not done."

"Well, your hair looks a lot better without it."

He brooded for a few minutes. "You'll never make a silk purse out of me, you know."

"I'm not trying. I like you as you are."

"With amendments."

"Very little ones. Do you *mind?*"

"No, not really. Not so that it matters."

We drove on a long way. I could still see he was thinking of it.

"Deborah, I sometimes wonder."

"What?"

"Whether this flop in my painting—whether in a way it's had its pay off—"

"I don't understand."

"Well, it's altered us, hasn't it? Our relationship, as you might say."

"Well, yes I—"

"You see, I wonder . . . I was always the one in charge, wasn't I, telling you to snap out of it, do new things with your leg, rise above it. But now, since then, in a way I'm crippled—in my chosen job. That failure meant a lot to me—more even than you imagine. Well . . . now we're on equal terms. D'you think you'd ever have come away with me if that hadn't happened?"

"I didn't come away with you out of pity, if that's what you mean."

"No, but I think it had some effect on you, didn't it? Like feeling you were helping me instead of just being helped . . ."

"Leigh," I said, "I swore when I came on this holiday not to think, not to ask myself questions, not try to sort anything out, but just to enjoy myself, to be. So I have. So I've done that. Well . . . I don't want *you* to start!"

Neither of us spoke after that. A real sense of contentment, just driving back knowing we'd eat dinner in the little restaurant of the motel, waited on by the white-coated Moroccan boy from Ceuta, drinking a bottle of wine while the candles guttered, and then going across to our chalet to make love.

By now we'd come to know each other with a physical intimacy that I still found not quite believable. Most times I completely forgot my deformity in his forgetting of it. For the first time my thin leg in nakedness of the whole body seemed natural, as natural as the good-shaped one, as natural as the curling brown hairs about his navel, as his strong broad loins. And I'm pretty fastidious over many things; small things easily offend. But there was nothing in him to offend; he had a sense of judgment, a lack of coarseness that many better educated men couldn't have equaled.

But in thought we were still infinitely apart; our minds didn't interlock in the least, they moved in the same ambience but separately, making contact as they could.

One day we were talking about Whittington's, and I told him of an Italian who had come in and asked them to offer for sale three Tiepolo sketches which in fact it

118

turned out later he had stolen in Rome. While they were examining these he had contrived to steal six small English water colors which were on view at the time and which he took back to Rome and put up for auction there. Only someone's quick eye and the last-minute intervention of Interpol had prevented the double swindle.

Leigh was disgusted, not because the Italian had tried to cheat us but because he had done it so badly.

"Lord help us! How could he *hope* to get away with it?"

"He nearly did. He'd twice done it successfully in France."

Leigh brooded a minute. "I suppose you do get things stolen from the auction rooms?"

"Very, very little. A pretty careful watch is kept on the small things, like jewelry."

We were lying on the beach, but partly under the shade of the beach umbrellas we'd bought, because we were both brown in places and sore in places. It's always difficult to get a consistent tan. He put his hand on my back, where the costume ended, and moved his fingers along my spine.

"I really think I'd rob a bank to be able to do this forever."

"You'd tire of it."

"Would *you?*"

"Not if we could be like this forever."

He laughed. "You see . . . God, I'm flattered."

I put my face against his shoulder, smelling the warm skin. "Don't be."

The sun stole an inch more of our shade.

"From here," I said, "Tarifa looks like a medieval Moorish town. The other morning I got up early when you were still asleep, and it looked as if it were floating in the sea."

"I wonder how often it's been raided and pillaged and burned," he said. "Maybe that's what I was cut out for, to be a pirate, not a painter, to take what I want and damn the consequences."

"You sound very lawless this afternoon, robbing banks and walking planks."

119

"Or getting other people to walk 'em. It's always the *successful* pirate you think of in your dreams, isn't it—yes, the successful bank robber—even the successful painter. Never the one who comes unstuck."

"You've not so much as sketched since you came. Don't these new surroundings make you feel—"

"Yes," he said roughly. "They make me feel."

"So?"

He kneeled up in the sand and sat back on his haunches. Bent double, his legs looked immensely strong. "This is the best time I've ever had in my life, Deborah."

"And for me."

"So although I'm happy as hell, there's the old canker gnawing underneath."

"If your—"

"Sometimes in the middle of all this happiness with you I feel I could tear the world in strips. Why the hell should I be given an urge and no talent to satisfy it! If I'm talking about robbing banks and turning pirate, that's why! I wish I could! By Christ, I wish I could!"

We were silent for a bit. Presently his hands unclenched and he slid down into a sitting position again and put his arm round my waist. Very quietly then he added: "I wish I could."

After I was ill the muscles of my foot and lower leg had been so paralyzed that my foot had flopped about like the foot of a broken doll. When at length it was decided that no more recovery could be expected, I had two operations (arthrodesis, they called it), one to fuse the bone of the ankle, and one the bones of the foot. This meant taking away the cartilages in the joints so that the bones could then fuse together solid. Following it, of course, there could never be any spring in the foot again, or any movement not initiated by the muscles higher up the leg; but it did give me something solid to walk on, and I'd managed pretty well with the stick and the irons and the built-up shoe. And later without the irons.

For a few winters I'd suffered hideously with chilblains

120

and my leg had swollen and gone puffy and blue; but now I had injections each autumn, carbolic injected into the lumbar spine, which wasn't pleasant but it worked miracles.

In ordinary shoes, without the support and the extra inch provided by the built-up shoe I thought I should wag from side to side in that horrible way you see some people doing; but I found, as I'd found on the beach, that somehow I was able to take the weight on the ball of my foot without the heel quite touching the ground. It was odd to do this, because I'd never actually tried it before, but one soon got into the way, and by throwing my weight a little more forward I didn't seem to need the stick so much. At first I only tried it a couple of hours a day.

So ten days went by. Our skin had reddened and flaked and browned, and now it could only darken with every new day's sun. Leigh had run out of money and I was at last able to use some of my travelers checks.

In all our talk no mention was ever made of Lorne. This I take some credit for. It's not always easy to love a man and be made love to all through such a fortnight, *knowing* of his still existent marriage to a dark-haired blue-eyed Irish girl, five feet four inches in height, with a lovely brogue, and *not once* to drop her name into the easy conversation of dinner or the taut talk of love.

Although by now I was so much in love with him—sexually in chains—that I would have married him any time, anywhere, given the chance; yet, intellectually, I didn't know if I wanted to be so tied. Certainly, I didn't want to have given myself on any *conditions*. I had come to Spain because I wanted to come, with my eyes open, with absolute freedom of choice. That there should be any obligation to him as a result of it was unthinkable.

In spite of his superficial self-confidence there was no offending self-confidence in his attitude to me. He never took me for granted, was often hesitant and groping toward an understanding of what I felt or did.

And one thing I loved him for was that sexually he had

121

little to teach: we learned what we learned together. For some obscure reason this seemed to convince me more than anything of the lasting quality of his love.

We flew home on August 24.

It was odd how slightly more difficult it all became once we returned to England. One's affair became brother and sister to all the other affairs going on in dusty Fulham flats, with ravioli cooked on gas rings, and rust on baths where taps dripped, and worn-down heels and black sweaters freckled with dandruff. On the twenty-sixth I went to Hampstead. Leigh had wanted to come with me, but in this I was emphatic, not even would I go in his car.

Back almost to childhood, for I had been born here; back at least to maidenhood, intellectual and aesthetic maidenhood, long nights of reading about life instead of living it. Let myself in. Both there. Friday a good night. Erica as usual had just had her hair done. Thinner she looked. More feminine. New blouse.

"Deborah, how nice! We've just finished dinner. Have you eaten?"

"Yes, thanks. How are you both?"

"*Very* well. Your father picked up a virus in Corfu, but he's better now. Let's go into the drawing room. Are you staying tonight?"

"Not tonight."

"You're very *brown*. Wasn't it far too hot?"

"No. Not by the sea."

"I don't know how you could go to that country," Douglas said, "where there's still so much oppression." He put his hand on my shoulder. "And poverty."

"A lot of them looked quite happy to me."

"That of course is the tourist's view." We went into the drawing room. "A glass of port to say welcome home?"

"Thank you."

"You're walking without your stick?" Erica said.

"Only partly. I left it at the door."

"But you used to use it everywhere."

"I think I can manage better than I used to."

122

We sat down. Douglas came over with the port.

"I don't think we should forget," Erica said, "what Mr. Adrian warned us of."

"What's that?"

"He said you mustn't overtax the muscles of that leg, the few that still function. He said you could only develop them to a certain degree, and if you tried them beyond that point they'd be likely to let you down."

"I'll risk it."

Douglas said: "No one has ever fully assessed the mind-body correlation. Remarkable things are happening every day for which there's no medical explanation."

"I don't think it's all that remarkable," I said curtly. "I'm only trying a new way of walking. I just got into the way of it while I was bathing."

"You bathed?" said Douglas. "Better still. In Spain I suppose it's different."

"There are a lot of cripples, yes," I agreed. "But in fact we were bathing on an empty beach."

"My dear," said Erica, "I'm sure Douglas didn't mean that at all—"

"I meant," my father said, looking at me with his frank blue eyes, "nothing more than to be pleased you were going in the sea. If I put it badly, I'm sorry."

We sipped our port, and Douglas talked of a protest he was organizing against the police. Five youths had beaten up and robbed a milkman on his round, and the story was that when they were arrested they themselves had been badly handled at the police station. Douglas had written to *The Times* and *The Guardian* and was getting up a petition to present to the local M.P.

Through all this Leigh was never mentioned. It seemed he was to be one of the very few unmentionable subjects in this house. With half a chance Erica would have rationalized. A barrow boy who painted. The unforgivable thing was that his paintings were old-fashioned.

I stayed till ten-thirty. Then Erica said: "When do you think of coming back?"

"I haven't quite decided."

"Are you at Sarah's?"

123

"Not just now."

"Sarah's coming here on Sunday with Philip. Why don't you come?"

"With Leigh?"

There was silence as she pushed up her glasses.

"If he would like it."

"I'll ask him."

"The trouble with sex," said Douglas, "is that it complicates life instead of—as it should—simplifying it. The essence of physical sex is that it should release tension. But in the act human beings nearly always build up within themselves bigger tensions than they break down. Hence Arabella, no doubt."

It was the first time I knew he knew about her.

Chapter 13

I tried to find a sort of middle course for the time being by going back to live at Ennismore Gardens. I made the excuse that it was difficult to get to and from Grafton Street each day from Rotherhithe, but in fact it was easier from there than from Hampstead.

He argued long, but I felt I *had* to live separately from him for a while, just to get my bearings. One night he told me he'd been to the labor exchange, and a week later he took a job as a bus conductor.

I said: "D'you need money that badly?"

"Well, soon will."

"Have you any time to paint at all?"

"Does it matter?"

I blamed myself for taking him to the galleries. Before that he had had doubts enough, but they had been doubts of success not certainty of failure. I felt I had helped to destroy him.

During this time we were making love, and there was no abatement of our need. But living separately was constantly raising problems, of meeting, of leaving, of spending the night. I always made a point of going back to Sarah's flat afterward. And the fact that we were both now working regular hours didn't help.

One night he said how much he wished we could get

married. This was the first time he had ever mentioned marriage, and I looked at him, trying to see how serious he was. When I did not speak he added with a scowl that Lorne, being a Catholic, would never divorce him. But, I said, if she left *him*, might it not be possible for him to divorce *her*—for desertion?

He said: "My God, if only I could . . . But anyway, you're too good for me."

"Oh, I'm a great catch with a leg and a half. But might it not be worth keeping the idea in mind?"

"I'll more than keep it in mind. I'll find out."

The next evening he met me with a wry face. "I went to a lawyer in the lunch hour. It's two years. She has to have been gone two years before you can file a what's-it for desertion."

"Well, that's—that could be worse. Isn't it eighteen months already?"

"Nearly. But it means over a year more before the thing is sewn up. And in the meantime I've got to put on an act of wanting her to come back."

"Would she?"

"I wouldn't think there's a chance in hell. But the solicitor chap, this Davis, said it might be worth having her watched. If we could prove adultery against her . . ."

"Would she be likely to?"

"Don't know. I was her first. It depends whether she's met anybody."

"What did you decide to do?"

"Have her watched. Expensive but it's worth it. I've *got* to afford that."

"You're sure she wouldn't divorce you?"

"Not a hope. She never misses Mass on Sundays."

"You're not a Catholic?"

"Me, no . . . I'm nothing. Remember the man in Shaw's play. 'I believe in Michael Angelo and Rembrandt, in the might of—of design, the mystery of color, the redemption of all things by beauty everlasting. Amen.' Some caper like that. That's near enough to what I believe in, in spite of being no bloody good at it!"

126

I said: "That's a lot to believe in, darling. It's a religion on its own."

Since we came back I'd heard nothing of Ted Sandymount or Jack Foil, but the following Saturday night Leigh took me for a drink to a public house in the Old Kent Road where a group called the Sunspots were playing, and they were both there, together with three or four other people I knew by sight.

It was a fantastic place because the pub was enormous but was so crowded that they had to have a doorman to regulate the numbers, and they only let us in in rotation as the same number came out. Once in, it was pretty nearly impossible to move or speak; you stood shoulder to shoulder with your neighbor, who might or might not have been able to get a drink, and there you stuck like a crowd at a cup tie, while every cubic inch of air over your head was full of the beat and howl of amplified trumpet and electric guitar. After we'd got a bit acclimatized Leigh took my hand and began to hack a way through the crowd. Almost everyone was young.

I thought, don't get scared of being closed in, forget claustrophobia, somebody's shoulder, somebody's back, somebody's hair, pity I'm not as tall as Sarah; crowd coming the other way; impasse; tack, Leigh, go round them. What'll you have? Right, two whiskies. Then he saw the others at the back of the room; Ted waved; whiskies in hand we began to fight our way.

At the back it was just tolerable. Ted got up and gave me his seat beside Jack Foil. Thick lips, pebbles smiling. "Miss Dainton. Nice to see you again. D'you come here often?"

"Never before. It's very crowded, isn't it?"

"What?"

"Very crowded."

There were broken bottles underfoot. A barman was squeezing through trying to collect empty glasses. His left hand had endless fingers, producing unnumbered bubbles of glass like a glass-blower in a factory.

". . . music?" Jack Foil shouted.

"What?"

"D'you like this music?"

"Yes, love it."

"Strange."

"What?"

"Very strange. Youth. I feel very old."

"Why?"

"Must be much oldest here."

I looked round. He probably was.

"Blood, rhythm, sex," he said.

"What?"

"What the young like, I suppose."

"Isn't just that . . ."

The group reached a crescendo and crashed into silence. No one applauded. Voices suddenly strident in place of the beat. Leigh was talking to two girls we'd met somewhere. They were quite pretty.

". . . worried about Leigh."

I turned back. Jack Foil's heavy voice did not somehow rise above the hum.

"I'm sorry?"

"A little worried about Leigh, Miss Dainton. Lost interest in painting, become objectless. Crazy for a talented kid like him to spend his life on platform of bus. Don't you agree?"

"I hope he'll soon get something better."

"Very fond of him. Look on him—like a nephew. Still think he can paint. A very pretty picture of you."

The next number began. It was a famous pop song. Ted shouted at us what were we all drinking, and then began to fight his way toward the bar.

"A part-time job, he needs," shouted Mr. Foil in my ear. Smell of Guinness and carnation scent.

"I didn't know his legacy was so nearly spent."

The pebbles smiled again. "Not a careful boy. Doesn't keep account of what he spends, so money dribbles away. Easily done. Have been trying to think of something for him."

128

The music got louder, more all-invading, then sank again. Someone dropped ash on my shoes.

"D'you mean working for you?"

"Well, or something. He's not skilled."

Leigh was laughing with the two girls, making rather a fuss of one of them. This twist in my stomach, any connection with jealousy?

"I hope you'll try," I said.

On the way home I told Leigh what Jack Foil had said. A curious expression crossed his face. "Well, I've done odd jobs for him before."

"Such as?"

"Oh, various. He's got lots of irons in the fire."

"What sort?"

"All sorts. He promotes things. I've told you."

We stopped at traffic lights. "Leigh, tell me what you mean."

"Well . . . You can't have supposed . . . Among other things, he's a fence."

"A *fence*? He buys stolen property?"

"Yes." We started off with a jerk that nearly took us into the car in front. "Don't ever tell anyone, will you?"

We turned into Westminster Bridge Road. "If you've worked for him before, is that how you've worked for him?"

"Oh, not exactly. Sometimes it's handy for him to have someone like me who can act as messenger boy, or delivery boy or what-have-you. It's been dead easy and no risk. And worth a fiver or a tenner. That's for half a day's work, and no tax deducted."

No more then until we reached the flat.

"Leigh," I said, "there must be something more worth doing than being errand boy to a crook."

He sat with his hands gripping the wheel. "When are you going to cut this out and come and live with me?"

"I don't know. Isn't this the best arrangement for the present?"

"Who for? Not for me, it's not."

That week Philip called in one evening, and while we were alone I mentioned this thing about divorce for desertion and he said: "No, it's three years, Deborah. You have to have deserted a person three years before he can file a petition."

"Oh," I said carefully, "I'm sure I was told it was two."

"Alas, no. I just happen to have been reading up the latest Acts because of a case we're doing next week."

When I met Leigh I asked him again. Again he said, two, until I told him what I knew and then he suddenly gave way and admitted he had been told three also.

"But why?" I said. "Why lie to me? It doesn't make sense."

"I—didn't want you to know. I thought you might not feel you could wait that long."

"But I was bound to find out sooner or later!"

"Yes, but later it wouldn't matter so much. It would be nearer the time then, wouldn't it?"

There was silence between us. "D'you know," I said, "I can't *bear* you to lie to me. It puts all our—our relationship in question."

"I'm sorry, love. I'm that afraid of losing you."

"But don't you see—if it matters that much—this is the way you *would* lose me?"

"Don't speak of it."

"But I must speak of it. Unless there's—there's honesty between us, and trust, there can't be anything. Oh, of course we can make love and go skating and that sort of thing, but that doesn't add up to what I want—or what you seem to want. It's back to the old thing we broke up on before. You don't cheat people you really care about."

"It wasn't meant to be that, honest," he said. "I'm sorry, love."

"Oh," I said, "I'm sorry too. Perhaps I'm blowing it up too big. But you do see, don't you, what I mean?"

"I see all right," he said. "Maybe I'll learn in time."

Whittington's asked me to go to see a house in Norfolk, a small Victorian mansion built by one of the beer barons in 1890 for his eldest son. Aside from the furniture there was a valuable collection of china and porcelain. Grant Stokes, who did furniture, drove me in his car, and we got there about eleven on the Thursday, having overnight things with us, since it was a two-day job. Mr. and Mrs. Bustard, the owners, had just inherited, and were going for a quick sale; he looked like something smooth and well pressed in the City and she had blond hair and ice-blue eyes and smoked and coughed alternately.

My mouth watered at the very sight of the lovely display shelves of Doulton and Sèvres and Dresden. I started in on the Doulton, but at once began to sense something wrong with it—after being constantly in touch for a number of years one almost smells the imitation—and I soon knew it for a forgery. I passed on to the next group of things—some lovely Dresden figures—and found them the same. By the time we stopped for lunch I had not found a single genuine piece. This went on all through the afternoon, and by six I was in a bit of a panic because I had covered all the show pieces, and they were forgeries without exception.

It's very awkward when this happens. These pieces had all been giving pleasure and satisfaction to their owners ever since they were bought seventy-odd years ago. So long as they remained as showpieces in a case in Norfolk, they fulfilled just the same purpose as the genuine pieces that they copied. But once they came into the market their value and charm had to be destroyed in the eyes of their owners—because no man who thinks a thing is genuine can prize it when he knows it's only imitation. This is something wrong with human nature, but there doesn't seem to be any cure. And often the owners—apart from the financial disappointment—don't appreciate being told.

Mr. and Mrs. Bustard did not. They came in full of a hard, well-groomed, patronizing good-will; but when I told them that the entire collection had been specially manufactured as copies of the originals, all in the same French factory about 1880, and that the whole lot was worthless, they froze up. I thought they were even going

131

to withdraw their invitation to us to spend the night. What they did do instead was cast doubts on my competence, and the meeting was thoroughly unpleasant all round. Grant Stokes, of course, backed me up, but he hadn't had a lot to do with porcelain and he couldn't speak with the authority of Maurice Mills. The furniture, he told them, was all fairly good.

We went on working through the evening. If you're a rich Victorian brewer and don't know an awful lot about antiques it isn't difficult to be taken in. If he'd been content to buy decent stuff of his own period it would have been worth far more than this.

But about ten o'clock, fishing in the back of a cupboard upstairs, I found a porcelain statuette about nine inches high and a foot long. It was a statuette of a Chinaman sitting down, with a disproportionately big brown dog beside him. The workmanship was exquisite, and I knew I had come on a treasure at last.

That one piece of genuine early Meissen—a perfect specimen of which perhaps only four were ever made—was the only piece of china of any value in the whole rambling mansion; but it took much of the sting out of the rest. We were there all the following day and didn't get back to London until seven in the evening, so Grant Stokes dropped me in Ennismore Gardens.

As I went up the steps I saw my father's Vauxhall parked almost opposite the front door. A second too late, I realized I'd left my gloves in Grant Stokes's car, and this took my mind off "coo-eeing" as I usually did to let Sarah know I was in. It was a pretty small flat, and I went through into the kitchen to prop my stick in its corner. As I did so I heard my father's voice coming through the serving hatch, which was half open.

"You see, Erica feels that she's not like you and Arabella. She's been delicate and handicapped and that makes her more a special charge on us all—a responsibility, as it were."

Sarah said: "I think you're wildly wrong to look on her as delicate. I think she's tough. I mean, when has she ailed anything ever—I mean apart from the effects of the polio? I can't remember anything at all."

There was silence, and then the chink of a glass. Douglas said: "Thanks. Oh, no, I quite agree. But one wonders how far stamina is impaired. Is she still sleeping with the man regularly?"

"I've no idea."

"She does come back here?"

"Yes, always. But it's not my business to ask, is it?"

"No. Oh, no. I thought she might be quite open about it, that's all."

I tried to turn silently to move away. Douglas said: "Erica's surprisingly concerned. She persists in trying to worry me."

"I honestly can't see why she should be so worried."

"Well, a pregnancy for one thing. Has Deborah sought any advice from you?"

"Hardly! Strange as you may think it, I've never yet slept with anyone!"

"Oh, I'm sorry, Sarah, I didn't mean it that way. I meant that you're so medically qualified. It would be rather a reflection on us all if she got caught, as Minta would call it. And I suppose Hartley can't marry her, even if he wanted to."

"No."

I got back to the door, trying to keep my breathing quiet.

"Have you seen the first wife?"

"I hardly know Leigh even. We've only met a half-dozen times."

Douglas said: "I wonder if she's in any way handicapped."

"Who?"

"The first wife. Of course Deborah is very pretty indeed, but most men would sheer off. The odd man who doesn't may find her bad leg fascinating rather than repellent. Deformity fetishism isn't as rare as you'd suppose."

I went out through the kitchen door but his cool, clinical, uncommitted voice followed me.

133

". . . Men of that type, with that peculiarity, are usually unsatisfactory as husbands and lovers. There tends to be some hidden inadequacy in their own characters . . . They seek—"

I went out, quietly closing the front door again, and went down the steps. I walked the length of the square and then turned toward Knightsbridge. I raised a hand to a prowling taxi.

Chapter 14

He was surprised and delighted; it was the first time I had ever gone to him uninvited; then he saw my face in the light of the studio.

"What's the matter? What's wrong? You'll stay the night?"

"If you'll have me."

"*Darling . . .*"

"No, I don't mean that way. Not tonight. You'll have to give me a day or two."

"What *did* they say? Were they blackguarding me?"

"Not specially. Don't ask me, I'd rather not talk about it now."

"But you'll stay?"

"Yes."

"Permanently?"

"I don't know."

I sighed, trying to shake off misery and anger and malaise, to share his pleasure and sense of adventure. "Don't you have a shift on a Saturday?"

"I've been going to tell you, Deborah. I'm out of a job again."

"Leigh, when?"

"I got the sack last Monday. I wanted to tell you on

Tuesday but I hoped I'd have something fresh by the end of the week."

"What happened?"

"It was one of these rush hours. I grabbed a man and shoved him off. He's threatening to bring a case."

"Oh, I'm *sorry*. You should have told me."

I made some scrambled eggs and we sat together in companionable ease. We talked only about his future that night. Then we went to bed and lay together quietly, and it was only in the last drowsy minutes that I moved closer to him and went to sleep in his arms.

In the morning he was up and out before I woke, and while I was in the bath I heard him come back.

"I went to telephone Jack Foil," he said. "I think he'll help."

"In what way, though?"

"Don't fret yourself. He's never yet been in trouble with the police."

"I don't like it," I said. "I wonder sometimes . . ."

"You *think* too much," he said, "that's the only trouble with you. D'you remember what you said in Spain? Just be. Exist. Just live. That's the only answer to life really. That's the only answer *I've* found."

After three weeks at the Studio, Rotherhithe, S.E.24, I had got used to the bus journey to Piccadilly, shopping on the way home, cooking for him at weekends, the companionship and the demands of love. Hampstead seemed to be something only now observable through the wrong end of a telescope.

I felt relatively little anger against Douglas. Or if it was there it hid itself within, or transformed itself into a deeper commitment on behalf of Leigh. I felt more than ever, more deeply than ever, that I had to help him make something of his life. Whether we ever married or not, we were partners working toward a common end: my realization of myself, his realization of himself. This was all.

Much of the time I was happy. He often seemed younger than his age because of this boyish sense of adventure and fun. He still spent money freely, but had accepted that I should pay for the food and drink that came into the place. He hadn't found work, but I knew he was seeing a lot of Jack Foil.

A district utterly strange to me. And lonely. No neighbors—except the great warehouses—and ten minutes walk to the nearest shop. It seemed a curiously respectable neighborhood. I didn't know whether this was part of the welfare state; but everyone seemed to be moderately prosperous, decently dressed, well found. The shops were unlike those I normally knew. The multiple stores, the supermarkets were only just moving in. For the most part shops were still privately owned, one story, personal, friendly. JIM'S PIE SHOP . . . BETTY'S FOOTSTORE . . . MARTIN'S FOR MEAT. People soon recognized you, called you dear, took an interest. They were a bit suspicious of my accent, but it soon went. There seemed scarcely any colored people, only a few Indians and Chinese. It was all very homely. I had somehow imagined Rotherhithe to be a slum area with wicked lascars and dark deeds by the docks. Anything but.

We had only one near quarrel, Leigh and I, when I told him of my visit to Norfolk and discovering one piece of Meissen among all the fake. He was thoughtful, tapping a cigarette around but not lighting it. "*Where* was it, this piece?"

"At the back of a cupboard, among some old candlesticks."

"Would the owners know they had it?"

"Oh, I shouldn't think so. There was so much junk."

"What size was it—a foot square?"

"The ornament? Oh, less."

"And how much d'you think it will fetch when it comes up for sale?"

"Oh, not less than £2000."

"Oh, my God!"

"What's the matter?"

He at last flicked his lighter. "Hadn't you a bag? Anything like that?"

"Of course. But what . . ."

"The rest of the stuff was junk. No one knew of this

137

piece. You could have just slipped it into your case. What a chance!"

"I'm sorry," I said angrily, "I obviously need an awful lot of educating!"

"Maybe you so. Maybe you do," he said, and got up. Then he turned. *"Sorry,* Deborah. I didn't mean any of it. Forget I spoke."

"Why should I? You won't."

"I know. But I spoke without thinking. It was just that we could have got probably seven or eight hundred pounds from Jack Foil for the thing. It was on a plate. And nobody would ever have known."

"Except that I would have known. And you would. Doesn't that count?"

"D'you think being free of money problems for a while would have made us think any worse of ourselves?"

I picked up a scattered newspaper and for no good reason began folding it. "I've worked for Whittington's for over seven years. Don't you think I owe them any honesty—even if I don't owe it to myself?"

"But you weren't stealing from them—or at least only a bit of commission. It's one of those cases, I think, where it would have done nobody any harm."

"I'm sorry!" I threw the newspaper down. "It is obviously something we shall never agree on."

There was a long silence. I don't know how long it takes to get through a cigarette, but we sat there unspeaking until he had stubbed the end in a stone ashtray. Then he got up and went out without a word.

Jack Foil's flat was over his antique shop in Old Brompton Road. You went up steps at the side and came to a door of reeded glass with a light over it, and as soon as you pressed the bell dogs yapped as if the electricity had been connected to their tails. He opened the door himself, and we went in between potted plants, with two very fat dachshunds monopolizing the conversation. Then his wife slid from between more potted plants and led us into a long darkish room lit with five lamps in black drum shades.

Wife about thirty: bleached hair on shoulders, tired blue eyes, good figure but wearing a size ten frock where she needed a twelve. Plants everywhere.

"It's my hobby," said Jack Foil, taking my elbow. "This is an Umbrella Tree—know it?—it comes from Australia; very nice, don't you think? D'you take whisky or gin? Sherry, then. Sherry, Doreen. This they call Mother-in-Law's-Tongue—ha, ha!—very long, if you understand, and wagging. Down, Rufus! Down! They get excited, you know, we don't have many visitors. Down, Paula! Leigh, you'll take whisky, I suppose? . . . This plant's called Scarlet Trails. Lovely red flowers in the spring, but they don't last. Comes from one of those American islands. There, it's dry sherry, is that all right for you? . . . Down, Rufus! Let me look at your shoes, Miss Dainton . . . Ah, you're all right; no laces. Laces have a fatal fascination for Rufus. If he can, he'll chew them right off. A friend came the other day and was *quite* annoyed. Sitting down, you know, he didn't notice until it was too late . . . Ice, Leigh? Ah, of course, I remember, no ice. Is Dr. Sarah Dainton your sister, Miss Dainton? She comes in the shop sometimes. Fancy, and I never connected! Very charming. Small silver pieces, as you know. She bought a Georgian silver tea canister. Only last week. Sit beside me and tell me what you think of this rug. You recognize it? Ha, ha! I was looking at it the day we met in Whittington's. But I wanted it for my personal use, not for the shop. The wife fancied it. Perhaps you think it's a pity, what with the dogs."

Dark hair on the back of his hands, like fur; unpleasant contrast with the gold of the two signet rings. Pebbled eyes, never quite normal in size, wobbled as the lenses moved. Smell of carnation. He looked sinister. Yet homely. A stout, heavy man of fifty talking, talking, with his two dachshunds snuffling at his feet, and green room plants giving a vegetable look, an underwater look to a room insufficiently lighted, and a blond corseted young wife flirting with Leigh and pulling her short skirt down to her knees so often that she drew his looks. (Yet a softer woman this, much, than the moneyed blonde in Norfolk.) Sherry dry and fine, Corona smoke, central heating, settee too soft, enveloped one like a bed. I had read a book once about a fat man suffocating a girl with a pillow. Careful. No claustrophobia.

"Yes, Mr. Foil," I said, "and is that a Stanley Spencer?" Are these all stolen pictures on the walls? Did that handsome diamond on your wife's finger come from some Hatton Garden robbery? But surely not. Surely you're too careful for that. "Well, I suppose he's one of the easiest of all painters to recognize." "It's what you were talking to me about that day—developing a style that isn't a mannerism. When we were talking about Leigh."

What risk is Leigh running in your company? Of course he talks big, about breaking the law; but isn't he *basically* too well balanced, too level-headed. . . .

"Leigh tells me you're going to be married, Miss Dainton. Of, of course, I know, there are obstacles but they can be removed, can't they. Time and patience. That's a Catherine Wheel Plant you're staring at—very nice and easy to grow . . . Oh, yes, I knew her slightly. But she wasn't his type. Type? Ha, ha, well of course there isn't any, is there? But you know what I mean. Leigh's rather an elite sort of chap, in spite of coming from a simple home. Deserves somebody like you, Miss Dainton, if I may say so."

Genuine benevolence in his voice? Never anything but courteous and kind to me. Another mistake of the conventional mind to suppose that a man who lived illegally was any less human or ordinary or, indeed, likable in his everyday life.

Leigh, I thought, was not quite at ease in his company. Less pugnacious, less jolly, more concerned to please.

He got temporary work in a clothing warehouse in Percy Street. Money good, but no prospects. One day he confessed to me he owed Jack Foil £500. I was appalled and wanted to help him to pay it back at once. He said no, what did it matter; but all that day and for many days afterward I worried about it. I had saved about £400, but he wouldn't accept any of it, saying: "Look, sweetheart, can I take from you now the cash I spent courting you? What sort of a lark would you call that? I know you want to help, and in some ways maybe you can help; but don't you see you just can't help *that* way!"

Most of the time now I never used a stick. In fact, I'd left it in a cupboard at Whittington's. I sometimes woke in the night with an unallayable ache in the small of the back, but this might have been caused by any one of the changes in my changed life. Leigh was encouraging me to dance: half of the studio was uncarpeted and he had a small record player and we tried there. He wanted me to go with him to a dance hall. "Darling," I said, "it isn't so much that I'm afraid of people pointing me out and saying, 'look at that freak.' I'm afraid of people pointing me out and saying 'look at that brave girl.' D'you get what I mean?"

"I get that you care a hell of a lot too much what other people think."

"Don't we all? You care too much what those silly dealers think of your painting."

"They're experts. And don't change the subject."

"It's all part of the same subject."

One or two weekends we went out of London, and he let me drive the car. I seemed to get into it pretty quickly, and actually, with the weak leg being the left one, I didn't have much trouble. The only real difficulty was the headlight dipper, but of course this didn't matter during the day. I applied for a test.

At Whittington's the big autumn sales were coming up, and I brought home a stack of catalogues. He thumbed through them.

"What a packet of folding money there must be in all this stuff! It isn't till you see it all listed that you realize. Hundreds of thousands of quid all humped together in those junk showrooms of yours!"

It was swan-feeding time—we did this twice daily— and we went out on the balcony in the evening light. A white vessel was just passing flying a Trinity House flag. It seemed to move as easily as a swan, gliding with the stream, completely silent. The water had a slightly pink glow like fashionable champagne. A premature light winked here and there.

"We ought to go into business together," he said, "as junk dealers. You with your strict honesty, me with my knavery. We'd be an unbeatable team—slap into the First Division."

"D'you know that's not a bad idea."

"What isn't?"

"We *might* go into business together—in an antique shop. I mean—I know almost as much as anybody about china and porcelain, and I've a working knowledge of a few other things. You understand a lot about painting."

He stared at me. The swans were coming downriver; four fully grown and six cygnets; they steered and maneuvered into a position where they could most easily grab the bread and meat we offered.

"We could work together," I said, "instead of on separate things. And what we made would be our own."

"What do we use for money?"

"To set up? Oh, I know . . ." Neither Douglas nor Erica had any personal capital behind them. They always claimed to have educated their children on overdrafts. "But it's worth thinking about. It's the first real idea we've had."

No more then, but the following morning he said: "I wonder what we'd need to set up. We could rent a shop somewhere to begin. But even then it'd cost the earth. Three thousand pounds I'd think to get started properly, to buy in a bit of stock, and to wait for people to come in and buy. I could ask Jack Foil."

"Don't."

"O.K., O.K. But we'd have to have money from somewhere. Even a barrow boy's got to buy his barrow!"

"Let's think of it for a while. Perhaps I can think of something."

I felt much happier just for having this to dwell on. Before there hadn't been any future; one went on from day to day, happy but blinkered. But this was a possible solution only just out of reach.

On November 3 I found our balcony piled with wooden cases, cardboard cartons stuffed with straw, three old chairs, coconut matting with holes in it, old clothes, a moth-eaten feather boa. You couldn't see out of one window at all. Leigh came in a few minutes after me and laughed at my face.

"This is the beginning of our antique shop, mate; I'm going to buy a horse and cart and collect junk."

"No seriously! Tell me."

"Well, you said you wanted a bonfire."

"D'you mean it? Can we?"

"I went and asked one of the dockmasters of the P.L.A. They don't mind so long as we keep it reasonable."

"And fireworks?"

"Oh, yes. I've got a whole bunch here." He picked up the parcel. "The lot. Other people are bringing theirs as well."

I laughed. "What other people?"

"Lay off. This is my joint still and I'm giving the party."

"But, darling, can we afford it?"

"No, we can't, but that adds an extra zing. Anyhow it's your birthday party as well—a week early."

"I didn't know I'd ever told you."

"You didn't. It leaked out when I was talking to Sarah last week."

"Is she coming?"

"You wait and see."

The fifth was a Saturday, so we could spend all day getting ready. I made a female guy out of the smelly old clothes. The tides were right. Leigh had made sure of that before anything else—but of course he couldn't start building the bonfire until four when the river ebbed. Even then it meant building on wet stones.

The night was a bit windy and overcast and dark but not cold. By six we could see other lights flickering here and there over the city and docks, and a few rockets and flashes. At six-thirty Arabella and a young man came. To my surprise it was not Bruce Spring, but I didn't catch his name and had no chance of asking her about him. Then four other people, including two I'd met at Ted Sandymount's. Then Ted himself, blinking and twitching; he'd been away on holiday, and his nose was peeling; whenever I looked at him all that evening he was picking at the loose skin on his nose. Then Sarah came with Philip Bartholomew and David Hambro. And then my father and mother.

When I saw them I glanced at Leigh half in anger, half in panic; but he pinched my elbow and a minute later I was kissing them coolly and welcoming them as if I'd expected them all the time.

Fortunately more guests came, so the shock was absorbed and embarrassment was breathed out in commonplaces. I was still half angry inside, but Douglas and Erica were never bad party-goers, and I wasn't surprised at the way they entered into the thing. I'd never been allowed fireworks at home, but now they said they found them "tremendous fun," and particularly in the setting of London River.

This setting, you had to admit, made all the difference. It was probably rather absurd—and yet it was beautiful. We started off with twenty rockets fired from bottles; then I had to light the bonfire with a torch Leigh had made, and everyone sang "Happy Birthday" in the dark flickering, spark-blowing night and drank my health in Rioja and bit into sausage rolls. The fire's reflection was mirrored in metallic gray and green and orange in the quiet lapping river. The pyre was soon a mass of flame leaping up to the feather-boaed witch on the top. Faces laughed, talked, peered, drank, in flickering setting-sun colors; then, as if arc-lighted in a pantomime, turned green, crimson and yellow as flares were lit on the stones.

A cruising river boat flickered its searchlight over us; a great rocket flowered and died, silhouetting Tower Bridge; Roman candles popped and spluttered; the witch sagged and tottered, flames licking, and then fell sideways upon the stones. Her hat struck the water and hissed and floated away. The red wine was too cold, the sausages too hot, but no one seemed to mind. About now I looked up and Mr. and Mrs. Jack Foil had come, were standing beside Douglas and Erica on the balcony looking down. Her ash-blond hair fluttered like a flag.

Another flurry of rockets; more crackers; then the men began to push together the remnants of the bonfire to encourage the blaze. The tide had turned and was creeping gently in, lapping at the stones at our feet. We had had our fun, it told us; time to go.

In the studio everyone crowded, talking at once. Wine had unlocked tongues; people too hot in coats now, dropping them in corners; clink of bottles; Leigh passing by me: "O.K., love?" "O.K.—devil." Smiles, loving smiles between us. "Well, I reckoned it a good idea, birthday and all that. Where's your glass, David?" Separated again. But together. I love him. God, it almost hurts. Don't let this end. Not the party but the love. A blissful amity. Founded on sex but almost independent of it. I'd die for him. Schemer. Scheming all this up. Still treating me like a juvenile. I'll show him.

My father's voice, lighter in timbre than some others but very clear. "It's a question of reaction formation. Obsessional morality was the obvious example in Victorian and Edwardian days. Now we see others at work." "Pyorrhea," said Mrs. Foil, close by me. "But then she's nearly twelve. Otherwise as healthy as could be." A hand on my arm. "Darling, a lovely party," Arabella said. "Fabulous idea and all." "Who's the new man?" "Benjy? Not really new. Sort of *da capo*." "Bruce?" "Oh, lots to tell you about him. Suddenly things went sour—desperately, tragically. It shows how wrong we would have been to marry." Ted Sandymount's sniff and snicker. "So I said to him I said, you can stuff that, what d'you think I am, an *au pair* girl?" Wine was running out, anyway, it must be getting on for ten. Sarah had miraculously produced two big trays of chocolate biscuits. Those *went*. *Everybody* took one, even Douglas. Good sign. Good party. Leigh by the door, face smudged with bonfire ash; I took the last biscuit, munched deliciously; people going now. Met Leigh's eyes; he wanted me. Go now; go everyone. "Thank you. Delighted you came." "Yes, wasn't it fun? We'll do it again next year!" *"Glad* you came, Erica. I think it's going to work out." "Goodbye, Douglas, thank *you.* For coming, I mean." "Mr. Foil . . . Well, Jack, then. Thank you, thank you." "Sarah, did you *bring* the biscuits?" "Next week? Yes we could, I expect. I'll ask Leigh."

Going, going now. Cars outside had choked the lane. Much revving of engines, people trying to maneuver, laughter, slammed doors. Ted here still, talking to Arabella, eying her as if he'd like to bed her; she eying him back, flirting as usual with anyone for the fun of it. Leigh came back from outside, looking at me again. The room a shambles. Cigarette smoke and ends, empty glasses, gloves someone had forgotten, burned out Roman candles in a jar, bottles on their sides not even dripping, a paper bag with Catherine wheels. Arabella's young man. "Thanks, Deborah, lovely to have met you. The car's outside and it's just raining. Goodbye, Leigh." Only Ted now. And Leigh knew Ted well enough to get rid of Ted.

Back to the door. We were alone.

We knew it had been a great success. We knew everyone had enjoyed it. We stood a moment and smiled at each other, and then laughed. Then we moved and met, and kissed, still laughing. We fondled each other, breathing a sort of deep fundamental affection, of which desire was only a part. But because of the amalgam breadth and depth were added in some chemical synthesis of which perhaps even Douglas would have approved. In the wreckage of the party we made love as never before, moving the very wells of body and spirit where for a while we dwelt together and alone. It happened. I know it happened like that. Even though it never happened like that again.

Deep in the breathing dark of the night he said: "You awake?"

"Yes."

"Why?"

"I don't know. I heard the rain. You?"

"I been thinking."

"Nice thoughts?"

"Of you—fabulous. But not all of you."

"Tell me."

He drew me against him. "No. Sleep."

We lay for a time, warm and deliciously drowsy. The wind was blowing and rain beat on the windows. All the more infinitely comfortable here. Twice I dozed, each time woke knowing him awake.

"What is it, darling?"

He moved his arm, stretched. "God, you were marvelous."

I lay with my face against his hand.

After a while he said: "Lucky about last night."

"What?"

"The rain kept off."

"Yes, it would have been a mess. What's worrying you, Leigh?"

"D'you want to know now?"

"Why not?"

"It's only five."

"Well, I shan't sleep if you don't."

Silence. He said: "I've been asked to ask you something and don't dare."

"What?" I giggled. "I can't *imagine* anything you wouldn't dare—"

"*No.* This is serious. Somebody like Jack Foil. Not Jack Foil but somebody like him. They want information."

"What d'you mean? What information can I possibly give them?"

"About Whittington's."

Silence. Mind move around in its little cell, probing, cold cell, the heat has been turned off. "What sort of information?"

"The sort of precautions that are taken at night."

"Against burglary?"

"That kind of thing—yes."

"Somebody wants to break in?"

"It's being considered."

Silence. I lay very still.

He said: "I don't know how they've come to think of you. I suppose seeing you here and *friendly* with people . . ."

"With Jack Foil."

"Maybe."

I breathed out on his fingers. "Well, just tell them no. Tell them to go and feed the swans."

"It's not so easy as all that. There's no one else they know who has an inside on Whittington's."

"Good, I'm relieved. Tell them to try Sotheby's instead."

"Whittington's is the place they've got in mind, see. Of course . . . There'd be money in it for us."

Stare up into the dark. Almost sightless dark. Voice and body beside me. Can be heard and touched and deeply loved, but not the brain activating . . .

"You're not seriously suggesting I should do it?"

"That's what I've been awake so long about. Beating it out, saying to myself, I've no right to ask her, and then thinking, it'd be five hundred. That'd get us in the clear with Jack and give us the beginning of a nest egg."

"Oh, Leigh, stop it! Don't be so utterly silly!"

Silence. "I know it's silly. I *know* it's silly."

"Well, then."

"It sounded plumb crazy to me at first, I promise you. But that's what I've been mulling over. When you come to think of it, it seems easy money for so little."

"So little?"

"Well, when you've told 'em what you know they may decide to do nothing at all. That's up to them."

"And pay us the five hundred? Oh, ho!"

"Maybe not . . . I don't know. I don't think I can reason straight tonight!"

Silence for a while. "I reckon the place is insured, is it?" he asked.

"What, Whittington's? Well, of course."

"I suppose if they were broken into, the publicity would be almost worth the upset."

Not the brain activating, not ever. Not even in the fus-ing fires of love.

"When did you hear this? When was the proposition put to you?"

"Last night."

"By Jack Foil?"

"No, someone else. Someone bigger than him."

"At the *party?* Ted?"

"No. One of the others. It's not important. You'll never guess."

"You should have kicked him out."

"That would have been *very* unhealthy."

Think this over. "Leigh, have you got mixed up with a *gang* or something? It sounds awfully melo—"

"No. Not that. Only people I know."

"You know some strange people."

"Yeh."

"Darling, they don't know *me*. So if they're so silly as to think . . . well, that's excusable. But for you to think the same . . ."

"I said I didn't dare ask you. But you pestered . . ."

"Well, you can't be surprised, surely, at the way I feel."

Long silence. I said: "Could you drink tea if I made it? Or Horlick's? Or . . ."

He said: "I'm *sorry,* Deb. Honest. I knew how you'd feel and yet . . ."

"Yet what?"

"It's so difficult for the likes of me. You get a propo-sition like this—you chuck it out. I get a proposition like this—and it sticks. So it makes you that much better than me—"

"Oh, rubbish—"

"Well, it does. But I've told you—we come from dif-ferent ways of living. My dad's on the railways. Mum died early and he had kids to bring up. All my life I've seen him *scraping. You* haven't a clue what that means. When you were short of money it meant you couldn't afford a luxury. When we were short of money it meant we couldn't afford a necessity. I was second eldest. I had to wear all my brother's clothes, when they were already rubbed threadbare by him. *Always* the cheapest food to try to make it go further. *Always* making do with fifth rate. Of course the money came in every week. We made do. But every penny gobbled up. Never a penny spare. I swore when I grew up I'd not be like that. I swore it through my teeth every time we went short. So you see . . . money means different to me. It means too much, maybe. But that's the way it is, Deborah. I can't change now. I'm not saying I'm right—I'm only saying the difference."

I began to feel a bit sick. "And . . . you'd like me to give information to thieves who want to break into my firm, a firm that trusts me, for £500. Just £500. You want me to betray them for that? I'd rather *give* you £500. I'd rather give it you so that you can say no!"

"Oh . . . forget I ever spoke!" He turned half away, and sighed, blowing out a long deep breath.

"I can't, Leigh. I want to know."

He said: "This business of honesty . . . we've talked about it before. *I* don't know. I'm not the Lord God. But who's honest and who isn't? I know you are, love; but how many others? Anyone knows—you can pick a hundred cases. Lord X. His great-grandfather was a dirty moneylender and bought property in Rotherhithe. His grandfather and his father were slum landlords, employing men to squeeze and bully their tenants while they lived in a great house in Sussex and owned a private yacht and what all. The property is half blitzed and half condemned, so the present Lord X sells it to a development company for £600,000. Is that honesty? By the laws of the land, yes. But how much honester is it than the Great Train Robbers? Who caused the most suffering? Look at half the Rolls-Royces in London today. Who owns 'em? Old men driving about, lechers, gluttons, sitting on fortunes. How did they come by their money?"

I took his hand. "Of course that's partly true. But you can always justify yourself in anything if you point your finger at other people. It's really only yourself you can judge."

He took his hand away. "You sound like a parson."

"No, I sound like a prig. You don't give me much choice, do you?"

"I'm sorry, I'm sorry. I've told you, forget I ever spoke."

There was a silence that lasted into minutes. Somewhere a clock chimed the quarter hour.

I said: "Forgive me, darling, for being like this. Don't think I think myself better than anybody else. Of course I was brought up in lucky, comfortable surroundings—I grant you that. But that doesn't make the difference—not really. It's just that there—there are—are things I feel I can do, things I . . . just can't see myself doing *at all,* under any circumstances. You're a much more generous, open enthusiastic person than I am—*kinder,* more thoughtful, so often unselfish. You beat me in all these things. But when you ask me to—to cheat the firm I work for—it—it isn't on. It's as if someone asked me to cheat *you!*"

"I'm sorry," he said again. "I'm sorry I asked."

Chapter 15

No word of it next morning. Up early, trying to make some order of the chaos before he woke. When he did he said he had a headache and would go out for the Sunday papers. He was away a long time and didn't get in until a few minutes before lunch. We ate without much conversation.

He was perfectly pleasant but cool. But what he'd asked was a lead weight in my stomach; that he said no more of it emphasized by omission.

Rain all day, and we didn't go out. There were enough bits of leftovers from lunch and yesterday to make a scrap supper. I went through my presents, a coffeepot from Douglas and Erica, perfume from Sarah and Arabella, stockings from the Foils, chrysanthemums from Philip Bartholomew; but the savor was lost. I wondered if I really was a prig. Or, even if I wasn't, whether I seemed one to him. This same big gap in our mental outlook. However much we loved, sometimes we might have been of a different race. Did he make any effort to understand me? Did I make any to understand him? At the party, thoughts across my mind: I'll die for him. But not lie for him—is that it? The big noble sacrifice, but not the small shabby one.

A busy day on Monday, and I stayed late, deliberately,

stayed on until the security guards came at seven. Home by bus. Nearly eight. He wasn't in.

When I was late we usually ate out, though I tried to avoid this by bringing food home with me, as it was so much less expensive. Tonight there was nothing in the house but eggs and bacon. I poured myself a gin and tonic and waited. He came in at nine-thirty, looking tired.

"Hello, love. Been waiting? Sorry I couldn't let you know. We ought to be on the telephone. I applied and then canceled it because we couldn't afford it."

Quite nice. Pleasant, cool, friendly, no resentment. But *cool*.

"There's only eggs and bacon, will that do? I didn't have time to get anything."

"Well I've—eaten a bit. Couldn't avoid it, really. You eat and I'll just have a whisky or something."

"I don't think there's any whisky. Two or three wouldn't drink wine on Saturday."

"Blast. Oh, a cup of tea, then."

I made tea but didn't cook myself anything. I buttered a couple of crackers and put cubes of Cheddar on them. He ate one and I the other. We talked a bit and then got ready for bed. He didn't say where he'd been and I didn't ask him.

I asked him on the Tuesday evening how they'd taken my refusal.

He said: "D'you mean? . . ." and blinked his heavy lids. "Oh, *that* . . ." He put his knife and fork down and cut a piece of bread from the loaf on the table.

We continued to eat for a bit. I said: "I suppose they didn't like it."

"No, they didn't. Not much."

"What did they say?"

"They asked me to ask you to think again."

"And what did you say?"

"What could I say?"

"That you would?"

"Yes." He looked at me steadily for a second. Queer look. Somber. No warmth in it. "Yes, I said I'd ask you to think again."

"Why? Why make it worse?"

He pushed his plate a couple of inches away from him with his thumbs. "I was trying not to make it worse. It isn't easy just to say no."

"Why not? You owe them nothing."

He shrugged. I said: "Or d'you mean you *do* owe them something? Is Jack Foil pressing you for his money? Is that it?"

He got up, thrusting back his chair so that it screeched. "Jack's a receiver, not a blackmailer. He's my friend."

"And the others?"

"Well, not so as you'd notice. They weren't very friendly today."

"Well, can they do anything about it, if I refuse?"

He shrugged again. "Your guess is as good as mine."

"But this—this is ridiculous. It's another form of blackmail—"

"Oh, it's not as bad as that—they're not thugs. Nobody's going to be beaten up, if that's what you're thinking. But this is a tough world, Deborah, so soon as you get out of the nice little suburbs. It only means—I'm only saying that it's not easy for me just to say no, just like that. I've got to think all round it. And so have you. So I'm playing for time. I said I'd let them know definite by next Sunday."

On the Wednesday there was a big miscellaneous sale at Whittington's which really took off from the start. Every auction room knows this can happen. Six sales will be quite normal, good business etc. The seventh seems to go from the first lot. People bid more quickly, they bid against each other at the right times, in the heat of it all prices rocket.

This was the sale in which we'd put the single Meissen piece. It fetched 3900 guineas. Two eighteenth-century candlesticks reached 580 guineas. A young American paid £3700 for a tiny jade toucan with emerald eyes; interviewed afterward, he said it was a Christmas present for his fiancée in Boston. Two or three of the less reputable dealers were there and were working in collusion, but private interference was so great that this time they couldn't do much to control the prices. One of Shaw's Prefaces, signed by the author, went for £10,000. I looked at the catalogue. *"Fabergé clock, the property of the Hon. Mrs. Anthony Justine . . . Chinese lacquer screen, the property of Lord Suppint . . . the property of the late Earl of Calshot."* All the property of someone, and all fetching ever-increasing prices. Money flowed like milk. An elderly woman in a print frock paid £7000 for a Stubbs while scarcely bothering to lift her eyelids, and another, 600 guineas for a Sheraton breakfast table. Money, money. Of course I could see what Leigh meant. The hideous discrepancy. Leigh's father was an ardent trade unionist battling dourly for his pay rise of 11/6 a week. Leigh looked at it differently. Leigh was in with an odd crowd and saw no particular harm in trying to persuade his mistress to sell a little information for a sum of money that represented 11/6 a week for sixteen years —and that tax free. You could see his point of view.

But Deborah Dainton had her standards. It sounded prissy but it was true. How far did they go? It was very odd. With a little effort one could probably produce a perfectly rational case for doing what Leigh wanted. The moral issue, as he said, was very confused. Nobody would come to any harm. One of the vast insurance companies might pay away a little of their profits. Nothing more. But Deborah Dainton didn't do it. Not if she wanted to go on living with herself, she didn't.

But what if she wanted to go on living with Leigh?

He was a bit strange all that week. No one could say he was sulky or moody or short-tempered or unkind. But a sort of thin transparency had come between us. This was perhaps not deliberate on his part, but it was as if I had damaged our relationship. He bore no ill-will but it had happened.

It's much easier to justify yourself if the opposite party gives you cause for complaint. If he'd snapped at me I should have felt better. So I began to snap at him.

On the Thursday he said: "All right. I'll go and tell them tonight that it's no sale. That satisfy you?"

"Yes."

"You don't sound as if it does."

"How can I?" I said, nearly crying, "unless I feel you agree with me."

"How can I when I don't?"

"You don't?"

"Oh, I don't know." He stopped. "Not just in those words anyhow . . . I honestly don't know what I agree with. One minute I think one thing, next minute the opposite. I know you, and I know it's a hell of a thing to ask you to do. But it's choosing between two things, isn't it, and neither of 'em's good. That's the trouble."

I bit at my finger. "D'you want me to leave you?"

"I thought we were going to get married."

"So did I. But this . . ."

"You'd break it for this? You can't care much."

"You ought to know how much I care."

He put his hands up to his face. "Why the hell did this ever come up? I'll go now. Don't wait supper. I'll have it while I'm out."

He went across for his leather jacket, put it on over his shirt, his face drawn as it might have been with pain. As he got to the door, I said: "Wait."

He stopped short. "What for?"

"Don't go tonight. Let's leave it a day or so. You haven't to tell them till Sunday."

"It'll make no difference. Best get it over."

"I don't want to be *left*, Leigh. I can't bear to be alone tonight in this studio. I feel—surrounded by all these buildings—they're all empty at night. Can't we . . . talk? Let's eat a meal and try to forget it. It's been on my mind night and day this week. Let's try for an hour or two to think of something else."

That night we made love but it wasn't a success. Not either way. The loving kindness had evaporated too and left only a sort of exhaustion of spirit. I woke about six-thirty and found him gone, the place empty. He came back at seven-thirty in time for breakfast, said he'd just been walking.

While we were having breakfast a barge came alongside the warehouse next to us and began to unload timber. The rattle of the derrick and the clank and thump of the timber did not encourage talk between us.

You don't stop loving a man because of one thing. Last Saturday was still so near that one kept harking back, trying to remember. I desperately wanted to comfort him, to care for him, to please him, but there wasn't any way. I felt now that whatever happened, even if I agreed, our feeling for each other was stained, spoiled. Whoever gave way, you lost.

He worked Saturday morning, and I didn't. I shopped for the weekend, in and out of the crowds, waiting in the butcher's, picking Cox's on a fruit stall, remembering tooth paste, limping—though not limping nearly as much —along the pavement, waiting at the traffic lights, shopping bag heavy on arm. People thronging, pushing; greedy faces, mean faces, kindly faces, ailing, lonely, drink-flushed, self-satisfied, oversatisfied, underprivileged faces, new faces wrinkled in prams, old faces ready for the box. All little egos, all wanting personal comfort, personal gratification, personal attention. I, I, the most important word in everyone's language. They differed from the crowds in Hampstead, which were better dressed, more casually at ease, more sophisticated, perhaps more decadent; but it was a superficial difference, not a fundamental one. All subscribed to the same motives, the same end.

And what was that end?

I could have cried in the street, wept with indecision. Anyway, to do what Leigh asked was "out" for me. Then what? Leave him? Would I be able to now? I seemed at this time to need him with an urgent emotional need. No one in all my life meant anything like him. We were lovers, companions, friends, helpmates; instead of being one against the world it was two. This was the fundamental thing: my whole life was changed because I was sharing it. It's the one vast difference between loneliness and

157

non-loneliness, the bridgeable and the unbridgeable gap. I couldn't do without him.

And since we became lovers our complete relationship had changed. I was no longer a step ahead of him, in that he was the wooer and I the chooser. He'd never suggested or implied that the pendulum had swung the other way. But if it came to the point might it not be so?

Did I need him more than he needed me? Perhaps you could only know when it was too late.

When I got home the barge had unloaded, so quietness again. A hazy sort of day, and the studio had absorbed some of the river damp, mirrors misted, chairs clammy. I dusted a bit, rearranged my plates on the mantelpiece, shortened the stems of Philip's chrysanthemums. Even with the windows shut I could hear a cox coaching his crew from the Wapping side of the river. "One-two-one-two-one-two."

I blew out an uncertain sigh. Maybe I was making too much of it all. Let him tell these people, no, and there'd be an end: in a couple of weeks it would all be forgotten. We'd go out tonight and ignore this silly sordid tangle.

On the table by the door was his post, which had come since he left. I never touched his letters normally, even his open flaps; but there were three today that looked like bills. They were. £33.10.0., £9.11.3., and £41.5.0. All accounts-rendered with *"please remit"* or *"an immediate payment will oblige."*

I went to his desk, got envelopes, wrote checks for all three, put them in my coat pocket to post them. My balance was going down. We were probably just paying our way with what we earned but I never saw his money and never knew how much he paid toward overheads, how much he allowed the bills to drift.

He was right. I'd never been short of money before. Wasn't now—yet. But might be.

I put two pork chops on for lunch, peeled potatoes, cut up a turnip. Then with a few minutes to spare I made a bit of pastry and tried my hand at a jam tart.

No luck with a different job for him. I'd tried to encourage him to look for something which would make use of his talents as a draftsman. It was very much up to me to help him in some practical way, but as yet I hadn't been able to find the way. To find worth-while work, a new view of life for him, a new self-respect. Worthy but dull? Wasn't it Nabokov who had said that the only alternative to banality was perversity? But we had the *potentiality* for happiness together, however it might be realized. God knew that was rare enough. Two against the world.

I was of course running him into extra expense merely by living here. Also, quite by the way, he was paying to have his wife watched.

When he came in I was looking through a book of his early sketches that I hadn't seen before. He said: "Your horrible firm'll be selling those at a hundred guineas a time in the year 2000." And laughed.

"Artists should always have children," I said, "then at least somebody benefits."

"Well . . . you said it."

Lunch was ready and we sat down to it. Joy to find his mood changed. This was the man I knew, could be natural with. I didn't ask the reason—if any—for the change, but gratefully took up where a week ago we'd left off. He'd bought tickets for an ice-hockey match, and we spent the afternoon there. In the evening we drove through Rotherhithe Tunnel and went to a public house on the Isle of Dogs, but this was less popular and less noisy than the one where we had met Jack and Ted.

I suppose I drank too much. Unusual for me; but I suppose this was the relief. On the way home I said:

"What have you decided to tell them?"

"Who? . . . Oh. I can only tell them what you've decided. But can it. It's been a good evening. We don't want to spoil it now, do we."

"Leigh"—I struggled with curious emotion—"you've never actually told me what they want to know—have you?"

"You haven't given me a lot of encouragement—have you?"

"Well, what is it? At least I ought to hear that."

159

We dived into the tunnel. "Details? I don't know 'em myself. They obviously'd like to know the general security arrangements, that's all. You can imagine as well as I can—what nightwatchmen, what alarms, when they come on, who's responsible—all that. If they think it's too tough an assignment they'll scrub it, as I said before. But until they know . . ."

"Can't they find all this out easily enough for themselves? It would cost a lot less than £500."

"They don't believe in taking chances."

Silence till we got home.

Ideas. If I *did* agree to help, it would warm our love again—so very important—but need I (privately) commit myself too deep? With the best will in the world, there was a limit to what I could find out. With a little less than the best will . . . Even if "they" refused to pay the £500, I would have appeared to do my best. So long as nobody suspected—Leigh especially.

"Ask them what they want to know," I said.

Conspiracy is the oddest thing. It spawns in the mind, and the mere circulation of thought carries the spawn into far corners. Conflicts develop in the strangest way. "Thou shalt not" can be eroded from many sides.

Of course it's not easy to be half committed—or not easy for someone who hasn't cultivated the talent of deception—this I would have realized on a less emotional evening. Yet even in the gray light of Sunday morning—and that of other mornings—I didn't repudiate.

You can be over seven years with a firm and yet have hardly any idea. Security precautions are just something you never take notice of. You leave at six or seven in the evening and come again next morning at nine-thirty. Doors are locked; men come on duty; but it's all of utterly no importance.

So when someone asks you, you have to start from scratch. And move cautiously for your own sake. (I hoped still that the whole idea would be scrubbed, as Leigh called it; if I had any influence it would be; but if it wasn't, if "something" happened, I wanted no finger of suspicion pointed.)

Sometimes I woke in the middle of the night and said, you fool, you screaming asinine little fool, you female Judas, you twisted little beast; and the man beside me was asleep, a heavy young man, solid limbed, white limbed, gentle handed, kind mouthed; so I said, well, there it is, you trade love for integrity; and what is integrity? Can you feel it, can you taste it, as you can feel and taste love? Four syllables; four socks on a line; and as significant, no more so—or only more so because of breeding and tradition. To whom anyway did I fundamentally owe any loyalty except to Leigh? And I would turn over and try to hold his hand, as if that were the only certain thing in a world that didn't seem to have a lot of certainty any more.

"They're not ordinary nightwatchmen," I said. "They're Safeguards. You know, there are lots of organizations now. Securicor are the biggest, I suppose. Safeguards send two men round every night. They come on at seven and stay till seven the next morning. We don't pay them. We pay the firm Safeguards so much a year for over-all protection."

"Is it always the same two men?"

"No, I think they change every week. I suppose that's part of the system."

"Are there burglar alarms as well? I've never seen any wires when I've called for you."

"Yes, there are two circuits. One operates on the windows and doors. I was looking today. It works by buttons. All the buttons are pressed down and then the alarm is switched on. If anyone opens a window or door the button flips up and the circuit is broken and sets off the alarm."

"The other?"

"It works in the strong room but I don't know how. It sets off separate bells on the roof if anyone goes in or opens the door."

"Where is the strong room?"

"In the basement. Not far from where I work. There's a safe inside, and steel filing cabinets and some shelves."

"What's the make of the safe?"

"I've no idea."

Leigh put down his pencil. "Well, it's a start."

"Yes."

He yawned and stared at the paper. "I honestly don't know what else they want, but I'd think a plan of the place would be useful. It's such a honeycomb."

"There is a plan on a wall in Peter Greeley's office; I expect I could draw a rough diagram from memory."

"You give me the diagram; I'll draw it."

"Now?"

"Why not? It'll show we're doing our best. That's what matters most." It was as if he had cottoned on already to my idea.

But it was three floors, and though I could more or less remember, I couldn't fit the rooms over and under each other. "Never mind," he said. "It'll do for the time being. Any idea what routine these Safeguard blokes follow?"

"I think they must patrol. I think they have machines they clock in at at certain times."

He nodded. "Where are their headquarters?"

"I've no idea. Won't it be in the telephone book?"

"Yeh . . . I was just wondering."

On the Friday he was late back and said: "I didn't see this man until today. He thinks it's a good start. But he wants more details. I suppose it stands to reason."

"Yes," I said, "it stands to reason, doesn't it?"

Hand on my arm. "Deborah, you've been a real sweetie, doing this. I hope you've not felt too bad about it."

I smiled. "I'm beginning not to know how I feel. You're doing a sort of Pavlov's dog on me, and in the end I shall be a nervous wreck."

"Don't *say* that." He scowled at me, but in worry not anger. "Not even as a crack. If this is doing anything serious to you, for Christ's sake, we'll turn it in."

Serious? What was serious? Seriously, I could no

longer judge; that far the jest was true. "Tell me what they want now."

He took out a creased sheet of typing paper. On it was written:

(1) Name of safe and number. *Very important* to get number right. You have to have safe open to see number which is always on middle bolt of the three that move to lock the safe when you turn the handle.

(2) Position of alarm switches. Where they switch off.

(3) Type of strong-room alarm and how operated.

(4) Any private line between Whittington's and Safeguard's head office in the Strand?

(5) Name of guards now doing duty.

(6) Who do they take over from at night, and who takes over from them in the morning?

Leigh was watching me as I read this.

I said dryly, "Well, there's no harm in asking."

"It's a pretty tall order, I must say."

"Leigh, I've been thinking over the people at our bonfire party. You said this man was there. I can't begin to guess who it is."

"Don't try, love. It's better not."

"You always make it sound so dramatic. Is Jack Foil in this?"

"Why bother to ask? The less you know, the better."

He looked very young. Sometimes I felt so much more than a year older. Perhaps I ought to have thought for us both, to have gone on refusing to do this thing. But although in character I was more mature, maybe better balanced, physically he was the master. I suppose if there's any excuse for me, that's it.

I needed an excuse during the next two weeks at Whittington's. I suppose in seven years I'd been in the strong room thirty or forty times and seen the safe opened every second visit. But I'd gone in casually with someone, or got one of the directors to open the door because I wanted the records of 1963 sales, or something of the sort. I'd done this with a perfectly clear mind and face, never bothering to think about it. But now I needed an excuse, and it took me ten days to think up something that sounded genuine to my own sensitive ears. Then I had to get John Hallows to open the door, which made matters worse, it being him. And then unlock the safe.

He left me for about three minutes which was more than enough . . . 951063 . . . On the middle bolt, as they'd said. Copied now on a corner of my catalogue. When he came in again to lock up I said: "Is this room on some sort of a burglar alarm at night?"

"Yes." He smiled. "Why?"

"I thought I heard one of the Safeguard men talking about it this week—"

"Yes, there's a trembler alarm over there. It's at the back there, between the cupboards. When it's set, if anyone opens the door or tries to break in, opening it alters the air pressure in the room and that sets the trembler off."

"Ingenious."

"Yes, if anyone tried to get in here they'd be in for a few nasty surprises."

"Good," I said, and *so* meant it.

"Answers to questions," I typed before Leigh got home.

(1) Safe. Pemberton. Number 951063.

(2) Alarm switches in director's private room on ground floor, controlling both systems.

(3) Strong-room has a trembler alarm.

(4) Cannot tell if there is any private line.

(5) Names at present Webster and Troon.

(6) They take over from a director and at least one of our own attendants. In the mornings, Mr. Sloane, foreman, and two cleaners arrive at seven, others at seven-thirty.

When I'd finished I pulled it out of Leigh's old machine and read it through.

I was helping—already more than I had ever intended to. But when and how to stop? For a few minutes I had been tempted to give them the wrong numbers of the safe, but to tell them any deliberate lie which later could be checked was asking for trouble of the worst kind. For Leigh as well as for me. So I was now co-operating in a prospective burglary. This was a confused dream, a sleazy nightmare. It was like being ill; you lost your sense of reality. You said is this really happening to me? and you answered yes, but it still had no conviction.

I screwed the paper in a ball, but before I could find the wastepaper basket Leigh came in, so I gave him the paper instead. This is the rationale of nightmare. Take only one step out of reality, and all the rest logically follows.

Chapter 16

Perhaps it is more like driving in an unknown town and taking the wrong spoke at a roundabout. You go on quite happily for a time afterward, not realizing your whole direction has changed and you're heading north instead of south.

The information was passed. No comeback. Leigh hadn't received the money but he seemed to have no doubt he would get it. He was in his cheerful mood and carried me along. Except for two Saturdays when he went with Ted Sandymount to watch Charlton Athletic, he seemed to see less of his other friends, and I began to feel that with luck we might break free of them even yet. Weekends, apart from the two matches, we spent together, Saturdays mainly looking for a shop or some small premises that we might rent.

Sunday mornings sometimes at low tide Leigh would wander off on his own along the river beach. It was more than I could do, what with the big stones, and here and there walls and jetties to climb; but he enjoyed it, came back knee-wet and muddy. I thought then that he would have really liked to live on an island like Gauguin, existing on a few pounds a year, carefree, responsibility free, free to laze and wander and paint . . .

Sarah got engaged to Philip, and Leigh and I twice

went to have drinks in his rooms. Although so different in temperament, Philip and Leigh got on together; I could see an agreeable future in their friendship. Once Sarah suggested calling at Jack Foil's antique shop but I headed her off.

Leigh wrote a legally dictated letter to Lorne asking her to come home, but she didn't answer. The agency reported her as living a celibate life, but Leigh told him to keep a man on the case.

One day I came home and met a good-looking young-ish-middle-aged woman leaving the studio. We just moved to each other as we passed, and when I got in Leigh was looking upset.

"Dad's next door neighbor. She's up here for the day. Says he's been ill."

"Why don't you go and see him?"

"I will sometime. But he's all right again."

"Do you ever write?"

"A couple of times a year, I reckon."

"Let's both go and see him. You never talk about your family."

"No . . . wait till we're married. He's conventional that way."

Shopping days to Christmas shortened with the daylight. Weekly we skated. I was good now, went on my own, didn't fall. Weekly theatre too but little music—except for pop music we couldn't enjoy the same things. Douglas and Erica asked us up. We went but it wasn't really a success, though everybody tried.

I took the opportunity of collecting more of my precious china and porcelain. Since meeting Leigh the pieces had come to mean less and less to me; no longer the almost animate comfort they'd once been; but I still prized them, and it was fun to have them all in the studio, arranging them and rearranging them. I explained each one to Leigh, explained why each one was beautiful to me, gave him an idea of its value. We talked about how we would build up a stock in the shop, what it would be good to specialize in.

Christmas came and went. This time last year I'd have

peered at myself with incredulity. Different person. Looking back, I now saw that little trappings of invalidism had been there—and incipient old-maidism perhaps. These gone. So I could stare both ways. Two or three at Whittington's remarked on a change. They didn't know the half.

On New Year's Eve, which was a Saturday, I took and passed my driving test. This was a surprise and a great thrill. I felt so elated and when Leigh came home for lunch he was just as delighted.

The rest of the day we spent alone. A quiet misty day, with all the river buildings wrapped in cellophane. A hazy sun hung over the river for a few hours and then went out. But no fog when night came; the same cold distant haze, the same brooding quiet. We put on the record player and listened to records until just before midnight, then went on the balcony. At midnight the clocks chimed and bells began to ring in the churches. Then suddenly all the ships in the port of London let off their sirens and fired Very lights into the misty night. It was like another firework display, like a Coronation, a flowering of a great city and then a dying. The quiet air quivered with the wailing, hooting, snoring noise; waves of it came backward and forward across the river, colliding, echoing. Buildings blanched as Verys fell, the cranes flickered against the pink sky. Then as quickly as it began it all stopped. The last of the lights faded, the city sank back into its shadows and the nearer ships fell silent. But away, far away, in Blackwall Reach and Bugsby's Reach and Woolwich Reach and Gallion's Reach, the sirens were still sounding like an echo of the first explosion, dying, dying, dying . . .

In the new year Leigh left the job in Percy Street, took another as a clerk in a drawing office in Margaret Street. A pound a week less, but more scope.

Jack Foil. One day at lunch. "May I share your table? D'you mind? A trifle crowded," he said, overlooking the empty tables. "Just come out of Sotheby's. Fine stuff going this morning but most of it over my head. Or over

my pocket—ha-ha. Whittington's have a dull week, all
that Victorian furniture. Just a snack, waitress. Just a
plane of underdone beef, cut thin, and a salad if it's fresh.
Miss Dainton, you're not eating. D'you prefer to be
alone?"

"Of course not."

"I've an envelope for Leigh, thought it would save the
postage—ha-ha!—the wife and I were saying only the other
day that we don't see enough of you both." Signet rings
flashed on furry-dark fingers. "That lovely party in November. Such an original idea."

I looked at the thick white envelope. "For Leigh?"

"Yes. A business matter. But you know about it. Very
helpful you've been, Miss Dainton." His piece of bread
had holes in it and he covered those rapidly with butter
like someone puttying the cracks. "Very helpful. You've a
very efficient mind, if you don't mind my saying so."

I left him in doubt.

"Your father and mother are very elite sort of people,
too—I hadn't had the pleasure before that evening. We
talked about collecting. They don't believe in it."

Ruminative silence till his food came. When he cut his
meat he held his knife between first finger and thumb,
like a pencil.

He said: "Is there a private line?"

"What?" I looked at him, startled. "D'you mean? . . ."

His eyes wobbled. "Yes. You didn't say."

"I haven't found out. I can't."

"We have to know, you know." He sprinkled vinegar
on his lettuce and then a touch of sugar. "Talk to the
guards."

"I don't know them—except just to nod to. I'm usually
gone before seven."

"Stay on. Exchange a pleasantry or two. A joke. A
pretty girl like you."

I wasn't eating now but I watched him eating.

"There's usually catches, that's the trouble. Little
booby traps, or things of that nature." He wiped the outside corners of his eyes. "Things the intruder doesn't
know about. Only make one mistake. Who's in charge of

169

security, d'you know? In the firm, I mean. Who deals with Safeguards?"

"I don't know." I did know; it was Smith-Williams.

"Find out, will you?" The lettuce crackled and a smear of oil ran down from the corner of his mouth. "It should be easy. Most people talk easily, love telling things when it's in confidence. It's lovely to have a secret and to pass it on. That's the way the world goes round."

I said stiffly: "Does Leigh know you're meeting me?"

His eyes were nothing but glass; he was looking down at his plate, disappointed that the thin beef was gone.

"I'm sure you'll help us, Miss Dainton. It's—part of the agreement, isn't it? I hope it's not asking too much."

It is, it is.

"There's no efficiency in the world," he said. "That's why I admire you. One of the elite ones, you know. You and Leigh, if you can set up in business together."

I said: "Are you the leader in this, Mr. Foil? Leigh says there's someone else but won't say who."

"You must come and see us again." He put his knife and fork together on the plate and smiled at me. "I've some new plants. Interesting. There aren't any leaders, Miss Dainton. It's just among friends, as the saying is . . . Don't forget your envelope!"

Two hundred pounds in ten-pound notes. Sight of them is curiously corrosive. (What you could buy; go into a shop with three or four; not earned; not taxed; free to squander. I'll have *this* and *this* and *this*; things I've always wanted; no, I'll pay cash.)

"You must give them back to him," I said, "so as to pay off part of what you owe him."

"No, he doesn't want it; he'd be insulted. This is a fair payment for what we've done, what *you've* done. I've done nothing."

"But it's essential to get clear of them, don't you *see?*"

"This isn't enough. I owe him five hundred. There's one thing certain: if you're going to kick clear you don't try to until you really can. That's straight common sense, love."

It was.

"This *mustn't* be squandered, Leigh." Lovely to squander, to dress well, to dine at the Savoy, to . . .

"No, that's sense too. It should go in a long stocking, so as we've made a start saving up for the shop."

"It won't get us far, but—"

"Well, there's more to come. Perhaps much more to come . . ."

"Mr. Smith-Williams," I said, "how do these safety precautions work against burglary? I mean to do with the Safeguards."

"Why d'you ask?"

"I was talking to my father last night about the burglary in Hatton Garden. He said he thought Securicor were best."

"They're certainly bigger. We chose Safeguards because they specialize in premises such as ours."

"What would happen if we did get broken into? Would they be responsible?"

"Oh, no, not unless we could prove negligence of some sort. But of course it's a very black mark against them if their precautions, for which a firm pays a pretty high rate, prove to be ineffective."

"There's a lot of inefficiency in the world." For some reason I quoted Jack Foil.

"That's a very cynical remark! I hope you don't find it in this firm."

"Oh, no." Laughing. "We're the exception!"

It isn't easy. You angle for information but the fish doesn't bite. And whose side are you on, fundamentally? "I can't get what they want," I say to Leigh, "they'll have to find out some other way." "Do what you can, love. When's the next big jewel sale?" "The end of February. Does that mean? . . ."

"It doesn't mean a thing. I'm in nobody's confidence. But that sort of date must be of some importance in their young lives . . . Anyway, forget it. I love you."

Easy to forget then. I'd thought once, right at the beginning, that first day, if one could only lift away one's thinking mind, put it on a shelf somewhere for the time being, forget the smart words and the smart answers . . . It was easier now, grew easier every day. Your individuality, nature, tastes changed—not drastically, dramatically, but subtly like a plant moved to new ground and growing in different soil. "What did you mean, Leigh, by saying there might be much more for us in this?" "Did I? Well, obviously three hundred more if we all keep our bargain." "You didn't speak as if you meant it that way."

His ways were changing too. His voice was less aggressive, he used expressions I used, swore less, didn't make so many little slips in grammar. I'd never said anything to him, but he seemed peculiarly apt to take on the color of his company—and most of his company, I suppose, was me.

To Jack Foil's again, and after drinks to the Caprice to supper. His wife in an expensive black taffeta frock, very short and deeply V-ed at the back, with a big frill running down the back and round the hem, so that to sit down she had to move it like a bustle. Seen from a distance with the ashy hair she would have passed for twenty-two. The present fashion for very short skirts didn't suit me. Our conversation tonight would have made Douglas and Erica groan; traffic problems, television, dogs, holidays abroad.

After supper when we went downstairs to the Ladies: "Do call me Doreen, won't you, I feel we're going to be friends. Jack's very fond of Leigh . . . Jack's never had a family—I'm his second wife, you know . . . Oh, I've only been married six years; I think maybe one of these days I'll produce, but it's a bit of a disappointment, especially with Jack being a family man."

"Has he known Leigh long?"

"Oh, it's about three years since he first brought him home . . . He did look sweet. Leigh, I mean. Half scared, half ready to fight. He's changed so much. Does Leigh talk to you much, Miss Dainton? There, but I must call you Deborah, mustn't I? Jack doesn't talk to me much, you know. He's always very sweet, but I sometimes think—oh, but really, I mustn't say it! . . . Well, I sometimes think he likes me most because I'm an ornament. You know. He's a *collector*. He's always bringing home beautiful things. Not that I think I'm beautiful, mind, but I'm an ornament—or he thinks so. Do you and Leigh *talk?*"

"Yes, quite a lot."

"You see, Jack doesn't ever *tell* me things. I never know what his plans are. He loves bringing me presents and dressing me up and all that, and he's always so sweet. You know. And you can *trust* him. Ever since we've been married I've never seen him look at another woman. He's sweet. But there's something brewing now, isn't there?"

"Is there?"

She tucked in a wisp of hair with the end of her tail comb. "Hasn't Leigh told you?"

"We hardly ever discuss Jack. We talk about—oh, music, painting, motorcars . . ."

Our eyes met in the mirror.

She said: "Leigh does paint ever so well, doesn't he. I saw that painting of you that Jack had. Really very good. But you're lovely, I think. Such coloring."

I smiled and turned away from her eyes.

"Are you afraid for Leigh?"

"Afraid for him?"

"Oh, you know. When you're fond of someone you"—with a tissue she wiped a corner of her mouth—"get afraid for them. Or I do. Whenever Jack's late I always think he's been run over or something. . . . D'you think it's funny for me to be satisfied with an old man?"

"I'd—never thought. But is he old?"

"Well, oldish. But I had a young one before. He only had only one idea what women were for, and he didn't know any better. Nor never would. It's nice to have someone like Jack. Dotes on you. Even though he never talks. Not about important things . . ."

When we got upstairs they were waiting, and Leigh was listening rather deferentially to what Jack Foil had to say.

"I'm terribly late tonight," I said to Maurice Mills. "Can I work on a bit? With Mary being away . . ."

"Yes, I'll let the guards know. But don't overdo it. A lot on this new stuff is practically undatable."

He was right. Some things any expert could identify, but in the last hundred and fifty years an enormous amount of china had been turned out anonymously by good factories which could only be assembled in large general categories. I could have left at seven easily. Last Saturday in that cafe in Evelyn Street a girl had come across to Leigh; skirt too tight; hair like a meringue. "Hi, Leigh, where you been hiding?" A couple of minutes of uncomfortable talk; he didn't introduce me; she moved off. I didn't ask. Two drinks later he said: "That girl Sue Jones, trying to butt in, trying to make out she knew me well." "Perhaps you've forgotten her." "No, it was just done to rile me." "Well, it did, didn't it?" "Yes, it sure did." "She certainly looked *me* up and down. Particularly down." "That's clottish. I thought you'd grown out of that feeling."

A tap at the door. "Excuse me, miss, I wondered, as you was still here, whether you'd like a cup of tea?"

"I'd love one, thank you. Shall I come for it?"

"No, I've got it here just outside."

Ginger-haired man of fifty. Bad skin, with shaving rash. Square jaw. Square nails not scrubbed. Blue uniform, just like a policeman, heavy truncheon in belt. *Safeguard* shoulder flash.

"Sorry if I'm in your way," I said. "I'm about ready to go."

"No, it doesn't make no difference to us, like. Stay as long as you want. We don't often have comp'ny so late as this."

"What time is it? Good heavens, nearly ten! I'll go in a moment now."

Sipping tea. Slightly worse-tasting if anything than the usual office tea. He sipped too.

"Has your partner got one?"

"Oh, yes, he's upstairs; I took him his first."

"I suppose one of you always has to stay by the telephone?"

"Well, that's the general plan. Not that it matters

s'much as all that. It is pretty safe here, y'know, against surprise."

"D'you have a private line to your own headquarters, or something like that?"

"Yes. We ring up every half hour. Give a code word to identify ourselves, see. Tonight's is . . . Well, last night's was *Lowestoft*. If they don't get it—if they don't get it every quarter and three quarter hour they know there's trouble and come round in force."

"That's terribly ingenious . . . But supposing you're investigating some noise and happen to be a bit late?"

"Oh, well, they're not so eager to turn out in the night as all that! They give us five minutes' grace."

Tea finished. Pretending a little left. Stirring the dregs. He was looking at the china.

"Lovely stuff you get in here. I said to the wife this week, I said, it's a good job you can't see all I see of a night or you'd be discontented for the rest of your life! It's true as true."

He looked like a retired Army sergeant. A fair pension, but this extra would make all the difference. Tough and not easily frightened. Jack Foil and his friends had better try some easier meat.

Suddenly he said: "Oh, I'd best be going. It's quarter past, and I have to clock in at ten-twenty on the first floor."

"Clock in?"

"We've three clocks in the place, you know, miss. We do 'em each by the hour, one every twenty minutes. If we let 'em over-run they set off the alarms."

"Isn't that clever!"

"Well, it's a good system. Let us know, will you, when you're thinking of going. We wouldn't want you to try and unbolt the doors by mistake!"

"I'll go now. If you'll—er—clock in and come down again, I'll get my coat."

I said: "They'll never break in, not in this world. When you were saying how careless Whittington's were, I thought, I expect they're not really careless at all!"

"You sound pleased."

"I am. Oh, I am. Relieved anyway."

"Why?"

"Doesn't it stand to common sense? Now your friends can try somewhere else, where I *can't* help them!"

"They may not want to."

"What choice have they?"

"I don't know. . . ."

"It seems to me, Leigh, that this is the perfect answer. No one can say I haven't done my part."

"They certainly can't." He was silent a minute. "There may be a way round all this, see. I don't know. We'll have to consider it."

"*We*'ll have to? It's their plan, not yours!"

"Oh, I know. But you get involved."

I looked at him. "How involved?"

"Well, as I've said before, they're friends. Jack is, and Ted. And the others in a way."

"So what does this come to?"

"Well, after a time, talking of it, you get drawn in. It's like a game—a sort of game."

"Nasty game if it goes wrong."

He looked back at me moodily. "I wasn't going to tell you this, but, as the whole thing may be off now, I'll tell you. They offered me a part of it."

No drama. Careful, no drama, now. "D'you mean actually in the breaking in?"

"Yes . . ."

"And what did you say?"

"I said yes."

". . . I see."

"Maybe you don't quite . . ." He leaned forward and took my hands. I tried to draw them away, but no good. He kissed them, knuckles up, then finger tips. "*You* always reason things out, Deborah. What about *me* for a change? What about me doing it? When they suggested it, when they first said how about it, I thought, this is crazy, but I didn't ask you, because I thought, God, a man's got to make his own decisions sometimes. And after a time, turning it over, it seemed to me—it seemed to me—here

176

have I been spouting to you, to myself, *I'd* do this, *I'd* do that if I had the chance. Well, here was the chance. You can't go on talking about raising the Jolly Roger for *ever*, and doing nothing when your number comes up. You bluff. And fate calls your bluff. And if you don't back it with your guts, then you won't listen to yourself next time you spout. You'll *know* you're an all-time sham!"

I got my hands back, but not before they'd responded to him, to what he said and did, like self-governing colonies, without my full consent.

"Leigh, we can argue about this all night—"

"I know—"

"—You're *wrong*. I don't think I can prove it but I just know this is the *wrong* way to do *anything*. Not morally wrong—that may be but I'm not talking of that—but wrong as a way to getting on. Just that. It doesn't work. It may seem to for a time, but sooner or later . . . It's like gambling and drug taking . . . In the end you can't win. Now that I know this I'm more than ever relieved!"

"Maybe . . ."

"I'm relieved because they'll *have* to call it off."

Jack Foil said: "You'll get the three hundred tomorrow, Miss Dainton. Or Leigh will if you want him to have it. You can see the picture now, can't you? I wonder what Whittington's pay for the service."

Ted Sandymount said: "You got a telephone check every quarter and three quarter hour, and a clock check at the hour, at twenty past the hour, and at twenty to the hour. That means there's never more'n a few minutes without a check. An' they're all the worst sort of checks —things that raise the alarm if they're *not* done."

"So do we give it up?" Leigh asked, hands in pockets, leaning against the wall between the windows. "Do we drop it?"

This in *our* studio; Jack and Ted arrive; just casually calling; make coffee; Leigh's friends; gossip about the district; I've been waiting but perhaps it's just what it seems; drop in and talk. Then it begins.

177

"Well, we'll just have to think about it for a day or two, won't we? Never despair, that's my motto."

"I been getting around a bit—" Ted began.

"When things are worked to a pattern," Jack Foil went on, "it gives people confidence. They think they've got it all fixed. Nobody can beat it, so they relax. But you can beat nearly everything with time and patience."

"You mean we don't drop it?"

He wiped the outside corners of his eyes. "They say I've got cataract. But it's early stages—doesn't really interfere. It must be fine to have lovely young eyes like you, Miss Dainton."

Ted was fumbling in the pocket of his big check velvet-cuffed jacket. "I got a list here of the Safeguard staff. I got it last week from Roland. A hundred and forty-two of 'em. I've been through 'em name by name, with all the records Roland's got. You don't recruit all that lot without a few slip-ups. Four of 'em have got prison records!"

"It doesn't follow," said Jack Foil. "You ought to know that. And besides . . . set a thief to—er—well, you know how it goes."

"There's two of 'em I'd bank on for certain. A man called 'Baker' Evans and another, Fullerton. One's got a record, the other hasn't. But you could get at 'em both— not for what they've served time for but what they haven't. Anyway, money's all they care about. Money'll buy 'em. I promise you."

"It's not much good, is it," said Leigh, "if they're like that and busy guarding a fur store in Hammersmith, or something."

"They're both on the right rota." Ted grimaced as he turned over the sheets. "Fullerton we don't know when, but it's 'Baker' Evans's turn to take over duty at Whittington's some time next month. It's a toss-up, like, but it might fit. If it just happened to be the right week. Or he might be able to switch it to fit."

Sip at the last of my coffee but it is cold. Hands and feet are cold. Still don't believe in this yet, but in the middle of the night I shall. Stop it? Accessory before the fact. I can go to prison too. But they're only *talking*. Still only

178

talking. No real plan yet. There's no leader in these three men. Who's the fourth? It won't happen. Pick up the coffee cups while they talk. It won't happen. That woman in the hospital paralyzed from the neck down. She said: "Well, there's always hope; and I find pleasure in little things. I never look further than tomorrow."

Tomorrow is Saturday, and it won't happen.

The weekend an oasis in the winter, two rare January days, sunny, mild, windless. We drove down to the coast —I drove most of the way—and saw people sitting in deck chairs on promenades. Also an oasis in our private life. We forgot the thing. We parked on Beachy Head and took the hood down and ate sandwiches of chicken fillets and ham and shared a big bottle of beer, and there was a lot of friendly talk and laughter.

Although we'd been together months now, our talk didn't often deal with our past lives. He seemed afraid of mine, perhaps because he thought recalling it separated me from him again, broke the "spell." When I asked him about his he usually shrugged it off with a word or two, like someone getting rid of an uncomfortable coat. One heard nothing of his brothers; vaguely I knew one was on the railways, the other in a shop, nothing more.

After we'd finished eating we got out and walked to the edge, looked over the white chalky cliff to a sea pale as porcelain. A seagull drifted here and there; no horizon existed; the sun shone soundlessly; voices echoed in a void.

He said: "Let's not go back tonight."

"What d'you mean?"

"Let's stay at some hotel. Let's see if they'll take us without luggage. We'll pretend you're an heiress and I've run off with you. A ward in chancery, that's what they call it."

I laughed. "We've nothing. No night things. Not a tooth brush."

"We can buy tooth brushes, if you're that fussy. Let's stay at some little pub in a village. With blackened oak

179

beams and open fires with iron kettles and a big double bed that you have to climb into."

"They always charge extra for double beds."

"Well, I'll pay. It'll be worth it."

I had a queer feeling in the back of my knees. "Let's be practical . . ."

"What for? It's Sunday tomorrow. I want to wake up in a village where the church bells are ringing. Maybe I'll even go to church. Come with me?"

"If you want, yes."

"Even after the double bed?"

"You're leading me astray."

"Fabulous thought. How astray can we get?"

I took his hand. "Let's enjoy the sun."

Surprisingly, we found what he wanted, a small village hotel six or seven miles inland from Seaford. One bedroom free and that a sort of attic, with tiny windows and beams dangerously low, and a floor that creaked and sloped, and a cistern that gurgled at intervals through the night. But it had the double bed. Leigh said we were having trouble with our car and paid for the room in advance, and no questions were asked. He insisted on signing the register as Mr. and Mrs. James Smith.

And we slept naked, and in the night I woke up to find his head heavy on my breast, and in the morning we sipped tea and listened to the sparrows chirping in the sun.

He said lazily: "This room reminds me of the one I had when I was a kid. It was the top room of a house overlooking Clapham Common. We just had the top floor."

"I thought you lived in Swindon."

"So we did—later. But we were a couple of years in London when I was a kid. Good job we moved."

"Why?"

"I got in with a crowd. That's when the good old J.D. began."

"What's that?"

"Juvenile Delinquency. Not that it amounted to much. I've told you, I'm a stinking coward when it comes to the

180

law. A couple of coppers round at the house, and a probation officer puts the fear of God into you. No more breaking windows or pinching sweets in supermarkets. So I stayed straight, s'welp me, until I met you."

"I don't think that's fair."

"No, it isn't. Forget I spoke."

Later we actually did go to church, Leigh in the rather hi-fi clothes he still sometimes wore in spite of my influence. I was far more at sea in the service than he was. He found the place in the Prayer Book and all that. Douglas and Erica, being unbelievers, had done nothing to educate their children in what they considered an obsolete superstitition.

Leigh knew the hymns, too, and sang away in a lusty voice that wasn't very musical but kept in tune. Afterward we all filed out into the respectable sunlight among the yew trees and the gray-faced gravestones. "Cremation's so much more hygienic," I said. "Yes," he said, "but it's too sudden. I'd rather rot."

Back to the hotel and off. We found a shop open and bought some food and picnicked at Birling Gap. The sun was blazing still but the air was colder, the brief spring nearly spent.

I said: "Let's not go back at all."

He stared at me and laughed. "Not at all?"

"Let's go away somewhere, somewhere else to live."

"Now who's being unpractical?"

"It can happen. Douglas told me of a doctor in London who suddenly resigned, changed his name, left his things to be sold up, and emigrated with his wife to France."

"But he had money, I'll bet."

"Oh, he had some. But they did work in France."

"You want us to go to France? Or Spain? Just like this? With an old motorcar and two tooth brushes?"

I sighed. "When is Jack paying you the three hundred pounds?"

"Tomorrow."

"I'd rather go without that than stay."

"Just decamp, eh? With the booty. And leave the debts. Where's your passport?"

"At home."

"So's mine."

We drove home reluctantly, slowly, with the returning traffic. A thin haze of early fog hung over London. When we got back to our studio you couldn't see the other bank of the river. After only a day of absence the studio smelled dank. I drew the curtains, shivering slightly. He noticed it and asked me if I'd caught a chill. I shook my head, because it wasn't that sort of chill.

The bright day is done and we are for the dark.

Chapter 17

The jewelry sale on February 23, which was a Thursday, would be the most important one of the year so far as our firm was concerned. The Plouth diamonds were to be sold, and the Maharajah of Gwalpur had sent a collection of emeralds of exceptional quality. Around these "big" offerings had been built a conglomerate of ninety-six lots ranging from pearl studs that might fetch £30 to diamond bracelets and rings that could go for two or three thousand apiece. The sale would start on the morning of the twenty-third at 10 A.M., and John Hallows would conduct it. During the preceding weeks much of the jewelry would come to accumulate in our safe, but such things as the Gwalpur emeralds would not arrive until three days before, when they would be put on view. The catalogues were sent out on February 1.

All this sounds exceptional, but of course it was not. We had four jewelry sales a year, and any number of others in which objects of great value in themselves or of great value to collectors were deposited with us and remained in our cellars or strong room until sold. The normal precautions, as even Jack Foil admitted, were adequate for all occasions.

The first week in February passed with no word spoken. Leigh said nothing; I said nothing; I caught no glimpse of the others. Perhaps it was all abandoned. Perhaps it was all arranged.

I had a card from Sarah inviting us to dinner on the twelfth, the Sunday evening, at her flat. The evening before, we went out as usual for a drink, and in the smoky noisy atmosphere of the pub I could stand it no longer and asked Leigh for news. Apart from variations of expression he really had three faces; the young, open, boyish one, which I saw most often in love, and loved best; the petulant, explosive, tormented one, without patience and without malice, which was rooted in his painting, his work, his drive to create; and the narrow, cautious one, eye-on-the-door, whisper-behind-your-hand, money envious, the one most rarely seen—at least by me.

This settled on him now as he said: "Must you know?"

"If you're in it—yes."

"We're going to have a shot on the twenty-second."

"How?"

" 'Baker' Evans has come in with us."

"D'you mean he's on at that time?"

"Yes, he comes on on the Friday before. It's a lucky break."

I waited for him to continue, but he didn't. The band was playing: *I'm Shy, Mary Ellen, I'm Shy!*

"Well?"

"Well, that's it."

"How are you going to do it?"

"You'd best not know."

"I think I've a right to."

"Yeh . . . I know you have. But why ask?"

"I want to know."

"Well . . . we go in at 2:30 A.M. on the Thursday morning. Evans switches off the two alarm circuits in the director's office and opens the back door for us—the one in Bruton Yard. We then overpower him, give him a cosh on the head and tie him up. First thing the other man knows—that'll be a bloke called McCarthy—we're in his room and it's four to one. We tie him up, break the strong room and blow the safe. We reckon about two hours at the outside."

"What about the telephoning?"

"Evans will know the code word. The man at the other end won't know it's one of us speaking."

"And the clock alarms?"

"They're all controlled by the two switches."

It was just a two-piece band in here: piano and drums, playing popular numbers of older days. Sometimes customers joined in the singing. It was all good-tempered, friendly, warm.

"How can you get into the strong room?"

"It shouldn't be difficult. Ted Sandymount got down there the other day pretending to lose his way. It's a glorified cellar."

"And the safe?"

"It's about fourteen years old; we know that by the number you gave us; and there are ways of getting in."

"Did you say there were four of you?"

"Yes, the other's the expert on safes."

"Is he the leader, the organizer you spoke about?"

"Not really."

"Did he come to our house in November?"

Leigh shifted uneasily.

"Leave it, Deb. D'you want another drink?"

"No, thanks. Let's go home."

When we got to Sarah's the next night, Philip of course was there, and Virginia Fisher and a young man she had recently acquired, a friend of Philip's who was reading law. I admired two new pieces of Georgian silver Sarah had bought. For dinner we had terrine, and a pheasant with onion stuffing, and a Stilton. (I missed the better cheeses; Leigh cared only for Cheddar.)

Other things I had missed, I found tonight. Philip had the voice for a barrister; deepish, clear, educated but not affected. The others all spoke well. Like coming back to my own people. For the first time I felt a sense of homesickness. Even the food was different from the snack meals we so often made do with. The wine was decanted, tasted extra good.

Of course I should have known that this leisurely gracious meal was really a far greater exception in the life of an overworked and underpaid young doctor like Sarah than it was in my own, but this didn't register. My feelings all stemmed from one thing: I didn't want to go through the next few weeks.

After dinner the talk ran near what was in my mind. It was Leigh's doing; but probably he couldn't forget it either. The other man, called Bingham, said something about the criminal law he was reading, and Leigh took him up on it, in the way he had once talked to me, said he thought the whole system was pie-eyed, because the punishments were wrong. It was time something was done to put things right in the book. Was anything being done?

Bingham laughed: "I'm not a law reformer; I'm just a law-learner. I can tell you more about the Romans than the Angles just now."

Philip said slowly: "Oh, there's always room for improvement. But it's not as easy as you think, Leigh."

"Why not?"

"Well, this distinction you draw between the crime that's anti-human and the crime that's anti-property. A lot of people do, but—"

"Well, isn't it right to do that?"

"No. Not altogether."

"Why not?" I asked.

"Well, to begin on the simplest level, if a man goes in for crime and decides all his activities shall be against property, how does he keep on the right side of the line he's drawn? He may never intend to hurt a fly, but supposing he's doing a job and is on the point of success, and then somebody unexpectedly gets in his way—does he meekly say, 'What a pity, I've failed,' and drop his loot and run? Or does he try to put the inconvenient person out of the way? This was the problem of the people who did the great train robbery. One man had the guts to stand up against them, and he was dangerously injured and his health impaired for life. Yet the newspapers led the way in admiring those criminals for their cleverness, not condemning them for their brutality."

"The judge did plenty of that," Virginia said. "Thirty

years was a bit thick, I must say. That's where I do feel the law goes wrong."

Leigh smiled at me. I didn't smile back.

Philip said: "People said at the time that the sentences were a psychological mistake, but I doubt it—"

"You think they were just?"

"They're still open to revision; you have to remember that. But people in the know thought the judge was right."

"Why?" said Leigh. "This is just what I'm talking about. *Why?*"

"Because crime at this moment in our history has to be *seen not to pay.* We're on a knife-edge in this country at the moment. You may think I'm talking like this because of my father's what he is; but it isn't just that."

Leigh put a lump of half-melted sugar in his mouth with his coffee spoon. "You have to admit, though, the really clever men were not all that bad. They're too *smart* to be; it doesn't pay them—"

Philip said: "Until about fifteen years ago there wasn't any organized crime in this country. Not really organized, planned, financed, run as a business. So it was easy to deal with. The police dealt with it. A few criminals got away but most got caught. It wasn't a serious problem, a problem that could get out of hand. But now it can. And it's on the verge of doing just that."

"How do you mean?"

"The sex criminal, the man who knocks an old woman down for her handbag—all that—they're just individuals—maybe worse *as* individuals but not a danger to the community as a whole. But in the last five years in this country we've come up against the real thing—which is the menace of big business. When big money comes in—finance—where crime is on the verge of becoming respectable, as it has done in the United States, then look out. This is the terrifying danger. How was that great train robbery financed? Perhaps from the London Airport robbery of the year before. In any event, there was whacks of money behind it. And where there's money there's danger. We've always reckoned that about 90 per-

187

cent of all people in this country are honest. That's to say, if someone offered them a bribe of £10—or perhaps even £100—they'd refuse to listen. But what if the bribe were increased to £1000 or even £10,000? How many people are honest then? And even if they want to be honest, there's all the other pressures that can be applied. Once crime becomes big business, run by apparently respectable people for respectable people, there's no end. You see, you see . . ." Philip leaned forward. "Jock Bingham here, is going to be a solicitor. He'll do well for himself, I'm sure, as most of them do. But if there's enough money, enough lawyers will be corrupted to defend shady clients on knowingly false evidence. If that becomes the case, then it becomes really much easier to teach the shady clients how *not* to get caught, than bothering to have to fake up the evidence to defend them. Then some of the police can be bought. Who knows that judges—a few judges—can't be bought, if the price is big enough? This is the beginning of the corruption all civil life. It's been proved so in the United States—thanks chiefly to the mistake of prohibition. Once the corruption is there it's the devil's own job to uproot. That's why the handbag snatcher is not so important, and that's why our laws are not so wrongly slanted as you think, Leigh."

There was silence for a bit. Leigh had refused a liqueur —he was never a big drinker.

He said: "Isn't this pitching it a bit high? I've met one or two people who have been against the law all their lives. And to talk to they're really not much different from you or me. They're professionals—most of 'em are known to the police and most of 'em don't mind—it's an occupational risk. They keep to their rules—as I've said before—and the police keep to *their* rules. It's like a game—a grim game maybe—but both sides play it. I still reckon these people are decent enough in their own wrong-headed way. They oughtn't even to go in the same dock as a child murderer!"

Virginia murmured a word of agreement. Philip shook his head and smiled and sighed.

"Individually you're right; socially you're wrong, for the reasons I've said. In the eighteenth century wars were fairly localized affairs fought out by professional armies. An enemy soldier then was a tolerable figure. But as soon as wars became total and involved all ages of non-combatants they became intolerable. That's what the criminal has become today. Just as in the international world we have to overcome war or we die, so in the civilian world we have to overcome crime or our civilization dies!"

"I think you're a perfectionist, darling," said Sarah, patting Philip's hand. "But I agree with you entirely, in spite of Leigh. I don't know what Father would say in this argument, because he hates all police forces!"

Philip said: "That's because he's had the privilege of growing up under their protection."

Talk broke up and no more was said of it. Except for all the dragging anxiety it was a pleasant evening. Strange, I thought, not for the first time, how much warmer Sarah made her home and her entertainment than the home we came from.

On the Thursday, when we were eating after we had been skating, Leigh said: "There's a shop I've found in Lambeth. I'd like you to see it."

"We haven't much hope, have we?"

"It's a tobacconist's at present, but the man has died and his widow's selling. It's in a frightful mess, but there's a lot of *room* behind. We could turn it into a showroom and live over. The licence for tobacco would be a help; it could keep things going while we've developing the other side."

"What do they want for it?"

"Seven thousand—chiefly for the good will, which is pretty nearly non-existent. But it's obviously worth that as site value. It's leasehold, of course."

"What's the rental?"

"Five hundred a year, and rates about one-fifty."

"We couldn't hope to get it! We couldn't pay a year's rent, let alone buy the good will."

"We might be able to in a couple of weeks."

Silence fell. I said: "Just what do you hope to make out of this thing?"

"The stuff must be worth £150,000 at a minimum. If we get a third of its value and split it four ways, that means £12,000. It would set us up."

"Until the next time."

"Oh!" He stopped explosively and peered through the window at the experts waltzing. "D'you think I'm looking forward to this caper next Wednesday? D'you really? Don't you know I'm absolutely petrified with panic? Of course I'm tough in some ways, you know that. But all my life I've been scared stiff of the law. In spite of all my talk. I've told you—this is a bit of a self-test. I won't allow myself to *be* that much of a windbag, to talk about wanting to be a pirate and then ratting at the one big opportunity. I'm going to prove that I've got the guts to do this. But once I've proved it, there's going to be no repeat performance, I can tell you! Let me get away with a few thousand, enough to set up in business with you and no questions asked, and you've got a law-abiding citizen on your hands! I'll be afraid to cheat at a parking meter ever after in case I'm pushing my luck!"

We went to see the shop on Saturday afternoon. It was on a corner of a district where a lot of old buildings had been pulled down and big offices built, and would probably never have the "dropping in" tobacco trade it had once had. But it was not far from the West End across Westminister Bridge. I thought it would cost two or three thousand to renovate it and make alterations, but Leigh said he was good with his hands and could do half of it himself. Once the deal was done he'd leave his job and work full time here. I could continue at Whittington's for a few months until he was ready for me.

I did not know if I could bring myself to continue at Whittington's at all if Wednesday went as planned. The nearer it came the more impossible it became to go there each day.

But I couldn't sleep on Saturday night for thinking of the shop. Even if only five thousand came to us we could borrow enough to make do. Leigh had wanted to put down a deposit on Saturday afternoon but I'd said wait. The widow, who seemed to take a fancy to us, said she'd keep the offer open for a week.

Even perhaps with three thousand, I thought, perhaps one could borrow enough. So one is corrupted. So Philip Bartholomew was probably right.

Sunday passed uneasily. Leigh spent the day sketching. I'd noticed sometimes before that tension sent him to his sketch book. He'd chain-smoked then. He could *really* sketch well. Seeing his pencil moving with such certainty on the paper, creating mass with a few disparate lines, one *wondered* why he should be considered to have no talent, one no longer wondered that he had as a boy been full of ambition. Remembering the Picasso film, how the master created enormous, powerful, significant designs with a piece of chalk, one could only see the resemblances not the differences. There was of course a gap, the gap created by genius; but how could it be so wide that one inspired scrawl commanded the admiration of the world, while the other was looked on as worthless?

Could it be that Leigh had a future as an artist in pen and wash, in crayon, in black and white?

In the evening I thought I'd go and see Douglas and Erica. They were both in, and unchanged. It was as if nothing had happened in their lives while so much was happening in mine. Perhaps it's a commonplace of youth visiting middle-age, to find this. The time of experiment, of stress, of adventure, to them was over. They were married, occupied, professional, on an even keel, from which they might not be disturbed until sickness or death. I deeply envied them their serenity, their lack of stress. Yet, of course, given the chance, one would not conceivably have changed.

Or only for a week. Let this week go by. Please God, if there is a God; please Freud, if Douglas is right, let this week go by.

I told them about the possibility that we might take a shop. They were cool, not enthusiastic, doubtful of its success. Their attitude would have been amusing if it hadn't been unamusing. In spite of their liberalism they were exactly like the rich snob parents of old, disapproving of a daughter marrying a working man. The only difference was that it was not a lack of class or money to which they objected in Leigh, it was what they considered his lack of originality and talent.

Strange smells that I'd once accepted as normal: ether, Mincream, Soochong tea. "What," I said, "would you say if I wanted to borrow money? For this shop, I mean."

"For the shop?" Douglas stroked his head. "As you know, Deborah, it's never been a habit of ours to *accumulate*. In principle we're rather against it. Not that there has been much incentive with three girls to educate." He laughed, giving his amusement plenty of air. "How did you *hope* to finance it?"

"Leigh has a legacy. But it's very small. I thought . . . I wondered . . ."

"Banks. They can help sometimes . . ."

I said: "But surely . . . A matter of a few thousands. We're educated people, established, never seriously in debt. Surely." I suddenly found it necessary to press this point, as if the point, finally secured, would ward off the dangers of Wednesday, as if, going home tonight, I could cry: all is well, Leigh, I have the money, don't take any part in this raid; see, I can save us both!

But Douglas and Erica, completely unaware of the danger in which Leigh stood, were unhelpful past endurance. They had no money of their own to lend; our aunts and uncles were "untouchables" in the true English sense. But if Leigh could find the money, why bother to look elsewhere?

Yes, Leigh maybe "could find" the money.

I traveled home, exhausted, exasperated, railing against parents who couldn't understand because no one could understand who hadn't been told in precise terms what was at stake.

Leigh was asleep when I got in, but he woke to greet me. I had no comfort for him, no glad news that he need

192

not take part. He would have taken no notice anyway. We were both too committed now to draw back.

Monday dragged. A day of petty irritations, of staff shortages because of flu, of clients disputing valuations, of accidents in the showrooms—a picture damaged and a vase chipped—of Peter Greeley in one of his rare unreasonable moods, of a complete page left out of a catalogue by the printers, and the catalogues *sent out* before anyone noticed, of fog outside and drafts in. When I left it took me nearly an hour to get home, and Leigh hadn't returned.

The big room was like a dank well. The nearness of the river meant that whenever there was fog we got the worst of it. I switched on all the heating there was and crouched shivering over the larger fire in my thick overcoat, warming my hands and listening to an exchange of distant fog signals. After about twenty minutes I thawed out sufficiently to move around and to begin to prepare supper. There seemed no reason why Leigh should be any later getting home from Margaret Street. I'd bought two lamb cutlets and I put these under the grill. He hadn't come by the time they were ready, so I didn't put the bacon and tomatoes on, as I'd intended. I washed the lettuce and made the dressing and settled to wait.

Two letters for him, one in a woman's writing. Not Lorne's, for Lorne's was backhand; I'd seen it in the kitchen on a grocery list. The other typewritten, from the solicitor. Another bill from the detective agency? I drew back the curtain, peered out. The fog was unrelenting, like an attack of melancholia. A few lights made aureoles in the yellow dark. I thought of Doreen Foil's remark in the Caprice: "Whenever Jack's late I always think he's been run over or something." And Leigh?

Back to look at the cutlets. They were all right but they weren't improving. Have mine? But I wasn't hungry. The fog had got into my throat. Fear death, to feel the fog in my throat, the mist in my face. . . . Who'd written that? Browning, I thought. A declaration of pious nineteenth-century optimism. Well, anything wrong with that?

The optimism might have been proved true or untrue, it didn't render the expression less valid. I was ever a fighter so one fight more, the best and the last . . . Well worn now, worn smooth with repetition, almost meaningless like the prayers in the Prayer Book; corney. What in its place? Not even a belief in human nature. Too much of the world was sick, poisoning itself with its own spleen. Time for a revival, a return to former values? But what values? Thou shalt not? . . . How could you turn back? It was against nature. So forward, into the darkness and the fog.

At nine I took the spoiled cutlets and picked at one sparingly. At nine-thirty footsteps.

Leigh, in his old leather coat, face sort of darkened with the fog; Ted Sandymount; Jack Foil; a stranger, middle-aged, gaunt. When I saw them I knew there was something wrong. Half-smiling, half-grim, they came in, found chairs, apologetic, polite; Leigh said, I hope you didn't wait, and what'll everybody drink, and sit down, Deborah, you're in this now—you're in this.

John Irons, they said his name was; a broad face, the color of fresh putty, black eyes set so deep you had to quarry to see their expression, a mouth that looked as if it had never spoken ordinarily but only dropped words out of the corner when no one was looking. But polite, good-mannered, quiet. And gaunt. Watchful. This was our friend, said Jack Foil. He made number four, so to speak. He was a top man at his job. The top man looked at me as if I were a Chubb safe, and then looked across the room and said nothing. We sat and talked. Three of them had whisky. Leigh and I made coffee. He seemed not to want to say anything in the privacy of the kitchen.

Smoke hung in a haze over the men as they talked and drank. The fog had come in here, only it was blue-colored instead of ochreous. Jack Foil cleared his throat.

They all stopped talking.

He said: "You've helped us in this, Miss Dainton— Deborah—you've helped us a lot, so it's only right and fair you should know what's happened. In fact, we've come specially to tell you."

I stared at him. I pulled my skirt down over my thin leg.

"There's been a real upset. One of those things you don't make plans for. You remember"—his eyes wobbled at me—"me saying to you there's a lot of inefficiency in the world. But you can be as efficient as you like and one unlucky mishap and all your plans are upset. This has happened now. No fault of anybody's. There it is."

I stared at him and then at Leigh. No one spoke.

"What is it?"

" 'Baker' Evans was due to take over at Whittington's this week from a man called Gaskell. They change weekly, as you know, one changing Friday, one Tuesday, so that it's not long the same two are on together. 'Baker' Evans was due to come on again at Whittington's last Friday. A return visit. Perfect. Just covered the time perfect. But there's been flu about; a lot of flu; and his partner went down with it, so they told him to stay on the weekend at Knight's the jewelers instead, where he was already. Fine. It still worked. Coming on at Whittington's tomorrow night. Running it a bit close, but he'd be there all right for Wednesday. Fine." Jack Foil twisted the signet ring among the fur on his left hand. "But now he's been put off again. His mate's down with pneumonia and five others are off. So they're having a stand-still, bringing on reliefs for a few unimportant jobs, leaving others where they are. So Evans stays at Knight's and Gaskell stays on at Whittington's with a fellow called McCarthy."

The foghorn droned again in the river. Dead silence in the studio. Leigh's coffee cup rattled as he put it down.

"So it's off," I said.

Jack Foil shrugged.

"Or it's postponed," I said. "Perhaps next month."

"The same sale won't be on then, will it?"

"There'll be others."

"What others?"

Silence. There was a constricting band round my lungs. After the early cold the studio was now overheated.

"Would you do it?" asked Jack Foil.

Chapter 18

"Look," said Jack Foil, "don't upset yourself, Miss Dainton. Calm down and have a little drink of this. Leigh, pour her out a finger or so. Just a dash of soda . . . *That's* right. Of *course*, you refuse. Anyone would at first thought. The way you were brought up—the elite sort of way—I see exactly how you feel. It's brought on you suddenly, but you see it was brought on us suddenly and we felt rather desperate in a way and thought, well, Deborah's done so *much*, been so *much* help. Maybe . . ."

"Well, I'm sorry."

"So are we all. But we won't press you; we'll leave you to think it over."

"Don't do that—"

"But before I go, just let me say what would happen. Just let me say, so that you can judge better. Just let me say . . . Wednesday evening, people leaving, you get ready to leave, hat and coat, gloves, scarf, all on. People leaving. Right! You leave, they think. But instead you slip into one of those cupboards. *You* know. They're all over the building. It's *made* for hide and seek. Lovely big cupboards. A bit dusty, maybe, some full, some half full, some empty: I've seen them. You sit down. You've a watch. It'll be a long wait. But not too hard really. No risk really. You wait. And at two-twenty, you come out, just when the guard's gone by; then you slip up to the boss's office on the ground floor, avoiding the telephone room where the other guard is, just slip in to the boss's office and switch off the two alarm switches. Right?" He wiped the corners of his eyes. "Then what? Then you just walk down the corridor to the back door, knowing the patrolling guard's upstairs, and let yourself out. And you don't lock the door after you. Then you go home. That's all. Don't even need to see us. Never see us. No connection. Off you go home. Finished. Done with. It isn't too hard, is it? I'll leave you to think about it."

"Please don't."

Mr. Irons spoke. "How do we get the code word? I couldn't promise to do the job in less than a couple of hours, minimum."

"Oh, that could be seen to," Jack Foil said. "Ted can tap the wire. He wasn't in the P.O. for two years for nothing. He can tap it about midnight. No difficulty there. If Miss Dainton could do her part."

"Look, Jack—" Leigh said.

"Oh, I know, I know. We'll say nothing more now. But I do ask her to think about it. I ask you both to think about it. She's done so much—helped so much—more than this, I believe. It's due to her we could plan at all. This . . . I know it's a bit over-facing at first sight, at first thought. But it means three moves, that's all. She pretends to leave and doesn't, sits in a cupboard. Move one. Move two, she goes up the stairs and switches off the alarms. Move three, she leaves by the back door and leaves it unlocked."

"Oh, it's asking a lot," said Ted, chewing his cigarette and twitching. "It's nerve. You got to have nerve."

"Miss Dainton's got nerve. Don't tell me different. She's one of those people you can see."

"Oh, stop it, Jack," said Leigh.

"Look, Leigh. I'm putting my cards on the table. I'm not," said Jack Foil, smiling at me, "I'm not bullying any-body. If this thing falls through because Miss Dainton won't help that's just very, very unfortunate. We're all a lot poorer, and *disappointed, very* disappointed because

197

we've missed all we planned to do. But don't tell me Miss Dainton wouldn't have the nerve if she so felt like it. That's not flattery or bribery or anything else. I'd put a lot of money on her if she felt like it. I try," he said, "to be efficient, so I think I know efficiency in other folk. Well, she may be a slip of a girl, and a trifle handicapped at that; but I'd rather choose her than any of you men here if I was in a tight corner!"

Leigh said: "You shouldn't have come here, any of you! You shouldn't have asked her!"

"Oh, shut up," said Jack. "She doesn't need your protection. Or advice. It's up to her. I've got confidence in her judgment. Come along, boys, we've said all we can."

The bedside lamp that we'd bought made three concentric light rings on the ceiling, like a target. Into the target area an insect was crawling—a small beetle. We were troubled with beetles here; they came in from the river or bred in the damp timbers of the balcony. Some I hated, but this was small and harmless. It moved very slowly, stopping now and then as if without purpose. Each ring was brighter than the last, and you could see it hesitating before moving into a yet clearer light. It should have had a shadow but its legs were too short.

Leigh said: "Let's go to sleep, love. The argument's over."

Over? But how over? Nothing conclusive, nothing decided. All my refusals accepted, but accepted in the way an advancing army accepts casualties without halting the advance. Two escapes, really, only two: hysteria or illness. Neither will I stoop to. But only blank refusal. Leigh on their side or mine?

"Go to sleep, Deborah," he said again.

"You really want me to do it?"

"How can I say?"

"Well, you can say."

"No . . . They'd no bloody right to ask you—that's what I feel at heart. But there's so much preparation been made, there's so much at stake—for us to gain. It gives

198

me the works to think of you getting involved in any serious way, in any *danger*. And I think, of *course* she mustn't, mustn't think of it. And then I think of you not doing it and all our plans coming to nothing and having to start at square one again—and I think of the shop we want to buy, and putting a deposit down and moving in and beginning to alter it, and having enough money to set up and buy a bit of stock and start in business together. And that makes the difference. It's awful. There may be other chances, of course, but they may be next year, or they may not ever come like this again. In any case *this* shop'll go. God, I don't know what to say, really I don't!"

"You've said it."

"Yes," he agreed. "I've said it. We've talked it out. Can you go to sleep?"

"No."

"Can't we put out the light and see?"

"No."

The beetle had crawled into the second brighter band, but then, disliking it, or perhaps being diverted by some current of interest perceptible only to itself, it turned and moved off into the grayer band again.

Which is the worst step? The first, the tiny movement over the forbidden line, into the forbidden territory—or a wild overrunning? Which is asking the most?

Leigh said: "Irons is a queer bird, isn't he?"

"Who?"

"John Irons."

"Oh, yes . . ."

"I only met him last month. Jack's known him for some time. The absolute pro. D'you know he told me he's never broken in anywhere since he was twenty? When it's ready for him, he walks in and does his part of the job. Like a surgeon, almost. Other people have to make all the preparation."

The beetle had come back again, seemed agitated, and then suddenly stopped dead and made no move, became just a mark on the ceiling.

"Of course he's been inside two or three times. He's

the only one connected with us with a record. It's a pity to have anyone the police know, but you can't do without one expert in this."

"I would call Jack an expert."

"Well, in his own line, yes. But he's too smart to have been caught. He organizes. But not often, that's the point. He lives off antiques. He stays in the background."

After a minute I said: "I think his wife's scared of him."

"Who? Doreen? Of Jack? Whatever makes you say that?"

"Aren't you, Leigh?"

"What, scared of Jack? . . . Why should I be? Maybe he's the leader because he's got the know-how, the connections. But scared . . ."

"So he is the leader?"

"Yes . . . so far as anyone is. He has the ideas. But it's all a pretty friendly set-up, as you can see."

"There wasn't anyone else at our party?"

"No . . . But in the early stages Jack wanted to be anonymous. It's just a precaution."

"You're always different when he's around."

"Different? How?"

"Oh, I don't know. Less positive. He takes sureness from you."

"Well, he's given me a lot in return."

"Has he?"

"He was the first person, ever, to treat me seriously as a painter."

The beetle had moved again, started forward into the brightest circle of light. It was in the bull's-eye. I don't know what attraction or repulsion moved in its primitive nerve centers, but it began to go round in a circle itself, moving as it were on a central pivot, as if afraid of attack. This went on for a minute or more and then, perhaps intimidated by danger I couldn't see, it abruptly abandoned its defense and scuttled off, from bright ring to less bright, to gray, to dark, and then was lost to view in the shadows of the corner.

"Put out the light," I said to Leigh.

Tuesday was even more foggy than Monday. It was a return to the worst conditions before smokeless zones. London Airport was closed, trains were canceled, ships were dockbound. Statistics were released, no one knew how gleaned, of deaths from bronchitis and pneumonia, although so far only two days of fog had had to be endured. I overcame my allergy for tubes and reached Whittington's via Rotherhithe, Whitechapel, Holborn and Green Park. The tubes were crammed, over-hot and over-drafty, people shuffling, docile, waiting, pressing, coughing. I came up into the sun-tempered haze of Piccadilly like Lazarus emerging from his tomb.

Whittington's was quiet. Traffic choked the streets but fewer people than usual came to the West End from choice. It was the second view day for the jewelry sale. Emeralds stared up from their glass cases cosseted in cream silk. The splendid Plouth diamonds shone with white fire. Parker and Davidson and Jones and Armitage were on watch. To those who came with expert inquiries the cases could be discreetly opened and the jewels examined, but never except under the polite but careful gaze of two of our men. At the door Anson and Harper, two more of our commissionaires, both ex-paratroopers, were casually ready to block any hurried exit. Of course it was not expected, had never happened, but it always *could* happen and therefore must be guarded against. The ordinary visitor, interested perhaps in investing a few hundreds in a modest diamond or two, saw nothing to remark.

Downstairs we were going through a miscellaneous collection of china which had belonged to Lady Stockton. Surprisingly enough it had never properly been itemized even for insurance purposes and some of it was difficult to ascribe and value. As we finished looking at each piece, Mary Fent wrote down what I told her and we stacked the piece in the cupboard beside the bookcases —those bookcases which were full of all the most authoritative reference books on china and porcelain ever published. This was not one of the big cupboards, being only half length with open shelves beneath. There was a big cupboard by the door, at present in an untidy mess with piles of old catalogues and art magazines and reports of sales in Paris and New York; on its left wall were pegs on which we hung our hats and coats and where my now discarded stick was propped. There were also two big cupboards in the passage outside. Both were crammed to the doors with miscellaneous articles which had been accepted for sale and then not sold. (Some had not reached their reserve and waited collection by owners who now appeared to have forgotten them; some we had withdrawn because they had been proved to be useless fakes before they were offered; some had been mistakenly accepted with better things and were being held over in the expectation that some day they could be fitted into a new sale of odds and ends.) At the end of this passage from our office was the private office of Smith-Williams, and opposite that a smaller but emptier cupboard. On this corner the passage made a T, the left-hand turn leading to the furniture department and stairs up to the ground floor, the right-hand one leading to the strong room, and beyond that to the small antiquities department and two rooms used for storing pictures.

I left that evening at six and was surprised to find Leigh waiting. The fog had come down again; it got into your nose and throat like diluted tear gas. He took my arm and led me among misted figures and the haloes of cars. We groped our way across Bond Street and walked toward Cork Street. I expected his little Triumph, but we stopped at a big old Austin waiting at a parking meter. Inside was Jack Foil. We all got in the back.

"Miss Dainton . . . It is easier this way than meeting at a house. And this fog makes difficulties for us all . . . I wanted to thank you . . ."

"Oh . . ."

"I think it will be easy for you. I think so. You've—er —picked where you can wait?"

"Yes . . ."

Leigh took my hand.

Jack Foil said: "We agree to your conditions that it should be at one-thirty and not at two-thirty. I quite appreciate . . . the waiting will be difficult—quite the hardest part of it, I should say. You have a good watch?"

"Yes."

"With a luminous face?"

"Yes."

"Then all is quite simple. Really simple, Miss Dainton —no real cause for nerves or tension, believe me. I've given Leigh a paper with it all typed out."

He paused. A man with a pear-shaped hat walked past: in the fog you couldn't be absolutely sure.

The heavy, almost-educated voice went on: "The Safeguard at the telephone rings his headquarters at a quarter to one, a quarter past one, a quarter to two. The Safeguard on patrol, clocks in in the basement at one o'clock, on the first floor at twenty past one, on the ground floor at twenty to two. You will leave your place of hiding at exactly twenty minutes past one, proceed slowly up the stairs and go into Mr. Greeley's office and switch off the alarms at twenty-two minutes past one. At this time you will know that the patrolling Safeguard is on the first floor, having just clocked in. You will then come to the back door and unlock it and open it and we shall be waiting to come in. As we come in you will go out, your job nicely done."

"How shall I get home?"

"Drive yourself. A young lady like you, who is easy to remember—if you'll pardon me—shouldn't be seen catching a late bus or waiting in a tube or perhaps be remembered by a taxi driver. Leigh will hire a Mini tomorrow and when he comes on this job will park it in Berkeley Square—on the south side—and you will pick it up there. You'll have a key. Do you know where Farthing Street is?"

"No."

"Leigh will show you. It's a cul-de-sac off East Lane, which runs off Abbey Street. His own car will be parked there. You just change cars and drive home. We'll pick up the Mini on Thursday."

I said: "What about the two Safeguards?"

"What about them?"

"You'll have to——"

"Oh, they won't be hurt, I can tell you. They'll take care themselves for that. They'll do their duty—naturally —but when there's four to one, they'll show common sense."

A man came out of the fog and tapped on the window. Jack Foil lowered it.

"Can you tell me which way to Burlington Arcade?" Australian voice.

"Straight down. Straight down this way and cross the street. You can't miss it."

After the window was raised there was silence in the car.

"One thing," said Jack Foil, and wiped his eyes. "One thing, Miss Dainton, if anything goes wrong at the beginning, don't try to carry on——just drop everything and pretend to be ill. If one of the Safeguards should see you, it's all up, because he'd identify you anywhere and through you the police would reach Leigh—and perhaps even me. If they come on you, say you twisted your leg and fainted, couldn't remember where you were. Or if they find you in the cupboard, say you went in to find something and felt faint and someone must have shut the cupboard door. I leave you to make up the best story. But get them to send for a doctor. I've given Leigh a pill for you to take before the doctor comes. It's a simple emetic —but it's much more convincing if you really are sick. Do excuse me for putting such thoughts in your head, but to organize you have to prepare. Efficiency—you remember we talked about it once."

"Yes, I remember."

The smell of carnation overlaid the smell of petrol and dusty leather.

"What time do we meet tomorrow night?" Leigh asked.

"Midnight. We pick up John Irons at 12:45, park here at 1:10. Perhaps the earlier time will be an advantage after all. In a manner of speaking the more people there are about the better."

I put my hand on the door handle.

"Our car's just round the corner," Leigh said. "What if it's foggy like this, Jack?"

"The forecast says clearing. But if it doesn't we'll meet an hour earlier in case of delays. One last thing, Miss Dainton."

I paused. He had sunk back into his corner and the thick spectacles only gave off a sort of aquarium light.

"This is a big effort for you, Miss Dainton, we fully understand. I never forget an injury and I never forget a favor. I'll see you and Leigh do well out of this. You'll do very well indeed. So good luck for tomorrow."

I was moving to get out when Leigh nudged my attention to Jack's outstretched hand. I took it; it was cool and very soft; the metal of the ring was colder.

"Good luck for tomorrow," he said again.

Tuesday was usually our West End night, but tonight we would have gone home had there been anything at home but silence and thoughts and waiting. Instead a light meal at a Chicken Inn and then the London Pavilion to see the latest teenage pop-singer hit. For about an hour the film was gorgeously noisy and actually squeezed the tension and the fear out of the center of one's mind. But the noise began to fail with repetition, and as soon as it began to fail it began to jar. So in the end I couldn't sit it out and we left at ten and began to grope our way home.

Eleven-thirty when we got in bed, and we both more or less realized at the same moment that we were unlikely to sleep. Leigh never used sleeping pills and I hadn't for eight years, and all there was in the place were six aspirins and two Veganin. We tried one Veganin and two aspirins each, and we sat up and made tea and then read for a bit and the clock struck two and then three.

I dozed on his shoulder, and nightmare and reality took turn and turn about, the way it does when you're a child and running a high temperature.

I suppose that way we slept, because much later I woke, warm and comfortable, the dark just giving way to the filtered light of dawn; I stretched my legs deliciously, the sheets where I parted them being just cool enough to give a sensuous pleasure to lassitude and ease. And it was minutes, or seemed minutes, before the drawn sword of the new day slid its cold steel between my ribs.

He was still sleeping. But I no longer slept.

Chapter 19

The forecast was right: the fog was clearing. Still thick in the morning, a genuine pale sunshine had broken through by midday. There was a breeze at London Airport. A few ships left the docks and moved downriver.

I went out to lunch and, as I should get no supper, had a fairly substantial one. As usual I ate alone. The food didn't go down but stayed in my stomach as if I had eaten clay. About three o'clock I felt so sick that I began to wonder if I should be ill and so wreck the whole plan before it started. We were still working on the Stockton china, and there were about a dozen pieces of valuable eighteenth-century stuff—jugs and mugs and vases—that I was almost certain were Lowestoft, in spite of the Meissen crossed swords on two of them—because factories were not above copying even trade marks. But Maurice Mills was out this afternoon, so, sooner than commit myself, I put the pieces aside for him to see.

I told Mary I was going out for tea, and this gave me a chance to walk a bit; then I went in a cafe and swallowed three cups of weak tea and waited to see if it would kill or cure.

It was nearly four when I got back, and someone said an old lady was waiting to see me, so I went to the counter at the back and found old Mrs. Stevenson. She had brought another couple of pieces of china, which I accepted because they weren't valueless; but I warned her she would be lucky to clear £30 for the two.

I thought, what would she think if she knew? What would John Hallows think? He'd probably pity rather than blame. Poor Deborah—so infatuated that she can no longer think straight at all. But after seven years . . . nearly eight. But he would be truly hurt—as most of the directors would be if they ever knew. It was *such* a betrayal.

On the way back I went through the showrooms. A satisfying number of people about, including several top-rank jewelers whom I knew by sight. It would be a highly sucessful sale tomorrow—if it ever took place.

Pains in my stomach. They seemed to be nerve pains, griping down the front of my belly and right into the groin. Nervous appendicitis. After working for twenty minutes I went into the ladies' lavatory and sat on a creaking bentwood chair in front of the damp-stained mirror and made up my face again. My grandmother, whom I could just remember, used little cool tear-offs called *papier poudre,* and sometimes she'd wiped my face with them when I was a child. No modern compact seemed to have the same comforting, cooling feeling when one was hot or worried.

A girl called Madge Stevens came in. "Feeling all right, Deborah?"

"Yes, why not?"

"I just wondered. Is it the usual thing?"

"Well, yes . . . I felt a bit green after lunch."

"I *thought* you looked it."

"Oh, I'm all right."

Madge Stevens straightened her stocking. "Funny how things change, isn't it? When I was at school we always used to call it the Curse. Now when it turns up I'm always so relieved that I call it the Blessing!"

I got up, smiling. "Well, it's your turn at the mirror anyhow."

Back to work, still fighting odd bouts of pain. Mary

had been called away so I took the opportunity of pretending to have to go to the cupboard opposite Smith-Williams's office. It was as I had seen it yesterday. Two mirrors, a folding camp bed, a copy of Rodin's *Le Baiser* about quarter size, two buckets and a mop, and some overalls behind the door. But room enough for me. If I ever got there. I had just shut the door when Smith-Williams came out of his office.

"Oh, Deborah, can you come here a minute?"

Like a criminal already caught, I went shakily into his office, answered some routine inquiry as if not properly awake. He had to ask me one question twice before I heard him, and I thought he looked at me appraisingly as I answered. Presently I escaped to my own office.

Five came and half past. Upstairs the showrooms would now be closed. In a few minutes John Hallows and probably Davidson, who had the longest service with the firm as a commissionaire, would go upstairs with strong boxes and open the cases and put the jewels in—the vivid viridian emeralds from Gwalpur, the diamonds collected by the late Jonathan Plouth, the paper millionaire—and bring them down and enter the strong room and open the safe and put in the boxes and lock the safe and lock the strong room; and then all would be secure for the night.

"Look," Mary said, "I think I'll slip off now, if you don't mind. It was such hell getting home last night."

"Yes, of course, you go. I'm leaving myself in a few minutes."

"Where's Mr. Mills this afternoon?"

That was what I was wondering. "I don't know if he'll be back again. But anyway he won't ask."

"O.K. Thanks." She slid off her stool, tall and gaunt and graceless and young. "Thanks, Deborah. Bye."

"Bye."

The directors usually went about six-thirty, though this was elastic either way. I wished I knew whether Maurice Mills would be back. If he came back he might well work on until seven-thirty, in which case it would be difficult to find an excuse to outstay him. On the other hand, if I *left* now and he came back at six he might be surprised to find us both gone. Or John Hallows might yet drop in about something and be similarly surprised. Also, the earlier I went to earth the more likely I was to be seen and the less unlikely it would be that by a thousand-to-one chance someone went to the cupboard.

I worked on.

At seven the guards arrived and the alarms were switched on. At that point the guards *had* to know if anyone was left in the building, because they had to switch off the alarms to let them out. Therefore if I was *publicly* in the building at seven I couldn't just disappear. I was marked until I left.

In haste I got up, shut the reference book I'd been using, dropped my pen, groped under the desk and couldn't find it. Starting up I jogged the desk and shook a cup and saucer to the edge. Rubbing my shoulder I looked out through the glass door and saw Smith-Williams talking to Davidson at the door of his office.

Put the cup and saucer in the cupboard out of danger. How long would they talk? Davidson, a big gray-haired ex-Guardsman—one of those who had defended Calais in 1940—was explaining something. He was expressive about it, pointing upstairs and shaking his head. Look at my watch. Don't panic. Do the Safeguards ever come early?

I got down on hands and knees and searched for the pen. It had rolled against one of the back feet of the desk. I stood up, wiping dust off my fingers. If Maurice Mills came back now he'd certainly stay on for an hour.

Smith-Williams was lighting a cigarette, holding his birdlike head sideways so that the flame didn't go in his eyes. Davidson, like the other commissionaires, never smoked on duty.

If I put on my coat and went past, turned left toward the stairs but skirted them, there was an alcove with three or four enormous old oil paintings leaning half across it. The lights in the passages were still on, wouldn't be dimmed until seven; but this alcove was halfway between lights and would be shadowy.

Twenty to seven. I put the ledger away, moved a few plates into places of safety, turned the key in the glass doors of the cabinet, picked up my bag. I fiddled in the smallest pocket of the bag, found Jack Foil's pill, put it back. I counted the money in the bag: about six pounds. I took out a compact, dabbed my face, dropped the compact in, shut the bag. I went to the cupboard by the door, took down my coat, struggled into it, tied a Spanish scarf round my hair. In the mirror my face looked pinched, the eyes out of proportion—like a bush baby or something. The pains in my stomach were coming and going like cramp.

They were still talking. I switched off the lights in the office and went out, walked toward the two men, ten paces.

"You'll never get young people to see it like that, sir," Davidson was saying. "There's no discipline now, even like in my time . . ."

"Good night," I said.

They both answered good night as I walked past my cupboard.

"Well, you can't have plain insolence, I agree," Smith-Williams said, his cigarette wagging. "Personally, I don't see . . ."

Turn left toward the stairs and, on impulse, into the Ladies. Sensible precaution. No one there, fortunately; all the other women had probably gone. Wait five minutes. At twelve minutes to seven I came out. Passage empty. No one on stairs. Three steps back. Davidson had gone, but Smith-Williams's office door was open. To go back and walk into the cupboard with that door open and Smith-Williams in his office was more than I could face.

Back past the stairs. Voices at the top of the stairs. Davidson and another man. Voices mumbling. Not coming down. At the end of the passage was the big furniture department, which was still lit up, but I couldn't see anything of Grant Stokes or either of his assistants. Abreast of the alcove. It wasn't as dark as I remembered: one of the paintings had been moved. I bent down to tie my shoe. Nothing moved either way. I straightened up, stepped over a nineteenth-century stool, round a rosewood trolley and slid behind the paintings.

Memories of childhood. Hide and seek with Sarah and little Arabella. The breathless, heart-thumping pain of crouching in a dark place while others *searched* for you! The stomach-twisting pains of fear. The giggling, half-hysterical leap when you *were* discovered. The hour-long times, the clever times, when you were not. Once I'd hidden in the chimney in the old washhouse that had then been attached to our house, and *no one* had found me. There'd been trouble then because everyone had got worried and been afraid I'd come to some harm. That was when I was nine, when confined spaces meant nothing to me at all.

At seven the lights went down. From now until morning pilot lights in the passages and single lights in the store rooms and display rooms. The minor offices, such as my own, were left dark.

So against all belief the first part of the plan had happened. Not as planned, of course, nothing ever did, it seemed; but I could get to my cupboard if I waited and chose the time.

Seven-twenty. Maurice Mills was clearly not coming back. Smith-Williams? On his way home to Canonbury and dinner? The commissionaires would all be gone. Think carefully. At seven the patrolling guard will have clocked in just near the strong room in this basement. At twenty past he goes up two flights and registers in the cashier's office. Therefore this basement should be empty of life at least until a quarter to eight. Wait then until twenty-five to eight—that gives everything time to settle down.

Fifteen minutes to crawl by. Count. Don't look at your watch until you've counted a thousand. Slow now. Counting I reach five hundred and feel I must look in case I'm overrunning it. Six minutes have passed.

I look at my watch then until seven-thirty. Now.

How easy it is to stumble or kick against something merely by taking too much pains to avoid it. Out into the passage. The stairs are dark. Smith-Williams's office in darkness. Turn corner, hand on handle of cupboard. Freeze . . . Our office is lighted.

Against the wall, trying to be invisible. Through the glass door I see Smith-Williams in there just coming out. I watch his hand on the door, then he turns back into the office and lights another cigarette.

Hand on cupboard door. Door open. It *creaked*. He's taken down one of our reference books, is poring over it, blue smoke spiraling from the cigarette. Gently into the cupboard. One foot, the other, draw in one's body, pulling the door with finger tips. Creak again. Through the narrowing gap I see him shut the book and return it to its shelf. Fingers on handle, turn slowly; shut, release handle very gently.

Darkness. Success. Footsteps close outside, another door shuts, a nick of light pierces a tiny crack in this door. He has gone back to his own office.

Smith-Williams left at eight. Before he left I heard him talking to the guard. It was Gaskell who was patrolling at present—I knew, from Monday night, the West Country voice. Gaskell was a much smaller man than his companion, McCarthy, red-faced, spectacles, with an expression as if he'd a nasty taste in his mouth. He'd been a prison officer and later a private detective. After Smith-Williams left, the tiny crack of light disappeared and utter silence fell.

I was at last able to grope about and find a comfortable position. I inched the buckets over to one side where there was less likelihood of accident. The copy of the Rodin sculpture was then eased gently after them. It was obviously impossible to get the camp bed unfolded, so I let it lie on the floor and squatted on it, letting my legs reach toward Rodin, and trying to rest my back against the wall.

Not a great success, but time was passing. And the acute pains in my inside had temporarily stopped. Immediate emergency over.

I was a lot more comfortable than I had been in that

chimney eighteen years ago. Odd I should have remembered that tonight; it had fallen into a deep trough of memory and had not been dredged up once in the last ten years. Possibly it had come up tonight because of hiding behind the pictures. Hide and seek, that was it. No claustrophobia in those days.

Don't think of that word now. You're not really confined here. You only have to turn the handle and the door will fly open. Only you daren't touch the handle, that's all.

Pity so dark. Even when one's eyes grew accustomed it was still like near blindness. Strange that crack, which had allowed in the light from Smith-Williams's office, let in none from the pilot light in the passage. Perhaps the light had failed. Odd if there was a power failure tonight of all nights.

Where was Leigh? Not yet nine o'clock. Perhaps eating a nervous meal on his own at the studio. And Jack Foil helping Doreen to wipe up and watering his indoor plants and then taking the dachshunds for a walk. Perfect domestic scene. Ideal husband. What excuse did he make to Doreen when he left the house later tonight? Or did she really know it all?

And Ted Sandymount? How did one tap a wire? What was more, how did one do it secretly? Presumably he knew. Post Office training? And the putty-faced, sunken-eyed Mr. Irons, quiet spoken, gentlemanly, gaunt. Was he by now gathering up his tools? Or did he have them in a special case, each instrument tempered and proved? And how would he bring them here tonight? In a private car, or by tube? Would he look like a commercial traveler, with a suitcase, seeking a hotel? Might he not be stopped by the police? They didn't go about with their eyes shut.

Pity so dark in here. Wish one had brought a torch: this was a bad oversight. Open the door an inch? It would be quite safe to do so at regular times through the night, because one knew certainly there would be no one on this floor.

But safer not. Stay where you are. Stretch your legs a bit. Left knee is aching.

Funny if I'd never had this bad knee. Funny if none of that had ever happened. I had come home from school one afternoon; Erica petulantly: "Oh, Deborah, not *another* cold in the house! We seem to have only just got rid of Arabella's." Next morning: "Did you remember the aspirin? Well, go to school, see how you are tonight. It's a pity to miss games. Take two or three hankies with you." That evening: "Do your homework and then bed; I'll bring you some hot milk. You're running a temperature, I can see." Temperature 99.4°. Not alarming. Nasty night. Streaming nose. Douglas in the morning, peeping in smiling. "What's the temp? 99°? Bed for you, I think; but get up for lunch, it'll do you good. Minta will be in to see you later. Bye." I didn't get up and didn't want any lunch, and Minta was cross because she thought I was saucy and didn't fancy what she brought up. Dreary afternoon, nose still running. Throat dry. Feeling mouldy. Missing the rehearsal for the school play. Miss James wouldn't like that. Out of bed to the lavatory, felt quite breathless. Very odd. Erica back at eight. "Oh, dear, *still* in bed? You're looking pinched. I'll come and see you after supper." While they were having supper it got worse. "Mummy, I can't breathe! Mummy, I can't breathe!" Sarah heard me. Douglas upstairs. One look at me. "Telephone for an ambulance."

Funny how one remembered things after all this time. "Mummy, I can't breathe!" Didn't do to dwell on it just now, the memory too vivid. How much air in this cupboard? If it kept out light, might it not keep out air? To have the door an inch open would be a wise precaution.

Footsteps. Gaskell round again. It must be ten. Three hours gone. Nearly halfway. Give him time to clock in . . . Think about something else. Music, painting, *skating*. Skating was lovely, smooth, sweeping, cold refreshing air, not like this stale cupboard air. Footsteps again; he was going back. I glanced at my watch to check, and was horrified to see that it had stopped. Stopped at ten past nine. Now what to do? I put the thing to my ear and heard it ticking.

Jogging in the ambulance. Erica came with me. Somebody in the darkness had said: "Hurry, she'll not live another hour."

Hospital—stretcher—wheel in. Room with a boxlike thing. Lift me in it. Only my head out. Torture? No, iron lung. Flat on back, head on pillow like a deck chair head rest, all body inside enormous metal coffin connected by tube to giant bellows slowly rising and falling. *Pushing* on your chest, pressing till you wanted to faint; then relaxing, then *pulling* instead, pulling till your mouth opened and air went in; relaxing, then pressing again pressing till the air came out. "Ease this off a bit, nurse," said a voice. Then Douglas saying: "Naturally one did not anticipate . . . The symptoms were unidentifiable." Another voice: "You didn't notice the loss of muscle tone?"

I put my hand on the handle of the cupboard and gently turned the handle. Gently pushed the door an inch. Light. Dim light but *so* welcome after the utter darkness. And *air*. Not imagination that it had grown short in the cupboard. I put out my head and looked each way. My office in darkness. Smith-Williams's in darkness. Upstairs two men. Shut the door so carefully; but it still creaked. Loose the handle, grope your way a foot back—something fell off the back of the door with a hellish clatter.

Frozen silence, heart lurching, teeth held, *wait*.

It was an overall that had dropped, but what the devil had made the noise? If Gaskell or McCarthy were coming down the stairs . . .

I squatted back slowly on the floor and waited. Nothing . . .

Five to ten. It was growing stuffy again. I could feel the iron lung compressing and expanding my chest.

You didn't really lose any feeling in your body when you had polio; it was all there, but helpless. You lay as if strapped in that iron coffin, not moving because you couldn't move. At first you couldn't even pass urine. The disease had never got up to my throat. They fed me liquids through a sort of teapot, but I couldn't take much. The whole coffin was on a sort of trolley and they wheeled you about on rubber wheels that squeaked. They

216

were all cheerful and peered at you smiling, and you wanted to scream and daren't because if you did a sort of bubble might form in your throat and make you cough and then you'd suffocate.

Three hours to go . . . It had been three days to go then. They took me out after about a day, but I began to die so they put me back. The nights were the worst time then, because you were supposed to sleep; but it was only the nurse who slept, and you were still troubled with the remnants of your cold, and your nose irritated and you couldn't rub it. And a tear came out of your eye and ran down your cheek and tickled and irritated all the way and *never stopped* irritating as it dried. And sometimes your nose was altogether blocked. But still the bellows went on, pushing, pressing on your chest until your mouth opened and the air went in again. It *was* torture because you were really dead and it was keeping you artificially alive. If you could just *die*, if you could just *suffocate:* a horrible few minutes and it would be *over*. But this: *in* and *out* and *in* and *out* and *in* and *out* and *in* and *out,* forever, all through the long dark hours; and if the mucus ran down your face and you whimpered loud enough the nurse would stir and bend over you and wipe your face and say: "All right, love? Like a drink?" And you'd shake your head and she'd move away and sit down again and you'd just have to concentrate on this terrible living that was being forced on you . . .

My head banged against the wall and I woke up. . . . Time? I'd been asleep. Nearly midnight. God, I might have slept all night through! But was it natural sleep? Wasn't it more half-fainting for lack of air? I could feel the machine working on my chest even now. I was terrified to scream because if I did a bubble would get in my throat and choke me. I was bound hand and foot. Paralyzed, dead and buried, all except my head; the thing beside me was like a steam engine puffing and sucking at the air. Pressure all round. Black walls weighing, black sides pressing, holding me down, blind in the dark, deaf in the dark, dead in the dark . . .

I thrust at the cupboard door, wriggled the handle, got

217

it open and stumbled out into the passage, gasping at the air. I could hardly stand, hair soaked in sweat, trembling, gasping to get breath. The only importance was to get out of the cupboard and never go back. *Never* go back, not for love of Leigh or all the money in England!

I lurched against the wall, nightmare still only just a step away, but reality slowly taking over, reason beginning to flex and stir. I shut the cupboard door and leaned with my palms and face against it. Not in there again. Not yet anyway. Must have a short break. Just a chance to recover. Then perhaps I could stand it again. Only an hour and a half now. Pity, having come so far, to fail now.

The door of Smith-Williams's office was ajar. At his desk was a big swivel chair that he often tilted back to put his feet on the corner of the desk. I pushed open the door, closed it again, groped to the chair, sat there.

Relief. Like being taken out of the box for the third time and finding that your lungs could go in and out of their own accord. Erica had cried. The only time I had ever seen her cry. Douglas wasn't there, but he came soon after, his blue eyes limpid with pleasure. "She's been very lucky," they said. "Full movement in the arms now, and we'll hope the legs will recover in the next day or so."

Footsteps. So I was caught. McCarthy. Well, it wouldn't be difficult to pretend illness. No need for Jack Foil's pill. He had come down the stairs pretty slowly and now he appeared at the junction of the passage, walking sleepily, swinging his torch. He turned his head and looked up the short passage to my office and then passed on. His footsteps receded. He was going to the clocking-in place. I sat still. He was whistling *The Londonderry Air*. I sat still. His footsteps stopped. There was a long pause. He had gone right on into the antiquities department. Footsteps coming back. Same pace. His torch was on now, flickering about.

He came to the T-join again, paused, flicked the torch toward my office. The light swept across Smith-Williams's office in passing, but was too high to show me up.

He went on. I heard him going right down the passage into the furniture department. Silence. Then back he came again to the stairs, began to mount them. His footsteps died away.

... With the back of my hand I wiped my damp forehead. So now I should be safe here for nearly an hour. Sitting in this chair in comparative comfort. When one o'clock came round I would slide down and lie under the desk until he had gone again. It was no part of their duty to search every office. I should be reasonably safe.

And so it was. One o'clock came, and with it McCarthy again. He followed an identical procedure. His light came nowhere near me. When he had gone I got up and sat down in the chair again, and began to watch the minute hand of my luminous watch. Only twenty minutes to go. My part was almost done. Perhaps for me the worst was already over.

Chapter 20

Twenty minutes past one. I got up, went to the door and
out. One of the men should now be on the first floor, the
other in the telephone office on the ground floor. The
pilot light burned at the foot of the stairs. I went up.

Showrooms haunted in the half light. A great Persian
vase loomed like a man standing in the doorway. The offices were down to the left; a light under the telephone-
room door; Mr. Greeley's office in darkness. Halfway
there I remembered gloves. "Don't forget to wear gloves
whatever you do," Jack Foil said. "I know your fingerprints will be about, but you might leave one in an inconvenient place." Too late to go back to the cupboard
where I'd dropped them off. A handkerchief; wrap it
round the handle of Mr. Greeley's door, go in. Enough
light from the passage to see.

A small square office; he usually kept it manned during
the day, though often he was himself upstairs. I knew exactly where the switches were: between the bookcases a
small cupboard where he kept drinks; behind the bottles
were the switches, two square brown bakelite boxes with
gray cables leading up the wall. The switches were white
lettered on red and marked on and off. Move the bottles
very carefully; a fingerprint here might tell a lot. Clumsy
work with a handkerchief, but I got them out and

reached in again. Both switches down. I pushed one up and then the other. Each made a noisy clack.

Wait, half afraid of a booby trap of some sort, perhaps a separate alarm that rang if the switches were touched. Nothing. I took away my hand and knocked over a glass.

It didn't fall out of the cupboard: it rolled along the edge and I caught it with my other hand in time. Gulp spittle, swallow fear, heart swelling. Fingerprint. Pick the glass up, put it in pocket. Safer now thrown on some dump miles away.

Silence still, but time passing. In three or four minutes McCarthy or Gaskell would be coming down. I went out. Light under the telephone-room door but no movement, no alarm. Perhaps the other man was dozing. Nearly half an hour before he made his next call to headquarters.

Now back past the head of the stairs, through the book-auction room, then the passage with the counter, where things were received, then the narrow hall, then the door leading to Bruton Yard.

It was of stout oak and locked with a five-lever mortise deadlock. Also a conventional key to turn, but this hardly ever used. Then heavy bolts top and bottom. Bottom one came easily but the top I could barely reach. Back to counter for chair. Another fingerprint? But this no matter: I was always being called to the counter. Bolts were different. Very careful with the bolts.

The top bolt came down, I pulled the chair quietly back, turned the mortise lock and flicked up the catch. Then pulled open the door.

A man came in, horrible, like a nightmare: I gulped, hadn't expected the stocking masks. Then another, who squeezed my arm. "Bless you, love." A third. A fourth. The fourth stopped briefly, said: "Car's in Berkeley Square, just where we said. Bye for now." Ted.

Then I was out in the foggy night, and the door was shut behind me.

Bruton Yard is a cul-de-sac which spreads out at its closed end into a modest little square. It is used as a rear entrance by a dozen firms whose premises back onto it.

There are two sodium street lamps, but our corner of the yard is in shadow.

The fog swirled in the distant lights of Bruton Street. Still a couple of windows lit in the building next to Whittington's, a firm of textile exporters. Seven cars and a furniture van parked about the yard. The old Austin saloon was one of the cars. Dustbins; a cardboard box lying on its side, an evening paper curling damply at the edges, empty milk bottles.

I shivered, wondering what was going on behind the door at my back. Since the guards could be taken separately, they *might* not resist. But still robbery with violence. Even if not hurt they'd be tied and gagged; so a much heavier sentence if things went wrong. And I as much involved as if I were in that building now. Accessory before and after the fact.

Ought to go. Five minutes' walk. But it meant walking through brightly lit, half-empty streets. And although my limp was not nearly so noticeable, no policeman would fail to notice that it was there. One-thirty, of course, not late for London. They'd never stop me or ask. Chances were I'd never even see a policeman.

But I did not move, needing time after the terrible tensions of these last minutes, almost waiting, listening, as if I should hear something from the building just left. Safe in the shadows of the yard.

A tabby cat moved across the light, came toward me mewing. I knew her, she came from one of the other offices, sometimes walked into Whittington's and was given a saucer of milk. Hand down and she rubbed against it. A touch of warmth and homeliness and sanity. I picked her up and walked a few yards with her and left her on a low wall mewing.

The end of the yard. There stopped to put on headscarf—a bit of protection and it would disguise my fairly noticeable hair. Then after fumbling in pockets realized the scarf was in the cupboard, along with my gloves. I had dressed up to go home to deceive Smith-Williams and had stayed so dressed in the cupboard until the enclosed space had made me feel queer. Then I had dragged off scarf and gloves and dropped them on the floor.

Danger? My scarf and gloves had every right to be in the building. I had once left a coat three weeks. But in that cupboard? If the police found them before I did, would they pick them out and ask whose are they? Easily identifiable, particularly the Spanish scarf. Why put them there? Once suspicious, many more questions? What time did you leave? Who saw you leave?

Two young men were coming down Bruton Street laughing and trying to hail a taxi. I kept in the shadow, but one of them saw me and gave a wolf whistle. I turned back into the yard.

Nobody here at all. Perfect silence. Stand away from the cold glare of the street lamps. Footsteps. Someone else in Bruton Street. I retreated, backing away, back to the oak door.

The tabby cat leaped into the light, making arches like a cantilever bridge, came mewing, then stopped dead. Some interesting smell took her interest. Head turned, she stalked away.

Had they locked the door on the other side? Almost certainly. But only five minutes had passed. I took out my handkerchief and tried the handle. It turned and I went back in.

Just as when left. The pilot light burning dimly in the passage and another above the counter. It was as if the four men I'd admitted had been sucked into the silence.

I went as far as the counter. A book open on it, a pair of scales, a used coffee cup. Go on into the book auction room, with its bookshelves, its central table, its rostrum. Footsteps. A man.

He looked at me like an animal ready to kill; hand behind back, hand raised; danger; but the hand dropped. "What th' hell?"

Strange voice—one I didn't know. "I came back. I'd forgotten my gloves."

His blurred face stared. Then someone behind him:

223

Leigh's figure. "Deborah! How did you get in? Why've you come back? . . ."

"I forgot my gloves."

"Christ! What a thing to do! Len, you were supposed to do the door—"

"I thought I 'ad . . ."

"The catch—I put it up," I said.

"Where are your gloves?"

"In the cupboard downstairs. Are they—have you . . ."

"What? The guards? Yes. Go and get your gloves for Pete's sake. Leave the door now till she's out of the way, Len."

"I'll watch it," said the stranger. "Or some bleeding copper . . ." He went past me.

I stared at Leigh. He said: "Hurry. We've no time to waste."

"Are they all right?"

"Who? The guards? Sure. We've not hurt 'em. The little one gave in without us laying a finger on him."

"And the other?"

"Len had to tap him. But it's a trick they have. You get it across the shoulders—back of the neck—and you're only out for three minutes. Now *hurry*."

"Can I stay?" I said.

"What in hell d'you mean?"

"I'm afraid of going to the car."

"But there's nothing to it!"

"If I'm seen—with my *limp*. There are not many girls like me about. If a policeman sees me he won't forget."

"Yes, but if you stay here . . ."

"I've been here half the night. What difference does it make?"

"But it breaks the arrangements."

"What does that matter?"

"Hell, I don't know what to say . . . O.K., Len?"

"O.K.," said the stranger, coming back. "Don't forget to lock it again when you let 'er out."

"She wants to stay."

"What?"

"She wants to stay."

Len shrugged. "It's not my show."

"It makes no difference," I said again. "I'm in this anyhow."

Leigh hesitated. "Go and get your gloves. I'll ask Ted."

Len disappeared toward the stairs.

I said: "Where's Jack Foil?"

"At home. Where d'you expect him to be?"

We moved together toward the stairs. Beyond were the showrooms and the two doors: the telephone room was still lighted: it blazed brighter suddenly as Len went in.

"Who is he?"

"We needed a fourth. His job is to guard the guards. Where did you leave your goddamned gloves?"

"In the cupboard downstairs."

"I'll come down with you."

We went together, his gloved hand gripping my upper arm tightly. "Did you have any trouble?" he asked.

"It was a long wait."

"It's over now. I *wish* you'd go."

"No. I'll . . . see it through."

I got to the cupboard and he flashed his torch. I picked up the gloves and pulled them on, tied the scarf over my head.

Footsteps on the stairs. Another man. "D'you want to stay, Deb?" Ted Sandymount.

"Yes. There's much more risk in that five-minute walk."

"Well, search me, I don't know. I don't know what Jack'll say." He hurried past us, walked toward the end of the building where the strong room was. An extra light burned there.

"God, you ought to be wearing a thing over your face!" Leigh exclaimed. "Take one of your stockings off. If you're seen . . ."

"Well, if the guards are both in the telephone room . . ."

"Jack'll be furious if you get in the way. I've got to help Irons."

"There's no reason why I should get in the way!"

225

He hurried off toward the strong room, and after a minute I followed him. Perhaps in my bones I knew that returning for scarf and gloves had been an excuse. I was too deeply committed with Leigh to want to separate from him now, too committed altogether to this thing. In any event there was no horror for me greater than sitting in a cupboard for six hours. This, in a sense, was a release. Ted Sandymount was on his stomach, doing something to the power plug in the wall. John Irons had pulled off his nylon and had loosened his collar; hands on hips he was staring at the strong-room door and whistling gently; he alone of the four men looked unhurried, as if he had hours to spend. When he saw us he raised his anthropoid eyebrows and muttered out of the corner of his mouth:

"This is a bit harder than you said."

"What's wrong?" Leigh asked urgently.

"Nothing's wrong but what can't be put right. But this door will take a lot of blowing. I suppose you don't know where they keep the keys, do you, lady?"

"Each director has a set. No one else."

"Hm." He patted the wall, where the corner of the strong room abutted on the passage. He was different, in his element, more talkative, where the others were less. "There must be a grill somewhere. You got to have air . . ."

Ted Sandymount said: "D'you want two points or one?"

"One'll do for the time being. There's a lift in the place somewhere, isn't there?"

"Just a furniture lift," I said.

"That's right. I may want extra power, Ted. But I'll let you know."

He took out a hammer and began to tap at the strong-room wall. After a minute he stopped and put a fruit gum in his mouth. He'd brought all his gear in a canvas cricket bag. It was odd; I'd thought he'd go to great pains to disguise what he carried, but this was the sort of bag any policeman would suspect, since no one played cricket

226

in February, least of all a gaunt, pallid-faced, black-browed man in his fifties.

"Chisel," he said to Leigh.

As if the feel of the wall gave him some guidance he began to chip at the brick about shoulder high, two feet from the corner. In five minutes he had made a sizable hole about a finger-width across and a few inches deep.

Ted had made his connections and plugged in the drill. It whirred noisily until it was switched off.

Irons looked at Leigh. "Carpets."

"What sort?"

"Any sort." He glanced at me. "She'll know where they are."

We went off together. There were big carpets upstairs but these would take too much lifting. We got one from Smith-Williams's office, one from Grant Stokes's, one from the passage. When we dragged them back, Irons was unwrapping a bag that contained slim sticks of things like grease paint. He took out one and gently peeled off the paper. Inside was a yellowish putty-like substance, and he began to ease and press some of this into the hole he had made. Ted Sandymount had pulled off his nylon and was tinkering with some thin wire and a little dry-cell battery not much bigger than a torch battery.

Leigh pulled off his own stocking; relief to see his features again after the distortion of the mask.

Irons had filled up the hole and was smoothing it over. Two wires were projecting, and he plugged the end with plasticine. He muttered to Leigh, "How about taking her ladyship upstairs?"

"I can go myself," I said, "if you want to get rid of me."

"What time's your next call to the HQ, Ted?"

"Ten minutes yet."

"Oh, well then we can get this over first."

I went up the stairs with Leigh. He was terribly tense —far more so than I was now. But even with me the first moments of release were already past.

The explosion was more a heavy vibration in the building than a noise.

When we went down Irons was pulling away the remains of the carpets. "It's got to be taken gently. We can't afford too much row. Another couple of charges'll do the trick."

"How long is that going to take?"

"Ten minutes each maybe. But we'll need more carpets. How would it be, dear, if you made us a cup of tea? We'll be glad of a cup of tea."

So I made them tea. It should have been slugs of whisky; this was too prosaic, too homely, the sort of chore you did for a carpenter or a plumber on a job. But it lowered the temperature; maybe Irons, the only pro, asked for this deliberately; if so his idea worked. To him only of the four, this was a night like others—he'd done this regularly all his life; he'd been in the nick three times, he said; twice caught on the job and once framed by the police; he *was* a workman, a skilled workman whose only distinctiveness was that his work happened to be anti-social.

I knew the tiny kitchen well, could do everything by the light of a pencil torch—there was a frosted window to the place, though it only looked out on the next building —and when we'd all finished I washed up and emptied the teapot and put the cups away. Ted Sandymount had taken a cup up to Len when he went along to telephone Safeguard headquarters. The word tonight was Harrogate, and this was his second call.

Last night he had been on the roof locating the wire. Tonight again he had been up there in the dark and had listened to earlier calls, so he knew roughly the sort of brief conversation that passed; but every time he had to ring increased the risk. And he could pass for McCarthy who, surprisingly with that name, was a cockney like himself; but he couldn't imitate Gaskell's west country voice; headquarters might expect Gaskell to take his turn sooner or later.

While I was drying and putting away the cups there was a second vibration, louder down here than the last. This was an old building, ramshackle and abutting on others in which people might be sleeping or a night watchman patrolling; I wondered how far tremors would travel.

For a time I didn't go back; Irons had said to keep away because of the fumes, and anyway I felt they did not want me around. I thought of the arguments in Sarah's flat. The ethics of crime was no longer an academic problem. Tonight everything was changed for me.

I sat on a high stool, tried to see through a flaw in the frosted glass whether there were any lights in the opposite building. There was a brightish one somewhere but I couldn't locate it without opening the window. It might of course be the headlights of the first police car to arrive, having been alerted by some extra alarm that we knew nothing of. They might now be completing the surrounding of the building so that no one could get away . . .

Leigh came sharply into the room: "I wondered where the hell you were! You didn't come back . . ."

"Irons told me not to."

"Oh . . . sorry. I didn't know that. I'm pretty geared up tonight. Sorry, love." He put his arm on my shoulder.

"Will it be long now?"

"Probably not."

"There's only about four hours left."

"It'll do."

There was the third vibration through the building. Cups rattled in the cupboard.

I said: "Why didn't Jack Foil take part in this himself?"

"It isn't his *line*. He makes the arrangements, organizes things, disposes of the stuff afterward."

"And takes none of the risks."

Leigh shrugged. "That's the way it works . . . Let's go."

Irons was getting in. The strong-room wall consisted of fourteen inches of brickwork—three four-inch bricks, with thick cement between. The first explosion had breached the first layer, the second had split the second. The third, working on already loosened and damaged bricks, had blown a sizable hole through into the room itself; and now, while Irons stood back, Ted Sandymount worked with a pick to break a sufficient opening to climb through. When it was done Irons led the way in and we followed.

He switched on the light. The room was in a mess; part of a steel filing cabinet blown away, papers scattered with ledgers on the floor, the room horribly acrid with the smell of the last explosion.

Irons and Ted went over to the safe. Irons had taken off his gloves and didn't put them on as he fingered the safe, trying, you'd think, with the ends of his blunt fingers to probe and test the quality of it. The safe itself stood about four feet high and three broad. It was finished in gray enamel with the maker's name, *Pemberton,* and the door handle and the keyhold guard in chromium plate. The door handle was long and rather slim and pointed downward.

Irons put in another fruit gum and chewed quietly.

"Well?" said Ted.

"Newer than I reckoned on," said Irons. "Later than I reckoned on. They've messed their numbers about, just to be awkward."

"How long will it take?"

"Ah . . . that's yet to be known, isn't it. But there was big changes between, say, '53 and '56. First we'll have this little key guard off."

"What d'you mean, changes?" Leigh demanded as he began to work.

"Well, up to '53 they was mostly still making safes of mild steel. Mixing the layers, maybe, but not so bad. But by '56 or so, safes was being made with an outer lining of steel and an inner lining of steel, and between them was this new alloy that's more or less drillproof. Of course you can get *through* it all right in the end, but it's a long job. I'm not sure about Pemberton's. They was always a bit out of line with the rest. It's years since I've had a go at a Pemberton."

He inserted a thin tube slimmer than a pencil into the keyhole. At its end was a battery and a switch. After he had slid about six inches in he switched on and bent to peer along the barrel into the keyhole.

Ted Sandymount looked at his watch. "Time d'you make it?"

"Twenty minutes to three."

"I'll be going up to ring them. You'd best come with me, Leigh."

"Why?"

"We've got to force an entry somewhere. It's not got to be left to look as if we were let in from the inside."

Irons withdrew his probe. They waited but he shook his head. "It looks round about a '56. I'll drill for a bit and see."

"Aren't you going to try gelly first?" Ted asked.

"No."

"Why not?"

Leigh passed him the drill which Ted had connected. Irons seemed in no hurry to begin, but put his hand on the top of the safe and tapped it in a familiar way. Words came quietly out of the corner of his mouth as if he was afraid a warder was listening.

"All safes since the war, more or less, have got this double-locking caper, what they call an anti-blowing device. If you blow the lock with gelly you release a spring that lets a new bolt fall into place that jams the door for keeps. So you're worse off than when you began. So then you have to drill holes in the door and find where the jamming bar is and lever it up with a couple of screwdrivers."

Ted looked at his watch again and grimaced and began to pull his stocking over his face. "So what?"

"Well, if you've got an older job—'53 or before—you're all right. But when you get this new alloy it's hours of work to make the holes, so then you try other tricks to see if you can save all that time and trouble."

Ted said: "Come on, Leigh. We'll be back in about twenty minutes, John."

"O.K., O.K."

I bent to pick up some of the fallen ledgers and put them in a pile beside the filing cabinets. The shrill whine of the drill began.

Chapter 21

You began to feel tired and cold; suddenly you began to feel tired and cold, and your eyes were heavy and your limbs ached. More tea? The last was only half an hour gone. Dead of night. The small hours. Four hours to daylight. Four hours to the arrival of Bob Sloane and two cleaners, to get ready for another day. The noise of the drill got on my nerves, and I slid out through the gap in the bricks and made for our office. Even here you could still hear the drill, like the distant noise of a bluebottle caught against a windowpane. It stopped. I turned back. It started again.

Somewhere upstairs, Ted and Leigh were faking a forced window. But it *must* look like an inside job. They'd first suspect one of the guards. Then . . .

The drill stopped. Irons cocked a black eyebrow at me as I squeezed back in, but he said nothing. He was changing the bit of the drill for a finer one. I began to move some of the broken bricks, piling them to where they would be less in the way. Footsteps. Ted.

"Well?"

"It's the reinforced type," Irons said.

"Hell's fire. What now?"

"We'll think a bit." Irons didn't restart the drill but took out another fruit gum. "Done your break in?"

"Yes. First floor. You can get up to it by crossing the parapet from next door."

"And the alarms?" So that hadn't been forgotten.

"I've still got to fix that. It means fiddling with some matchsticks and a few bits of rubber . . . What you going to do here, though?"

Leigh came down as he was saying this. His face was flushed and tense.

Irons said: "Doing it straightforward will take me best part of three hours—"

"Three—"

"But I've told you. There's ways of cheating. I'll try gelly now. Just a baby charge to begin—say half an ounce in the keyhole—see if we can blow the lock without jamming the handle."

Ted pulled off his mask, made a face as if he was going to sneeze. "It's those phone calls that give me the willies. Bloke at the other end wanted to chat this last time, said it looked as if the fog was coming back, and it'd be hell getting home if all the trains were late. Next time we'll be talking about wives or something!"

With firm fingers Irons was squeezing the yellow gelignite into the keyhole. Then he got out a pencil and gently pressed it in, added more, pressed it in, added more.

"Look," said Ted. "There's ten minutes before the next call. I'll go and fix those alarms while you're doing that. We can't help, can we?"

"No," said Irons composedly. "No one can help."

"Right. Then come on again, Leigh. Maybe we can plug, maybe we'll have to cut the wires."

They went off again.

Irons looked at me sidelong as if he didn't want to be seen looking.

"It's no good getting in a flap. That's half the trouble, getting in a flap. Opening a safe's one of those jobs where you've got to use your loaf. Make a mistake and you add hours to the work. Now this safe—it's strong and not too old as safes go. D'you know there's still safes in use in London built in Victoria's day? D'you know one of the biggest insurance companies in London has its main safe thirty years old? Strong, mind you, strong as a bank vault, but not modern, no modern ideas." He covered the keyhole with plasticine and trailed the thin wires across the floor.

"You want more carpets?"

"No, these'll do. But it depends whether I use 'em." He went to his cricket bag and rummaged in it. "I'd advise you to keep out of here—else you'll have a headache."

"What if this had been a new safe?" I said. "Bought this year or last."

"Well, there's ways round everything, if you've the will and the tools, but it gets harder every year. There's safes made now you can't get through with a drill, no, nor with oxy-acetelyn neither. Can't touch 'em. But there's a thing called a thermic lance—French brought it out after the war for cutting into Jerry's strong points—well, that'll go through anything—concrete, steel, rock. I've seen it used. Phew!" He pulled out a long circular piece of black rubber.

"But you don't use it?"

"Me? No. That's out of my street. Anyway, you don't want it here. Anyway, the heat kills you. The fumes'd gas you out in a cellar like this and the heat'd burn up any bank notes in a safe before you got to 'em. All right for jewels or gold maybe—but the oxygen you use . . ."

"What's that?" I said pointing.

"A bicycle tire. We'll just see if it works—"

The lights went out.

I heard Irons curse in the darkness, and groped my hand back against the wall. After a minute he put on a pencil torch. Neither of us spoke then. The light traveled slowly round the strong room. For the first time he was rattled; I could hear him breathing.

At first dead silence. In it a car accelerated away. Then closer sounds came in—muffled voices, soft footsteps. We waited: Irons reached in his pocket for something that looked like a cosh. *In flagrante delicto* came into my mind. One of Douglas's favorite expressions. *In flagrante delicto.*

Footsteps down the stairs, another pencil torch. Above us something was knocked over; Irons moved quickly behind one of the cabinets. Torch out. Darkness.

The other torch flickered through the hole. "Are you there?" Leigh's voice. "Where are you?"

"Here!" I said.

"Haven't you got a light at all? The bloody lights have fused. John——"

Irons put on his torch again; Leigh's nylon-flattened face peered in like something out of a Hammer film.

"We were fixing the alarms: Ted said if we didn't cut them no one would believe it was an outside job. He must have crossed the wires. Lucky he wasn't killed!"

"Damn you," said Irons, and the simple word sounded worse than an obscenity. "You give me a right shock. What's he doing now?"

"He's gone to check with Len, tell him and see the guards are safe. Where are the fuse boxes, Deborah? Any idea?"

"No, I don't——"

"Damn the fuse boxes," Irons said, suddenly urgent. "We got to get a move on with this now. You"—to me —"can you take both torches, hold them so's we can see. I want you t' help me with this safe, Leigh. But for Pete's sake mind the wires. I want the safe turned side on to those shelves. Watch the wires!"

"If you need the drill again you'll need the power."

"Maybe. Maybe I won't need it——"

Ted came clattering down the stairs and pushed his way in, scattering mortar and bits of broken brick. "Deb, d'you know where the fuses are? Leigh's told you—I goofed high and big. John——"

"Mind those wires!" Irons snapped. "Maybe we can manage with this light——"

"We've *got* to find it. Any passing copper might notice there's no lights anywhere."

"I think they're in the kitchen," I said. "There are electric boxes in the corner cupboard——"

"Show me——"

"What's the time, Ted?" Irons said. "It must be——"

"For Chrissake, yes . . . Wait. I'll do that first. You go with Deb, Leigh, see if they're what we—"

"I want Leigh *here!*" said Irons. "I got to move this 'ere safe a few inches if we're to try to—"

"*You* go, then," Ted said, grasping my arm so that I winced. "See if you're right, but don't touch *anything.*"

He went with jerking flat-footed strides up the stairs as I made for the kitchen. I was right: there were eleven fuse boxes, three meters. As soon as I knew I went back to the strong room, found the two men, by the light of a single pencil torch propped on a filing cabinet, heaving with crowbars at a corner of the safe, trying to shift it away from the wall. They had moved it perhaps an inch.

"I don't see—" Leigh gasped, "what the hell—you're driving at."

"You don't have to," said Irons, bunching his muscles and heaving again. "Now *together!*" Another inch.

Leigh pulled off his mask and leaned exhaustedly against the safe, wiping his sweating face with the stocking. For a few seconds they both rested.

"What are you getting at?"

"Look," said Irons. "I told you. All safes have this anti-blowing device. If I set off that charge in the keyhole and it breaks the lock, the new bolt falls and jams the door worse'n ever. Right?"

"If you say so, yes."

"Now look. How long does it take that new bolt to fall into place? Half a second, fifth of a second, tenth? Eh? Well, supposing you just judge right and the charge of gelly is just enough to crack the lock without jamming the handle an' all. And someone happens to be pulling on the handle to turn it just when the charge goes off. The part of a second'd be enough to turn it before the new locking bar falls. So then the bar doesn't jam the door because the handle's already been turned. The door's open. Right?"

"I don't know. I don't know how they work. But any goddam fool who had his hand on the handle when the charge went off'd lose his hand."

236

"I know, man, I know! That's why I brought this here in my bag." Irons picked up the bicycle tire.

"I don't see—"

"It's got to go from the safe handle to that shelf bracket. It's the only thing I can see that's strong enough and just the right height. But we'll want to move the safe another six or eight inches."

Leigh still looked unconvinced, but he bent to help, and the strain and stress began again.

Ted was looking in, pulling off his stocking. "O.K. Were you right?"

"Yes."

"Show me."

We went down the passage to the kitchen and I showed him.

"Was it all right again—the phone call?"

"Yes, it was another bloke at the other end." He took a deep breath and peered at the switches. "Now, the whole flaming lot of the lights have gone so it must be a main fuse. One of these three. Can you shine the light?"

He climbed on a chair and I shone the light. As he clinked open the second box he gave a grunt and scraped around in his pocket, took out a bit of old fuse wire, switched off all the switches, and pulled out the fuse. Three minutes and he replaced the wire, put back the fuse, shut the box.

"Now wait for it."

He pulled down the switches one after the other. The pilot light outside the kitchen door came on. "Thank Cripes for that!"

Sweating he slithered off the chair and stood a minute, then went to the sink and sluiced his head and face in tap water.

I went back ahead of him to the hole in the strong room, from which the full light now shone. Irons and Leigh had moved the safe about another two inches. They had no more crowbars, but Ted took over from John Irons, and slowly, with infinite stress, they made the last few inches.

Irons picked up the tire and looped it round the built-in steel bracket that supported a shelf. Then he tried to stretch it to meet the safe. It just reached and he looped it over the safe handle, so that the handle was being pulled round to open.

Under Irons's directions they began to lever the safe away again so that the tension on the tire grew until it could grow no more. Satisfied, Irons paid out the trailing ends of wire until they were through the hole into the passage. I went out first, and the others followed, leaving Irons to fix the carpets. He did this, taking care that none of them got in the way of the handle or the wires; then he followed us out and we all crouched down out of reach of the blast. I watched Irons fumblingly connect one of his wires to the little battery and then just touch the terminal of the other.

The explosion in the confined space was sharp, and hit the ears like a gunshot; the basement echoed and vibrated. But none of the lights went out.

Irons led the way back in, pulled away the carpets. The tire had slipped or been blown right off it, but the handle had turned. Irons put his hand quietly round the handle and pulled. The safe door came open.

Of course I had seen them before in the showcases. I had seen others just as beautiful and valuable displayed, discussed, examined, auctioned. Jewels were nothing new to me. But because of what we had done, these had come to have a special and terrible significance. All the effort of the night had been aiming at this one moment, all the preparations, all the sweat and risk and terror. A few small glittering bits of mineral stone; to peer, to finger, to stare; it seemed ridiculous, slightly obscene. After a minute I drew back and let the three men bend over them.

Even they for a while seemed startled and without purpose, as if their ideas had not led them further than this; then Ted Sandymount picked up an attaché case, and carefully the jewels were taken out of their boxes and dropped into the cotton wool with which the attaché case was lined. I looked at Leigh's expression. It wasn't triumphant yet—tension still stretched the muscles and drew in the mouth.

John Irons was the only one who looked satisfied. While the others put away the jewels he took up a dampened cloth and began to wipe the safe door and sides and top and everywhere that could possibly have been touched. Part of the time only he had worn gloves.

It was twenty-five minutes to four. If this trick had failed, three hours of drilling would have been running it almost too fine.

Ted Sandymount saw me look at my watch. "I got to do it once more. If we're ready in ten minutes I'll put the call through just before we skip. That'll give us a full half hour—thirty-five minutes—before anyone gets suspicious. Nearly through, John?"

"Just to pack my things. Just to pack my things."

"You, Leigh?"

"Ready right away."

"Which car shall I go in?" I asked.

"I'll come with you in the Mini," Leigh said. "It'll be safer that way."

"I got to deliver these," said Ted Sandymount, twitching as if he had a fly on his nose. "You come with me, John?"

"Yes. We got to drop Len too. Do that first. Len's had the easy street."

"Anything else to pick up?" They looked at me.

"No," I said quite coolly. God, was I going to become practiced at this? In five hours I was due back at Whittington's, a simple innocent girl.

Last minute searches. Anxious thoughts. Anything forgotten? A button? A fingerprint? A handkerchief? A torn coat leaving a thread of tweed behind? A cigarette end? A pencil? A footprint? A lipstick? A laundry mark? A torch?

"How are the two guards?" I said to Ted.

Irons was carefully stowing his things, methodically, like a plumber at the end of his day. Ted was changing back the plug that had worked the drill. Leigh had piled the carpets in a heap, had pushed the door of the safe shut with his foot, was now standing half out, waiting for the others, his face still stretched as if the nylon mask had pulled it out of shape.

"Shall we go ahead of you?" he said.

Ted screwed in the end of the plug. "If you like . . . No, wait. One opening of the back door is enough."

Irons finished stowing his things. Ted sat up on his haunches, looked at his watch. "We've five minutes to wait yet. You three go up and wait in one of the showrooms while I put the call through."

A last look round the wrecked room. They all dragged on their masks. "Put something round your face," Leigh said to me. "For Pete's sake."

I tied the scarf round my hair so there was a piece left to go over my face. We left, went up the stairs to the ground floor. Ted walked along to the telephone office, went in. We sat on a couple of settees in the first showroom, like prospective clients waiting for the auction to begin. The room next door was where the auction should have started in seven hours time.

The door opened but it wasn't Ted.

"You've not been some bloody time, you 'aven't," Len said, coming up with us. "Two and a 'alf hours! Why, I—"

"Shut your gob!" said Irons.

"Well, you can't hardly breathe in the thing. I been half-dying in the thing!" He put a gloved hand up inside his stocking and tried to mop his face.

We waited.

Another car in the distance, and I thought I heard a train hooting.

"Anyone know what the fog's like?"

"Clear."

"Just our bleeding luck."

I didn't sit next to Leigh. Whatever we felt for each other, this was not the time to feel it.

The squeal of brakes. I looked at my watch. A quarter to four. John Irons's tennis bag lay in the shadow like a dog at his feet. Ted had taken the all-important attaché case in the room with him.

I heard the ting of the telephone as it was lifted. For the last time tonight the code word "Harrogate" was being used. At four-fifteen there would be no call. At four-twenty the guard at the other end would send a general alert. By four-thirty at the *very* latest the emergency squad of Safeguards would be round at the building, probably with police too. It gave us at the most forty-five minutes—forty to be sure. No time for loitering. No time for going back for things overlooked. Pains in my stomach back now. I kept remembering I'd dropped a comb or left my handkerchief in the strong room; the pains got worse with each fresh twist in my brain.

Ted came out.

"Right. Let's go."

Down the passage past the reception counter to the door. Ted shot the bolts back, opened it gently, peered out. A fine misty light. The faint humming noise of London even at dead of night. He was a long time looking. Len prodded him. Ted slipped out. Len followed. Then I. Then Leigh. Then John Irons, who gently turned the door knob behind him.

Pulling off nylons. "I'll thank you to keep your bleeding hands to yourself," Ted snarled at Len.

"O.K., O.K."

"You go first," Ted said to Leigh.

Leigh took my arm. "All as planned for tomorrow?"

"Sure. Sure."

We left, stepping into the bright sodium light of Bruton Yard. Silent cars. Silent shadows, black striping the concrete. The tabby cat mewed round my legs, but I couldn't stop to stroke her. We walked arm in arm. Came to the narrowing mouth of the yard. Turned left into Bruton Street. A car came down, passed by us traveling slowly. Chauffeur driven. Safe. A taxi stopped at the corner, a man paying it off. Bruton Street a mile long. The corner at last. Berkeley Square. The big showrooms and the expensive cars. *Very* bright. As light as day. Waste of electricity. We had to walk a quarter of the way round the

241

clock to reach the car. No word between us. We were strangers linked only by a common purpose.

Police. Two policemen stood talking at the entrance to Berkeley Street and Hay Hill.

Leigh changed sides so that he would block me from their view. "Cross here," he said.

We crossed diagonally, making for three cars still parked. The policemen had their backs to us, but at a big old car fifty yards short of the Mini, Leigh stopped.

"Wait. I don't want them to see us get into the car. Maybe they'll move."

They didn't. They stood there talking. They stood there while the green lights went yellow, went red, went yellow-red, went green again. No traffic, but the robots worked in a dead world. Someone was walking along the park side of the square, approaching where we were standing. Leigh put his arms round me and began to nuzzle his head against my scarved hair. A single man, walking slowly. We didn't look at him as he went past.

Footsteps retreated. At the same time the two policemen began to move. But they turned round and walked slowly west. We watched them go past, watched them move slowly off toward Hill Street.

"Now."

The last hundred yards. He went on ahead, unlocked the door of the car for me, was already whirring the starter as I came up, got in.

The engine fired, choked and stopped. It was a cold night. He tried again, and this time the engine fired and began to run.

We drove off.

Before I got home a fierce headache was setting in. When I got in I was sick, and the headache became even worse, as if my skull was opening and shutting. Leigh had it too but not as badly. We used the last of the aspirins and lay together but it was practically impossible to sleep. I was sick again and at seven o'clock felt terrible.

Leigh was frantic because he rightly saw that the whole

242

plan might come to bits if I didn't turn up at nine-thirty as if nothing had happened. He cursed me for wanting to stay and cursed himself for letting me. If I'd gone home as planned none of this would have happened: Irons had warned about the gelignite.

At seven-thirty he went out for more aspirins and gave me some in brandy, but this made me sick again. I got up at seven forty-five and had a sip or two of tea and then went back to bed again.

Leigh said: "Look, love, take it absolutely easy for another hour. Then get up slowly and I'll drive you there."

He switched on the radio at eight but there was no mention of what we listened for.

At a quarter to nine I got up and took a bath. He coaxed me to try to eat something but the sight of food was enough. I took another three aspirins, in tea this time, and my head began to throb less violently. I could open my eyes and move without nausea. He took six aspirins himself and watched me like a man watching a racehorse on which he's staked his whole fortune.

I can't express the dread I had of going back to Whittington's that morning. It seemed inconceivable everyone shouldn't know exactly what I'd done. It seemed equally inconceivable I shouldn't show it on my face.

Back in the car—after so short a time—my legs, both legs, shaky and weak. Leigh helped me in, drove me very fast to the West End. He talked all the time, maybe trying to take my mind off what was ahead.

Weather fine today and milder. A west wind was blowing the last of the fog away, and traffic was thick. He put me down at the corner of Grafton Street. There was no hope of his being able to stop, but as I felt blindly for the handle to get out he said:

"Remember, this is the last bit. We're in injury time. Get through today and we're on velvet. Remember, love, you're doing it for the future, for that shop, for marriage to me—God help you—for setting up in business, for our future together. I wish to God I could help you. I'm just praying and keeping my fingers crossed. I'll not come for you tonight because the less I hang around here the safer it is for both of us. But I'll be waiting at home for you, Deborah."

"I feel I *look* awful."

"You don't—honestly. That bit of make-up has given you a top-of-the-milk look. Nobody'd possibly think a thing. Listen, when you go in, don't be remembering what's happened at all. Think about our holiday in Spain —all the fun we had. Think about shopping in Cadiz. Think of the next time we can go. We could go there for our honeymoon."

I got out. From there I could see the entrance to Whittington's, and beyond the cars at their parking meters I could see, immediately outside the main door, two cars with blue lamps on their roofs.

Chapter 22

"Come in," said Detective Inspector Malcolm. "Miss—er —Dainton, isn't it? Sit down, please. Just a few routine inquiries."

Peter Greeley's office on the ground floor; just three of us, the other being a constable taking things down.

"Miss Dainton, you've been with the firm—is it seven and a half years?"

"Yes. It will be eight in May."

So far less trouble than I'd thought. All in such confusion that no one had time to remark on pale face, tired eyes or—possibly—guilty look. Place closed to the public, staff and principals all sitting about in one big showroom, police moving everywhere, no business.

"What time did you leave last night?"

"Oh—about half past six, I think. Or it may have been a bit later."

"Were the guards here then?"

"I don't think so. I didn't see them."

"Do you usually see them?"

"Not unless I stay late."

"What time do you usually leave?"

"Between six and six-thirty."

"You were a little later last night?"

"I had quite a bit to do. And I half-expected Mr. Mills to come back."

We hadn't been allowed downstairs at all. Stopped almost in the door. Directed into the big showroom. They said it was to allow the police a free hand—fingerprints —photographs.

"Who was in your office when you left?"

"Nobody. Miss Fent had gone about twenty minutes before, and I switched off the lights as I left. Mr. Smith-Williams was still in his office—or at his office door— talking to one of our commissionaires called Davidson."

"Which door did you leave by?"

"The back entrance. The one into Bruton Yard."

"Why? Was that usual?"

I opened my eyes a little. "I don't really know. Sometimes I leave one way, sometimes the other."

"Was there someone at the door? Did someone see you leave?"

"I can't remember. Most people had left by then."

"Was the door open or shut?"

"Shut. But not locked."

"Did you—thinking back now—did you see anything suspicious, anyone loitering near the door when you left?"

"No. The yard was still about half full of parked cars."

"Was it possible, d'you think, for someone to come in that way, unseen by any of the staff, and hide in the building?"

"I don't know. I suppose it could have happened."

Just looking out of the corner of my eye I could see the drink cupboard which still stood open, the bottles pushed to one side as I had pushed them, the alarm switches switched up into the OFF position: I tried not to look at it: I tried not to let my head turn that way. One glass missing. The glass I had taken home and broken and thrown in the river.

"Where do you live, Miss Dainton?"

Well, it had to be faced. "At No. 23, The Lane, Rotherhithe."

"Do you live alone?"

"No . . . I live with Mr. Leigh Hartley, who rents the studio."

The constable looked up slowly, but not at me, bit his pencil. Inspector Malcolm had a strong-boned face, close-cropped hair with a ridge where his hat came, a scar on his lip.

"You're—not married to Mr.—er—Hartley? You'll excuse these personal questions—one tries to fill in a general picture."

"Mr. Hartley's already married but separated from his wife. He's at present trying to get a divorce."

"When you hope to be married?"

"Yes. When we hope to be married."

"How long have you been living there, Miss Dainton?"

"Since—it would be last October."

"Before that?"

"I lived with my sister in Ennismore Gardens."

"How long have you known Mr. Hartley?"

"Since last April."

"What is his—what does he do for a living?"

"He's a clerk in Rodwell & Lloyd, in Margaret Street."

"Does the firm—this firm, I mean—know of your association with Mr. Hartley?"

"I don't think so. It didn't occur to me that it was their business."

"No . . . Your address, then, with them is still Ennismore Gardens?"

"It may be my parents' house in Hampstead. I lived at home until about June of last year."

"What is your father, Miss Dainton?"

"A doctor. So is my mother. And my sister."

"Quite a medical family, eh?" Inspector Malcolm plucked at his scar. "Do your parents mind your living in Rotherhithe?"

"They have three daughters. We all live away from home."

". . . Yes. It's the general trend these days, isn't it. I have a daughter myself who'll soon be wanting to spread her wings. More's the pity . . . Well, thank you, Miss Dainton—that's about all for the moment. I hope you

247

won't mind having your fingerprints taken. We're doing the whole staff including the directors—it's a question of elimination, you see."

"No, of course not." I got up as he did.

"Oh, Miss Dainton, one thing," as I got to the door. "Did you know how the alarm system worked?"

I turned, would have been glad for once of my stick for support. "The alarm system? I knew there was one." How hard to keep one's eyes from that cupboard. Perhaps it would be more natural to let them stray. I let them stray.

He said: "Ah, I see you know where the switches were."

"I knew there were switches there. I didn't know quite what they did. I was in this office at Christmas when Mr. Greeley opened the cupboard and took out some bottles."

"What we're trying to establish, really, is how many people are likely to have known how the alarms worked. It seems certain to us that whoever broke in had a very close knowledge of the whole set-up, and if a fair number of people in the office knew of it, aside from the directors, one or another may have talked—quite innocently —and given secrets away."

"I suppose we all knew a little," I said. "But I don't think any of the girls knew enough to be *really* helpful to a thief."

"You'd be surprised what people can pick up," said Malcolm. "They go about mixing in a friendly way. They hear one thing here and another there; piece tiny bits of information together and gradually build up a picture and make a plan. The really good finger man, as he's called, is very astute and very practiced . . . Well, thank you again . . . Er—send in Miss Fent, will you, Rogers."

At twelve Peter Greeley sent us all home. A surprise but I suppose one might have expected it. Once the staff had been interviewed they could only get in the way and hinder investigations. In the building there were at least six plain-clothes policemen; as well as a man from the forensic science laboratory, a photographer, a safe specialist from Pemberton's, a loss adjuster sent by Lloyds and the Chairman of the Safeguard organization.

"Opening tomorrow at the normal time," Peter Greeley said, smiling grimly at us. "Business then as usual. This is just one sale that won't take place—at least for the present."

All the directors were taking it philosophically—partly perhaps because they were fully insured, partly because there was no other sensible way to take it. I realized that in that Leigh had been right—burglary when it didn't involve violence was an impersonal thing. Apart from McCarthy with his bruised head, nobody was *suffering* for this theft. It amounted to a transfer of money from an insurance company into the pockets of certain individuals who had risked their freedom for gain—who still risked it. There were no sorrowing widows, violated girls, aching hearts or desolate parents. This was the line Leigh had drawn at Sarah's flat, and except for the one act of violence against McCarthy, they had succeeded without overstepping it.

Only Smith-Williams seemed to take the robbery as a personal loss. He had persuaded Whittington's to employ the Safeguard organization, and he'd been responsible for the general precautions; it was an affront to his own competence that all this had failed, and his manner implied that the staff had in some way failed too.

Mary Fent was delighted at having the day free and, as we fended off several reporters, suggested we should have lunch together and then try to get in at the matinee of the latest musical; but my head was still throbbing so I made an excuse and left for the East End by bus.

Very tempting to ring Leigh and tell him I was free and suggest lunch; but I had a feeling that I was still on sufferance, still being observed by some God-like eye trained on me from Scotland Yard, and that the least variation from the norm was best.

So I sat in the bus and read the midday edition of *The News*. "West End Jewel Haul. Night raiders grab £200,000 from strong-room safe at Whittington's. Guards coshed." While the bus bumped and bobbed, my eyes fled over the print—foolishly surreptitious, as if as a member of the staff concerned I should not be fascinated anyhow. "Effected an entry by means of first-floor window—daringly planned—inside knowledge—alarms jammed and then cut—four masked men—guards overpowered—code messages continued to be passed—strong room dynamited and safe smashed—Gwalpur emeralds —Plouth diamonds . . ."

I knew it all.

"Police under Detective Inspector Malcolm conducting extensive inquiries . . ."

I knew that too. But where would it stop? Not for weeks. Not for months. Patiently, quietly ferreting.

River full, a welcome sight after being invisible for three days. I pulled the curtains of the studio back farther to let in more of the wintry light. It was a fluid, shimmering light such as you get nowhere else in London, born of sky and reflected river. Wind was blowing the low clouds gustily across, but here and there were streaks of green of a quite improbable color as if put there by an inspired artist—the way Bach in the midst of formality makes his point by a sudden discord.

The studio smelled dank again, and I put on a fire and kicked off my shoes and warmed my feet. But it was my heart that needed warming, and not even Leigh could do that.

For I had realized that in this enterprise neither he nor I had seen far enough. How *could* we buy the shop in Lambeth, how *could* we put down even the deposit with a promise of more to come, while the police were searching and ferreting as they would be now? At this stage they wouldn't actually suspect anyone in the firm, and they might never do so; but a young woman who had just gone to live with an artist-cum-clerk in Rotherhithe, who had thrown over her family and connections for this rather sordid entanglement, would be much more under their eye than the same young woman going home dutifully each night to her doctor parents.

Supposing, then, she and the man appeared to have no money, and suddenly produced seven thousand pounds to buy a shop, wouldn't they ask where it came from? This was the eternal problem of the thief in modern society: if he stole money, how spend it without rousing suspicion?

I went in stockinged feet to the window, sat there for a time watching the wind licking the river, watching cloud and smoke mingling in gray-brown wraiths and wafting away. Somewhere the gulls were crying.

Headache threatening again. I went into the kitchen and put on the kettle. While doing so I cleared the breakfast mess which we'd both been too preoccupied to tidy up. Then I lay on the bed and drank tea.

The tea was like new courage seeping into my veins. It was like a shot of morphia after pain. Anxieties began to relax. They were all there just the same but they hadn't such power to hurt. The police might suspect much but they would first have to prove. They might even never suspect at all . . . It was so easy to find yourself guilty when you knew you were.

I must have fallen asleep and dozed for upward of an hour. The bell woke me. Half past two. I started up: too early for—but police—or telegram—or baker—or . . .

As I opened the door a woman was turning away. She stopped and looked at me, startled. She was the woman I had seen here once before, Leigh's father's next-door neighbor.

I smiled in relief. "Did you want Leigh?"

"Oh—er—well . . . I just called . . . Is he . . . ? He's not in, I suppose?"

"No, he won't be back till about five-thirty. Can I give him a message?"

"Well, no . . . that is, yes . . . I left a note . . ."

She seemed scared. Good-looking, as I realized before, fortyish, fresh young skin, good eyes with very clear whites, brown hair with curls round her forehead. Navy blue twin-set with tweed skirt, navy mohair coat.

I realized I was standing on a letter, picked it up, smiled again. "Is this for Leigh?"

"Yes . . . I rang just thinking he might be just in. But I didn't expect—to find—er—anyone else . . ."

She hadn't expected me. "I'm never normally home at

251

this time; but . . . You're a neighbor of Leigh's father, aren't you?"

A shadow crossed her face. "Is that what he says?"

"I thought he did. Do come in for a minute. It's cold here."

She hesitated. "I oughtn't to. Leigh told me not to come round."

"Well, he won't be home for hours yet, and I've just made a cup of tea. Like one?" I felt a need for company, ordinary decent female company, and she seemed nice. You could talk to her about everyday things.

She still hesitated. "I don't think I ought, miss—er—"

"Dainton."

"I don't think I ought. You see, I don't want to upset him."

"Why should you upset him? Anyway you can't if he never knows you've been."

She fumbled nervously with her gloves and looked round as if expecting someone at her elbow. "Well . . . I really don't know."

She came in. I put her letter, marked by my shoe, on the table where the post usually went, and encouraged her into a chair by the electric fire. Of course the tea was cold, but I put the kettle on again. When I came back she had slipped off her coat and was warming her hands, which had seen a lot of rough work. We discussed the fog until the kettle boiled, then I went and made the tea and brought it in on a tray and we sat and sipped together.

"Is Mr. Hartley not well again?" I asked.

She flushed. Color came to her face very easily. "Oh . . . Leigh's told you that, has he? No, he's not well. He gets bronchitis in the winter, and this year it's been much worse. We wonder if he'll be able to keep his job. He's not due for a full pension yet for five years."

"D'you want Leigh to go and see him?"

"Yes . . . that's what I do want. He hasn't been near us for nearly a year. Of course his dad didn't approve of the way he was living, and said so; and it made for poor feeling; but I'm sure Joe—that's my husband—would be glad

252

to see Leigh to talk things over. I think it would really do him good just to meet him and talk to him again."

Light dawning. "You're not Mr. Hartley's neighbor then—you're his wife? You must be his second wife—Leigh's stepmother. I wonder why he never told me about you!"

The woman sipped her tea. "No, I'm not his second wife, I'm his first. I really don't know why Leigh should be ashamed of me!"

Emotion then. Two women, both rather weepy—though I think she didn't see mine for her own. Soothe her agitation while trying to soothe something in me. Alarm bell. Why, why? No sense, no reason. Teacups clattering shakily. I expect I misunderstood him, Mrs. Hartley. No, no, that's what he likes people to think; I shouldn't have told you; he'd be furious with me. Well, he'll never know.

A cigarette, perhaps? Well, a cigarette. Leigh's packet on the mantelpiece, three left. No matches. Oh, thank you, I've a lighter. Click, click; flame flickering near moist eyes, draw in, hide behind the smoke. Do you not smoke, Miss Dainton? No; I did once for a bit but I gave it up. Joe doesn't now, he used to; I don't at home because it makes him cough.

Embarrassed silence. Another cup of tea? No, thank you, I really must go. Do stay a little longer; happy to have met Leigh's mother.

She about half-finished the cigarette while I busied putting the cups back on the tray; then quite suddenly she said: "I really don't think he's *ashamed* of me. Not really, you know."

"I'm sure he isn't. Why should he be?"

"But he likes to make things up. He likes to feel different from other people. He likes to think things are different from what they really are. To be an orphan, to sound motherless. It's an attitude. He was always a good boy but he used to make things up, still does. His schoolmaster used to say it was his way of escaping from real-

253

ity. His dad used to get very cross—didn't make allowances. I hope—I hope it hasn't upset you, Miss Dainton, I hope you won't let it get back to him."

"No, of course I won't. But . . ." clinging to a last disbelief ". . . you look too *young.*"

"Oh, thank you. I'm forty-four. Maybe I haven't gone gray; maybe that's it."

"You were very young, then, when Leigh was born."

"Twenty-two. It seems young now." She saw something in my expression. "Did you think Leigh was older? I *mustn't* talk any more. I shall say something I shouldn't. I'm always *talking* too much, Leigh says."

"No, no. Go on." In spite of the tea my hands were very cold, circulation suddenly poor. "It doesn't matter. Leigh and I are very fond of each other. This won't—make any difference."

She said: "What lovely hair you've got, Miss Dainton. Has Leigh painted you?"

"Once or twice." I laughed dryly. "Not as often as he painted his wife." And waited.

The clock ticked. "Oh, Lorne," said Mrs. Hartley, fumbling with her handkerchief. "D'you know I hardly knew her."

So that was all right. Not just an excuse not to marry me. Hands out to the fire; but draw them back because they're not awfully steady.

Mrs. Hartley said: "Only twenty at the time. Very impulsive, but Leigh *is* impulsive. I met her—I met Lorne —for the first time at the church. It was awful."

"What was awful?"

"Well, nine o'clock in the morning and only four people there, and the Catholic priest would hardly look at us because we were Protestants. It was over in five minutes. We might have been lepers."

"Was this in Swindon?"

"No, a church near here."

"Do you live in Swindon—or in Clapham?"

"Oh . . . In Clapham, Miss Dainton. I've been there all my married life."

"And Leigh lived with you?"

254

"Yes—until he left home. His dad was against it, him leaving home at nineteen without a proper job. At least he didn't think it a proper job, working part time for this man, Mr. Foil."

"Did he work for Mr. Foil?"

"Oh, yes, before he came here. Didn't you know—Mr. Foil has an antique shop. Leigh worked there."

"I didn't know."

"His dad wanted him to go on the railways. Said it was steady and he could paint in his spare time. Leigh's painting and drawing was always a bone between them. Joe never believed in it. But you think he's a good painter, don't you, Miss Dainton?"

"Oh yes. He's good."

The sky had cleared while I dozed and the clouds were reflecting a reddening sun. The derricks on the other bank looked briefly like flamingos bending to drink at the edge of a lake. A string of barges moved downstream, sliding quietly with the tide.

"His dad says I spoiled him, him being an only child; but I didn't really, Miss Dainton, not really. He was brought up well, and well looked after, and that always shows, doesn't it. He'll make good yet, I'm always saying to Joe. Don't worry, I say. Joe thinks because we had it hard, he has to." She drew at her cigarette uneasily. "I really must go."

"Where do you live, actually?"

"Right overlooking the Common, the top floor. It's a house that's been divided up. No. 28, Albert Road. It was lovely tea. Thanks."

"Don't go. I've often said to Leigh I wanted to meet his family. Did you say he was an only child?"

"Yes. So was I. Perhaps it's in the family, like. But he was luckier than me. My mum and dad both died when I was four. I was brought up in an orphanage. You wouldn't think—or I hope you wouldn't think . . ."

"No, I certainly wouldn't!"

"I went into service, first. But then I got into a shop. John Lewis's, it was. In Oxford Street. As an apprentice. I was doing very well. But the war came and I joined the

ATS and after a couple of years I met Joe and we got married and I had Leigh. After the war Leigh was still a tiny baby and you couldn't leave him all day long to go back into a shop. But after he went to school I went into service again. Not regular, of course. Daily woman, by the hour. You get paid quite well, and it helped out. We could buy things that we couldn't have on Joe's money. A fridge. Vi-spring mattresses. A bicycle for Leigh." She smiled suddenly. "D'you know, Miss Dainton, we've never had anything on the H.P. all our lives. It's old-fashioned, I know, but we don't believe in it. I still go out two days a week, and we save what I get till it's enough to buy something. At Christmas we bought an electric toaster, chromium, one of those that pop up when the toast is done. But it doesn't work too well. We joke about it. One side toasts pale and other side dark. Joe says it must believe in a color bar . . ."

"Have you been," I began, "were you artistic yourself?"

"No, not from me. I never could draw at all. But his dad paints lovely water colors of flowers. He always says he hasn't got a garden so he has to paint one . . . But it's a hobby with him, you see. He thinks it ought to be only a hobby with everyone. With Leigh. That's why they fell out."

"Was it your husband's sister who left Leigh the legacy?"

"What?" She stared. "Oh, that bit of money. No . . . it was his grannie, Joe's mother. He won prizes at school; two drawing prizes. But he wouldn't work at other things. He's clever, you know that."

"Oh, yes . . . I know that."

We sat in a strangely companionable silence. While she was talking I had listened to her light, pleasant voice. There was nothing there of Leigh's harshness. It was almost without accent.

I said: "Leigh's never told me much about this legacy. But I'm afraid he's spent it now."

She said: "Oh, Grannie Hartley didn't leave any

money, but she left a little house, and we sold that. Half went to Joe and half to Leigh . . . Yes, I'm afraid he's spent it long since. That's what Joe doesn't like—living above yourself, he calls it."

"I know what you mean."

"And Joe thinks Mr. Foil is the wrong influence. Joe thinks that's wrong." Mrs. Hartley got up. "I really must go. It's been nice."

"It's been very nice."

"Leigh's told me about you, of course; but he—he sort of doesn't want us in his new life, I think that's it."

"If you were my mother," I said, "I'd want you in my life."

She flushed again. "Oh, d'you mean it? It's lovely to hear you say that . . . Really lovely. Don't tell him I've been, will you, dear?"

"I'll say I found the note. Actually I'm only here by chance—because of something that happened in my office . . ."

He got back at six, looking just the same. Clear eyes —like his mother's—narrow nose, curly, tight, untidy hair, heavy lids, brilliant teeth. Leigh. My love. My lying love.

He was full of questions. He wanted to know every detail . . . He didn't look at all tired for the loss of a night's sleep. His headache had lasted till midday but unlike mine was now gone. I turned the questions. The jewelry, he answered, had gone straight to Jack Foil. For two or three days more nothing would be done; then it would be moved by easy stages to Amsterdam. The money would take time to come through.

Until the visit of Mrs. Hartley I'd been pressed by fears of the police. Though these fears still stalked I felt unable —at least temporarily—to discuss them with him. I'd been standing on rock and part of the rock was quicksand.

He didn't mention the shop in Lambeth.

I pointed out the letter and he opened it.

"From your father?"

"Well, more or less. He wants me to go and see him. Maybe I will. Next week, maybe, I'll take a day off and go."

I said: "Was it your father's sister who left you this legacy?"

"What? Oh . . . sort of. It was an aunt."

"How much did she leave you, Leigh? How much have you got through?"

He took my shoulders and kissed me. "It's gone, that's what matters. It wasn't much. But now there's a lovely lot to come. God, I was scared last night. I was so scared at the beginning that I could hardly think straight. D'you remember how I snapped at you when you came back? Sheer funk. I never thought I'd be so weak in the knees and paralyzed with funk."

"I was scared myself."

"You didn't show it. You were bloody marvelous. I shall never forget the way you played along right through to the end."

"That's the way I'd like it."

"What?"

"To be able to play along right through to the end."

He shifted uneasily, sensing something in my voice, I suppose.

"D'you know," I said, "I never knew you'd worked for Jack Foil in his shop?"

"Who told you?"

"Ted."

He looked at me, but his gaze seemed to be centered more between my eyes than actually looking into them.

"Yes, I worked for Jack for about nine months before I got the legacy and moved in here. It was interesting but I got bored. Then I came in for this money and moved."

"Was this after you married Lorne or before?"

"Oh, before. Look, Deb, I've got to go out again. I—"

"How did you first meet Jack Foil? You've never told me."

"In a pub. Ted first and then Jack. I was in a dead-end job pushing a pen, but wanting to paint, aching to. I meet Jack and he says he'd like to see some of my stuff. I show it him and he takes one for his antique shop—a flower painting of all God damn things—and sells it, *and* sells it! Maybe he wasn't as surprised as I was. But he took an interest from the start. The first professional ever to see real talent in what I did. And he's never lost faith, that's still more!" Leigh took up his leather jacket and began to struggle into it. A piece of the lining had come away, and he made a couple of attempts before finding the sleeve. "After I'd known him about six months he said would I like to work in his antique shop, as a sort of assistant and general helper. I jumped at it, because it meant I could get time to paint."

"Did you know he was a fence then?"

"Not on your life! He wasn't such a fool as to confide in a youngster."

"Leave your jacket tomorrow," I said. "I'll mend it."

"What? Oh, I only did it yesterday. Look, I don't know what time I'll be back."

"Where are you going?"

"With Ted to lose that old Austin. The risk's very slight but there's just a slight one—you know, some copper took the number while it was parked outside Whittington's, that sort of thing. The idea is to ditch it. What's the time now—just after half six? Oh . . . should be back well before ten. But don't wait up if I'm late."

"Leigh," I said as he moved to go.

"Yes?"

We stared at each other but I said nothing. I was looking for some warmth, some reassurance, some companionable glance which told me we were still two against the world.

"What is it?"

"Oh, nothing."

He smiled cheerfully and was gone.

Chapter 23

Prowling taxis don't prowl in the East End. I got one at Tower Bridge. Albert Road is on the north side of Clapham Common, and No. 28 is a corner house with a view of the common through the bare trees. There were three bells and I pressed the top one. After a while Mrs. Hartley opened the door. She stared.

"Oh, miss—er . . . Oh, I didn't expect. Is anything wrong?"

"No, no, but I just wanted to see you again for a minute or so. Do you think I could?"

"Why, yes." She hesitated. "Come in . . . I'm afraid it's a long climb . . ."

I followed her up two flights of stairs.

"You must think it strange—my coming so soon after you called."

"No, no. Pleased, I'm sure."

"It was just that I thought . . . Leigh was out and I thought . . ."

We went into what originally had been an attic but was now, for all its sloping ceiling, a well-furnished sitting room. Everything was neat and in good condition. Style modestly modern. A gas fire licked its white gums and kissed at the television, which flickered back. Between them sat a short bald man with a mustache. He wore a shiny blue suit and was in his shirt sleeves.

"Oh, Joe, this is—Miss Dainton. I'm sorry, Miss Dainton, we weren't expecting visitors." She hurriedly switched off the television and put on another light.

Mr. Hartley got up and shook my hand and looked awkward. I said I hoped I wasn't spoiling his program, and Mr. Hartley's chest rattled and he said no, it was a poor thing: sometimes you just went on looking because it was too much trouble to get up and switch off.

Polite conversation. He was about five feet six and stout, with a thick neck. His voice was much more like Leigh's, hadn't the roundness of his wife's, and you could see where Leigh got his stockiness from. His mustache was trimmed to look fierce, but his eyes had a way of twinkling when the cough didn't empurple them. A good lot older than his wife.

We talked about the railway and the weather and the troubles of housing. They had three rooms on the top floor: a kitchen, a bedroom and this sitting room. Three years ago the house had been bought by a Pole who had tried to turn them out. The people below had been intimidated and had gone.

"Not us," said Mr. Hartley. "Not that it's much to look at but we've nowhere else. Then they put colored people in the flat below. Now I'm not anti-color. If you don't believe in the brotherhood of man there isn't nothing to believe in. But this became a whorehouse. Couldn't get up and downstairs. Fighting. Shouting and screaming all the night. Couldn't sleep. I went to the County Council. Man there said he couldn't do nothing. Wasn't his business. If we didn't like it, hadn't we got somewhere else to live? Relations? Well, I ask you."

"I'll put the kettle on," said Mrs. Hartley.

"What did you do?" I asked.

Joe Hartley had a discussion deep in his chest. It was an earth tremor without being an earthquake. "We hung on, Miss Dainton. It was, well, I can't properly describe it. I was afraid for the wife, oftentimes with me on night

261

shift. But she wouldn't move either . . . In the end it was all right. The police done it—did it for us. Cleared them out. So we're still here."

"Was Leigh living here then?"

A shadow on the plump red face; eyes losing their fun. "No. He'd gone before then."

I said: "You know, I expect, Mr. Hartley, that Leigh and I are—in love with each other, that I'm living with him?"

His eyes seemed to go to my thin leg, then moved on. "The wife told me."

"I expect you don't like that."

"There's worse things."

I said: "I know I'm putting things badly—too bluntly —but I felt I had to come and see you after meeting Mrs. Hartley this afternoon. It was only this afternoon, but I wanted to see you."

"I like people to be straight." His smile was half-interrupted by the earth tremor in his chest. "I like that. But why did you want to see me particular?"

". . . I felt I wanted to talk to you."

"About Leigh?"

"All sorts of things. That chiefly."

"Has he been telling you lies?"

I ran a hand down my cheek; it seemed to hurt. "Does he do it so often?"

"The wife told me she'd seen you. It's hard to get a grasp of my son. *I've* never been able to Miss—er— what's your Christian name?"

"Deborah."

"Deborah. I never have, I tell you. He said he was an orphan, was that it?"

"He said that he had no mother. I . . ."

"It don't make sense, do it?" Mr. Hartley bent down to clear his throat and his bald head shone in the light. "What's it you want to know, Deborah?"

". . . It's just with seeing Mrs. Hartley . . ."

"Ask what you like. I don't mind."

"Well, I've been left feeling so confused, not knowing

262

what to believe. This legacy, for instance? It really did exist?"

"From his grannie? Yes. Three hundred and fifty pounds it come to. It wasn't much but it gave him ideas. He was working for this man Foil, and he thought he'd branch out and become a proper artist. Foil found him this flat, this studio in Bermondsey, and he went to live there with no proper work to do."

"Three hundred and fifty pounds? But that wouldn't keep him!"

"Nor did it for long. Mary tells me he's working now. That'll be good for him. Perhaps you've been good for him, Deborah."

"But how has he lived for two years?"

"Ah, that's for him to tell you. Perhaps he's worked on and off. We don't know."

Mrs. Hartley came in with a tray of tea. The crockery and the way it was laid showed she knew how it should be done. She put the tray on the oak gate-legged table and put up one leaf. The chairs in the room had flowery chintz loose covers and the curtains were of yellow ribbed nylon.

We were helped to tea. "Lovely flower pictures," I said.

"Ah, those are my husband's, Miss Dainton. Aren't they nice? Remind you of spring. My favorite is those wallflowers."

"That's what Leigh should have done." Mr. Hartley supped at his tea. "Paint for pleasure, work to live. Maybe he would have but for this man Foil. Though I don't know. He was always a queer lad."

"Is he seeing much of Mr. Foil now?" Mrs. Hartley asked.

"Yes . . . quite a lot."

"Possessive, that's what they call it," said Mr. Hartley. "Possessive. He got hold of Leigh, influenced him, like. More than I ever could. Likes people running after him, doing little jobs, at his beck and call. Queer, men like that. Queer. Not queer in the other sense, mind. He's got a wife. Sort of baby doll. Though I did think once, I did

263

think once he might be queer in the other way, the way he took it when Leigh married Lorne Riley."

I put my cup down. It wasn't Rockingham but it was a pretty good imitation. "Didn't Mr. Foil like Leigh's wife?"

"Well, part of the trouble, I reckon, was that he done it—did it without telling Foil. Leigh took up with this Lorne girl about three months after he'd moved into the studio, and I reckon Leigh thought Lorne had a bit of money put by and between them they'd be able to manage without Foil. Well, he didn't like that at all. By then he thought he owned the boy." Mr. Hartley stopped and rumbled. "Am I saying too much?"

"No. Please go on. Don't stop him, Mrs. Hartley."

Mrs. Hartley said: "Joe, it wouldn't have broken up if they'd been really in love. Mr. Foil just helped it along."

Mr. Hartley said: "He just helped it along. But that's why I wasn't sorry to hear Leigh had taken up with someone else. It shows he's still able to order his own life. Has Foil tried to break it up between you and Leigh?"

"No . . . He seems to approve. I don't know why."

Mrs. Hartley offered me another cup of tea. I shook my head.

"D'you know," said Mr. Hartley, wiping the ends of his mustache, "I remember when I was a lad hearing a parson say: 'Christ commands you to love your enemies. He doesn't say you've got to like 'em.' Well, d'you know, I sometimes feel that way about my son, God help me. I love him—of course I love him. But I can't truly say I really like him!"

"Joe! What a thing to say! In front of someone who—who—"

"Oh, I know, I know. But it's not that I'm saying there's nothing good in the lad. He's full of good intentions. And agreeable enough, most of the time. Couldn't wish for a better lad to share a day off. And serious in some ways. Oh, it could have been worse, much worse."

Mrs. Hartley said: "All that's true and much more. And never one to go after the girls much—rather shy."

"Shy," I said. "I wouldn't have thought that."

"He hides it by pretending not to be. You think he's full of confidence and really he's terribly short of it. I say to Joe he's got much more confidence than Leigh has but he doesn't need to bluster and show it."

Talking for a few more minutes. Somewhere in the conversation another poisoned arrow. Sometimes you get them shot into your soul, but you can't exactly locate them. It was something I'd said myself; that was curious.

Time to leave. I must go. Mr. Hartley got up and had a conversation in his chest and then said goodbye. "Come again, please. I believe you'll make a man of him."

Mrs. Hartley insisted on showing me out. We went down the first flight in silence, but as we began the second, she said: "You must think it awful, Joe saying what he does about Leigh."

"No. He's a very honest man."

"He is, Miss Dainton, he is. To him, telling untruths, cheating even in small ways, stealing even in the way they called 'winning' things in the army—he can't stand any of them. It's never done him much good in his job, all the same. He's never got any promotion because of it . . . And it never helped him to get on with Leigh, who has this artistic temperament, half dreamy, half practical, like. He couldn't understand why he had a son he couldn't understand." She laughed nervously. "If you see what I mean."

We got to the front door. She peered at me anxiously. "If you're in love with each other I hope nothing we've said will spoil it."

"Of course not."

"There's so much good in Leigh. We never had trouble with him as a boy. And as for leaving home . . . well, it wasn't much here to have to sleep on a pull-down bed in the sitting room, it wasn't much privacy for a boy to have, or a place to keep his things. You can't wonder that he jumped at the chance to leave."

She was holding the door so that I couldn't go through it. I wanted to go now.

"You're a lady, Miss Dainton, aren't you. I can tell. Haven't you always found Leigh gentlemanly?"

265

"Yes."

"I mean it's all the little things that count. Modesty for himself and for others. He has a sort of taste, a sort of delicacy. D'you know, from when he was eight he never let me in the bathroom when he was in the bath—would always lock the bathroom door. And—and he always puts down the toilet seat after using it. And he never took liberties, never was vulgar. He swears a bit, but I've never known him use a vulgar expression. Some people may laugh at these things, but it's so easy to be slipshod, not to care. I think those things count."

"Yes," I said.

She let me go and I left.

Down Latchmere Road toward Battersea Bridge. On the bridge I stood and leaned over the coping looking up the river and at all the glittering lights. A pleasant evening, and mild. All fog had gone; the wind had dropped; London hummed like a great pink-flushed beehive newly awake after three days of coma.

I knew now where the poison lay. But it could still be poison of my own imagining. How prove it one way or the other? Taxi. An address in the Old Brompton Road. Not far this time. Lights flickering everywhere. As light as day almost, but different. A sort of twilight that impinged on the mind. Green and red, safety and danger, love and hate. Jerk and stop, swing and turn, stop and jerk. Green and red, love and hate. Yellow like pain. An hour's sleep last night. An hour today. But lack of sleep doesn't always blur the preceptions; sometimes it refines them, gives them a cutting edge. Lack of food too. What eaten in the last twenty-four hours? Tea and brandy and tea and brandy and tea. Sweetened hemlock. Great ghosts and phantoms moved in the taxi.

I got out, paid him, he drove off; I looked up at the shop. Closed of course. Eight o'clock. Never noticed the name before. *Sefton Antiques*. Even with the name of his own shop he was in the background. In the window were two Hepplewhite chairs, a Georgian silver teapot on a mahogany three-legged table, wine-glasses on a tray, bound copies of *Punch* for 1891–5.

Up the stairs to the glass door. A very faint light somewhere, but at first, after I had pressed the bell, nothing but the distant yapping of dogs. Wait. Footsteps after all. Doreen Foil. Hair loose. Flowered housecoat. Mules. Cigarette.

"Deborah! Why I . . ."

"I came round for a minute. D'you mind?"

"No . . . er—no. Lovely . . ." She drew back and I went into the greenhouse-foliaged hall, followed her into the long living room. She flapped vaguely across and made light here and there while we were talking.

"Jack isn't here. He's away. Did you want to see him?"

"No . . . Leigh's out and I was feeling lonely, and a bit strung up."

She sat down opposite me, drawing her housecoat modestly over her knees in a way she wouldn't have if she'd been wearing a frock. We talked about nothing much. The dogs were still yapping, and she confessed that when Jack was away she often kept them in the spare bedroom all day because they got on her nerves. "I take 'em out twice a day, but it's such a drag. I don't know why they can't have boxes for their business, like cats." Spilling ash, she offered me a cigarette and then a drink, or coffee. I said no, thanks, but I was almost passing your door and—was she expecting Jack back tonight?

"I'm not sure, dear. He said not to wait up. Not that I'm likely to, after last night!"

I looked at her, startled. "Last night? What had you to do—"

"*Well* . . . it was this Silver Cross Charity Ball at the Hilton! Jack had often said he'd take me but I never thought he would. He took a party—six of us—it must have cost him a bit as tickets were five guineas, without wines. We didn't get home till after three. I've been yawning my head off all day!"

"Lovely," I said. "You are lucky." Expensive, but cheap as an alibi. "I think I will have coffee, if it's not too much trouble."

"No. Sure. It'll only take a minute." She was different, easier tonight with Jack not here. I must get something out of her—but what was there to get? She pushed her loose hair behind her shoulders, her eyes a bit glazed with lack of sleep, flapped her way past the Umbrella Tree and the Scarlet Trails, dropped ash by the further door, went out. "Shan't be a minute."

Room silent. Light, confined within black drum shades, was only permitted out on sufferance. Plants drooping, watching. Mother-in-Law's Tongue, Catherine Wheel Plant; aquarium light. Shelved books, good crockery. Get up to look at that. An open desk. Papers, letters, cheque book, invoices. What chance? What to look for?

Slap, slap, slap. "Forgot to ask, dear, d'you like it black or white?"

"Black, please."

"O.K." *Slap, slap, slap.*

Room silent. An open desk. Four drawers. If she wore her mules you could hear her moving. She wouldn't suddenly take them off. Three or four minutes to make the coffee. Pick up cheque book. *Sotheby's,* £295. *Cash,* £50. *H. S. Seaton,* £25.10.–. *Silver Cross Society,* £31.10.–. *Leigh Hartley,* £20. *Cash,* £50. Letters . . . "Acknowledge receipt of chair." "Dear Mr. Foil, Please see if you have other Georgian spoons of the King pattern." Waste of time. Drawers . . . First locked. Second drawer, mass of papers. Square envelopes, out-of-date bank sheets, bills, travel folders, dinner menus, photograph (unrecognizable). Try another drawer. Bottle of gum, secateurs, ball of green twine, seed and plant catalogues, Gardener's Diary. Last drawer . . .

I stopped. The room was silent but there was some sound, some movement. I stared all round, and all the plants stared back. Supposing Jack Foil came up the stairs . . .

But the dogs were silent. I opened the last drawer. Whittington's catalogue, profusely scribbled over. A letter in Leigh's handwriting . . .

Slap, slap, slap. I jumped back a foot, pushing the drawer, not able to grab the letter. She came in.

"This—is a lovely plate," I said.

"Oh, that . . . Yes, it's Spode or something. But of course you're an expert, aren't you?"

"Who told you?"

She looked surprised. "Why, Jack said so. When we met the first time . . ."

I took my coffee and we sipped and talked. I tried to lead the conversation round to Leigh, but she had nothing new to tell.

I said: "I suppose Jack still pays Leigh a salary, does he?"

"Oh, that I wouldn't know. Jack's got a lot of irons in the fire. One day he's down at the docks, next day he's up at Hurlingham. He has a meat business, did you know? And a building yard. Maybe Leigh still works for him, I wouldn't know."

"But Leigh comes here often, doesn't he?"

Doreen sipped the drains of her coffee and left a little brown mustache. "You're not jealous, dear, are you? I promise you, you haven't need to be. There's nothing like *that* about Jack."

"No. No, that's not what I mean. But you see Leigh and I want to get married, and he's awfully evasive about money. I wondered if you knew."

" 'Fraid not. But I'll ask Jack if you like. In a roundabout way. But he's cagey, too."

"It doesn't matter."

"Well, tell Leigh to keep in with Jack, that's my advice, Deborah. It really is. If he keeps in with Jack he'll be all right. It'd only be if he fell out with him that it might be all wrong."

I said: "I must go. Leigh will be back. Tell me one thing, Doreen. How long have you known my sister?"

"Your—sister? I never have."

"Yes, you have. Dr. Dainton."

"Oh . . . Dr. Dainton. The tall girl . . . Oh . . . God knows; not very long."

"Longer than you've known me?"

"I can't remember."

"Do try."

269

"What does it matter? . . ." Doreen screwed at her earring. "I suppose we may have. She came in the shop one day and Jack invited her up to meet me and to see the room plants. It's his pet hobby."

"Did she talk about me?"

"When? Then? I wouldn't know."

"What I'm trying to get at is . . . Had you heard of me before—say before last April?"

Doreen shook her head. "Honestly, I wouldn't know. Why?"

"When did she come in to see the plants? Would it be before last April?"

"It could have been. God knows." Doreen bent and lit another cigarette with a silver lighter so massive she could hardly get her hand round it. She paused. "Wait? Is that Jack now?"

The dogs were barking.

After a minute she relaxed. "No, it's somebody next door. Paula's so damned edgy these days that she barks at everything, and that sets Rufus off. D'you think dogs suffer with change of life? I mean bitches?"

"I expect so," I said.

The telephone box is at the corner of Old Brompton Road and Juniper Street. I hadn't a threepenny piece but I'd plenty of sixpences.

Purp, purp, purp, purp, purp. Press the sixpence in. "Sarah?"

"No, this is Virginia."

"Hello. It's Deborah here. Is Sarah in?"

"No, she's at the hospital."

Oh, damn, blast, damn. "D'you know when she'll be back?"

"Haven't the faintest. You know what it's like; they expect her to work all hours."

"Yes . . . yes. I see."

"What's the matter? You sound agitated."

I took a grip of my voice. *"No,* not a bit. It was just something I wanted to ask her. I'll try again in an hour or so."

"Can I get her to ring you?"

". . . No. We're not on the phone."

"O.K., dear—I say, what about this robbery at your place? That was pretty sensational, wasn't it?"

"Oh, *that*. Yes, it was." Come to think of it, Doreen hadn't mentioned it. Didn't she know where I worked or wasn't she as innocent as she pretended?

"Any theories? D'you think it was an inside job?"

"I doubt it. Just a gang of smart crooks."

I hung up. Out of the box I hailed a taxi, but when I gave him the Rotherhithe address he said he was off duty in twenty minutes and going north.

So I went home by bus.

Didn't take too long really. The bend of the river somehow helped. The East End bustled this evening as noisily as the West. Past a cinema where Leigh and I had sometimes been: a fifty-times-life-size woman in a swim suit leered down among the colored lights, bosomy, with long beautiful legs.

I got off in Jamaica Road, turned up among the quieter places, the warehouses, the storage sheds. Smell of the river. No little red car outside. Nothing had changed, nothing had stirred while I had been away. I let myself in.

I put on all the lights, stared round the room with its big sagging dusty velvet chairs, its tall windows, its stacked canvases, its empty easel. Outside, the river still moved, London glittered and glowed. I didn't draw the curtains. Leigh's desk. All the time I lived here it had stood open, papers and bills and receipts and oil paints scattered. But although I had used it to write letters, cheques, the occasional note, I had never pried into it. This was no great virtue—or if it was a virtue it was only practiced by instinct. Only once, when he refused to tell me his debts, had I threatened to search it.

But must *not* search it now.

Sit and wait. *Must* not jump to conclusions. Must reserve judgment, as Philip's father would say. Judge only on fact, not on suspicion.

Sit and wait.

Chapter 24

At ten I went out again, to the telephone opposite the *Brunel,* the pub that Leigh would never let me go in because he said it was no place for ladies. (Curious what he would, and would not, let me do as a lady.)

Virginia answered again. Sarah still not home. As I returned to the studio Leigh was just parking his car.

"Hello, love. Been out somewhere?"

"Yes . . . I was ringing Sarah."

He followed me in. "Lack of a telephone's a damned nuisance. Anyway we shall *have* to afford it now."

"Why?"

"In our new place, I mean."

"Oh."

He took off his jacket and threw it toward the pegs behind the door. It hit them but fell. I picked it up and hung it with my own coat.

"Thanks," he said.

"Have you eaten?"

"Yes, a sandwich. It'll do."

"All right about the car?"

"Yes, but it took some losing—more than I thought. What's the matter? You still look pale."

"Do I?"

"Yes, frightfully." He came over and kissed me. "How's the head?"

"Better. But I'm tired, I expect. After last night."

"That's why I wouldn't have been surprised to find you in bed and asleep. D'you know," he gripped my arms and smiled into my eyes, "I expected to be flaked out myself by this time; but although I'm ready for bed I don't feel tired. I reckon it's all the excitement. And the way things have gone with such a bang. Whoo-ee! Nobody's been, I suppose?"

"Nobody. Shall I make you coffee?"

"I can make it if you're fagged." He followed me into the kitchen.

"Did Ted come back with you?"

"I dropped him at his place. Perhaps I *might* have a bite of something if there is something . . ."

"There's cheese and some eggs. Shall I—"

"Cheese'll do." While he foraged I made the coffee and we drank it together and ate pieces of cheese on butter biscuits. This was one of his favorite snacks. I didn't know what I was going to say to him—if anything. Perhaps there was nothing I could say, yet.

"What was the trouble about the car?"

"Oh, not trouble really. Ted drove it, and I followed in the Triumph. It was just picking a spot."

"Have you seen Jack?"

"No." His eyes questioned. "He's out of London making his contacts."

"What about the shop?"

"The shop? . . . Oh, we ought to see it tomorrow, oughtn't we."

"Well, we've got till Sunday. She said she'd keep it till then."

He chewed reflectively. "We could put down the deposit. It'll be a few weeks before our share comes in."

"What is our share going to be?"

"We'll have to wait for Jack for that. I'd say ten thousand or near it. Everything's gone like clockwork."

"So far."

"Why? What's wrong? Something *is* wrong. Deborah . . ."

"Perhaps it's only something wrong with me. The reaction."

"You should have gone to bed, love. You know how ill you were this morning. Phew! I began to sweat! If you hadn't turned up at Whittington's as usual . . ."

"It's the human element, always letting one down."

"But you *didn't*. You made it fabulously. I don't know what we should have done without you."

"You'd have done nothing," I said, pouring another cup of coffee. "There was nothing any of you could have done."

He watched me in silence. "That's true. That's certainly true." He added: "Jack realizes that."

"I know he does."

Leigh swallowed a last corner of biscuit. "What had Sarah got to say? Did she mention the robbery?"

"She wasn't in. Virginia answered." My blood was thumping painfully. If I attacked I should have all the advantage of attack, but I knew I should really not be able to use it. Wait. Judge only on fact, not on suspicion. If I spoke now I should be desperately, emotionally upset at the first words.

"Did Virginia mention it?"

"Yes. She said did I think it was an inside job? I said I thought it was just some smart crooks."

"How right you were . . ."

I finished my coffee.

He said: "The light's pretty terrible in here," and got up to switch on the other lamp.

"No, leave it now."

He came across and stroked my forehead and hair. "Bed for you, love. You're tired out. You'll feel quite different in the morning."

When I got to Whittington's the next day a couple of detectives were still there, but men were already repairing the blown wall of the strong room, and the broken window and other damage had already been put right. It was surprising, though, how much disorganization the burglary had caused, and about eleven Mr. Greeley called the staff together and said, much as he regretted stealing back from us the half-day's holiday we'd had yesterday, he'd consider it a favor if everyone would come Saturday morning to try to get the rooms completely back to normal by Monday.

After this, instead of going downstairs again, I went to the coin box in the main entrance and dialed Sarah's number. When she had been on duty late she often slept on, but I wouldn't wait longer than this. But there was no reply. The ringing went on and there was no reply.

I worked till 12:45 and then went out to lunch. Still slightly dazed, still bitterly thinking.

Usual cafe. Busy today. A waitress I knew smiled and waved me toward a table where two people were just getting up. It was a table for four, and the two still occupying it were German girls, one very blonde, both pretty. They smiled at me as I sat down and I smiled back. Then they went on with their conversation.

Not hungry. Stare dismally down the menu while the waitress licks her pencil; I choose a Dover sole, sit back as she leaves, loosen my scarf. Try Sarah again. The telephone here is coin box without the privacy of the box, but it will serve.

The bell went endlessly on. Either she was already out again or had never come home. Back at the table the two German girls were just beginning their meal.

Someone coming to the table. A shadow blocking the light, coming to the vacant seat. I shifted a bit.

"Miss Dainton, how nice! Well met, as you might say. D'you mind?"

A shadow indeed blocking the light. The one that lay across us all.

"Excuse me, ladies. I'm sorry; I'm a big man. These small tables are very difficult. No, please don't move."

Cuffs not very clean today, showing against the furry wrists. Diamond links, stain on waistcoat. He would have passed for many things other than what I knew him to be; a lecturer in Oriental Art at a minor university, a

275

well-to-do publican, a middle-grade solicitor with a thriving divorce practice.

He ordered sausage and mash. "My common tastes. You'll excuse me, Deborah, there's much to be said for simple fare, the food of ordinary people . . . In fact I often eat here when I've been to Sotheby's."

"We're a bit disordered at Whittington's," I said, pulses beating suffocatingly, "owing to the burglary."

"Of course. I read about it. Very clever, wasn't it. Very clever indeed."

"We don't know yet."

"How do you mean?"

"Well . . . whether they'll be caught."

Pebbles glinting like prisms, he looked at the German girls. "I doubt if they will be. People who plan such a clever robbery . . ."

My food came. I forced myself to begin.

He said: "You called to see me last night."

"Yes . . . Well, no. Doreen. I called to see Doreen."

"She said you were worried about something."

"Was I? I don't think so."

"She said you looked worried."

"Oh . . . I expect it was just—late nights and that sort of thing."

"That sort of thing . . . Yes. You were asking her, though."

"What?"

"Asking her questions. I thought perhaps you were worried."

"Why should I be?"

"Doreen said you were asking about how long we had known your sister."

"Yes . . . Well, we just talked. We talked about a lot of things. That was just one of them."

A long silence between us. His food came. The German girls were laughing, sharing a personal joke.

I said: "Leigh was out. I felt lonely. I thought I'd call. Doreen seemed pleased."

"Oh, yes. Yes, she's a friendly girl." He piled floury

276

potatoes on his fork and put them in his mouth. "She said you were also asking about Leigh."

"Was I? We talked about him. It's natural, isn't it?"

He smiled. "German. Such an ugly language. And yet it sounds pretty, coming out of pretty mouths."

"Please?" said the blonde girl.

"I beg pardon. I was thinking aloud." To me he said: "You were—first class the other night. Leigh's told me. Ted's told me. It's just what I thought—what I expected. The elite person always stands up to test."

"Thank you." I passed him the tomato sauce.

"But," he said, "these things have an aftermath, a backwash. The higher strung you are, the worse it is. Don't let it get—into your system."

"Oh?"

He eased his stomach against the bleached pine table-top. "All is going very nicely now. Your part is over. My part—the hardest part, in some ways—is just beginning. But don't worry. All will be well. Ask no questions. It's better really."

"Is it?"

"Just now we've got to be careful, but later on—who knows—we might plan a little holiday together, just the four of us. I know Doreen has quite a liking for you—as I have a liking, you know that. Have you ever been to Majorca?"

"No."

"We might go there together, this summer, the four of us. I know a little place. It would be rather jolly."

I hadn't finished the sole but I put my knife and fork together. I watched him cut a slice of sausage.

He said: "But just for the present be careful. Better not to call. It might be remarked, who knows? Later on —we can celebrate, just you and Leigh and Doreen and me. Ted if he wants, but Ted is rather—a rough diamond, as the saying is. He doesn't quite blend. You know what I mean."

"I must go," I said.

"So soon. I was hoping . . ."

277

"What?"

He smiled with blind eyes. "That you'd stay. D'you know, Miss Dainton, I can't get used to calling you Deborah. I was going to tell you—oh, but it sounds boastful—I was going to say that when a windfall like this comes in I always give some of it away. Usually to waifs and strays. Or the physically handicapped. The Purley Heritage for thalidomide babies—that sort of thing. It helps."

"What?" I said bluntly. "How does it help?"

"It helps to be able to. D'you know that Toc H saying —'The rent we pay for our room on earth.' That's how I feel when a windfall comes in."

"I'll remember that," I said.

I couldn't ring again during the afternoon. Anyway the probabilities were that Sarah would have another spell of duty until five or six and then have the evening off. This was a pattern which had occurred before.

I might even go round to see her after work. Leigh had said he would not be back early tonight. I think in the euphoria of success he was going to call and see his parents, but this was only speculation.

Over the length of the afternoon the tension built up in me so I couldn't concentrate on anything at all. Numbers and pottery marks blurred, voices reached me from a distance. Twice Mary Fent asked me if I was ill. She said she felt like a touch of flu herself.

Every day at Whittington's nowadays became endless. This was Friday. On Wednesday none of it had yet begun. Only my adventure, my aberration perhaps, had begun months before.

About five, I saw Inspector Malcolm talking to Smith-Williams. They were going through a list together. Missing jewelry or the suspects on the staff?

I left as it was going dark. When it came to the point I couldn't face the possibility of a fruitless journey to Ennismore Gardens. Wait at a telephone booth. Many people still in the streets, the last of the office people and senior staff from the shops, drifting away to trains and movies and home and TV and books and bed. The commonplace life, the ordinary human life which somewhere on the way I had lost.

In. Dial. "Sarah?"

"Yes?"

"Oh." Now it had come I had lost the words.

"Deborah? Sorry I was out last night. Anything important?"

"Well . . . I just wanted to ask you something."

"Say on. But, ducky, how are you? Did the robbery upset you?"

"I'm all right—"

"Odd we should be talking about that sort of thing when you came to dinner—"

"Sarah, this is just a homely little personal thing; but d'you remember when Leigh and I met?"

"Do I not! When I threw that party I didn't realize I was laying a gunpowder trail!"

"Before then—before that night—did you know Leigh well?"

"No, I'd met him twice. Both times with David Hambro."

"So did he know you had a sister?"

"He probably knew I had two. David could have told him even if I didn't. So what?"

"What I'm trying to find out is whether he knew that one of your sisters was medical and the other wasn't."

"What on earth can you want to know that for at this stage? He soon did know when he met you!"

"But did he know *before* he met me? Try to think."

Silence at the other end. Suddenly I didn't want her to answer, wanted to close my ears and my eyes, to hang up the receiver and leave the box and go home.

"He *probably* did. I think at David's he asked me about my family. It's not an unnatural thing to discuss."

"Did he—" I stopped, choking, not able to go on.

"What is it, darling? Are you upset? I can't tell whether you're upset or—"

"I'm laughing. Sorry. Sarah, it's just a silly joke." I snorted and held my throat. "Just one other thing. D'you remember that apple green Rockingham plate you and

279

Arabella clubbed together and bought me for my birthday
—the birthday before last?"

"Yes, of course. Have you bust it?"

"No. Where did you buy it?"

"That's our business!"

"No, seriously, Sarah. I must know."

"From that shop in Old Brompton Road."

"Sefton Antiques?"

"Yes. That friend of Leigh's who was at your firework
party. Foil."

"I suppose he asked you in to see his indoor plants?"

"Not then. Later."

"How much later?"

"Oh, dear. I don't know. It was Christmastime. Not
this Christmas. The one before."

"Thank you, darling, that was pretty much what I
wanted to know."

Chapter 25

I was feeling queer, so this time it was lucky the taxi driver would take me.

Jog along. Lean back in the dark impersonal womb of the cab hidden from the peering lights. Still some mistake? Still only a hunch? Pray that it was. Pray for error. Pray for shame at a shameful suspicion. Pray that Leigh perhaps would be home after all, to talk, to comfort, to reassure. To lie?

The small middle window slid down. "Which way from 'ere?"

"Turn left. It's off Rotherhithe Street."

So again into the quieter places, the warehouses, the parking lots, the storage sheds. Like last night. Like all the nights. Again no car outside. I paid the taxi driver, went in.

Lights. Fires. I slumped in a chair in the kitchen, put a damp tea towel to my head. For a time I seemed to lose awareness of my own identity. Minutes passed. Then I got up, took off my coat, went back into the studio. It was too late to feed the swans.

Leigh's desk. The bottom drawer only, I remembered from dusting, was locked. The letter of his I had seen last night at Jack Foil's showed that correspondence passed between them. It might be innocent, but in any case Leigh by nature was less careful than Jack and might have failed to burn . . .

I sat and stared at the desk. To do this would be to take the step that was not retractable. To make a move of enmity between us that was not retractable. No going back. Better wait until Leigh came and have it out with him direct. But how did you have it out with a man you loved but did not trust? Love destroyed judgment, suspicion destroyed love.

Wait a bit. Eat something. I'd only swallowed a few mouthfuls at lunchtime. I went into the kitchen and opened the tiny fridge; there was nothing that attracted. Back in the studio. Look through tonight's evening paper. Already the sensation of yesterday was forgotten. Whittington's had no more claim on the attention than the half hundred other places which had been robbed in the course of the last year. It was not even mentioned. The press were concerned with a new parking scheme, a baronet's divorce, a story of rape in a respectable suburb.

I threw the paper on the floor, picked up a magazine, but that soon followed it. Time was passing. Come soon, Leigh, come soon.

I went to the desk. It was a plain oak desk with three drawers, six cubbyholes above, a flap that let down, one brass support broken. It had probably been new from Waring & Gillow or somewhere about 1925. Ink stains and paint stains, papers overflowing. Suddenly I began. Quite suddenly I began. I began. I started at the top left-hand cubbyhole and began methodically to search . . .

For twenty minutes I searched, until the sweat came out on my forehead, and my hands were trembling. Absolutely nothing. But the bottom drawer was still locked. I had always noticed it while dusting, while hardly remarking—certainly not resenting—the fact. I had been through the cubbyholes and the other two drawers. Absolutely nothing.

I went into the kitchen and put on the kettle for coffee and came back with an iron rod Leigh had found on the beach one day. It had a beaten end like a screwdriver, and Leigh used it for opening cases. It was now used to open a drawer. •

Not nicely done. John Irons would have hated the mess. I split the wood all round the lock, bits of it flaking onto the linoleum, before the lock gave way. I felt as if I were destroying some part of Leigh, and some part of myself.

. . . Books, letters, receipts. Drawer only half full. Catalogue from King Charles Shop, Carnaby Street; travel folder of Southern Spain; manual of birth control; photo of his mother; passport (he'd be twenty-three in April); school reports in a rubber band; new paperback of *The Perfumed Garden;* copy of the will of Annie Hartley, deceased; tenancy agreement for the studio.

Letters. One from his mother dated three weeks ago. *"Dear Leigh, I don't understand why you never came near us once all through Christmas, the present was nice, and thank you for it but it isn't the same as you just even calling in for an hour or two. Your Dad . . ."*

Lorne's handwriting. Four letters. But the latest was dated last May. *"Dear Leigh, Thanks for yours. Its no good writing like that because Im telling you its all over between us. As weve agreed all along havent we. And its no manner of good raking up Stevies name for he never ment a thing to me as you well know. You still havent sent my manicur set which was a present from a friend when I left Cork so you might send it please. And theres that book of wildflowers with those bits pressed in it we collected that day in Suffolk you could send that too. Im staying here the summer as summer is the busy season. Then maybe its back to Ireland. Ive paid two of the bills you sent on but dont think I should pay the groceries. Lorne."*

Letter in a man's hand—asking for the last payment on Triumph Spitfire.

Tin box. Unlocked. In it money. About twenty pounds in notes; some insurance stamps; foreign stamps cut off envelopes. Four or five brief scrawls on exercise book paper. One, which had had something pinned to it, was folded over. It was just a few lines of writing, signed *J.F.*

It said: *"This is the final from the Vosper thing. You did well to get on to it so quick, but you've got to realize that the boys in Switzerland did the work so they take the big cut. J.F."*

There was another one which still had a paper clip attached. The clip had gone rusty with the damp air, and the money enclosed had long since been used. This said: *"If you can make it all right with her take her to Spain. Sunshine is very useful for softening ladies up. I'll foot the bill. J.F."*

The water had boiled away. The kitchen was full of steam. I switched off the electricity and tried to vomit in the sink. Nothing came up.

I went into the tiny bedroom and collapsed on the bed. I lay diagonally across it, head without pillows, stretching my stomach.

I was walking hand in hand with Leigh across the soft green slopes toward Beachy Head. It waved like a sea, and in the distance were yellow cushions that seemed sometimes to be cushions and sometimes to be toadstools. Leigh's hand was clammy, and I came to understand that Leigh also was a part of the decay of the world. Nothing grew but what grew in cellars and breathed poison and foul air. Corruption, death and decay. The contamination of disease that I had suffered at the age of eleven was nothing to the contamination that my mind and soul suffered now. The room was beginning slowly to go round. Every second I stared at the yellow toadstools the spinning world went faster.

I rolled off the bed and fell to the floor, body on the carpet, knee bruised, face on the cold linoleum.

Time passed. I lay very still. If I made no move perhaps it would go away. Yet nothing could take away the fetid and sticky emanation of the truth.

The distant clock chimed a half hour. Raise head. Get slowly to feet. Weak, frail, cold.

On top of the wardrobe were the two suitcases in which I had brought most of my things to this place.

Shakily I stretched up, lifted one down, opened it. Open wardrobe. Underclothes, stockings, skirts, hardly know where to begin. Shoes, frocks, summer coats; as always, more grew even in a few months than had ever been brought by case. And there was the porcelain in the next room. None of it broken yet, even after two moves. *"Dear Leigh, please send me the Coalport plate painted with flowers by William Cook. I have paid the two bills I owe but not the groceries . . ."*

Hands still shaking like malaria. I folded three summer frocks, laid them in; two skirts, a couple of blouses. Ten minutes to pack the case. That done, I clicked the catches, lifted it off the bed, looked up at the other case, could not somehow begin on the next.

Couldn't act. Couldn't rest. Back into the studio. A ship was going past the windows, gaily lighted. I opened the French windows and stood out on the balcony to watch the lighted ship disappear round the bend of the river. It was like the last of my hope and my love.

Sheltered here, not cold. I thought of the firework party, when all had gone so well. I thought of New Year's Eve and the Very lights and the echoing sirens, echoing in the distance. I thought and thought, and there was nothing my mind could touch that wasn't contaminated.

I thought more clearly of all the time since last April: the early meetings, the separation, the coming together, the portrait, the holiday, the break with my family, the suggestion first put forward in November and the gradual procession of events since. I thought of learning to skate and learning to dance and learning to drive. I thought of learning to love.

When I got back in the studio I was shivering. I put on heavy winter coat and scarf against a cold that was not the winter cold. Yet all this time my mind was exploring the shock, even while my body still cringed from it. It was like someone badly wounded whose mind moves ever more rationally and clearly, even while death is creeping up toward it.

One last thing. One last point to clear up. I went out,

leaving all the lights on, walked to the nearest telephone box, opposite the *Brunel*. I looked up a Temple Bar number. Still no threepenny bits. A sixpence went in.

"Safeguard headquarters."

"Oh," I said, "I wonder if you could help me. I wanted to know how Mr. Evans was. Whether he was back on duty."

The man's voice said: "I'm sorry, we don't answer personal calls."

"Oh, *I'm* sorry. I understood he'd been very ill. It's his niece speaking. He didn't tell me he'd been ill at all."

A pause. "Hold the line, please."

I could hear faint whispering. After a minute or so the same voice said: "What name was it?"

"Evans." I gave an apologetic laugh. "Sometimes people call him 'Baker' Evans, I think."

"What's your name, caller?"

"Clara Evans."

Pause. "I'm sorry. There's no one of that name employed in our organization."

"Are you sure?"

"Hold the line, please."

Another pause, and then a new voice came on. "Miss —er—what is the name? Miss Evans? Where are you calling from?"

"A call box. I only rang to inquire about my uncle, if he was better."

"Your uncle being employed by our organization?"

"Yes. One of the security guards."

"Would you give me your full name and address, please."

"Clara Evans of—of 121 Sutton Street, Hampstead."

"I don't think we can help you, Miss Evans. What is the number of your call box?"

"Oh, it doesn't matter." I hung up.

I came out of the box, stood a minute leaning against the side. This was a half-developed, half-condemned area in which waste land, new tall blocks of flats and tiny old houses jostled each other. The small seedy pub with the green blinds looked more like a film set than a piece of

London, for the house on one side had been pulled down, and on the other was a gaunt acre of dumped rusty corrugated iron with two ruined cottages in the middle. The green blinds of the pub stood separated from all other lights. I walked across and went in.

It was early for a crowd even though Friday night. The barman was fiftyish, big and square headed, and there was something wrong with one side of his face. I ordered a large brandy.

So deep had the knife gone in that ordinary feelings no longer registered. Lame—it didn't matter. Venomous, assessing stares—they didn't matter. Wrong change. A cackle directed at me from a girl in carpet slippers. I drank the brandy—no judge but it was harsh stuff.

Prostitutes no different from West End prostitutes. One fat one had holes in her nylons through which bulged little balloons of flesh. Cheapest dresses—*couldn't* they afford better than that? But maybe the dresses didn't count. Three Scandinavian seamen; blond, bony, bad types. A Slav of some sort, unshaven for a week and drunk already. Two spider-legged English boys with long hair. A middle-aged man in a boiler suit. Two old women in carpet slippers.

Silence while I drank. They were watching me. The barman with the plastic surgery face went on sweeping the counter round and round with a dirty yellow rag. Then he blew his nose on the rag and stuffed it in his pocket. I ordered another brandy before the first had gone down. He stared at me and took my glass and pressed it up against the upturned bottle. This time I gave him the right money.

"Lost your way, dear?" It was one of the old women.

I stared back at her. No fear. I knew as much of evil as these people. They couldn't harm me the way I'd already been harmed. What was violence?

Then one of the tarts giggled to draw attention to herself and began to chat to her friend. One or two of the men still watched me, but talk began to break out again. I heard nothing of their talk. It was like the humming and crackling of a radio when the station has closed down.

The barman had said something. "What?"

"Bin 'avin' a day out?"

I put the glass down.

"What's wrong wi' yer leg? Accident?"

The brandy was alight in me, and grief, the uttermost grief, was turning to a terrible anger.

"Mine was a car," he said. "Went through the bleedin' screen. Six bleedin' cars piled up one on top o' t'other. Two stiffs, and me wi' me face pulped like minced liver. Twelve weeks in 'ospital. Nother o' the same?"

"Yes."

One of the men who had been sitting back was at the bar, standing beside me. It was the Slav. I paid for my third drink.

"Never been able to go in a flamin' car since," said the barman. "I git the shivers, minute I put me foot in, like I got bleedin' flu. Shock, they say."

" 'Allo," said the Slav, and put his hand against my thigh, stroking it. I lifted the glass and looked at him with all the grief and anger and hatred. To dash the glass into his face, to make *him* the next for twelve weeks in hospital! . . .

He stepped back. Something had communicated, even though I said nothing, even though he was drunk.

" 'Alf pint?" said the barman.

The man nodded. "You come 'ome with me, eh?" he said, smiling, but the smile was half-hearted. I didn't answer. He was part of the background. If he had struck me he'd still have been part of the background; just something on the periphery of hateful life.

Every now and then since I came out, feelings had come over me as if my head and my heart could contain no more and would swell up and burst. But brandy was helping; it was a solvent, an anticoagulant, helping reason and hurt and hate and disgust and anger and misery to flow. I could consider the idea of killing myself—not as an act of insane despair but as a rational way out. I could consider the means; I had no drugs; the river, of course, was the answer. I could think of the other alternatives to suicide.

I finished this brandy. On the wall of the pub, above the bench where two of the girls were sitting, was a row of comic cartoons: *Gin and It, Black and Tan, Mild and Bitter*. The women thought I was looking at them, and one of them opened her mouth, put her finger in and made an obscene noise.

Somehow I got out of the pub. I was feeling stronger, colder, clearer, but I only remember standing in the shadow of the wall outside and watching the drunken Slav come out; I remember watching and wondering if he would see me. I didn't hide, because it didn't matter.

After he had passed I walked home. It was twenty minutes to nine when I got back. No car.

I went in. The lights burned. I had not shut the door onto the balcony properly and it had blown open. I shut it and sank into one of the leather chairs.

Time passed. Maybe if I'd had someone to talk to then: a friend, a mother, a sister, a priest . . . It needed to be talked out in this time of clarity. To talk, to rage, to weep. This was a venom, a poison which should have been let. Suck out the bite of the snake. Otherwise I'd die. My heart was adrift.

But out of the sickness and the self-damnation, out of blasphemy and derision, out of hate and impurity, an intent was showing up, like a hard seaweed-covered rock as the sewer tide went down.

I went to the desk, dragged a chair over, sat down. Think. Whom would this affect? Everybody I knew and hated. Everybody I knew and loved. Think. This is another form of suicide, slower acting, more disgraceful, with perhaps some life to be lived at the end of it. Think. This damns all, more effectively, *far* more effectively than a sodden corpse drifting out with the morning tide. This too is worse for me, far worse for me. Death is tidy; it shuts the door, draws a line in the ledger, shames gossip, *de mortuis nil nisi bonum;* poor girl, it was a frightful pity, and we never knew the *reason*—well, of course it was *thought,* but the post mortem showed she *wasn't;* anyway who cares about that these days? . . . The coroner said . . . I'm sorry for her parents; and of course

Leigh Hartley who, though perhaps a bit of a lay-about, was *devoted* to her; no reason, my dear, no, no reason . . .

Death is tidy. This solution is untidy, *untidy*. And disgraceful. And full of the light of pure, baleful reason. But *this* is the one I want; this, God helping me and giving me strength, is the one I intend to *take*.

Address the envelope first and then there can be no error. A very short address. *"Detective Inspector Malcolm. Scotland Yard. S.W.1."*

What I write is quite brief. After all, there's no need to elaborate in writing. Talk will do that. A statement, that's what they call it, isn't it, a statement will do that. *"I, Deborah Dainton . . ."*

I am quite explicit, all the same; quite explicit as to what I say and what I do not say. Leigh Hartley, Ted Sandymount, Jack Foil—especially Jack Foil. *We* planned, *we* executed. Whatever alibis have been arranged, *we* executed. Yes, there was an expert safebreaker, but I never saw his face. Why implicate John Irons? He was—so far as I know—no part of the conspiracy. I'm no judge, to assess and condemn. I'm only stating my part and mentioning those who planned it.

Surprising how quickly it can be put down. It flows easily off the pen, for there's no need to qualify or discriminate. Ten minutes. Barely ten minutes. The only hesitation remembering Ted Sandymount's address. That done I signed it. Sealed it in an envelope. Gum on the tongue. Even a stamp handy in the drawer. Post it at once. Post it before.

"Hello, love," said Leigh. "Did you think I was never coming?"

Chapter 26

I get up. Still wearing overcoat, I put letter in left-hand pocket.

"Hullo. You are a bit late."

"Doing a bit of duty work, you know. Can't say I enjoy it but it's nice when it's done."

"Doing what?"

"Oh, just something I had to attend to."

I went into the kitchen, and he followed me in as he had done last night, while I put on the kettle. He hadn't noticed the splintered wood on the bottom drawer of the desk. We made casual conversation. For some reason it didn't lag. It no longer meant anything.

We drank coffee. He said he was more tired than last night, how about me? I said, oh, yes, more or less. Bed then soon?

He ruffled his hair. "I must say you're still looking a bit flaked-out. Was everything all right today?"

"Yes . . ."

"See anything of the police?"

"They were still about."

"I reckon we're on a good pitch. They haven't a clue."

He sucked the half-melted sugar out of his spoon. His eyes were clear and untroubled.

"They've asked me to go in in the morning," I said.

"What, Whittington's? That's a bit thick."

"Well, it only makes up for the half day we lost."

"Ted wants me to go and watch Charlton tomorrow afternoon. I may. Should be a good match."

I said: "It was funny how we met, wasn't it? In the first place, I mean."

"Who? Us? Why?"

"I say it was funny how we met. You and I. If you hadn't come to Sarah's—to that party—none of this would have happened."

"I know." He stirred uneasily. "Do you regret it?"

"Oh, that's not really the point. Sometimes I think these things are designed."

"Designed? What d'you mean?"

". . . Don't you ever read your stars? I'm sure I've seen you."

He laughed, but not absolutely happy about it. "Lovey, we met, and it was the best day of *my* life, I promise you. So why ask impossible questions? This is the moment to look ahead—not back."

"Leigh, I met someone—quite by chance. Someone who knew you as a boy."

"What? Who?" His eyes were suddenly wary.

"It doesn't matter. But this person—this man—this man says you haven't got two brothers, that you're an only child. And he also says your mother is still alive."

A siren hooted on the river and Leigh put down his coffee cup. His face had closed up.

"I'm sorry."

"It's true?"

"Yes."

"But why tell me this?"

He rose. "I'm awfully *sorry*, love."

"But why? If you've lied to me before, there's always been a purpose."

"These weren't meant to be lies."

"Then what were they?"

"I can't *explain*. I . . . I go on. I lead myself on. I have a way of talking. Sometimes it's easier to make a thing up than to tell the truth."

"Even when it helps nothing?"

"Even then."

"How many lies have you told me about Lorne?"

He turned. "None! I swear. Honest. Not one. It all happened as I said."

"But how many other lies are there between us? What else is true?"

"Everything! . . . Oh, lovey, it's just this bloody silly habit I've got sometimes of—of making a drama of something. Sometimes I make up a story like I make up a painting. It's a composition. If—if the river's green maybe I paint it blue. It looks better to me that way, that day. Well, that doesn't matter because next day I can do another picture with another color if I want. But when it comes to stories, once I've told them to somebody else, then I'm stuck with them for good. Once I've told you— because it sounds dramatic—that my mother died young, I've got to go on with that forever. It—just comes out, and I curse myself afterward."

"Did you curse yourself afterward for making up the story of having to wear your brother's outgrown clothes?"

He flushed, and for a moment I saw the likeness with his mother. "Well, no, it wasn't true in detail but it was true in general. I *have* been put to counting my pennies and making do—all my life. That's *true*. It's just what I've been saying—I can't hold my tongue sometimes because I want to make it seem more dramatic. But the real essence is still true."

"And did you ever live in Swindon?"

"No."

"Why Swindon? What's wrong with Clapham?"

"God knows. I keep—trying to build up a life, a separate life. I keep trying to cut away from the old."

"So one of these days you'll be telling some nice new girl that you never knew anyone called Deborah Dainton."

"That's not true! You know it's not true." He came across and kissed me but I turned my face away. "Oh, look . . ." He rubbed his nose against my ear. "You know different. This is basic."

293

"Do I?"

"Debby, Debby, use your loaf." This very gently. "When I met you I wanted to leave *everything* behind— all my past. I still do. But I *never* want to go on from here. This is where I belong . . ."

We stood for a moment, and then moved apart. He hadn't noticed that I'd been drinking brandy; or, at least, he didn't mention it. I began to put the coffee cups under the tap but he stopped me. "Leave them, love. Let's just go to bed. Let's curl up together quietly, like, and leave everything for the morning. If you want to, I'll try to explain more then. But everything will seem different in the morning."

Without much more said we got undressed and into bed. He took me in his arms, but passively, with no intent. We lay there for a time. He seemed once or twice to doze off—his breathing got heavier, then lighter again. Over his shoulder I looked up at the packed suitcase on top of the wardrobe. The light was out but the curtains were partly drawn back, and light from the river reflected on the ceiling like crinkly leaves turning. This bed thy center is, these walls thy sphere.

It must have been half an hour or more before my utter silence woke him. "Can't you sleep?"

"Not really. You try on your own."

"You're still mad at me for telling you those half-truths?"

"I was wondering what will happen to the swans when we're gone."

"When we're gone?"

"Well, if we take this shop."

"Oh, someone will feed them. Anyway . . ."

"What?"

"I suppose someone will take the place before they pull it down. They're sure to want it soon for more warehouse space. I'll be a bit jealous of the people who take it."

"Perhaps you'd rather stay on here. Ten thousand is a lot of money."

He was silent, almost listening to my thoughts. "What's

294

wrong? I suppose I've upset you with these silly lies, but I thought you knew me well enough . . ."

"I thought I did."

"What is it, then?"

A siren hooted again. "I had a terrible dream."

"When? What about?"

"Oh, I can't tell you. Other people's dreams are so boring."

"Tell me if it'll help to kill it."

"That I don't know."

"Well, tell me."

Long silence. He nudged me.

"I had a dream. About a man. Fat and middle-aged. An antique dealer."

Silence. "Any connection with Jack Foil?"

"Oh . . . I don't know. This was . . . a bad one . . . He—he went to all the sales. Sotheby's, Christy's, Whittington's. He had all sorts of interests but he was always greedy for more. He saw all the beautiful things in these places. Often he'd buy things, but that wasn't enough. He wanted the bigger things. And he wanted to steal them. He'd stolen before but not perhaps in quite this way."

I could feel a difference in the muscle tension of the arm that was around me. "So?"

"So he longed to break in. But it was hard to do. Then one day a girl came into his antique shop looking for a present for her sister. She said it had to be good, as her sister was an expert on porcelain and held a position of responsibility at Whittington's."

"Christ, Deborah, what are you talking about?"

I lay quiet in his arms. "Want me to go on?"

"Yes . . ."

"This antique dealer asked some more questions then, found out that the sister wasn't married or engaged—and wasn't likely to be because she had a deformed leg . . . Now he—the antique dealer—had a lot of friends that he helped or patronized one way or another—and among them was a young man. He was genuinely fond of this young man—paid him enough money to live on in return for being at his beck and call. Maybe the young man helped other ways, I don't know. So he suggested to the young man that he should contrive to meet the sister who worked at Whittington's, and see what she was like. If it seemed a promising territory he could try and make her —as the saying is. He thought—"

Leigh roughly shifted his arm from round me, sat up, switched on the bedside light.

"He thought," I said, "that if the young man went the right way about it and the girl wasn't too bad-looking he might be able to get her obsessed with him. He would obviously stand a better chance because she was so lame and not likely to have appealed to other men. Then of course if he could—if that happened—breaking into Whittington's would be easy."

Screwing up his eyes against the light, Leigh reached for a cigarette packet, pulled one out with fumbling fingers, tapped it on his thumb nail. "Who in God's name told you this?"

"It was just a nasty dream."

"Cock . . ."

"All right. I worked it out for myself."

"How long have you known?"

"You don't deny it?"

He swallowed. "It's hard to deny, God help me, because it's partly true. But it's only half the truth!"

"What's the other half?"

He stopped tapping the cigarette but didn't light it. "Oh, Deborah, what a thing for you to find out! Christ, I —I don't know what to say. Who *told* you?"

"Who knows? Ted? Jack? Anyone else?"

"No. No, of course not. But they wouldn't—couldn't . . . Oh, Deb, what a flaming mess! But if you guessed as much as this, you must surely have worked out the rest too!"

I sat up, pushed myself up the bed to lean against the headboard. "What else should I know?"

"*Well* . . . it began like that—or more or less like that. I can't bear to think that you know—you were never, never meant to know—but I've got to be honest with you: it did. But it was only an *idea,* just a general thought, no more. Meet her; see what happens. Nothing more than that. It began that way but it hasn't ended that way, has it."

"Hasn't it? I thought it had ended exactly that way."

He made an impatient gesture, got out of bed, pulled the curtains across, came and sat on my side of the bed. "What d'you think? D'you think I've been play-acting all this time?"

"When did you stop?"

"For Christ's sake! Pretty early on. I fell in love with you. You can't have failed to notice that!"

"But when did it stop, Leigh? When did it stop? When did the play-acting stop?"

The cigarette was still in his hand but he had bent it. He flung it on the floor. "There wasn't an exact moment. Not exactly. But early on. You see . . ."

"You'll get cold sitting there. Put the fire on."

He kicked the switch with his bare foot. "You see . . ."

I said: "You came to that first party with instructions. You'd got to find the girl and make a fuss of her—see how she took it. Isn't that it?"

"Not in so many words. There wasn't any 'got to' about it. It was a suggestion. See if it was worth following up."

"And it was."

"You bet it was! D'you think I'd have gone after someone I didn't like, just to please those two?"

"I don't know. But you found 'going after' me interesting?"

"It got me right from the start. *You* got me right from the start. I didn't *need* any pushing on from behind!"

The bars of the fire were reddening slowly, like a sore place.

"But there must have been a point, somewhere, where there was a change, if there was a change. Was it before we went to Spain?"

"Yes, yes, yes, long before. From the very beginning, I tell you. It pleased me—in a way—to be able to suit them and suit myself at the same time . . . But I suppose if there was one time when I realized how serious it was for me, it was when you found I was married and cut me off. I found I couldn't get on without you."

"Certainly the scheme couldn't get on without me."

He leaned over and put his hand on my arm. "Look, look, look, I tell you it wasn't *like* that! I swear it wasn't like that. I've been crazy about you. How can I prove it? Haven't I proved it already?"

There was silence. "You say you love me?"

"Christ, yes! You know I do."

"But when you fell in love with me, didn't it ever occur to you to stop 'using' me? Feeling as you did and doing as you did should contradict each other."

"No, they don't because I needed money, *we* needed money, to be able to set up together. I swear I'll never deceive you in anything important again! I *swear* it, Deb."

"You even used the information I let slip to get your friends to steal the Vosper tiara. How did you feel about that? Didn't it ever trouble you?"

"It troubled me like hell. All of this has troubled me. I've felt so much of a heel so often. But I've had one excuse, and that seemed to me *just* to make things excusable, and that was that I was doing it for *you*. If—"

"You were doing it for me and for yourself and for Ted Sandymount and for Jack Foil. But chiefly for Jack Foil."

He swallowed and pushed a hand through his hair. His face in the shadowed light looked strangely handsome; his pajama jacket was unbuttoned and showed his white throat and strong young body. "All right, I'm a heel. I'm a rotten stinking gett. But I *love* you. Does that mean anything to you in any language any longer?"

I said: "It's queer how Jack Foil planned it all. How he played the fish—through you—and the fish swallowed the bait just as he arranged it."

"Maybe it seems like that to you now, but it hasn't *been* like that!"

"There never was a man called 'Baker' Evans, was there?"

"Who? 'Baker' Evans? Of the Safeguards, d'you mean?"

"Yes. There never was such a man. Because—"

"I didn't know that! I swear Jack told me—"

"Jack reasoned that if the whole plan could be prepared before I was asked to co-operate as a full partner and then this fictitious man fell ill, I'd give in and do his job. If he'd asked me at the beginning to stay behind and open the door for you, I'd have turned it down with horror. It was all carefully phased—tailor-made to fit my fears and my conscience."

"Now you're making him out cleverer than he really is. He's only played it as it came—"

"Once I'd taken the first step he must have reasoned each one would follow in its proper place. How you must have talked about me, discussed me over the drinks!"

"I never have! I—"

"Did you tell him everything, everything I said and did, so that he could plan more easily? Did you tell him we were all right in bed, and so—"

"I love you and you're beautiful!" He was staring at me.

"Or did you tell it all to Ted Sandymount so that he could repeat it to his boss?"

"*Really* beautiful—"

"Did you snigger about it? Ted would—"

"I love you when you're white and angry," he said. "I've never seen you angry like this before."

"Did you snigger about it?"

"Oh, *Deborah* . . ."

"I'm not going to be much use to you from now on, am I? We can't have two robberies in the same place. My chief use is gone."

"Don't *talk* like that. You can't possibly believe that all our love-making has been sham!"

"Oh, you've enjoyed it in a way, I suppose. I certainly have. It's been a—an experience for me. But I'm no more use to Jack Foil, am I? He may want you to do the same with some other girl. He certainly won't want you tied up both with a wife and a mistress!"

His hand moved up my bare arm. "You know I want to marry you as soon as ever I'm free."

"I don't know anything!" I said passionately. "I don't know whether you've even been to a solicitor about it! I don't know if you've spent money having Lorne watched! I don't know even if you've been working these last months!"

"How can you say that when I—"

"You never brought a bus conductor's uniform home. I wondered at the time that you could go right in without any training at all—"

"Deborah, you *fool!* Don't you think—"

"Oh, *that's* true! I am a fool. That's what you've made me!" Emotionally, ever since he came back, I'd been so cool, physical weaknesses gone, reason working, mind clear and steady. Now a first terrible crack, emotion squeezing through; mustn't let it.

He took my hand and kissed the fingers. "I know how you must feel—"

"Do you?"

"Yes. You think you've been cheated, played for a sucker all along the line. Well, so you have—though it was never so deliberate, never so planned from the start like you think. At least, not by me it wasn't. But I admit all the rest, and I ought to be kicked round London for doing it . . ." He straightened up and took my chin gently and looked at me with his clear eyes. "O.K. *Accepted.* You don't know what to believe. I've lied to you about so many things. All right, I wasn't a bus conductor. I dreamed it up for the effect. It sounded right to me, to take that sort of job. But I *did* take this other job later. And I *did* go to a solicitor about Lorne because I *did* want to divorce her and marry you. That's different. That's for real. You must see that's for real."

I did not speak, and he pushed my hair back from my forehead.

"You say you can't believe anything I've told you. But you can believe your own eyes, can't you?—you know about us living together? And your own feelings: you can believe them. You can understand I wanted to paint and make a living by it. It's the urge I've had in my guts ever since I was so high. Nobody really believed in me until I met Jack Foil. Lorne never did. But *you* did. You did for a bit, when I was painting your portrait. When you came back to me after that first row, I got to the point where I was ready to throw everything else over: Jack and Ted and the rest. *Right over.* You coming back gave me that glimmer of *hope*—just a glimmer that I'd really be able to paint and do something with it. I felt with your faith in me I was ready for anything. If I could have kept that bit of *hope* I'd have turned on Jack and Ted and thumbed my nose at them. I was *going* to. I'd made up my mind to. To throw them over."

"But you didn't."

"No, because I went to see your two friends in the West End, and they tore my painting to strips! It tore me to strips too! You were with me. You know that."

"Yes, I know that."

"You slept with me that night—half out of sympathy maybe. Did I seem like a practiced seducer? Did I? Have I ever? To tell the truth I've always been a bit scared of women—something the way I've been scared of the police." He smiled crookedly. "So we went to Spain together—"

"At Jack Foil's suggestion."

"Maybe. But you've got to sort that out too. Because he suggested it, it doesn't make what happened there untrue. If that was play-acting while I was there, then I wouldn't need to paint for a living: I'd be a Laurence Olivier in no time. So then we came back and you came to live here. And I was a sort of split personality, because I was following along a general sort of road that would lead to us going for Whittington's, with your help. But I was only doing that because it all made sense with the way I felt about you. Cheating you and playing fair with you meant doing and saying the same things."

301

The fire was bright now, warming us; the bed and his body took a glow from it.

"Lovey, do you believe me?"

"Nothing makes any sense any more."

"Some things do. You must know that some things do." He put his hand on my shoulder and slipped the nightdress strap down. Then his hand closed gently round my breast. He kissed me. I pulled away but he followed.

"No, Leigh."

"Yes, love."

"Don't you understand—that tonight . . ."

"It's the only answer," he said.

"How *can* it be?"

"Because it is. Because there can't be any lies in this. If this doesn't answer your doubts, then there isn't any answer."

"But don't you see—" I said.

"What?" he said, and stopped me from speaking.

I wanted to say: but that by itself can't begin to be an answer; because I'd never really doubted his sexual pleasure; it had been too obvious; as maybe mine had too. But that by itself wasn't an answer. Just as before, there was this lack of contact, this lack of merging of spiritual plasma—all the more to be missed because of the intimate merging of our body moistures when we made love.

And we made love tonight. Against all reason and sense. Almost against desire. And in spite of it, after all that had gone before it, the nervous stress, the bitter heartbreak, the consuming anger, the vile coldness of betrayal, after all that, everything came as it should. This I can never explain.

When it was over he lay for a long time with his curly head on my shoulder, breathing deeply onto my skin. Sleep was coming on us both. God, it was so inappropriate but so welcome! It was like a gentle death, creeping into the limbs quietly, stealing away the hideous nervous tautnesses of the day, moving into the body, so that gradually even the mind relaxed its grip. They are not long, the weeping and the laughter, Love and desire and hate . . . Sleep. Tomorrow was another day. Decisions, fears, bitterness, eviscerated love, sex desires, self-contempt, fierce hatred, angry pride, pressures of conscience, pain, pleasure, even the acts of breathing and limping: they could all wait. Down under the surfaces of sleep, gently diving, drifting away from life—surfacing briefly as he moved away. "I got you that time," he said. Beginning to drift again. Fire was still on but not the light. Warm orange red on ceiling and wall. Marks. Bars. Prison bars. Saloon bars. Jack Foil peering. Cataract. But it's too early to operate. Decisions, fears, bitterness, eviscerated love. Eight hours. Hours of death. Gently diving again. Under surface. Last prickings of eyelids. Warm naked sleep. Nothing to fear or decide for hours and hours. No pain. No pleasure except the relief of quiet oblivion.

Chapter 27

Morning light. He was bending over me. "I got you a cup of coffee, love. It's eight—so we'd best be stirring."

Pain. Morning light and pain. All the old conflicts. Monks from an inquisition, waiting round the bed to attack again as soon as the victim recovered consciousness. To thine own self be true. But where is thine own self, in which corner of the mind hiding? Conscience, thou shalt not; pleasure, I want, I want; revenge, I will repay; forgiveness, as we forgive them; suspicion, where still is the truth of it all? Perhaps there is no such thing as thine own self but only an aggregate of impulses, as there is no dictator in a democracy but only an aggregate of voters. And when no majority emerges there is chaos.

Chaos. I got up, bathed, heard him whistling as he made breakfast. On top of the world. No remorse for deceit now. All forgiven and forgotten. He had put it all behind him with a single act of conquest, a single sexual act. Was it conceivable? No, I underrated him. All the same he was happy knowing that everything would come all right in the end.

But what was "all right" to him? Marriage to me? Setting up in business, with me? Settling down, with me? Was this really his aim? How far had it been the bait to make the fish snap? He was in love with me, he said. But even if he didn't know it, the idea, like a hormone, had been implanted in him by Surgeon Foil. Leigh believed something with complete sincerity while it existed in his mind, but whether it was true or not by objective standards was another matter. Was marriage even *my* aim now? I was as deeply involved as ever—no doubt of that —but further from understanding than I had ever been. Humpty Dumpty had had a great fall. The pieces at the bottom of the wall no longer made any recognizable shape.

We sat together at the kitchen table, eating toast and marmalade and drinking more coffee like a homely married couple. He chatted cheerfully, but there was a wariness behind it. It wasn't lost on him that last night's subject had only been most sketchily explored. There was so much, so very much more to say. For the moment he was avoiding it, as someone avoids changing the dressing on a wound. Let it heal a little. Let it rest.

He said he'd drive me to work this morning, it didn't matter if he didn't get there himself till ten; anyway he'd be leaving in a week or two. What time would I be through? About one, I expected. Then I'll meet you too. No, don't do that, you were going to watch Charlton with Ted. Well, I can do that afterward: but it's not important; Ted can go on his own. No, I think I'll stay in the West End for lunch; I promised to see Sarah. How would it be if we met for lunch and then drove over to see the shop, paid the deposit? No, leave it till tomorrow as we'd agreed.

Then how about this evening? Do a show or something. No energy needed; shall I pick you up at Sarah's at six-thirty? I'll shop around, get the tickets. I'll get something that starts at eight and then we can have a slap-up dinner first. Perhaps so, I said; perhaps we could do that.

Time was getting on, so I put on my coat and went out to feed the swans. They were nearby today and came quickly, strong feet paddling. Leigh came out with me and stood watching, an arm on my shoulder. A string of barges was in midstream, moving quite silently with the tide. Washing was hung out on the leading barge. Smoke drifted downstream from some boat that had already passed. A streak of washed blue in the sky was gradually clouding over. Smell of the river, fresh and cold.

We turned to go in. He had never mentioned the broken drawer, though by now he must have seen it. He put on his short coat and we went out to the car. I slipped a bit as I got in and he came quickly round to see if I'd hurt myself. No. All was well.

All was well. Before switching on the ignition he turned and looked at me. "God, it was fabulous last night. I never *thought*—after what you must have *been* though . . ."

"I never thought either."

"You were marvelous. Honest, you nearly always are." He switched on and pushed the starter. It fired almost at once. "God, Deborah, you've changed since I first met you!"

I stared through the side window at the door we had just closed.

"Does anybody else ever tell you?"

"What, Leigh?"

"How much you've changed. Don't they ever say?"

"Sometimes."

"Perhaps they don't all know as much as me."

"Maybe not."

He put the car in gear and we moved off. Soon we were in traffic. "I sometimes think—"

"What, Leigh?"

"I think of how you were when we first met. You were *bright* enough, and pretty, of course, *marvelously* pretty; but, sort of grown in. In a groove. Settled to be someone who didn't have as much fun as other people."

"Different fun."

"Yes, different fun." We stopped and started and stopped. The traffic seemed no easier for being Saturday morning. "But it didn't need to be different, did it. Now . . . you skate; you do it as well as me. Remember that first time, how furious you were because I tricked you into going. And the second time, when you really tried it,

306

the way we staggered and slid and lurched, like a couple of drunks." He laughed.

"I remember."

"'And you drive a car now. And you swim. And you dance. That's something great, I think."

"I think so too."

"We must do other things together. It's only an attitude of mind that stops you. You realize that."

"Yes, I realize that."

"D'you remember the first time I came to your house, to that cocktail party? It wasn't my world."

We crossed Waterloo Bridge, slowing to a crawl as the traffic knotted at the lights below Aldwych. Cars three abreast, panting, throbbing, buses looming, people walking, fumes rising; move, stop, move, stop, as the other city accepted us, took us in like a transfusion into a vein.

"That's all over now," he said. "We share the same world. Yesterday, finding this out, you must have felt *terrible*, you must have hated my guts, you must have *hated* us all. I can only say thank God you didn't walk out on me before I had a chance of explaining."

Into the Strand. We seldom came this way because there are better ways of avoiding the congestion.

"I can see how you must have felt last night. I don't think you ever really have liked Jack or Ted, have you? Now you must feel . . . But it's partly a question of adjustment, isn't it? It's a question of seeing things in the round, if you know what I mean. Profit and loss account. In a ledger. You've lost something, been hellish hurt; but also you've gained. And I reckon if you look at it calmly you'll see you've moved out of the red, love. We've both moved out of the red."

"Literally," I said, "as well as other ways."

He laughed. "That's good. That's very good."

Charing Cross a complete blockage. Trafalgar Square.

"Drop me in Waterloo Place."

"Why? I can go on into Jermyn Street and round."

"I think I'd like a short walk."

"You'll be late."

"It doesn't matter. Nothing matters today."

He glanced at me. "I hope you mean that in the way I want you to mean it."

"I hope I do."

We stopped opposite one of the big airline windows. There was a mirror in the back of the window and you could see our little red car, with the endless buses thundering past.

"Sure you wouldn't like me to meet you for lunch?"

"No, thanks."

"I'd *rather*. I *want* to see you for lunch."

"No, thanks."

"It'd be better, Deb."

"No."

". . . Then I'll pick you up at Sarah's at six-thirty?"

"All right."

He put his hand on my hand. "You've forgiven me for this awful thing I did? Or part forgiven? Or just begun to forgive?"

"Oh," I said, "it's that balance sheet I have to think of. All the recreational therapy you've seen me through."

He looked at me earnestly. "You know it wasn't that, or even anything remotely like that. D'you think I didn't *enjoy* it? You must be crackers if you think that."

"It's just an idea one has."

"But there's nothing that's happened, nothing at all, was as *designed* as you think. Nobody's motives were clear-cut. Honestly. Motives never are. You're cleverer than I am, so you ought to know that."

"What about love?" I said.

"What about it?"

"Is that ever clear-cut either? Isn't it all a jumble of sex, hate, passion, self-love . . . ambition . . . calculation . . . ?"

"Is it?"

"I don't know. I'm asking you."

After a minute: "Stop thinking. I've said it to you before, love. Stop wondering and trying to work everything out and—and trying to see into other people's minds. We're all—groping. The only way is to make the best of things—to—to strike a balance and to let life lead you along. It's the only way to make anything of it at all."

"Supposing it leads you wrong."

"It won't. Not with me here. You'll go on enjoying things, you bet your sweet life. We'll make big time when this money comes in."

I moved to leave, but he said: "Wait, I'll help," and got out first and came to hold my door. It was the first time he'd done this for months. He stood there as I got out, and for a second or so I could see the whole scene plainly reflected in the mirror window. A small red car with a sturdy, ruffle-haired, polo-sweatered young man opening the door for a pale, pretty cripple. She had a delicacy of face that really belied the strength of her body and showed nothing at all of what was going on in her mind. And her thin leg stuck out like a stick, unhidable, unavoidable, incurable, ridiculous. Solicitously he bent to help her, and although her face told nothing, his seemed to be smiling with a partly hidden—but only partly hidden—pity.

Being helped made it more difficult, made the movement seem infirm. She straightened up, brushed her skirt down so that the thin knee was hidden.

He kissed her. "I love you, Debbie. You bet your bottom dollar on that. In a way—in a way I'm *glad* you found out. Because now you know the worst about me. This thing—although you might not believe it—has stuck in my crop for a long time. Now we can start afresh. When you've *really* forgiven me, that is. We're on the level from now on. And we're going places from now on —you must believe that."

"I love you, Leigh," she said smiling.

The mirror reflected their brief kiss. Then she stood there while he got back into the car, slammed the door, started the engine, waved a hand, moved out with the traffic. The mirror reflected her standing there with raised hand after he had gone.

She turned and looked in the mirror. Perhaps something in its angle made her look even more lop-sided than she really was.

Walk up to the corner of Piccadilly. The red car was only just disappearing round the corner into Regent Street. She opened her mouth to call, but no sound came. Turn left along Piccadilly. Other shops, other windows, all reflecting girl in green coat with headscarf and black kid gloves, dark stockings, green shoes. Stretch click, walk on your toe, stretch, click, walk on your toe. No built-up shoe; just a bad limp that you were pretending you were disguising. But who believed in the pretense except yourself? Not anybody. Certainly not Leigh.

Past Simpson's, past St. James's and the Garden of Remembrance, past Hatchard's, time to cross.

Cars flooding. How simple to be knocked down now. But they'd not kill you if you wanted to be killed. Another broken leg would solve nothing.

Safely across and up Bond Street. Stretch, click, walk on your toe. It was ten minutes to ten. A feckle of rain in the February wind. The figure was keeping me company, limping from window to window, disappearing and bobbing up again in a glass door. It was the *doppelganger* of German folklore, dancing attendance on me, imitating, mocking, showing me the other side of the coin. Love, hate, truth, lies, pleasure, pain; stretch, click, walk on your toe; with swift, slow, sweet, sour, a-dazzle, dim . . .

I stopped at the corner of the street where no image could mock me. At the corner was a post-box. In my pocket I reached down and felt the letter crisp in my fingers.

The strength of decision. What had Leigh said? There's nothing clear-cut ever. So there is no truth but only opinions? There is no self but only impulses? There is no absolute but only qualifications? . . .

I took out the letter and looked at it. Address carefully written—no evidence of stress on the part of the writer. Queen's head on the pale blue stamp. Where was Jack Foil's head? Hadn't he had them printed yet?

Careful; not let spite, bitterness, revenge . . . Then what motive if it was not a motive of destruction? But if all was destroyed, what was left but destruction?

I lifted the letter to put it in.

" 'Scuse me," said a voice, and a middle-aged man reached past me and put four letters into the letter box. They dropped with a rattle.

He walked away. Tear up the letter. Tear it up and drop it in bits into some fire. Postpone.

Put it off. Put it off a day or so, just for second thoughts. But what were second thoughts? A belief that now one knew the whole truth and accepted it? Weren't second thoughts the greatest danger of all, the danger that no decision would be come to again? A degeneration of mind and will so that one fell into a mental paralysis more absolute than poliomyelitis? Was this the next stage, the final stage?

Balance sheet. What was integrity? Four socks on a line. Can you feel and taste it as you can feel and taste love? But what was love if the taste was gone? How far would sex go alone? You were sort of grown in when I first met you; in a groove. Who knows, we might plan a little holiday together, just the four of us; I know Doreen has quite a liking. It's a different kind of fun, different kind of fun.

I dropped the letter. It fell on the pavement face down, and I stared at it. A middle-aged woman glanced at my leg and bent to pick up the letter, handed it to me with a smile. With a smile I thanked her and dropped the letter in the box.

Whittington's almost back to normal this morning. Police gone. Showrooms closed but the full staff there as usual. Furniture being brought in through the back door in Bruton Yard. Men in yellow overalls carrying a big Victorian wardrobe. On Monday a sale of coins and medals; they'd been on display yesterday. There was one Victoria Cross.

The Stockton china not yet finished. Maurice Mills was checking some of my attributions. All of them up to now he agreed with.

Death and hell, there was no farther to go. This was the end of the line. They are not long, the weeping and the laughter, love and desire and hate . . . I worked with him for half an hour, then could go on no longer, excused myself, wandered upstairs through the empty showrooms. I saw John Hallows, who smiled at me.

"Morning, Deborah. What's this, I see you're using your stick. I haven't seen you with it for months."

"This?" I looked down. "It was in the cupboard. I took it out when I came. No . . . I haven't used it for quite a long time."

ABOUT THE AUTHOR

WINSTON GRAHAM is one of England's most famous suspense writers and is the author of such widely read novels as *Marnie* and *After the Act*. His works have been translated into fourteen languages and made into five motion pictures. With *The Walking Stick*, he adds new luster to his much respected literary reputation.

A MONUMENTAL
NOVEL OF
FORBIDDEN LOVE.
BY ANN FAIRBAIRN

FIVE
SMOOTH
STONES

FIVE SMOOTH STONES is the
story of one man's initiation into
love. A passionate love—rare and
tender, consuming and tragic—a
forbidden love...

A Bantam Book/$1.25/ Where paperbacks are sold